# A HILLTOP IN TUSCANY

Books by Stephanie Grace Whitson

CONTEMPORARY FICTION
*A Garden in Paris*
*A Hilltop in Tuscany*

HISTORICAL FICTION
PINE RIDGE PORTRAITS
*Secrets on the Wind*
*Watchers on the Hill*
*Footsteps on the Horizon*

DAKOTA MOONS
*Valley of the Shadow*
*Edge of the Wilderness*
*Heart of the Sandhills*

KEEPSAKE LEGACIES
*Sarah's Patchwork*
*Karyn's Memory Box*
*Nora's Ribbon of Memories*

PRAIRIE WINDS
*Walks the Fire*
*Soaring Eagle*
*Red Bird*

NONFICTION
*How to Help a Grieving Friend: A Candid Guide for Those Who Care*

# STEPHANIE GRACE WHITSON

# A Hilltop
# in Tuscany

BETHANY HOUSE PUBLISHERS
*Minneapolis, Minnesota*

Published by Bethany House Publishers
11400 Hampshire Avenue South
Bloomington, Minnesota 55438

Bethany House Publishers is a division of
Baker Publishing Group, Grand Rapids, Michigan.

Printed in the United States of America

**Library of Congress Cataloging-in-Publication Data**

Whitson, Stephanie Grace.
    A hilltop in Tuscany / by Stephanie Grace Whitson.
        p.   cm.
    Summary: "Liz Davis' life is going exactly as planned. But just as things seem to be perfect, her whole world comes craching down. Can she find her hilltop in this valley? The sequel to 'A Garden in Paris' "—Provided by publisher.
    ISBN 0-7642-2936-2 (pbk.)
    1. Americans—Italy—Fiction.  2. Mothers and daughters—Fiction.  3. Widows—Fiction.  4. Tuscany (Italy)—Fiction.  I. Title.
    PS3573.H555H55     2006
    813'.54—dc22

                                                              2005032032

# ABOUT STEPHANIE

A native of southern Illinois, Stephanie Grace Whitson Higgins has resided in Nebraska since 1975. She began what she likes to call "playing with imaginary friends" (writing fiction) when, as a result of teaching her four homeschooled children Nebraska history, she was personally encouraged and challenged by the lives of pioneer women in the West. Since her first book, *Walks the Fire,* was published in 1995, Stephanie's fiction titles have appeared on the ECPA bestseller list and have been finalists for the Christy Award and the Inspirational Reader's Choice Award. Her first nonfiction work, *How to Help a Grieving Friend,* was released in 2005. In addition to serving her local church and keeping up with two married children and three teenagers, Stephanie enjoys volunteering for the International Quilt Study Center and riding motorcycles with her blended family and church friends. Widowed in 2001, Stephanie remarried in 2003 and now pursues full-time writing and a speaking ministry from her studio in Lincoln, Nebraska. Write to her at 3800 Old Cheney Road, #101–178, Lincoln, Nebraska 68516.

# A Hilltop in Tuscany

# ❧ ONE ❧

"YOU SHOULD SEE HER, Jeff." The voice on the phone wavered. "You should see what that jerk did to our little sister."

*Bruises? Swelling?* "Hold on, Danny." Jeffrey Scott interrupted his brother. "It's been snowing here. I've got to pull my car off the road before I wreck it." Glancing in the rearview mirror, he changed lanes and quickly whipped the Tahoe into a convenience store parking lot. Ripping the earpiece out of his ear he tossed it in the empty passenger seat, grabbed his cell phone, and climbed out of the car. "All right," he said. "Tell me again." He walked to the front of the vehicle and leaned on the hood while he listened.

"She's got guts," Danny was saying. "Somehow she managed to barricade Gary in the bathroom while she packed for the kids. Got them all downstairs and into the car before he broke out. She said he ran out the front door of the apartment complex just as she was driving off. Got herself to the hospital."

"Hospital?" Jeff stood up and began to pace back and forth in front of the SUV.

"Yeah. The ER doctor didn't want her to drive this far, but you know Sarah. Even a cast on her arm wasn't going to stop her from getting the kids to a safe place. Colorado to California in record time.

She pulled into my driveway around midnight last night."

Jeff bellowed, "He broke her *arm*?! Gary Henderson is a dead man. If he ever gets within a hundred feet of her again—"

"Hey, man," Danny interrupted. "Calm down. This is exactly why Sarah didn't want me to call you."

"She didn't want you to call?" Jeff forced himself to lower his voice. "Why not?"

"Because," Danny said, "you have enough going on in your life without thinking you have to slay a dragon for your baby sister. And those were Sarah's exact words."

"I don't have anything going on in my life that's more impor—"

"Yeah, right. Except planning a huge wedding. And a job. And a fiancée who only recently discovered that her perfect father wasn't perfect—and wasn't even her father." Danny paused. "Look, man. Sarah's right. You and Liz have enough going on. You don't need more on your plate right now. I wouldn't even be calling, except I know you. You'd be even madder a few days from now when you found out I hadn't called right away."

"Listen, Danny. Liz is okay. Really, she is. I'm not saying our trip to Paris was a breeze. But in some ways, it was the best Christmas we could have had. She got a reality check about Saint Samuel Davis and ended up being closer to her mom than she's been in years. In fact, after a rocky start, Christmas was great."

"Saint Samuel, huh? Do I detect a note of bitterness?"

"You do," Jeff said. "But it's my problem to deal with. And I will." He stood up again. "But right now, I want you to tell Sarah that she should—"

"Move in with me," Danny said. "I know. And she's agreed to do that. Permanently. She says she won't press charges against Gary, but—"

"That's absurd," Jeff insisted. "Let me talk to her. She's got to listen. A divorce isn't enough. She needs a protection order."

"She doesn't. Not really," Danny said.

"And when did you get *your* law degree?"

"It doesn't take a law degree to know Gary's not gonna be a problem to his wife and kids. Not for a long time. If ever." Danny paused. "He's in jail."

Jeff frowned. "I thought you said Sarah was refusing to press charges."

"He's not in jail for what he did to her."

"For what, then?"

"Armed robbery. Accessory to murder."

"Wow," Jeff said. "Wow."

"Very articulate, Mr. D.A."

"How do you know this?" Jeff's ungloved fingers were beginning to feel numb. While he waited for Danny to answer, he climbed back into the Tahoe and closed the door.

"Long story. But I've checked it out and it's the truth." Danny went on to describe Gary Henderson's bumbling plunge into serious crime. "Helped one of his cronies hold up a gas station—the day after Sarah took off with the kids. And they have the whole thing on video-tape. Gary was too stupid to wear a mask. Real tough guy, huh."

"I don't get it," Jeff said. "I talked to Sarah before Liz and I left for Paris at Christmastime, and she sounded great. Gary had finally landed a job. They were even talking about going to church."

"Yeah," Danny muttered. "Apparently our little sister has been painting a rosy picture of reality so her two big brothers wouldn't, as Sarah puts it, 'do anything stupid.'" Danny paused and Jeff could hear him taking a big breath and blowing it out. "Which was, of course, my first inclination when I opened the door and took a look at the latest. Believe me, bro. I had the same reaction as you. Beat the guy to a pulp now—talk later."

"What do you mean the latest? He's hit her before? She never told me he'd actually hit her. Did she tell you?"

"Selective revelation—that's our little sister," Danny said. "Don't feel bad. At least she had a somewhat logical reason for not telling *you*. Not wanting to upset the wedding plans . . . not wanting to upset Liz's already-upset world." He paused. "But there wasn't any reason for her not to tell me. I've got nothing going on but watching paint dry."

Jeff smiled in spite of himself. His brother, the restoration expert, could make a joke in just about any situation. Still, Jeff wasn't ready to calm down. "Let me talk to Sarah," he demanded.

"She's not here. Had an appointment with a counselor. She's interviewing a few before she decides, but she realizes the kids might not be as unaware as she was hoping."

*The kids. What was going through their little minds?* They were stair-step children, having arrived in a successive rush that transformed their once sprightly mother into a round-faced, plumpish earth mother. Jeff could picture them now, six-year-old Josh giving his two-thumbs-up gesture whenever something good happened, four-year-old Andy, mimicking his big brother's every move, and Hillary, the middle one, a five-year-old blonde who loved to play dress-up and pirouette on her little pixie feet. Thinking about the kids settled it. "Tell Sarah you called me," Jeff said. "And tell her Liz is fine. And tell her we're coming out."

Danny protested. "Don't do that, man. It's not necessary." He paused, then said more forcefully. "We're all grown up now, Jeff. You don't have to mother either one of us. And Sarah's right. You and Liz have enough on your plates right now." His voice was pleading. "She's doing everything right. And she's going to be fine. I'll let you know if that changes." He laughed quietly. "You should see what I'm seeing right now. The kids are out back with Diego. They're spoiling him rotten. He's forgotten he's a dog. Again."

The image of Sarah's three children surrounding Danny's spotted Great Dane brought a brief smile to Jeff's lips. But that image faded to one of his redheaded sister sporting a casted arm. He glanced down at his watch. "We'll be there right around bedtime. Let the kids stay up. We'll get a hotel room. I know your place isn't exactly set up for a family reunion."

"You probably can't get a flight out this late in the day, and even if you could, a last-minute trip is going to make getting through security a hassle. Why don't you just cool off and wait a few days? Check in a couple of weeks from now when Sarah is feeling better and the kids have had a chance to adjust."

"I thought you said Sarah was doing fine."

"She is. But . . ." Danny hesitated. "Look, Jeff. Don't take this wrong. But you know Sarah and Liz don't exactly . . . they aren't exactly close. That's all I'm saying."

"So I'll come alone," Jeff said. "But I'm coming." He could sense Danny giving in, reassigning beds in his house, trying to schedule these unexpected events into the "Franklin Planner single life" he'd constructed for himself.

"You probably won't be able to get a flight out on such short notice," he said.

"I'm engaged to a tycoon, remember? What good is that if I can't make use of the corporate jet once in a while? Look, I'm on my way to meet Liz at the estate right now. And we're going into a weekend. I won't be cramping anyone's style by pulling a few strings. Liz can call her pilot and get things rolling, and I'll be there in a few hours."

Jeff paused, waiting for Danny to clear organizational space for what he jokingly called the Davis Factor in his brother's life, and then he continued. "So, I'll fly into Santa Rosa. Don't bother to meet me. I'll rent a car." He revved the Tahoe's engine, nestled his cell phone back into its cradle, and put the earpiece in place. "I appreciate what you said about Liz, Danny. Really. I do. But she'll completely understand that I want to see Sarah and the kids. And that I need to come alone. If you think it's going to start a round of false guilt for Sarah, then just don't tell her I'm coming. It'll be a surprise, and after I get there I'll convince her I came because I wanted to, not because I thought you guys couldn't handle life without me." He added, "I'll also assure her that Liz wanted me to be with you guys."

Jeff could hear the relief in his brother's voice. "Okay, man. . . . Okay. If you're sure." Danny paused, then said, "So . . . we'll see you tonight."

"If you think it will help distract them, you can tell the kids I'm coming. But make them promise to keep the surprise for their mom. Tell them I'm bringing pizza. Valentino's. Cheeseburger."

HE'D BEEN DEAD FOR over two years, but Samuel Davis's absence still seemed to spill out of his office door every time Liz walked by. She was supposed to be across the foyer in the library helping Irene set up for a meeting with the wedding planner. Jeff would be here any minute. But here she was again, standing in Daddy's office doorway, fighting back tears. How she wished it still smelled of Old Spice. How she wished she could turn back time . . . engineer a cure for cancer . . . bring Daddy back. She stepped through the door. She didn't need to switch on the light to know the interior of this room. Dark paneling, deep wine-colored carpeting, heavy damask drapes . . . and at the exact center of the wall of windows opposite the door, a massive carved desk.

Crossing the room in the dark, Liz paused to lay a hand along the back of one of the two chairs opposite her father's. The gray leather was cool against her palm, and she smiled as she remembered Daddy's explanation when she brought up the obvious—that two sleek, and somewhat uncomfortable, gray leather chairs just didn't fit the rest of the room's opulent décor.

*"Don't go out of your way to make people comfortable,"* Daddy had said. *"At least not at first. You can always have a seating area where your better clients and friends lounge. For the others . . . Well"*—he had winked at her—*"it never hurts to remind them who's the boss."*

As Liz moved toward Daddy's cushy leather desk chair, she realized that his advice had served her well. There was a sitting area in her office downtown just like the one clustered around the fireplace on the opposite wall in this office. And, while Liz's office didn't have a fireplace, she had created warmth with a reproduction print of a beautiful garden, sofas upholstered in butter-soft leather, a perpetually well-stocked bar, a coffee urn, and chocolate truffles. People who were invited to sit in Liz's "circle of power" knew they were special.

She paused at Daddy's chair, inhaling again. No Old Spice. But there was still a faint aroma of old cigar smoke—comforting and sad at the same time. Pulling her father's chair out, Liz sat down in the still-dark room. It had remained untouched since the day Daddy died. Even when he was alive, Daddy's desktop never varied. Samuel Frederick Davis preached the gospel of organization, and he walked his talk. In addition to the clean desktop, Sam's office boasted organized files and no mixing of paper clips and rubber bands in the center desk drawer. The end of each workday saw only two things left atop his desk's polished surface—a spotless light-gray ink blotter and his favorite Waterman fountain pen cradled in an Italian marble tray Liz had ordered for Father's Day the year after she joined the company.

This evening, as she sat at his desk with her eyes closed, contemplating the planning of the wedding he wouldn't be able to attend . . . her lonely walk down the aisle, her grief rose up and clutched at her heart stronger than ever before. Maybe, Liz thought, maybe it hurt even more now that she knew the truth. Getting up with a sigh, she crossed the dark office to the heavy damask drapes and drew them aside. As evening light spilled through the leaded windows and onto the wine-red carpet, Liz peered outside at the barren landscape and once again tried to come to terms with the revelations of this past Christmas.

It hadn't been all bad, of course. When she thought about it, Liz had to admit that, had she met Jean-Marc David a different way—at a cocktail party, for example—she would have been fascinated by the handsome owner of a famous yacht called the *Sea Cloud*. She would have been drawn in by his smiling Nordic blue eyes, and grateful for the new interest in life her mother seemed to have when they were together. She would have liked him. She *did* like him.

What she didn't like was the way they'd met—Liz intending to surprise her mother by following her to Paris and arriving just in time to see her in Jean-Marc's arms. What she didn't like was the way her personal universe had been shifted off-center by her subsequent real-ization—and Mother's admission—that Liz hadn't inherited her blue eyes from Daddy. Both her eyes and her propensity to hiccup when she laughed came from Jean-Marc David. What she didn't like was the undeniable fact that her mother still had feelings for Mr. David. And, Liz thought, crossing back to her father's desk and slumping into his chair again, in spite of the fact that she was trying to support her mother's new life in Paris, she really didn't like the idea that Mimi was half a world away while her daughter tried to keep an impossible number of plates spinning.

No, Liz decided, if she were honest, she'd have to say that Christmas in Paris had been . . . Was there even a word for it? Maybe not. But sitting here in Daddy's chair, she could think of a few titles for the movie version. *Christmas in the Twilight Zone. The Worst Christmas Ever. The Christmas from* . . . No, Liz thought. Not that. It hadn't been that bad. But for her, it had been worse than the one right after Daddy died. Maybe, Liz reasoned, that was because Christmas in Paris had birthed a new sense of loss . . . and new questions about the truth that had always been just beneath the surface of her mother's ever-present sadness. Try as she would, Liz could not get her mind around the idea that Mimi had loved someone else besides Daddy, had pretended that part of her life didn't exist for all of Liz's life—and then decided to go back to it . . . and perhaps, back to Jean-Marc David. Closing her eyes, Liz leaned her head back against Daddy's chair, wondering.

She must have dozed off. When the cell phone tucked in her suit pocket vibrated, Liz yelped with surprise, instantly upset with whom-ever it was. If the wedding planner cancelled one more meeting, he was fired. And if Jeff didn't show up—

"What's the matter?" her mother asked. "And don't tell me noth-ing's the matter because I can hear the stress in the way you just answered the phone."

Liz cleared her throat. "Oh, Mimi, I thought you were Jeff or the wedding planner, calling to cancel our meeting tonight." She looked around at the office. "I'm just a little overwhelmed, that's all. There's so much to do. . . . Wait—what are you doing calling at this hour? It's 6 P.M. here. It must be the middle of the night in Paris."

"Just think of it as a well-timed call," Mimi said. "I couldn't sleep, so I've been thinking about what needs to be done before your wedding. I wanted you to know that I've hired some help for Cecil."

"You've . . . what?" Liz leaned forward.

"I've hired some help. We both know Cecil's getting too old to handle the estate grounds. And the fact that your wedding is going to be in the garden is the perfect excuse to get some help without hurting his feelings. George Kincaid's niece Allison is majoring in horticulture at the university. She'll be going out on Monday after class to talk to Cecil about helping with the spring cleanup as soon as the snow melts."

*George Kincaid?* Liz rolled her eyes. Her mother's propensity for hiring friends and the relatives of friends had always irritated her. And Mimi was doing it again.

"I hear that silence," Mimi said. "And I know what you're thinking. Just because I was right about giving George a chance to prove he's permanently sober and can handle designing Daddy's memorial wing at the hospital doesn't mean a thing when it comes to his niece's landscaping skills."

"I was not thinking that," Liz protested.

"Of course you were," Mimi insisted.

What was the point in disagreeing? Liz thought. They were supposed to be getting along better these days. Taking a deep breath, she said, "It's an established *estate,* not a project garden for a student. I want to walk down a *lush, green* aisle in a garden spilling over with *blooming* flowers and *healthy* shade trees. Would you really be thinking of hiring a student if it weren't that you know George Kincaid and you're trying to handle things from half a world away?"

"Allison isn't just any student," Mimi said. "And I'm in Paris, Lizzie, not on the moon. I have a phone and a computer, and I can communicate with florists and gardeners and caterers nearly as well as I could if I were living in Omaha. And certainly as much as I would be allowed to anyway."

Liz glowered. "What does THAT mean?"

Mimi chuckled. "Calm down, sweetheart. It's not an attack on your character. But it's the truth. You're a detail person, and you always have doubted my abilities when it comes to the details of social productions. And your wedding is turning into quite a production." Mimi paused. "And I don't mind, so don't get mad. A girl only gets married once, and you have the right to have whatever you want. I'm just doing what I can to lighten the load, honey. Allison is proof. By the way, I've talked to her. Checked her out. She's at the top of her class. Very knowledgeable. And she's worked at Mulholland's every summer since she was in high school. She reports to work there the day after graduation as one of their landscape architects."

"So what's hiring George's niece going to cost us?" Liz asked. The quiet on the phone was loud.

When Mimi finally spoke up, she was off the topic of the wedding. "Is there something you're not telling me about Davis Enterprises? Are we having financial problems? Because if we are, I can call Luca Santo, and he'll help me put this Left Bank apartment back on the market—"

"No," Liz interrupted. Why did Mimi always shift into martyr mode? "It's not that. Not that at all. Everything's fine. I want you to have the apartment. Enjoy it. I'm just—" She sighed. "It's hard to keep all the plates spinning right now, that's all. The hospital wing, foundation meetings, wedding plans . . . and just the everyday stuff of business."

"Being overwhelmed is pretty normal for a bride-to-be," Mimi said. "And you aren't just *any* bride-to-be when it comes to responsibilities." She paused. "Aren't there some things you could delegate to your intern?"

Liz closed her eyes. "I haven't met with him yet."

"Really?"

She was talking in *that* tone of voice now. The one she called "quiet encouragement." The one Liz always thought of as "barely masked disapproval."

"I predict Ryan will be a great help," Mimi said. "Try to get him involved as soon as possible."

*Oh, yeah,* Liz thought. *It'll be just great to have one of the foundation board member's sons shadowing my every move during one of the most stressful times in my life.* Ryan Miller. Liz hadn't seen him since he was in junior high. All she knew about him was he was a Creighton University basketball star. The kid probably didn't know a balance sheet from a blueprint. He was probably majoring in cheerleaders. He probably had a business IQ of about 70.

"I've got another idea for you," Mimi said.

"Really?" Was it her imagination, Liz wondered, or had she just sounded exactly like her own mother?

"Why don't you move back home to the estate so you can oversee things yourself?"

"What?"

"You heard me. Move home. Didn't you tell me you and Jeff were going to sell your condo before the wedding, anyway? Do it now." Her voice gained momentum and enthusiasm as she spoke. "Think about it, Lizzie. It's the perfect solution. No more cooking and cleaning. And Irene and Cecil will love it. Irene's been grumbling about her and Cecil rattling around in the empty house." Mimi paused. "In fact," she added, "you and Jeff might want to give serious thought to the idea of making the place yours. Permanently."

Liz had to hand it to her mother. After a lifetime of predictability, the woman was morphing into someone who announced one surprise after another.

Mimi's voice gentled. "Ask Jeff what he thinks. I personally love the idea of coming to visit my grandchildren in the home where their mother grew up. The place could use the laughter of children. It's little more than a mausoleum at the moment."

"But . . . but . . . aren't you . . . ever . . . coming back . . . to . . ."

"I don't think so," Mimi said, anticipating the question. "I love it here. I really do." Her voice warmed with enthusiasm as she continued. "Make the house yours. Redo Daddy's office for yourself."

As Mimi rattled on, Liz looked around her at her father's office, her heart pounding. Of course Mimi didn't know she was sitting at his desk right now.

"Consider it my wedding gift," she was saying. "With one condition: you have to give me 'Granny digs' so I can visit. Maybe those rooms at the east end. Have Mona call me. I'll get some ideas, and she can oversee the project while you and Jeff are on your wedding trip. You won't have to do a thing."

"You mean those tiny rooms where Cecil and Irene used to live before you built the apartment over the garage for them?" Liz said.

"Yes. Exactly." Mimi must have taken Liz's comment as acquiescence. She was picking up steam as she talked. "Your father would *love* the idea that you'd taken over his office, sweetheart. And . . . Jeff could have the library. Mr. and Mrs. offices—I love the sound of that—one on either side of the foyer. Do you think Jeff would go for it? It makes so much sense!"

"But Daddy's—"

Mary interrupted her. "There's no reason to maintain that house as a shrine, Lizzie. Start with the old office. Let Mona help. She'll have some fabulous ideas." Mary's voice gentled. "I know this is a lot to think about, honey. But at least think about it. And talk to Jeff. And as far as the wedding goes, do what you want. If you don't like Allison, get someone else."

Liz drew in a deep breath. If Allison Whoever was getting hired by Mulholland's, then she knew her stuff. And if Mimi really wasn't moving back . . . She looked at the west wall of the office where a framed watercolor of the Davis estate had hung for the last few years. The idea of living here . . . with Jeff . . . was . . . too good to be true. And if anyone could work decorating magic on a tight schedule, it was Mona Whitcomb.

"Be *happy*, Lizzie-bear," Mimi said. "The oncology wing is a wonderful thing. It's the perfect way to honor your father's memory. And the way you've taken up the mantle and run the company is something to be proud of. But in the end . . . it's *you and Jeff* that really matters. *Love* him, Lizzie. Fill that empty house with children, and above all, love that man."

After they said good-bye, Liz laid her cell phone atop Daddy's desk, leaned her head back, and closed her eyes. Mimi had made perfect sense. Every idea she had was a good one. Except that now Liz had several more things to add to her hopelessly long to-do list. *Sell condo. Move home. Redo office. Office for Jeff. New master suite.* And, Liz thought with another sigh . . . convince Jeff that it was the right thing to do.

"*Here* you are."

Liz looked up to see Jeff's form silhouetted in the office doorway. "Is it time?" she said, and jumped up without waiting for an answer. "I guess I must have been daydreaming." She snatched her cell phone up, slid it back in her suit-coat pocket, and headed for the door.

"We have to talk," Jeff said, taking her hand and leading her across the foyer and into the library. Irene had already brought in the coffee and, Liz noted with pleasure, made some miniature versions of her cinnamon rolls for the meeting. She reached for the silver coffeepot and began to pour them each a cup.

"I don't want any coffee," Jeff said.

For the first time, Liz really looked at him. "What is it?" she asked, and set the coffeepot down. "What's happened?" She reached for his hand, and together they sat down on an upholstered bench in front of one of the room's bay windows.

"I got a call from Danny on my way out here. . . ." Jeff began.

"You have to take the jet. You have to go out there," Liz said. "Can you leave now? Tonight?"

"I love you, Bitsy." Jeff's voice was warm with emotion. He kissed her, then continued. "You read my mind. I was hoping you'd understand—even if it does mean I can't help you with . . ." He nodded toward the library table where their wedding guest lists and various other notes and charts lay waiting for the arrival of the wedding planner.

"Understand? What's to understand?" Liz said. "They need you. You should go. Don't take offense, sweetheart, but I'm pretty sure I can handle all that." She gestured toward the table even as she reached for her phone. "I can't remember what Dave said his weekend plans were, but if there's a problem with him flying you, we'll get someone else. In the meantime"—she stood up—"go pack your bags."

Jeff stood beside her while she waited for her pilot to answer. Once arrangements were made, they walked toward the back of the house together.

At the door, he paused long enough to ask, "Would you mind—could you call Valentino's and get some cheeseburger pizzas ordered for whatever time makes sense for me to pick them up?"

Liz frowned. "Sure, but—"

"The kids love it. Remember?"

"Oh, right—sure. Taken care of." How did he do it? Remember little details like that? She could remember the phone numbers to a dozen different suppliers, but she never remembered personal details about people. It was one of the things she loved about Jeff. He noticed those things.

"Thanks, hon." He nodded toward the library. "I'm really sorry about—"

"Don't be," Liz said. "Mimi just called a little while ago. She reminded me that I need to simplify things as much as possible . . . and delegate. And she had some other ideas."

"Really?"

"Which," Liz said, "we will talk about later. After you've had a chance to be Sarah's knight in shining armor. Again."

"I love you, Bitsy," Jeff said, and smothered her with a last set of kisses.

After Jeff was gone, Liz called Valentino's for pizza and Vivace to cancel their reservations for a late dinner. Taking a deep breath, she made her way back to the library, feeling both irritated and relieved that the wedding planner was now half an hour late for their meeting. Once in the foyer, she glanced toward Daddy's office. How lucky she was to have had such a man to raise her . . . and to have Jeff in her life now. Sarah Henderson would be better off without her worthless husband. Liz was glad for her. Glad for those kids, too. And, she realized with a glimmer of guilt, she was also glad that for once in her life Sarah had run *west* to Danny for help . . . instead of coming *east* to Jeff. And all Liz Davis had to do was order pizza. And meet with the wedding planner. And manage the company, and the memorial project at the hospital, and the sale of her condo. And the move home. And redo Daddy's office. By herself.

# ⁊ TWO ⁊

LUCA SANTO SAT AT HIS kitchen table, oblivious to the beauty before him as the sun glinted off the church spires of Paris. Reaching for the brown wrapping paper he had earlier torn off a package, he ran his finger over the nearly illegible handwriting and smiled. No wonder it had been delayed. Luca could hardly decipher the address on the package—and it was his address. It was a miracle it had even made it to the right street. The shop owner a few doors up had delivered it a little while ago with apologies. He was sorry for the delay—he'd been gone on holiday. But it was here now.

Laying the wrapper aside, Luca ran his hand over the rough surface of the old Bible. It had not been easy to follow what he hoped at the time was an urging from God to hand it over to his best friend a few weeks ago. But the Jean-Marc David who had come to Paris to meet an old flame seemed to have mellowed since, as a young motorcycle racer, he had refused to listen to what he called his friend's "religious nonsense." And when he had left Paris with a promise for future visits, Luca gave him the Bible. And prayed . . . with so little faith that now, looking down at the note that had accompanied the Bible's return, he felt ashamed.

It had taken him a while to decipher Jean-Marc's handwriting. But now Luca didn't even need to look at the note to remember every word.

A Hilltop in Tuscany

*In time, I will tell you firsthand. But for now, I return your cherished
Bible to its home. I will purchase my own as soon as I reach Fiesole.
Perhaps Celine will think her papa mad. Again. But that is nothing
new. You will understand what I mean when I say it is as if the clouds
that hovered over and around the ship of my life have lifted, and for the
first time I see the horizon. Things are coming clear.*

It should be, Luca thought with chagrin, the best piece of mail
he had ever received. And it would be. If only it weren't for the last
line.

*And now, I entrust my dear Mary to my dearest friend, until I can
capture something of who it is I am becoming.*

She was *his Mary*. Which was, Luca told himself, as it should be.
Hadn't they loved one another in their youth? Hadn't they been reunited for this very purpose? It was obvious from Jean-Marc's note
that, at least for him, the old feelings had come to life. *His* Mary. It
was probable, Luca told himself, that the only things that had kept
Jean-Marc David and Mary Davis apart at Christmas were the unexpected arrival of Mary's daughter in Paris . . . and the fact that Mary
had held herself in check for reasons Luca could only assume were
spiritual. He knew Mary Davis was serious about her faith. At
Christmas, when they were reunited, Jean-Marc had been agnostic at
best. But if Jean-Marc's message was true, things had changed. The
spiritual barrier between him and Mary was gone. Hunkered over his
breakfast table staring at the note, Luca reminded himself that any
good friend would rejoice at such news.

Luca's thoughts turned to Mary and Jean-Marc's daughter, Elizabeth. Even while she was forced to come to terms with her new
reality, Elizabeth Davis had reached out to her mother, embracing
Mary's new life in Paris. She had even enlisted Luca's help to find the
perfect apartment . . . and to surprise her mother, not only with a
new home in the city of her choice, but also with a wonderful violin
so that Mary could pursue another old passion—music. Elizabeth
must have been struggling with the news of her own parentage, and

yet she handled it in a way Luca admired. There was nothing more to keep Jean-Marc and Mary apart. Any good friend would be happy for them both. And he was.

Bowing his head, Luca thanked God for what he had witnessed in his new friend Mary Davis's life over the past few weeks—and for his part in it. He'd been so careful to be nothing but a friend since Jean-Marc's departure to attend to his yacht and then to his daughter Celine and the twin grandsons living in Italy. Luca had forced himself to call Mary less often than he would have liked . . . to always ask about Jean-Marc . . . to be polite . . . guarded . . . no more than a good host to a new inhabitant of the city he loved. But he had not counted on Mary being so lovely, so gifted, so alive. He had not expected the sound of her laughter to haunt his dreams.

A man couldn't be held responsible for his dreams, could he? Even now, as he swept his hands through his gray hair, Luca tried not to dwell on the memories: Mary stepping out of a limousine at the opera on New Year's Eve in a shimmering black gown . . . Mary closing her eyes, taking up the bow and playing her violin . . . Mary protesting but finally agreeing to don the leather racing jacket with the yellow accents . . . Mary tucked behind him on his Ducati, breathless with the thrill of an early morning ride . . . Mary.

This, Luca thought, had to stop. Grabbing the brown paper addressed by Jean-Marc, he crumpled it in his hands. Standing up, he crossed the small kitchen and put it in the trash. He poured himself another cup of coffee and sat down again, forcing himself to open the Bible and read. He could not concentrate. He began to read aloud, but the words coming into his ears fell back out again.

The sound of a door opening in the courtyard below his window brought him back to the moment. He stood up and looked down in time to see his nephew Enzo and Enzo's cousin Adolpho Valerio opening the crate surrounding the latest arrival for Luca's Ducati dealership. As the motorcycle came into view, the boys made admiring sounds. When Adolpho glanced up toward his window, Luca shouted a greeting and promised to be right down. He was grateful for the distraction. Anything that would take his mind off Mary Davis was welcome today.

It was, Luca thought, as he headed for the stairs, unthinkable. Especially for him. A man his age. A confirmed widower. Except that it had happened. He didn't know when. But at some moment in the recent past Luca Santo had fallen in love again.

LIZ STARED AT THE wedding planner in disbelief. "You can't be serious," she said. "I called months ago. We'd already set the date."

"You *called*. You didn't *confirm*." The wedding planner, Byron Allbright, looked up from his calendar.

For the first time Liz realized that his green eyes were obviously contact-enhanced. She cleared her throat. "Well, let's regroup. Since we both agree I *called* first, it seems to me it's reasonable to expect that *you'd* be working *my* wedding and letting your assistant do the other one."

The guy actually smirked. "That's not the way we do things," he said. "The policy is, the *confirmed* customers have priority. Always." He tapped his pencil on the calendar. "And it says here that you were to confirm the first week of January." He looked up at her. "But you didn't."

He'd used about three times as much hair gel as he needed to slick back his hair. Which was *not* in any way an attractive style for his narrow head. Maybe it was a new approach to a comb-over. That was probably it. He was balding prematurely. And that earring. Oh, puh-leeze. You had to be manly to get away with that. Jean-Marc David could do it. This little weasel looked like . . . like a weasel playing dress-up. And now he was scolding her for not making one phone call? Liz wanted to scream at him. *I had other things on my mind besides calling you. I was losing my father all over again. To a stranger with his arms around my mother. The first week in January, I was too preoccupied to keep up with my to-do list, you moron. Can't you get that through your thick head?*

Instead of screaming, she grabbed one of Irene's miniature cinnamon rolls and crammed it in her mouth. She knew she must look like a rebellious child as she stood there, chewing, glaring at the wedding planner everyone at the club raved about—and purposely not offering him one.

Once the roll was swallowed, Liz poured coffee. The silence in the library was having its effect. Allbright shifted his weight from one foot to another. He was looking down at the wedding guest list. Perhaps, Liz hoped, he was noting the names on that list and regretting his policy just a little. The mayor of Omaha. The senator from Nebraska. The owner of the *World Herald*. His cheeks were coloring a little. Liz took another drink of coffee. Her hand wasn't trembling anymore, but she noticed the wedding planner's *was*.

"Well, then," she said. "I guess that's that." She reached for the coffee tray and picked it up. "I've got to get these back to the kitchen. It's getting late, and I try to respect my housekeeper's policy to be finished in the kitchen before ten." She smiled. "If you'll follow me, you can let yourself out." Without waiting, she headed for the foyer.

"But . . . surely we can work something out," Allbright stammered.

Liz shook her head. "I don't think so," she said. She looked over her shoulder. "You see, it's my policy never to allow myself to be treated like I'm anyone's second choice." As she stepped into the foyer, she heard footsteps as Allbright rushed around collecting his coat, his briefcase, his hat. She hadn't liked that hat, Liz remembered. It was so . . . affected. Jean-Marc might look great in a beret, but this guy absolutely did not.

At the sound of the front door opening, Liz turned around. "I'll expect a bill for your time," she said. "And I'll also expect you to cooperate fully with the new wedding planner when you are contacted about the details we've already arranged." She paused. "You do have a policy of cooperation with your peers, I expect?"

"Of course," was the reply—edged with a tinge of feigned hurt at the suggestion of anything else.

"Fine, then," Liz said. "Close the door behind you if you don't mind. I have a phone call to make." She retreated toward the kitchen. The door didn't close immediately. He was watching. Let him. She was Elizabeth Samantha Davis, and she could make a great exit.

## Mary

IT IS BARELY dawn on Saturday morning when my telephone rings. It is Liz . . . wondering if she woke me. Whenever my daughter asks stupid questions, something is wrong.

"Tell me what's wrong." I glance at the clock, realizing that it's about midnight in Omaha.

"I fired the wedding planner tonight. Jeff wasn't at the meeting and the guy was so *impossible*. He just stood there with his planner open staring at me and reminding me I didn't *confirm* like I should have that first week in January. So he's no longer responsible. He was going to have his *assistant* handle things because he had another client who *confirmed*."

I'm thinking that isn't quite as unreasonable as Liz seems to think . . . but I am also accepting a full measure of motherly guilt. After all, my life was the thing that rocked Liz's world when she should have been confirming her wedding planner. But then I realize what else she's said. "Why wasn't Jeff there?"

"He's on his way to California—" She pauses before adding, "For the next chapter in the *Life and Times of Sarah Henderson*."

"I thought Sarah lived in Colorado."

"Not anymore," Liz says. And she explains.

My own emotions run the gamut from disbelief to rage against a man I've never met but have always disliked because of the grief he has brought his wife and children. When Liz finally concludes the saga, I interject, "That man—no, scratch that. That *creature* should be put in a cell, sewed up inside a sheet, and given some of his own medicine."

"He's lucky he's in jail in Colorado and Sarah's brothers are in California or he'd be getting some of his own medicine—although likely in a back alley. I've never seen Jeff so upset."

"How long is he going to be gone?"

"Long enough that Sarah won't need a protection order," Liz says.

"Not Gary. Jeff. Is he going to miss work?"

"I don't think so," Liz says. Pauses. "I don't really know. He hasn't called yet. But I don't suppose work really matters at the moment, does it? I mean, he *has* to be with his sister now. That's the most important thing. Sarah and the kids."

I know this tone. She's trying to convince herself. "Of course that's important," I agree. "But so is his obligation to his employer. And to you."

"Right."

"Let's hear the rest of that sentence, please." I try to tease her a little, hoping it will lift her mood. "You can't fool your mother, Lizzie-bear. What else is going on I don't know about?"

Do I imagine it, or is she sniffling a little? This is not the Liz Davis I know. "I'm such a selfish brat," she finally blurts out. "I *know* he needed to go. I even helped. I arranged for the jet to fly him out. I ordered pizza for him to pick up for the kids."

"But you're worried about how this is going to impact the next few weeks in your own life. You need Jeff there." I pause. "Did you even get a chance to talk about the move?"

"No. But how can I even think about that? What kind of person worries about redecorating and wedding cake when her future sister-in-law has a broken . . . life?"

"A normal one," I say, trying to be kind. But I also want to be honest. "And a sometimes selfish one who's always been the center of her own world, always been handed whatever she wanted by her doting and powerful father." I scoot to the edge of the bed as if by sitting up I can somehow make my words hold more weight with my daughter. "You're not a terrible person, Lizzie—but you also aren't used to waiting on someone else before you can make a decision and move forward. You're used to being *first*. Isn't that pretty much what you said when you fired the wedding planner?"

I expect self-defense and anger, but Liz only sighs and mutters, "Pretty much." She sighs. "I know you said I'm not . . . but I feel like I'm a terrible person."

"Everyone struggles with doing what's best when it conflicts with what they want, honey. We've all been there, done that. And the fact that you don't really like Sarah very much doesn't help."

"I do so like her," Liz protests. "She's Jeff's sister!"

"And she's very different from you. The two of you don't have much in common. You chose the business world, and she chose a family. If you will recall, you had trouble understanding someone else in your life who made that choice. Until very recently."

"You're different," Liz says quickly. "You have talents. Gifts. Interests."

"So does Sarah Henderson," I reply just as quickly. "But ever since you've known her she has been financially challenged. She's had a worthless husband dragging her down. You can't hold it against Sarah for not finding time to wander art galleries and develop a private self."

"I don't hold it against her," Liz says in her most defensive tone. "She's a great mother, and I admire that. But she could have bought a clue and a diaphragm. No one has to have three kids in three years."

"Oh, Lizzie." I sound like a mother now, scolding a naughty child. I stand up and head for the kitchen. This conversation is going to require some caffeine. "Whatever you think of Sarah, you need to rethink your idea of motherhood. It's not something a girl with gumption does on the side while she develops other gifts. It's a full-time job for some of us talented, gifted women."

"Time-out."

I don't think it's fair, but I have to honor her request. My daughter and I are very different people. When a conversation escalates, we've agreed that either of us can call a time-out. We're using it less and less as we've gotten closer, but this is clearly a conversation that's leading us into waters we are not ready to sail.

"This isn't about me and motherhood. It's about me and Sarah."

"Well, that's an easy subject. You have to keep trying. You have to support Jeff as he supports Sarah. In fact," I say, launching another ship of hope onto choppy waters, "why don't you go out there? It would be a great show of support, and I bet it would mean a lot to Jeff."

"Go out there and do what?" Liz protests. "You know how they all are when they're together. It's like no one else exists. The last thing they need is me horning in."

"Toss a softball around with the boys," I suggest. "Take Hillary to Wal-Mart for some new clothes."

"Wal-Mart?"

Did she really just shudder? How did I raise such a snob? Oh, well. Another time-out topic for another day. "Not everyone outfits their children at Gap, Lizzie. Taking her kids there will only make Sarah feel like you're putting her down." I can hear Liz thinking. She may be a snob, but she loves Jeffrey James Scott, and she knows good advice when she hears it.

"You're right," she says. "I should go. If he's still out there in a few days, I'll do it."

She rushes through a list of all the things facing her in the week ahead. She is right—she really can't get away right now. "Good girl," I say. "I'm proud of you. It's going to be very hard for you, but you are going to have to figure out a way to share Jeff until he's sure his family is taken care of. Maybe it will help to remember that his loyalty to his siblings is one of the very things that will bless *you* in the future. He's going to be a wonderful father someday."

"Someday," Liz says quickly. "With emphasis on the 'some', *s'il vous plait*."

I protest even as I pick up the teakettle and pour steaming water over the loose tea leaves in the basket suspended over my cup. "I'm not pressuring you for grandchildren." I chuckle. "Although if I thought it would do any good . . ."

"It won't," Liz says abruptly.

"Time-out," I tease, and change the subject. "Can you get me Danny's address? I'll send flowers. Unless you already have." When Liz sighs loudly into the phone, I feel compelled to ease her guilt. "You've had quite a Friday of your own, sweetheart. I'm functioning on a good night's rest. You're still in the throes of the event. Not to mention the wedding planner dilemma. I'll add your name to the card, if you like. And make the bouquet outlandishly huge."

"If I do end up flying out there, I'll take more," Liz promises before asking, "But . . . what am I going to do about finding a new wedding planner?"

An idea pops into my mind.

THE IN-LINE SKATERS just outside Notre Dame Cathedral now know me as *ze Moto-Maman*. All of that began after the second time they saw me perched behind Luca on what my future son-in-law calls Luca's "screaming-yellow" Ducati. First, of course, the boys noticed the ride. They were practically drooling the first night Luca parked it across the street from the cathedral. When I climbed off and removed my helmet, the incongruity of the gray-haired woman and the racing bike resulted in nudges and whispers, then smiles. The fact I was wearing leathers—outlandish racing leathers with yellow lightning bolts shooting from the shoulders across my back toward the waist—only emphasized the anomaly.

I had laughed the first time Luca suggested I wear them. But then Luca's nephew Enzo dared me to try them on, and somehow I learned to feel at home in them. In *those* leathers on *that* motorcycle, hidden inside a full-face black helmet with a reflective visor . . . part of me feels newly free. It is probably egotistical, but I will admit that

I enjoy the look of surprise on strangers' faces when I remove the helmet and shake out my gray hair. This whole motorcycle thing has made me feel alive in a new way. I am not what people expect. I like that. And I must admit that when I am with Luca Santo, I am not always what *I* expect, either—which I also like.

So, since I have become Moto-Maman, the in-line skaters always shout a greeting when Luca and I drive by. Luca finds it amusing. I love it. It is part of the reason that, whenever I cross the bridge onto the island where the great cathedral has stood for centuries, my heart sings.

But on this Saturday evening in Paris, as I walk down the Boulevard St. Michel, rain transforms the intersections and sidewalks into mirrors that reflect the lights spilling out of shops and restaurant doors. I usually pause to admire the sugar-based art on display at a confectioner's shop, wondering how it is possible to create such thin sheaths of fine chocolate and then form them into leaves and flower petals. This evening, as I pass by, I barely glance in. I am relieved when, from the opposite end of the open plaza at the cathedral's entry, I realize there are neither skaters in the street nor throngs of tourists just outside the doors waiting to get in. Fewer people will mean more silence within the vast space, the soaring arches, magnifying the unspoken encouragement to look up toward heaven for help, to give burdens to the One who soars above all creation.

I slip into the cathedral and sit toward the back. Closing my eyes, I listen, reminding myself to breathe evenly and to relax into the Everlasting Arms. I whisper Liz's name. *Here I am. Again.* When words don't come easily, I take comfort in the sound of shuffling feet as a few tourists make their way up the side aisle toward the famed rose windows. Surely, some of those feet are attached to people whose lives are far more complex—and challenging—than mine. Thank God he can handle them all, the devout and the profane, the sincere and the hypocritical. I admit to feeling a bit hypocritical. Have I come to Notre Dame because I *need* to pray for Liz . . . or because Luca Santo isn't available to advise me? After Liz and I hung up this morning, Luca called and cancelled our luncheon date. Abruptly. I don't know what's wrong, but his voice was different. It was clear he didn't want to talk. I tried not to take it personally, but I was looking forward to asking his advice about whether or not I should go home to help Liz.

*"I'm not trying to make you feel guilty for staying in Paris,"* Liz had said. Which, of course, succeeded in doing only one thing: making me feel guilty for staying in Paris. I wonder when, exactly, does the magic moment arrive when a parent can dispense with the guilt over all their parenting failures? I've been wrestling with the question itself for only a few hours. I've been wrestling with the guilt for what feels like a lifetime.

I thought I was starting this new life in Paris with Lizzie's blessing. She bought my apartment. She bullied Monsieur Rousseau into selling her a violin I don't deserve so I can study my music again. I thought she approved. But I can hear the stress in her voice every time she calls me. And I don't know what to do. When I think about returning to Omaha, I am overcome with dread. It is the last thing on earth I want to do. I've been telling myself not to let false guilt motivate me. But today I'm wondering if what I've been calling *false guilt* is really God's voice. I only have to look around me at the various artistic representations of saints—and of Christ himself—to be reminded that sometimes being devout means doing the things you dread and trusting God to help you through it.

I sit in my chair for a long time, my head swimming with questions, my heart calling out for Luca, who would have the answers— or at least be able to point me to something in the Bible that would help. Luca would know. When, I wonder, did *this* happen? When did Luca Santo become such a presence in my life?

I leave the cathedral and walk the short distance to the brick wall that borders the Seine. Behind me, I hear a roar and turn just in time to see a flash of yellow as a scooter crosses the bridge just to the north. My heart thumps. Again, I wonder. When did this happen? When did my thoughts of Luca Santo broaden from admiration for his spiritual knowledge to . . . loving the way his almost-white hair sweeps back off his weathered forehead? When, I wonder, did I first realize that he resembles some of the more mature male models pictured in Parisian designer ads?

*This is absurd. You came here to pray about Liz. So get back inside and pray.*

But I want to call Luca for advice.

*He doesn't have any children. He won't know what to say.*

That doesn't matter. His voice is so soothing . . . and he's wise in his faith. He'd have something helpful to say.

*Have you forgotten that he cancelled lunch? Have you forgotten that it was obvious he didn't want to talk on the phone?*

Gripping the concrete railing before me, I manage to take myself in hand. I am supposed to meet Jean-Marc David in Florence in a few weeks. And his daughter Celine. And her two boys. He's taking me sailing.

I scold myself. Snap out of it! You are *not* going to fall in love with Luca Santo! It's ridiculous. And absurd. At your age. Imagine! Which is, I realize as I watch a *bateau mouche* make its way up the Seine, exactly the problem. I can. Imagine.

SUNDAYS, LIZ REMINDED herself, were supposed to be restful. She could almost hear Daddy opining about the wisdom of a day of rest. Of course, Sam Davis's version of rest meant breakfast at 6:30 instead of 5:30, church instead of the office, and golf instead of meetings with business associates in the afternoon. More often than not, Daddy's evenings on his "day of rest" meant dinner out with board members—dinners that everyone present knew were only thinly disguised meetings.

As she rolled over in bed and looked at her clock, Liz realized Daddy would not have been pleased with his daughter's version of rest. After the fiasco with the wedding planner on Friday night, she'd decided there was no reason to drive back to her condo and had scooted up the back stairs to her old room. Snuggled beneath a down comforter, she'd fallen asleep instantly. It was so good—so comforting—to be at home, she'd driven to her condo yesterday, packed an overnight case, and come back. Jeff had called in the afternoon. Sarah and the kids were all right, but he needed to stay for a few days. His boss was being great about it. They had things covered at the office. In fact, Jeff said, Henry Widhelm had given him a few things to do while he was in California. Something related to a case or a partner. Liz wasn't quite sure, and Jeff wasn't very detailed. Their call was cut short by a chorus of young voices shouting for Uncle J to come and play.

So here she was on Sunday morning. Alone. With Cecil and Irene having taken the day off to drive over to Council Bluffs to visit family, the day loomed before her. She should be delighted. Stretching lazily, Liz hunkered back down under the comforter, only to be roused by the sound of sleet slapping against the bedroom windows. *Great. Just great.* Oh, well. She'd make herself something to eat and head into the library. She'd left the wedding folio spread out in there. If she was going to take Mimi's advice, she had to have some fast answers ready by tomorrow morning.

With a sigh, Liz climbed out of bed and got dressed. At the bottom of the stairs, it happened again. Daddy's office door called to her and she went in. This time, though, instead of sitting alone in the dark, she went straight to the windows and pulled back the heavy drapes to let in the morning light.

Perching in one of the window seats just inside the bank of leaded windows, she studied the office from this angle. She had never really thought about there coming a day when this room might change. What she needed to run Davis Enterprises had long ago been removed from file drawers and the computer hard drive—the process overseen by Daddy himself in the days before a combination of chemotherapy and pain medication muddled his brain. She got up and spun slowly around, surveying the familiar space with a combination of appreciation for inheriting it and horror at the thought of changing it. But she would have to change it. Mimi was right. Moving home and using this office would help tame the swirling vortex that was her life.

She crossed to the wall opposite the fireplace, to the teak radio cabinet, smiling at the memory of Daddy and his vinyl. He never wanted to listen to music any other way. They had argued about it, with Daddy steadfastly refusing to be converted to CDs. What, Liz wondered, would he think of her iPod? She slid the record cabinet lid open and pulled out an album. The music a person liked said a lot about them. Sometimes it even brought them back for a while. She could remember a time when her mother had made her stop listening to one of these. . . . Which one was it? She couldn't remember, but Mimi said it was just too painful.

Flipping through the albums, Liz recognized the one with the song she was looking for. Bobby Darin. "Beyond the Sea." Pulling the record carefully out of its dust jacket, Liz put it on the turntable.

*"Somewhere beyond the sea . . . my lover stands on golden sands . . ."* She listened to the song once . . . twice . . . and again. Mimi had made her stop playing it, claiming it was too painful now that Daddy was gone. *"No more sailin' . . . move on out, captain . . ."* But on this side of Christmas in Paris, Liz could not help wondering if hearing the song was painful because it reminded Mimi of Daddy . . . or of Jean-Marc David?

*"Don't you want your mom to be happy?"*

If Jeff had asked her that once, he had asked it a thousand times. And Liz always insisted the answer was yes. Duh. It was just that the idea of Mimi being happy with a man she had loved before Daddy was just . . . weird. And now, in the space of a month, Mimi had invited not just one new man into her life but two. Luca Santo's name had begun popping up in her e-mails and phone calls. They went to the ballet. They had dinner. They rode *motorcycles,* of all things. Liz still shook her head at that one. And Mimi had made it clear that she wasn't coming back to Omaha to live. It was a lot of adjusting to ask of a daughter, even without the subject of fatherhood being in the mix. Sitting here in Daddy's office encouraged what-ifs and if-onlys.

*You can torment yourself with suspicion, or you can believe what Mimi said. She loved Daddy. She never once had contact with Jean-Marc after she and Daddy were engaged. Daddy knew she was pregnant when they got married and he didn't care. In fact, he was glad, because he couldn't father children. It's all true. Why do you keep torturing yourself with these thoughts? It's absurd.*

Turning off the record player, Liz moved back toward the windows to check on the weather. She was relieved to see the sleet had stopped. She didn't like the idea of Cecil and Irene Baxter driving in bad weather. She rubbed the crease between her eyebrows. If she wasn't careful, she was going to need a Botox injection to keep from looking like a worried old woman at her own wedding.

Surely Jeff wouldn't mind if she updated this one room here at home. Surely he would see Mimi's wisdom in suggesting she move home until the wedding. He would understand her desire to create a comfortable home office for herself. Even if it was only for a little while. Moving here permanently—living their married life here— would be a dream come true. But that, Liz realized, was not a topic to be brought up over the phone. Not while Jeff was so distracted by the crisis in Sarah's life. Not while he was interviewing lawyers so her divorce could be handled smoothly. Not while he and Danny were helping Sarah check out counselors for the kids.

She felt the creative energy start to flow and began making decisions. Some future generation would likely curse her for painting coffered paneling, but what did that matter? At least for now, it was *her* coffered paneling. She could do what she wanted. She would paint it. Taupe. She wondered if the abstract painting she had seen at a gallery opening just last week had been purchased. It would be just the thing for . . . No. No painting above the fireplace. Too predictable. Maybe this would be the excuse to finally own a piece of Chihuly. She'd been enchanted by the artist's glass creations since first seeing his exhibit at the Joslyn. Yes, Chihuly would do nicely. One piece. No, *three*. Three pieces of Chihuly glass on the mantel. And above them . . . nothing.

*Chihuly.* Definitely pricey if this was a short-term situation. But in her heart, Liz didn't think it was. Jeff had always loved this place. He'd love living here even more. She got up, moved to the windows, and drew the heavy drapes aside. White. She wanted white. Something light and airy. Steel furniture. Retro? Maybe. Mimi was right. Daddy *would* approve of her using this space to continue his legacy at Davis Enterprises.

Light poured into the room, dropping an oblique pattern of window grids onto the carpet and drawing attention to the photos on the mantel by reflecting off the sterling silver frames. Liz went to the mantel now, smiling at the black-and-white Glamour Shot of herself next to the picture of Mimi perched atop the middle of the backseat of the convertible Austin Healey, waving at the camera like a beauty queen. It was so strange to be here in Daddy's office while Mimi dined with Luca Santo and looked forward to meeting Jean-Marc David and being on his yacht in Italy. She wanted Mimi to be happy, but still . . . it was hard.

*"When the going gets tough,"* Daddy used to say, *"the tough get going."*

"All right, Daddy," Liz murmured aloud. "I hear you." She had heard Mimi, too. And Mimi's idea for the ideal wedding planner fit perfectly with Liz's plans to redecorate Daddy's office. She could take care of both in one phone call, first thing Monday morning.

"MONA AND COMPANY. May I help you?"

Liz sat at her desk, tapping her planner with the tip of her pencil. "Mona, please. Tell her it's Elizabeth Davis."

"She's in a meeting, Miz Davis. May I have her call you?"

"You're new, aren't you?" Liz stopped tapping with her pencil.

"Yes, ma'am."

"Mona Whitcomb thinks early morning meetings are for plebians," Liz said. "She never schedules a meeting before ten. Now, look under the blotter on your desk. See that list? Those are your top-dollar clients. My name is on that list. So pour Mona a second cup of coffee and tell her who's on hold."

"Y-yes, ma'am."

Liz had barely crossed to the sitting area and settled in a club chair when a husky voice came on the line. "Elizabeth Davis . . . darling. How *are* you?"

"Redoing Daddy's office," Liz said. "I'm moving home."

"Everything's all right, I hope?"

Mona was always ripe for gossip. "Everything's great," she said. "I just want to be closer to oversee the wedding preparations. Mother suggested I redo the office so I can work from here if need be. And it's so . . . *him*. I need to make it . . . *me*."

There was a pause. Liz could picture Mona scrambling for the file that would remind her what Sam Davis's home office looked like. "All that leather and darkness—" Mona shivered audibly. "Not you at all. You need color. And that albatross of a desk—"

"I want the desk," Liz interrupted.

"Of course you do," Mona recovered immediately. "It's a wonderful memento of your father. You should keep that *and* the fountain pen on the sideboard."

How did she do it? Liz wondered. Mona always remembered something about the rooms she decorated—some little detail she *didn't* do. The fountain pen on the sideboard was a Pelikan limited edition called Pyramids of Giza. Daddy had bought it long after Mona & Company finished the office. But Mona had seen it. And she remembered. Her memory for that kind of detail was one of the things that had enabled Mona Whitcomb & Company Interiors to become known as Mona & Company. If you didn't know Mona and what she did, you couldn't afford her anyway. She didn't even advertise in the Yellow Pages anymore.

"I don't know about the pen," Liz hesitated. "I know he would approve of what I'm doing, but . . . this is going to be hard."

"We'll do it together," Mona said, her voice warm, commiserating. "When would you like me to come? This afternoon? I could shuffle a few appointments and be there around 3:00. Or tomorrow first thing? You decide."

"Thursday afternoon," Liz said. "Jeff's in California on business, and I might join him at the end of the week. I'm staying out at the estate this week because I've still got some things in Daddy's office to deal with. Thursday will give me—and you—time to prepare." She paused. "And there's something else I want you to think about."

"I'm all ears."

"Now, don't say no right away, just because it isn't something you're known for."

"I know you were in Paris this past holiday, dear," Mona said. "And I won't be offended if you saw something there you don't think I've seen. In fact, I'll thank you for putting me on to some fabulous new trend. Your taste is impeccable, Liz. So what is it I need to know?"

"Oh, it's not so much something you need to know," Liz said. "As something I hope you'll do." Before Mona could ask another question, she blurted it out. "I fired Byron Allbright Friday night. And I want you. It was my mother's idea. And she's right. You'll be out at the house a lot, anyway, for the office project. I want a wedding that screams 'style'. No one does 'style' like Mona & Company. No one."

Mona was quiet for so long Liz began to wonder if they'd been disconnected. Except she could hear the woman's nails clicking atop her desk—whether with anger or thought, Liz couldn't tell. She spoke up. "I know you aren't a party planner," Liz said. "And you probably consider that kind of thing beneath you. But my wedding isn't just any party."

"I don't know the first thing about ordering invitations and flowers," Mona said.

"You don't need to. That's already been done. If your new assistant could keep up on making sure things are on schedule, that's all it would take. Those details are at more of a secretarial stage than anything," Liz said. "What I need is someone to help with the site. Someone to help with the style . . . the décor of the event. It would mean so much to me, Mona. I'd be in your debt. You could name your price." Liz paused and then put her last card on the table. "I'd be the envy of Omaha if you did this for me. No one would ever forget it. Or you."

"And," Mona said, "I'd start getting calls to plan bar mitzvahs and baby showers."

"You wouldn't," Liz insisted. "But even if you did, you could always price yourself out of the market. I need you, Mona. Please say yes. Or at least don't say no. Not until you've thought about it. We can talk again when you're out at the house. Think about it until then. If you say no on Thursday, I won't pressure you anymore. I don't know what I'll do, but I won't pressure you about it again."

"See you Thursday," Mona said.

Liz could imagine her jotting herself a note—it would be on a bright pink Post-it note—and sticking it to the whiteboard on her office wall, which served as the only planner Mona would allow into her life and baffled every customer who saw it. How the woman kept anything straight was a mystery. But she did.

# ℐ THREE ℒ

As Liz descended the few steps to the tarmac on Sat-urday morning, Jeff's heart raced. Hurrying to her side, he swept her into his arms, kissing her lips, her forehead, the side of her neck.

"I can't . . . breathe," Liz said. And then she held on tighter, whispering, "Don't let go."

When they finally parted, it was with breathless laughter. "I missed you," Jeff said. "So much."

"I've missed you, too."

"How's the moving process going?"

"It's under control."

"And the wedding plans?"

Liz laughed aloud. "I didn't think it possible, but Mona said yes."

He pulled her arm through his and headed for the car as Dave unloaded her luggage from the company jet.

"You should have seen it," Liz said, while they opened the trunk. "Already on Friday she'd drawn up a sketch of what she's calling 'the set.'" She laughed and shook her head. "I never cease to be amazed at that woman's memory. You'd think she'd been out to the estate and measured everything." She pointed to a folder sticking out of a small bag. "Those are the drawings. All ready for your approval."

"I approve," Jeff said, and closed the trunk of the car.

"But you haven't seen——"

"I've seen everything I need to see," he said. At her quizzical smile, he winked. "My oh-so-stressed bride is smiling. She's happy. And excited. That's all I need to see. You can tell Mona yes. And," Jeff added as he followed Liz to her door and opened it, "you can tell her to expect a very big tip from a very happy groom." He kissed her again. "I'm so glad you came, Bitsy. Now hop in—we're taking a little drive up the coast."

THE PROMISED "LITTLE DRIVE up the coast" was something Liz would never forget. She might have been to Paris, but she'd never driven a coastal highway, and repeatedly, as they rounded a corner and yet another vista of ocean and cliffs and rocks came into view, Liz exclaimed over the beauty.

She had yet another opportunity to be amazed when, a little before noon, Jeff pulled the car over. "What's up?"

"Lunch," he said, and motioned toward the horizon. "On the beach," he said.

"But . . . there's nothing . . ." Liz looked at the empty backseat. No picnic basket. No blanket. Nothing.

"There will be," Jeff said, getting out and coming around to open her door.

And there was. She didn't know how he'd done it, but he'd arranged for a seaside banquet. On a private beach. Sheltered from the wind, Liz could almost believe it was spring. They ate lobster and fresh fruit and savored a fine bottle of Beaujolais. After lunch, they snuggled atop a luxurious beach blanket, watching the waves while an obviously practiced crew swept away all vestiges of their lunch . . . and disappeared.

"You," Liz said, kissing Jeff on the cheek, "are just about the most wonderful man on the earth."

"Just about?" Jeff said, teasing. "What'd ya mean just about? What do I have to do to get top billing?"

"Marry me," Liz said.

"Already have . . . in my heart," Jeff said.

"Marry me and move home with me."

"Already plan to," Jeff said.

"You didn't hear what I said," Liz replied. "I mean move home—to the estate."

She snuggled closer and caressed the back of his hand. "It was Mimi's idea. She said we should think about moving there after we're married. She said we should redecorate—have Mister and Missus offices just off the foyer downstairs. Make it our own. Her wedding present." She cuddled close again—trying and failing—to interpret Jeff's reaction to the monumental idea she was presenting as casually as possible.

"She's never coming back to Omaha to live?" Jeff asked.

Liz shook her head. "But she loves the idea of having an apartment of her own for when she visits. I got the distinct impression that, although she's adamant about not coming back to Omaha, once presented with grandchildren, she might reconsider." It was a slight exaggeration. Mimi hadn't really talked all that *much* about grandchildren. But, Liz reasoned, it was a justified fib backed by good intentions.

"Hmm," Jeff said. He took a deep breath and reached up to stroke her hair.

"So. That's the latest from Paris," Liz said. "Mimi thinks we should *both* sell our condos and move out to the estate. And . . ." In their months together, Liz had learned not to press Jeff for quick decisions. She decided to change the subject and began to talk about Annie Templeton and Adolpho Valerio, Mimi's young musician friends. "We're invited to Annie and Adolpho's wedding in April."

"April . . . what?"

"Eighteenth," Liz said.

"Where?"

"Florence."

"Not London? Isn't Annie from London?"

"Apparently Annie's parents are less than thrilled with the idea of the wedding."

Jeff frowned. "But I thought her parents liked Adolpho when they met over Christmas."

Liz shrugged. "They did. But then the prospect of a spring wedding came up, and they began to sound less enthusiastic. When Annie didn't fold, her parents threw a fit. Demanded she wait at least a year or they wouldn't have a thing to do with it. So . . . enter Luca Santo."

"Luca?"

Liz nodded. "He and Adolpho are related somehow." She paused, trying to remember. "I think that nephew of Luca's who works in his shop . . . Enzo—that's it. Enzo is Luca's nephew, and Adolpho is Enzo's cousin. Anyway," she said, "I guess Luca considers Adolpho to be family, and he made a call to his sister in Florence, who lives in the Santo family villa, and . . . presto. Adolpho and Annie have been invited to have their wedding in Italy."

"I can't imagine a wedding where the family on both sides isn't supportive," Jeff said. He nuzzled Liz's cheek. "I'm glad we don't have those worries."

Liz agreed. "Mimi said Luca's sister is the one actually putting the whole thing together. Lucia sounds like a typical Italian-mama type. It's going to be quite event." She sighed. "I hate to say this, but I don't know how we can possibly go." She closed her eyes, waiting, knowing Jeff wasn't going to like hearing her plead business as an excuse.

"I know you have a lot on your plate right now, Bitsy," he said. "But family is important."

"Annie and Adolpho aren't family. They're friends of Mimi's in Paris. None of us even knew them two months ago."

"I wasn't really talking about Annie and Adolpho," Jeff murmured as he went back to stroking her hair. "The fact that their wedding will be in Florence provides a good opportunity for you to build some new family ties. Didn't Jean-Marc tell you his other daughter lives near there?"

Liz shrugged. "She's actually in what looks like a suburb—although I realize they don't think of it that way. But—"

Jeff kissed the top of her head. "That's perfect. We can go to the wedding with your mother, and then you'll meet Celine and her sons and spend some time with Jean-Marc." When she didn't respond, he squeezed her shoulder. "Relax, sweetheart. It's something to look forward to. Jean-Marc David is one of the best sailors in the world. And he's your *father*. Do you have any idea how many people in the world would like a chance to step on board the *Sea Cloud*? You're going to love it."

Liz sighed. The thought of meeting "the other daughter" tightened the ever-present knot in her stomach. "I did what you wanted," she said. "I added Jean-Marc to *our* guest list." She paused. "But if I'm honest, I have to tell you I hope he doesn't come. Just because we've e-mailed back and forth a few times doesn't mean I'm ready to go sailing off into the sunset with him. And the idea of meeting a half sister I didn't even know existed until a few weeks ago isn't very attractive at the moment, either. It's too much, Jeff. It's just too much."

"None of these things have to make it a negative event, Bitsy. An Italian wedding set in a villa overlooking Florence—how bad could it be?" He cupped her shoulder with his hand and gave her a little shake. "You might consider that the news is probably a little nerve-racking for Celine, too."

Liz snorted. "Except that she's probably not as surprised about my existence as I am about hers."

"What's that supposed to mean?"

Liz shrugged. "Just what it means. I don't imagine Celine is all that surprised. After all, she *knows* Jean-Marc. He's been her father all along. He's been a wanderer. And that's by his own admission. In e-mails."

Jeff was quiet. Again. He was always quiet when she said something he didn't like. She sat up a little straighter and shivered. The beach was losing its charm. But she would wait him out. She had to learn to do that. And she would. But as quickly as she determined to do it, she realized she couldn't. Her stomach was writhing. The pounding surf was getting to her, too. She had to break the silence, distract him, return to safer ground. *Reasoning*. No emotion, just *logic*. She took in a deep breath. "If we take Mimi up on her offer, that means redecorating the house. Not just my office. That's going to take up even more of my time," Liz said. "I just think it makes sense to postpone the 'family' reunion until things are more . . . reasonable. The hospital wing will be finished in the fall. You and I will have had a chance to adjust to being married by then. And maybe Mimi will have decided which man—if any—she's going to make a part of her life. Again. Or anew."

"*Which* man?"

"She talks about Luca Santo. A lot."

"Of course she does. He's the only person her age she knows in Paris." Jeff put his arm around her and nuzzled her cheek. She could feel his warm breath against her skin. "I don't see that Mary has to make a choice. A woman can have more than one male friend—don't you think?"

"Sure," Liz said. She changed the subject. Again. "Just remember that the next time I have dinner with an intern."

"That's different," Jeff said.

"It isn't," she insisted.

"It is when the boys have a raving crush on you. More than one has stared at you like he'd like to have you for dessert."

"You're jealous," she said, turning to look him in the eye. "That's so . . . completely adorable." She leaned over and kissed his cheek, then the corner of his mouth. "Unnecessary," she said, leaning against him. "But adorable." She kissed him on the lips. He wrapped his arms around her, and Liz forgot to be stressed about . . . anything.

It was Saturday afternoon. Adrenalin had powered Liz through the previous few days. A mere forty-eight hours after signing with a real estate agent, she got the call that her condo had sold. The buyer was paying cash, but he wanted immediate possession. What Liz had initially claimed impossible was being accomplished this very afternoon—thanks to her Realtor's personal friendship with a local mover. When she got back to Omaha, her personal belongings would be waiting for her at the estate. And the Realtor had located a climate-controlled storage facility for her furniture. The week was a blur, but she'd arrived in California and even brought a massive bouquet of flowers and more Valentino's pizza for Jeff's family. And now, as she sat alone at Danny Scott's drop-leaf kitchen table looking out on an idyllic scene . . . she wanted to cry.

How strange that the very thing she had intended to bring them closer only emphasized how far apart she and Jeff really were. Jeff was a natural with kids. He didn't have to *pretend* to like playing with Sarah's two boys. He entered into it with a sparkle in his eyes that Liz had never noticed before. He laughed. He roared. Crawled on all fours like a horse, oblivious to the grass stains on his Lord & Taylor pants. When Hillary, the "string bean" with long limbs and zero body fat, joined the fray, the boys headed for the sandbox Danny had built this past week. *"I want them to know I love having them here,"* he had said when Liz exclaimed over the recent addition to the bachelor's carefully landscaped and immaculately manicured backyard. While Josh and Andy ran cars over imaginary roads in the sandbox, Jeff produced a Frisbee. The look on his face as he and Hillary tossed it back and forth was pure enjoyment. And later today they were going to Wal-Mart—for *Jeff,* who wanted some sweat shirts and blue jeans. For himself.

"Hey, Bitsy." Jeff came into the kitchen, out of breath from his romp with the kids. He tousled Liz's hair, kissed the top of her head. "You should come outside with us. It's a beautiful day."

Liz smiled. Shook her head.

"Come on, baby," Jeff pleaded.

"You go on." She tried to give it a positive spin. "They're having a great time with you. They don't need me putting a damper on things."

"What do you mean, damper? You can toss a Frisbee, can't you?"

Liz shrugged. "Hillary stares at me like I'm a creature from another planet. The boys do their best to pretend I don't exist."

"So come out to the sandbox," Jeff cajoled. "Sit down and run a truck over the road. Make engine noises. Bulldoze sand. Build towers, tear them down, start again. It'll be fun."

"In a minute," she said.

"Suit yourself." He was back out the door, coffee cup in hand.

Liz closed her eyes. She really could not think of anything more boring . . . anything she would like to do *less* than crawling around in a sandbox with two little boys. She took another sip of coffee. Was it her fault she had never learned to play? Of course not. It just wasn't her. Maybe she was missing the parenting gene, after all. She certainly had no desire to procreate at the moment. What had it done for Sarah? Three kids—boom-boom-boom—and a descent into poverty. Liz didn't see the point. It wasn't like the woman's life was happy. Gary Henderson had been a loser from day one, and Sarah had to have known that. And now Sarah Supermom was going to have to get a job, and the kids would be . . . where? What kind of day care could Sarah possibly afford?

Liz sat up straight. That was it. There *was* something Aunt Liz could do. She smiled, inwardly rejoicing that at last she had come up with a way to make Sarah like her. Not that that was the intent, but surely Sarah would think better of her. She would talk to her tonight after the kids went to bed, while Jeff and Danny were immersed in one of their stupid video games.

WITH A JOKE ABOUT the brothers warring in the room behind them and a comment about the "beautiful sunset," which, in truth, she had barely noticed, Liz settled next to Sarah on Danny's patio. "I've been thinking," she said, "that you should let us help out with the kids' day care." She took a sip of coffee and waited for Sarah to jump up and down and thank her. But apparently Sarah hadn't read the script.

"Thanks for offering," Sarah said, "but we'll be fine. We don't have the details worked out yet, but Danny and I think we can handle it."

"How?"

Sarah frowned. "Did you think I was waiting for Jeff and you to fly in and rescue me with the big bucks?"

"No . . . I—"

"Like I said, Liz, thanks, but Danny and I—"

"But why burden Danny with it?" Liz blurted out. "When we can—"

"When you can just write a check and make it all better?" Sarah tugged on a red curl.

Liz glanced at her future sister-in-law, who had put her coffee mug down and was staring into the distance, her lips pressed together, her brow furrowed. Something was clearly wrong, but Liz couldn't imagine what.

Sarah took in a deep breath. "Look, Liz, don't think I don't appreciate your offer. I do. And I know you can't understand this, but the truth is that my brother doesn't *feel* burdened to have the kids and me here. He *loves* those kids. And although I can't quite imagine why, he loves me, too." She forced a smile. "I'll stay home with my kids during the day while Danny's working. I'll get a job working nights, and Danny will take over the evening shift. So we don't need day care, and we won't need your money. Although—" she forced a laugh—"if you insisted on starting a college fund, I wouldn't try to talk you out of it."

"But," Liz reasoned, "you'll both be so tied down."

"That's one way to look at it," Sarah said. "I prefer to think of it as parenting."

"I didn't mean it that way," Liz said. "All I meant was you're young. You should be able to go out for dinner once in a while. You should be able to have a social life."

"I will. There's a baby-sitting co-op at Danny's church. As soon as I'm able, I'm going to sign up. Even with working, I should be able to earn an evening on my own every few weeks."

"Every few *weeks*?"

Sarah shrugged. "I don't really have any deep desire to escape my children, Liz. Right now, I'm more into cocooning and reassuring them they are *safe* and we have a home. There's going to be counseling to go to—for a while at least. I want to try to minimize the effects of . . ." She bit her lip.

"Then let us pay for the counseling," Liz said.

Sarah sat back in her chair, considering. "All right. That, you and Jeff can do. He's already mentioned it. And thank you."

"Is there anything else?"

"Sure," Sarah said.

"Name it. Clothes? Toys? There's an FAO Schwarz at the mall. We could take the kids—"

"Liz. Stop. I don't need you to throw money at my children. I don't want to make you mad or anything, but really, they're fine. They don't need a lot of stuff. At their ages, they'd have more fun building a fort with the boxes than playing with the toys inside. If you want to help . . . just go out and play in the sand with them. Let them see normal grown-up people having normal fun. That's the best thing for them right now. They really don't need a lot of stuff. They just need consistent love from the semi-normal adults in their lives."

Liz forced a smile. "Love in the form of a sandbox?"

Sarah nodded.

That blasted sandbox.

# ❧ FOUR ❧

"CHURCH? DID I JUST hear my little brother ask if we want to go to *church*?" Jeff nearly choked on the late-night pizza he and Danny had ordered in to fuel their Nintendo wars. When she saw Jeff look her direction, Liz shrugged and took another bite of salad, hoping to stay out of the conversation.

"Yeah," Danny said. He looked at Sarah, who nodded encouragement. "It's good for the kids. A place to maybe find some friends. Some decent ones."

"All right," Jeff agreed. "I can see that. But what are you gonna do—open the Yellow Pages and hope for the best?"

"I . . . uh . . . well," Danny cleared his throat. "I've already taken them with me. To mine."

"To your . . . what?"

"My church."

Jeff snorted with laughter, but Liz knew that Danny was serious.

"This," Jeff said, exchanging a look with Liz and leaning back in his chair, "I've got to hear."

"There's not much to hear," Danny said. "I was hung over one Sunday morning last fall, and there was this guy on television preaching. Only it seemed different from the usual television preacher."

"He wasn't asking for money?" Liz quipped, not caring about the sarcasm dripping from her voice.

Danny shook his head. "Nope. In fact, when it came time to take up the offering, this guy said something about visitors being guests and that the place was supported by members and no one should feel obligated to give."

"You're kidding," Liz said.

"That's what I thought, too. Anyway, I can't really explain all the differences, but they were there. So I started listening." Danny shrugged. "And then I decided to check it out." He broke off. "Look, if you two want to come, great. If not, that's cool." He glanced at Liz. "It's not like I've turned into a Jesus freak or anything. But the kids liked it when I took them last week. Hillary came bopping out of the classroom with a clothespin covered with white cotton balls, and she told me the story of the little lost lamb. She was *smiling*. And at this point in their lives, I figure anything that makes those kids smile is worth my effort."

"What's Sarah think of all this?" Jeff asked, turning toward his sister.

"Sarah thinks it's great," Sarah replied. "Sarah thinks that maybe, just maybe, if she had gone to church instead of Billy's Bar, she wouldn't have this." She held up the cast.

"Don't do that to yourself," Liz protested. "Battered women always seem to think it's their fault. You didn't do anything to deserve that."

"I didn't say it was my fault," Sarah said. "But I wouldn't have met Gary if I'd been going out with church people instead of to Billy's Bar. I think that's pretty much a given."

"But if you hadn't met Gary," Danny said gently, "you wouldn't have those terrific little people in your life." He nodded toward the kids' bedroom.

Sarah smiled and turned to Liz. "So . . . are you coming with us in the morning? Because if you are, I'll need to clean out the backseat of the van."

"We'd love to come," Jeff answered for them both.

"But we can drive the rental," Liz added. "Jeff can ride back with you, and then I'll be able to head straight to the airport when it's over." She looked at Jeff. "I have that meeting Monday morning with Derrick Miller's son."

Later as she and Jeff said good-night, Liz said, "Well, Danny may not be one, but I think you do have a Jesus freak in the family."

"You mean Sarah," Jeff said.

"I'm not surprised," Liz reasoned. "She's been traumatized. Religion offers sanctuary." She did not say the rest of what she thought. Which was, *it'll pass as soon as she gets back on her feet*. She chuckled.

"What's so funny about Sarah finding some comfort in religion?"

"Nothing," Liz said. "It's great." She laughed quietly. "I was just trying to imagine the two uncles delivering the kids to Sunday School tomorrow morning. I've imagined you in all kinds of places, doing all kinds of things, Jeff, but this was not one of them."

"I know," Jeff said. "It would seriously mess with my debonair reputation in the Midwest if it got out." He bent to kiss her.

"Your secret's safe with me," Liz said, returning his chaste kiss with gusto. *And don't go getting religion on me. Our lives are complicated enough right now.* But religion would be good for Sarah and the kids, who were too young to go to school and make friends. And the sooner Sarah found new friends, the sooner Jeff would stop worrying about her and come back to Omaha and the real world.

## *Mary*

I HAVEN'T HAD this much trouble concentrating on a sermon since Sam died. But in that other life no one expected me to actually *listen* to the sermon. Sam and I went to church to be seen, not to be changed. Things are different now. At least they have been different until today. This Sunday morning, with Luca Santo seated at the far end of the pew just behind mine—on the opposite side of the church—all I can think about is him. Why didn't he sit with me? Is he watching me? Is my hair okay? Should I have worn my green sweater? After nearly a week of silence, he finally called me yesterday. We're having lunch after the service. And the sermon might just as well be in Yiddish for all the good it is doing me.

Why, Luca thought, had he chosen a seat where Mary was constantly in his line of sight? He should have sat closer to the front. He wasn't going to hear a word of the sermon, even though he had gone through the motions of opening the Bible to the passage the pastor had cited. A sermon on the topic of waiting on God would be good for him. But when he opened the Bible, there was Jean-Marc's note. As if he didn't have the entire thing memorized by now. As if he hadn't spent the better part of this last week pacing around his apartment, wrestling with himself about friendship and loyalty and . . . waiting on God.

Well, no matter. After lunch today it would all be settled. Romantic thoughts of Mary would be a pleasant part of his past. He would be able to concentrate on the new shipment of motorcycles arriving this next week . . . and the upcoming trip home. As for Annie and Adolpho's wedding in Florence, and Mary's attendance, it wouldn't be that hard to keep his distance once Jean-Marc got off that blasted yacht of his and declared his intentions.

Luca's finger traced Jean-Marc's handwriting and the words he'd written. *My Mary,* he had said. Obviously, the two of them had an understanding, and whatever smiles Mary Davis had sent Luca Santo's way were smiles of friendship. And nothing more. It had taken the better part of a week, but Luca finally had that in hand. And today at lunch, he and Mary would rejoice in Jean-Marc's newfound faith as friends, and that, Luca thought, would be that.

*Mary*

AFTER THE CHURCH service, Luca and I take the metro back to St. Germain. We talk about everything and nothing.

When we come up out of the metro, he takes my hand and leads me down a narrow street and into a tiny café crowded with diners. Our waiter recognizes Luca, and the two enter into a spirited discussion about some obscure detail of motorcycle design. Finally, the waiter leaves to retrieve coffee for us, and Luca opens his Bible, pulls out a slip of paper, and hands it to me. I reread it twice, focusing on the last sentence, where Jean-Marc has written, *I entrust my dear Mary to my dearest friend.* Looking up, I try—and fail—to decipher the expression on Luca's face. Finally, I ignore my personal misgivings, paste on a bright smile, and lay the note on the table between us. I hope Luca doesn't notice how my hand trembles as I stir my coffee. He does.

"I would have thought Jean-Marc's news would bring a smile into your eyes, *cara mia.*"

"Actually," I take a sip of coffee and clear my throat. "Jean-Marc called me. Yesterday." I force a smile. "He doesn't use the same vocabulary we do, but his faith seems genuine." *Listen to yourself. Where's the joy? What's wrong with you?* I shake my head. "I'm so ashamed of myself. My faith is so small. I've been praying for him . . . but I never really believed God would answer yes." I pause, realizing I am near tears. "I've been talking to God about a lot of things lately. And he hasn't been saying much. But then, this." I touch the note. "It makes one feel very small."

Luca's voice is comforting. "I know what you mean. Sometimes God seems to be ignoring us. And then, he does the last thing we expect. Sometimes the very thing we have wondered if he *could* do." He smiles. "Like you, I have sometimes had little faith when it comes to our friend Jean-Marc David."

I shrug. "At least your 'little faith' is limited to just one thing."

Luca frowns. He leans forward and touches the back of my hand. "Tell me, *cara mia.* What is it?"

"Nothing new," I reply. "The same old questions and doubts. The same worries about Liz. The wedding. Her future. And—" I hesitate, then blurt it out. "I think perhaps I've relied too little on God and too much on you. I've gotten into the habit of calling you first . . . and praying second." I finally manage to force myself to meet his gaze. "It's no wonder I've worn out my welcome with you."

"You could never do that."

He says it quickly and with conviction. For just an instant I think I see something more than duty to an old friend in his eyes. But it is gone so quickly that I tell myself it is only my imagination. He pulls his hand away, picks up Jean-Marc's note, and tucks it between the pages of his Bible. "My dear friend Jean-Marc has given me a charge to watch over you . . . and I accept it. Willingly."

He smiles politely. And suddenly I realize what it is that really bothers me about Jean-Marc's note. *I entrust my dear Mary to you.* It reminds me of Sam, who always had someone assigned to look out for me in new situations. When we were first married, I thought it was sweet of him to take such care with me. But as time passed, I began to realize what it really was. Sam didn't trust me. He didn't think I could handle life. And while I can tell myself that Jean-Marc isn't Sam, and this isn't the same thing at all . . . it still feels as if a cool wind has blown between me and my two friends. As if, at Jean-Marc's request, Luca has become my caretaker. As if, having finally broken free of my past, I am once again being handled. I tell myself I'm overreacting, but I can't quell my emotions.

"I've said something that upsets you," Luca says, frowning.

I shake my head.

"Yes," he insists. "And you must tell me what it is so that I do not repeat this mistake." His voice is gentle. "*Per favore, cara mia . . .* tell me."

I can't look at him. Instead, I look out the window. Clear my throat. Sip coffee. When I finally look across the table, Luca's expression is troubled, his eyes warm with what I desperately want to be honest affection. Taking a deep breath, I lean forward and say, "This all feels a little too familiar." It is clear he has no idea what I'm talking about. I look down and fiddle with my fork. "Sam thought I needed caretaking, too."

Luca immediately protests. "Jean-Marc does not think of you in that way. Nor do I."

"I appreciate you saying that. But just in case there's been a mis-understanding—" I stop to pray my voice doesn't shake when I say what must be said. "I'm not looking for a replacement for Sam Davis. You need to know that. And so does Jean-Marc. I enjoy the company of men. But I don't *need* it to be happy."

Luca waits so long to respond that I think he must be counting my heartbeats. Certainly it's pounding loud enough for him to hear it. But then he chuckles and waves his hand in the air. "You American women," he teases me, "always so intent to make your own personal declaration of independence." He winks at me. "*Capisco, cara mia.* I understand what you are saying." He flashes a smile and raises his coffee cup in a mock toast. "To friendship," he says, then leans close and murmurs, "And now we can have the dessert . . . as *friends*?" He winks again.

What's to be done . . . but to laugh and nod and order *crème brûlée*? And so I do. I even kiss Luca on the cheek when we part—just to show him . . . something. I'm not sure what.

Back in my apartment, I sit down at the beautiful grand piano in my light-filled studio and congratulate myself for clearing things up . . . and then I have a good cry—for the purpose, I tell myself, of getting Signor Luca Santo out of my system for good.

MONDAY MORNING FOUND Liz running late. The restaurant the Scott family went to after church was one of those "feed at the trough" buffets that gave Liz the creeps. Josh spilled a huge glass of Coke . . . in her lap. Andy squirted ketchup halfway across the table, and when a spot landed on Hillary's new church dress, she wailed. Liz promised to buy her a new one, but it was Jeff's pulling Hillary into his arms that finally calmed her down.

Arriving at the airport already frazzled—and regretting the hasty departure that amounted to little more than a peck on the cheek from Jeff—Liz got the news that her pilot had had to file a revised flight plan because of weather over the Rockies. It was nearly three in the morning before she finally landed on her doorstep . . . and later than that before she fell asleep. If Irene hadn't taken it upon herself to unpack some of the boxes the moving company had piled in her bedroom at home, she would have had no chance of making it to work on time Monday morning. Meeting with a new intern was the last thing on earth Liz wanted to do. But if she could get through it, she could then look forward to meeting Mona out at the house for lunch. Jeff had been noncommittal about them living at the estate after the wedding, but he told her to go ahead and update her father's office, saying that would be a good move for the immediate future no matter what happened with the Davis estate long-term.

Liz's most recent memory of Derrick Miller's son included a flash of blond hair, muddy Nike-prints on the marble entryway hall at home, and a bug jar left in the guest bathroom when Ryan had once accompanied his father out to the house for a meeting of Creighton alumni. She remembered Daddy's expression changing when he saw Ryan in tow with his illustrious father—and how Mimi had deftly "removed the boy" with a promise of one of Irene's cinnamon rolls and a bug collecting expedition around one of the ponds while the men talked. But it was obvious that muddy Nikes and bug jars had long been set aside when Margaret showed the grown-up version of Ryan Miller into Liz's office.

"You *cannot* be Ryan Miller," Liz said, hopping up from her desk chair and holding out her hand.

The young man flashed perfect white teeth and shrugged as he swallowed Liz's hand in a firm handshake.

The two stared at each other for a moment before Liz motioned to the sleek red leather chair opposite hers. "Sit down. Please."

Ryan folded his long frame with a grace that belied his age and settled back. "If you don't mind, I'd like to say something right up front," he said, and without waiting for Liz to give him the floor, he continued. "I just want you to know that I appreciate this meeting. It was Mrs. Davis who mentioned the internship to my father, and while I totally appreciate what a superb opportunity working for Davis Enterprises is, I don't want you to do this out of any sense of obligation."

When he paused and licked his lower lip, Liz had the sense of being inspected. His eyes were dark brown—so dark the iris and pupil blended together. Eyes like that in a woman would have made a novelist wax poetic about pools of . . . something. In an athletic young man with the bearing of a man far beyond his chronological age, they were powerful. Ryan Miller just might become a force to be reckoned with some day, no matter the business he chose.

"What I mean is," he said, and leaned forward, "I want more than anything to learn from the best, and in this level of the construction industry, in Omaha—maybe in the Midwest—I know that Davis Enterprises is the best. But if my presence is payback to an old friend, then—" he paused momentarily and looked past Liz toward the skyline in the distance—"then I'd rather be cut loose before we even start. Most of the guys in my business class are counting on their fathers' connections to get them ahead, and they're lazy because of it." His gaze hardened slightly and his voice dropped a little lower. He drew out the next words, "I don't want to be one of them. I want to earn my way."

"Well," Liz said. "That's a very impressive speech." She waited for the boy to look at her. "But you're . . . how old?"

"Twenty-three," Ryan said. "I know. That's a little old to be serving an internship. I had some trouble in junior high. Got held back a year." He smiled. "I thought it was the end of my life. Actually, it was a good thing. I think I'm more mature than most of my peers. More ready to be an asset to a company."

"Chronological age doesn't make much difference. What I was getting at," Liz said, "is—exactly what is it you know that would enable you to be an asset to Davis Enterprises? You're to be commended for your good attitude, but do you have any specific idea how that could work out, given your lack of experience?"

The boy didn't answer. She liked that. He was thinking. Or at least pretending to think. His head tilted a little to one side. White-blond curls fell just over the collar of his crisply starched dress shirt. Liz almost wondered if he had borrowed one of his father's ties for this meeting. She didn't think he was the type to own a tie. He was the jock—the rising basketball star, the golden boy of the team. She could imagine all the college girls turning their heads when he walked by, a golden Goliath striding across the campus on his way to . . . whatever classes it was he took. She decided to ask.

"I've had the usual stuff. Economics. Accounting. Marketing. Some basic construction classes. A couple of CAD design seminars. And Spanish."

"Why Spanish?"

He shrugged. "Personal interest." He smiled again, that easy smile learned at the country club by the sons of fathers who were busily smoothing the way for the next generation. "I figured I'd be ahead of the game if I could actually talk to my crews once I get my own business going."

"That's what you want? To become my competitor?"

He shook his head. "No, ma'am. I want to specialize more than Davis Enterprises does. I've got some ideas about residential planning that—But you asked how I could help Davis Enterprises."

"Well, the fact that you speak Spanish is great," Liz said. "The population in Nebraska is shifting. We have a lot of Latin and Hispanic citizens. If you're fluent, you might be able to help us find and benefit from the best of their work ethic—which I've often found to be very strong."

Ryan reached into his suit-coat pocket, pulled out a piece of paper folded in quarters, and held it out to Liz with arms so long Liz thought of a praying mantis. "Actually, I have something else you might be interested in. I took the liberty of talking to Mr. Kincaid in preparation for this meeting," he said. "And based on our discussion, I ran some numbers on the oncology wing project," he said.

"You . . . ran some numbers?"

He shrugged again. "Just a hunch. Mr. Kincaid said he'd mentioned using GFRC, but said you weren't open to the idea." He nodded at the paper. "That's a spreadsheet showing the long-term benefits if you were to use it." He continued before Liz could say it. "And you're thinking it's too late, but it's not. The switch could still be made. And it's consistent with Davis Enterprises' commitment to using local suppliers whenever possible." He smiled his easy smile. "You should really think about it. Mr. Kincaid's idea is a good one."

Liz studied the figures for a moment and then laid the paper down. "How do you know George Kincaid?"

"He's my adopted uncle," the young man said. "His wife and my mother were best friends. I stopped calling him Uncle George when I was about ten years old. That was when my dad and mom broke up . . . and Betty Kincaid died. So he sort of faded out of my life."

Liz got up from her desk, walked across the plush carpet to the sideboard where a perpetually fresh pot of coffee sat—Margaret rebrewed a pot every few hours throughout the day—and poured herself a cup. She kept her back to Ryan while she considered this new revelation—the spreadsheet proved George's proposal was a good one—and the disconcerting ease with which Ryan Miller offered to give up the internship while at the same time providing evidence that silently argued that he was well worth the investment of time and money any company would care to make.

"Coffee?" Liz asked.

"Thanks, no."

She turned around. "Don't tell me," she said. "You don't drink coffee. Unhealthy for an athlete."

He shrugged again. "Not the best for anyone's health," he agreed. "But I'm not really into preaching my personal gospel of health." He smiled.

"Good," Liz said. She set her coffee cup down and lit a cigarette.

"Except when it comes to second-hand smoke," he said. "That's . . . um . . ."

"Crossing the line?" Liz said.

"Yes, ma'am. I . . . uh . . ."—Was he actually blushing?— "respectfully . . . think so."

"Good," Liz said, and put out the cigarette. She smiled, walked back to her desk, set down the coffee cup, and held out her hand. "Welcome to Davis Enterprises, Ryan. I like a man with the guts to stand up for himself without being a bore." Watching the boy's color continue to rise, Liz settled comfortably back at her desk. "Now," she said, peering down at the paper Miller had handed her moments ago. "Let's talk about these figures." She held it out to him, but he didn't take it.

Instead, he presented George Kincaid's case from memory. "You'll see there," he said, "on about the fourth line down, that if we replace the current materials with GFRC—"

"But GFRC hasn't been used in a project of this magnitude anywhere in Nebraska."

"So what," the boy said. "Let Davis Enterprises be the leader. Like you were back in the '70s with state-of-the-art glazing on the Hillman Building."

Liz looked up with surprise. "You've done your homework."

"I didn't have to," he said. He smiled again. "My father used to rant and rave about Sam Davis and how he'd bested him on this business deal or that. I started paying attention to Davis Enterprises at an early age."

"Know thy enemy?" Liz said.

"Well," Ryan said, "something like that. Except that Dad's merger with Davis Enterprises changed his opinion. Your father was more than generous."

"We needed the equipment. Your dad wanted to sell. It was good for everyone."

"That's exactly what he said," Ryan agreed. "And then he said that if I wanted an internship that would make future employers stand up and take notice, this was the one to land."

"I'll have to thank him for the kind words," Liz said.

"But," Ryan said, "I still want you to say no if this is strictly a favor to an insider's kid."

Liz picked up the sheet of paper and waved it. "I'd be a fool to turn down an intern who has this kind of business mind," she said. "When can you start?"

"How about today?"

Liz laughed. "You have classes. I mean, when are you finished with this term?"

"I've already talked to most of my professors. Two classes are night classes, and the others agreed to let me finish the term as an independent study."

"Your professors are that flexible?"

Ryan shrugged. "It didn't take very much to convince them that an internship with Elizabeth Davis was an opportunity not to be squandered."

Liz slid open her center desk drawer and looked down at the small calendar that lay open but out of sight. "I've got an appointment in about an hour. Think you can wait until tomorrow to get started?"

Ryan grinned. "Whatever you say. You're the boss."

"You just keep talking like that, Ryan, and you'll go far in the industry." Liz laughed.

He stood up and held out his hand. "I've taken enough of your time, Ms. Davis. Should I wear a hard hat or a suit?"

"We'll start with a suit," Liz said, rising and shaking the strong, massive hand. She looked up at him, realizing that next to his towering, lanky frame, she felt almost petite. "We'll tour a few sites and talk some more. Maybe have lunch. Then I'll have a better feel for where you'd fit in."

He nodded and flashed another smile, "So arrive in a suit but maybe have a hard hat in the car?"

Liz grinned. "Hard hat on call. Definitely. But you don't have to provide your own."

At the door, he paused and turned back. "Thank you, Ms. Davis. I'll do my best for you."

As soon as the office door closed, Liz sank back down into her chair. The boy was young enough to be . . . well, her younger brother. But he seemed so at ease in his skin, so relaxed sitting in the chair across from one of the most powerful women in Nebraska. It was an attitude that might have irritated her in any other young man. But in Ryan Miller, the towheaded god of the Creighton basketball court, it was . . . reasonable. In a woman it would be called alluring.

Taking up the paper he had left her with his facts and figures, she looked them over. He was right. Of course that was no surprise. George Kincaid had been right, too, but Liz had refused to back down. Now she might have to. Strangely, she didn't mind. It would be good for her intern to see that one thing a good boss did was know when to admit they had made a mistake.

"Bitsy." Jeff stepped inside the massive front door, tossed a bouquet of roses toward the decorative table in the middle of the foyer, and pulled Liz into his arms. "This," he murmured as he held her, "has been the longest two weeks of my life." Grabbing her hand, he led her across the foyer and into the darkened library.

When she came up for air a few minutes later, Liz sighed with happiness. "Phew," she said, brushing her hair back out of her face. "That's a relief!"

"What?" He sat up beside her, straddling the padded library bench, pulled her against his chest, and rested his chin on her head.

She chuckled. "When you had so many good things to say about California, I was a little afraid you were going to report your own born-again experience and announce celibacy as a new calling."

Jeff nuzzled her ear. "Nothing quite that earthshaking happened. Although that church and the people in it are . . . interesting. We ended up taking the kids to a midweek program, and then—don't laugh—the three of us went to a Bible study at somebody's house while the kids were tearing around the church gym."

"Seriously?" Liz moved away so they could face one another. She reached over and switched on the lamp at the edge of the table next to them. Laughing, she rubbed the lip print off his cheek.

Smiling, Jeff traced the back of her hand with his index finger while he spoke. "Do you remember in Paris how when Luca Santo prayed over dinner it was like he was talking to someone sitting just across the table from him?"

"I guess," Liz said.

"Well, Danny's church people are like that. Frankly, it was weird to sit in a room with about a dozen people with Bibles open on their knees." He looked around at the cherrywood shelves full of books. "Is there a Bible in here anywhere?"

Liz shrugged. "Probably. I don't know. Why?"

"No reason. Just curious." Jeff said, and looked back at her. "I can tell you one thing—I knew I didn't belong to whatever club they have going." He paused before adding, "The funny thing is, I don't think I'd mind."

"Mind what?"

"Being in their club. Believing I could just call up God and he'd answer."

"So. The next time you visit Danny and Sarah, are you going to climb off the plane with a Bible tucked under your arm?" She chuckled. But Jeff didn't get the joke.

"Don't make fun," he said. "Whatever it is that's going on out there, Danny's serious about it. So is Sarah."

*Of course not,* Liz thought. It was not allowed to make fun of the favored brother and sister. Liz could feel their tug on Jeff, even from over a thousand miles away. She forced herself to stay calm. "I'm not making fun, sweetheart. I already told you I think it's great. For them."

Jeff was quiet.

Liz tried again. "So how is Sarah? Healing up?"

"Yeah. She and the kids are going to be seing a counselor at their church for a while. She seems comfortable with the idea."

"Does that mean Uncle Jeff is a little less worried about things in Marin County?"

"It does," he said. "And I've figured out a way to be a little less worried about things here, too." He looked around at the room.

"Really? What's to worry about? I'm handling things fine."

Jeff kissed the back of her hand. "Of course you are. Elizabeth Davis always handles things fine. But you *have* been stressed out. So. Here's the deal: I'm not sure about starting my marriage living here." He tapped Liz's mouth before she could protest. "But I *am* certain that selling your condo and moving here until the wedding was a great idea. And"—he nodded toward the door leading into the foyer, and ultimately to Sam's old office—"like I've said before, whatever you and Mona have decided to do with your home office is fine with me, too."

Closing her eyes, Liz reached up and took his hand, guiding it to her waist and murmuring softly.

Jeff kissed her cheek, then looked at his watch. "If we're having dinner at Vivace, we need to get going. I still have to unpack and get prepared for an early meeting tomorrow." He got up and pulled Liz up beside him. "Big meeting with the big cheese."

"So soon after you get back?"

"Something's been brewing while I was gone. Don't know what, but one of the guys in the office was hinting about it on e-mail last week. Wouldn't clarify. Just hinting. The guy drives me nuts sometimes."

Liz followed him out into the foyer. "Come on up while I change," she said, and headed up the stairs. "Maybe we should skip dinner."

Jeff shook his head. "Irene and Cecil wouldn't approve. I'll just go back to the kitchen and say hello to them. We'll go as soon as you're ready." He shrugged. "Who knows, maybe you living back at home will be a good thing for lots of reasons. Maybe it'll do us good to be old-fashioned."

"I *am* old-fashioned," Liz insisted. "I'm all for monogamy and morality and all that. I just don't think we should be expected to live like monks."

"It's only a few months until the wedding," Jeff reasoned. "And we don't want to give Irene and Cecil—or anyone else—reason to be upset with us. Besides," he added, "once we start our family, we're going to have to have this all figured out. Standards. Rules."

"That doesn't have to be such a big deal, you know," Liz said.

"So . . . what kind of rules are our kids going to be raised by?"

"Human kindness. Honesty. The Golden Rule. All the things our parents taught us."

"Danny and Sarah and their pastor seem to think there's more to it than that. And that abstinence before marriage is a good thing."

"More power to them," Liz said. She continued up the stairs. "We have time to work it out, sweetheart. Could we just be married for a while before we draft a plan for family life?"

"I don't know," Jeff said, looking up at her. "There's something very appealing about the thought of having a little girl with your blue eyes. . . ." He put his hand on his heart. "Wow. She'll have me wrapped around her little finger from day one."

"Slow down, Superdad, slow down," Liz said, waving him toward the kitchen. "Go ahead. Say hello to Cecil and Irene. I'll be down in a minute." She leaned over the railing and blew him a kiss. "But you're missing out on the best part of a homecoming."

# ℘ FIVE ℘

*Mary*

*As I ponder Luca's advice to "tell the mountains in my life how big my God is," rather than my usual tendency "to tell God how big the mountains are," I'm still not certain how it all works. But in these three weeks following our luncheon, it has seemed to happen in my life. Daily I hold up Liz and Luca and Jean-Marc to God . . . and pretty much tell God the mountains are too big for me. And daily he levels them out to the point that I don't feel quite so surrounded by trouble.*

*Jeff has been back from California for a week, and Liz seems to be less frantic about everything. I'm amazed by this because she has more to do than ever. Why she's taken on creating an office for Jeff that he hasn't even said he wants yet, I don't know . . . but I'm trying to learn to supply opinions to my powerhouse of a daughter on an as-requested basis only. With Liz, that usually means never. One thing is obvious: She's much more at peace when Jeffrey Scott is in town. Which probably bodes well for their future together. Jeff makes her a better woman. I hope she realizes that.*

A knock at my door pulls me away from my journal. I have been inhaling the aromas of Mrs. Delhomme's baking all morning long, so I open the door with a *merci* on my lips, but it dies in my throat because it is not Mrs. Delhomme. My hand goes to my unbrushed hair and then to the lapels of my bathrobe. I overlap it to hide the plunging neckline and look up into Nordic blue eyes.

*"Bonjour, chérie,"* Jean-Marc murmurs even as he bends to kiss me on either cheek. He hands me a huge bouquet of lilies and then laughs aloud and chucks me under the chin to help me close my mouth.

"Madame Davis?" All I can see are Mrs. Delhomme's black shoes as she descends the stairs from the floor above me . . . then the hem of her apron . . . and finally, her aproned self with towel-covered plate in hand. She looks from Jean-Marc to me and back again, pausing on the second step from the landing.

If charm were a disease, Jean-Marc David would never have lived to be an adult. In the next few minutes he introduces himself, makes Madame Delhomme blush and giggle like a girl, accepts her *brioche,* and almost makes me believe that my unkempt hair is becomingly tousled. I try to gather my composure and go to my bedroom to get dressed while Jean-Marc rattles around my kitchen making coffee. I feel a little like I've come through one of the storms at sea Jean-Marc has told me about—the ones that leave him simultaneously breathless and refreshed.

When I finally return to my kitchen—I have not taken time to apply makeup—I am treated to the sight of this outrageously handsome man pouring coffee into one of two cups he has arranged on a tray. He has plucked one blossom from the bouquet of flowers and laid it across what I presume is my plate. And if I had not already been struck momentarily dumb with surprise, I would have been by what happened next. Jean-Marc David bowed his head and said grace. Aloud.

"Thank you for eyes to see and ears to hear, for land and sea. Please guide my ship in all her ways and may the steps we take lead us to you." He says amen, and when I open my eyes he asks me about my plans for the day, insisting that I not change anything on his account. He apologizes for coming unannounced, shrugging, "You must forgive me, but hearing your voice on the phone became more and more inadequate. I wanted to see your face." He looks down at his watch. "Now tell me, when you have this meeting with Annie."

"Ten o'clock," I reply, "but I can change—"

"No, you must change nothing. I want to see Luca as well. Can you have dinner tonight?"

"Of course." He sits back in his chair, savoring his coffee, studying me. I can feel myself blushing. "Is something wrong?" I reach up to touch my hair.

He smiles and slowly shakes his head from side to side. "Not one thing," he says. "Everything is as it should be. Finally. For all of time and eternity." He leans forward then, and begins to talk. Storytellers are usually eloquent speakers. Jean-Marc is one of the best. When he finishes I realize that the greatest story he has ever told required no eloquence at all. Simple words—*sin, debt, paid, cross, faith.*

"I never knew," he murmurs, shaking his head back and forth. He looks up at me, and the smile is rich and warm and filled with love. "Some days, it is as if I have never seen the sky or the sea until now." He gestures helplessly, "It's as if there is new life all around me . . ." He sighs.

"There is," I remind him, reaching out to put my hand on his heart. "Right there."

He takes my hand and kisses the back of it before letting go and asking about Liz. The sun streams in my windows and from upstairs I hear Mrs. Delhomme . . . singing at the top of her lungs. We smile, and for the next hour we are two friends sharing our lives and, on occasion, two parents discussing their daughters.

AS USUAL, MONA produced a miracle. With the aroma of fresh paint still in the air, Liz sat behind the desk of Daddy's—no, *her*—new home office and smiled. In less than a month Sam Davis's dominion had been transposed from a dark lion's den to a light and airy work space for a thoroughly modern woman. Daddy's legacy was preserved with the massive desk—and the teak record cabinet, which Mona had had transformed into a bar. Instead of sliding open, the cabinet top now lifted up, bringing with it an array of bottles and serving glasses, all poised in an ingeniously designed rack. As for the vinyl, Mimi had been the one to solve that.

"Throw them out," she had said abruptly when Liz asked about them.

"I can't," Liz said.

"Are you a fan of old music, Elizabeth?" Mimi asked.

"Well, no . . . but—"

"Neither am I," Mimi had said, which surprised Liz and raised that question again about who exactly Mimi was thinking of the day she told Liz not to play "Beyond the Sea" because it was too painful.

"But, Mimi—"

Liz heard her mother sigh. "All right, then. Here's another idea. Have Irene make a list of the titles and artists, and I'll find out if they have any value. If I recall correctly, there are a few Beatles albums. They're probably worth something. Maybe we can sell them all and donate the money to the foundation. Is that better?"

"Much," Liz said.

"All right, then. I'll handle it and let you know."

And within a few days Mimi had arranged for a record dealer to stop by for Daddy's collection. She said that whatever he offered would be a fair price. He was probably going to get at least twice what he paid for them, but that was how the game was played, and they shouldn't begrudge him the profit.

Both Liz and Mary had been surprised when the dealer made his offer, which included fifty dollars for one Beatles album and nearly that much for a Bob Dylan. And once again, Mimi surprised Liz by telling her that both the Beatles and the Bob Dylan were actually hers. *"Daddy was more Bobby Darin back then."*

Mona had loved Liz's ideas for the office—except for the taupe walls. "Buttercream," she had insisted, looking over her polka-dot-framed glasses and raising her eyebrows.

Liz laughed. "We're talking paint, Mona, not the wedding cake."

Mona tossed her magenta-colored mane of hair over her shoulder. She went to the fireplace and posed, clicking her ridiculously long fingernails on the mantel. "You get to keep those awful gray chairs and the albatross," she said, pointing at Sam's desk. "I get to paint the walls buttercream." She gestured dramatically. "It's what Dale suggested. And he should *know*."

Liz had wavered. And rightly so. If the renowned artist, Dale Chihuly, was suggesting the backdrop color for his art, she should probably listen. "All right," she said. "Buttercream." She chuckled, "But I'd better like it."

"When have you *not* liked Mona's interior spaces?" The woman feigned a pout.

"Touché," Liz said.

And Mona had been right. The office was stunning. Buttercream walls and Dale Chihuly—not on the mantel but floating above it—a transcendent sculpture of blown glass that dazzled Liz every time she saw it. She had felt at home in her new office from the moment Mona unveiled it. Until about five minutes ago.

Now, she sat staring at her computer screen, frowning, twisting a hank of hair nervously around her index finger. With a sigh, she got up and crossed the room. Lifting a diaphanous white drape, she ducked beneath it and opened a window. The chilly night air shocked her skin. Rubbing her arms to warm them up, she turned back to stare at the computer screen glowing in the dark with the words *Password Protected*. What, she wondered, was going on?

The record dealer had scrawled a note on a sheet of yellow paper torn from a legal pad.

> *I was playing your father's vinyl to make sure it wasn't scratched— just so my eBay customers would know, not because I thought you were selling junk—when I came across these in an otherwise empty album cover. I've already got three* Breakfast at Tiffany's *to sell, so it's no problem for me. But maybe you've been missing these? I didn't do anything with them but put them in this envelope and send them to you.*

Liz hoped she could believe him. Mimi had said he had a good reputation among the antique-buying eBay crowd.

And here she sat, at Daddy's desk, with three mystery disks—dreading the idea of yet more surprises from the past. He had personally made the labels. Liz recognized the extra little swirl on the *J*s and the *G*—something Daddy always did when he wrote with his fountain pen. *JMD, GTK, JJS*. The letters didn't match up with any building projects Liz could remember—at least not since Daddy started using a computer. She ejected the password-protected disk labeled *GTK* and inserted the one labeled *JJS*. And stared as the name *Jeffrey James Scott* appeared on the screen. This one wasn't password protected.

Liz moved the mouse and waited. These old computers always took so long—*click, click, click.* Finally, there it was. Everything anyone could want to know about Jeffrey James Scott: his mother, Lily . . . his siblings. His ancestry. Education. Daddy had even checked for a criminal record. And whoever had done this had been thorough—talked to old girlfriends, even—and turned up not one thing negative about Jeff or Lily or Danny or Sarah. Jeff's father, on the other hand, had remarried. Been indicted. Had a long rap sheet that included, among other offenses, charges filed by his third wife for spousal abuse. He was currently in the Ohio State Penitentiary serving a five-year sentence for felony assault. If Jeff knew that, he had never mentioned it. He had always said, *"I haven't heard from him since the day he walked out on us, and that's fine with me."*

Sam Davis had apparently personally transcribed his conversations with whomever was digging the dirt for him. And after every session, he had written his impressions, his decisions. As Liz read, she saw her father's opinion of Jeff change. For a while, he had apparently considered forbidding Liz to see Jeff again.

*While there's no evidence at the moment that J. is inclined to follow in his father's abusive footsteps, the family history raises a red flag. Elizabeth will have to be told soon. I can see the charm beginning to work its will in her. Better to hurt her now than put her at risk.*

That entry was dated a month after Jeff had been introduced to Liz's parents out at the house. Thinking back, Liz wondered what had happened to prevent Daddy's moving ahead with his plan to end their relationship? Whatever it was, he hadn't said a word, and in time, Jeff had apparently proven himself to the point that Daddy decided to let it go. A month after he was planning to intervene and try to end everything, he mentioned letting Jeff drive the Austin Healey as a way of "giving his seal of approval." That was the last thing on the disk, save a brief note that said, *Talked to Jeff. Satisfied. Will retain this file for future—just in case—but trusting it will never be needed.*

"Well, Daddy," Liz muttered as she pondered the computer screen, "you certainly cover all the bases." She longed for a cigarette. She'd promised to quit smoking a year ago and had done pretty well—until Mimi's move to Paris and Jean-Marc David's subsequent entrance into her life. But in the last couple of weeks, thanks to the patch on her left upper arm, she hadn't lit one cigarette—except for the one she used to test Ryan Miller, and she'd put that one out without smoking it.

Jumping up, she went to her bag and took out a piece of the gum she kept for emergencies. Her jaw was working hard as she returned to Daddy's desk, sat down, and moved the mouse to bring the screen back to life. Daddy had known Jeff's bank account numbers. His income history. How much he paid for rent. Even that he owned a Roth IRA and contributed to it regularly.

Sitting in Daddy's chair looking at the information, Liz's emotions roller-coastered between warm gratitude that her father obviously loved her deeply and wanted to protect her, and hot anger against a man so domineering as to ferret out information behind everyone's back. She had to tell Jeff. She couldn't. But she had to. He deserved to know. Why did he need to know? What purpose would that serve now? It was just Daddy being protective. Controlling. Domineering. No, Liz thought, she wouldn't mention it. And then came the niggling thought that Sam Davis had seemed sure that his daughter would do his bidding—even to the point of breaking up with Jeff. The idea that someone was manipulating her life was unsettling. Even if he was motivated by love, Daddy had carried it too far. What made him think he had the right to do such a thing? She moved the mouse. *Click-click.* Closed the file. Was this how Mimi had felt? Manipulated, controlled . . . not allowed to *be*?

Getting up from the desk, Liz went down the hall and into the kitchen. She made herself coffee and headed back up to the office. The second disk revealed what she had suspected. *JMD* was Jean-Marc David. This disk was more disturbing, because it revealed that Daddy had kept track of Jean-Marc for years after Mimi and he were married. There was a long list of dates and locations. And notations every time Jean-Marc had purchased a different boat. Daddy had known Jean-Marc owned the *Sea Cloud*. Daddy knew about Celine Dumas. He even knew her husband's name—and had noted the date of their divorce. Why, Liz wondered, would he care about that? What would make him keep track of Jean-Marc?

The third disk waited. Who, Liz wondered, was *GTK*. She wasn't sure she even wanted to know. What purpose did it serve to see this side of Sam Davis? What if he *was* controlling and manipulative? Couldn't she accept that and still love him—love the man without loving everything about him?

*That's what Mimi did . . . her whole life.*

Liz stared at the computer screen for a long time, pondering the realization that this night of learning hard things about Daddy was helping her identify with her mother. For all that she had learned about the secret side of Sam Davis, no real harm had been done. Maybe he was controlling and manipulative, but that didn't mean Liz couldn't do a lot of good with the money and power he had accumulated. *That* could be a legacy both she and Mimi could be proud of, no matter what the disks said about the private Sam Davis.

Liz went to bed telling herself the third disk labeled *GTK* didn't matter.

She woke wondering about George Kincaid's middle name. He'd

been a good friend, Daddy always said. It was a shame about the drinking; a tragedy what had happened to his career; almost unthinkable how he had fallen from the pinnacle of his profession to the bottom rung of society. *"But friends stand by friends,"* Daddy had said. And that's what he did. Didn't he? And after Daddy was gone, Mimi took up the cause. Even when it caused a terrible fight between her and Liz, Mimi had defended George—insisted that he be the architect for the hospital wing being built in Daddy's memory.

*Maybe,* Liz thought with a little shiver of dread, *Daddy knew something about George Kincaid that needed to be kept hidden?* And if that was the case . . . what would it mean for Davis Enterprises now, when George was working so closely with everyone on this new project? *Maybe,* she told herself, *you are worrying about nothing. You don't even know his middle name.*

## Mary

STANDING ON MY balcony overlooking the courtyard below, I close my eyes and inhale. God is in his heaven, and all is right with the world. While I'm not certain exactly where the line originated, I am basking in a sense of "rightness" since Jean-Marc's surprise appearance at my door yesterday morning. His joy is contagious. Dinner last evening was delightful. There was no male-female tension. Only friendship. And this morning, I feel newly confident that the future holds good things for the people I love . . . because the God who loves them all holds the future.

Outside the inner sanctum of the courtyard, Paris is awakening, but here, inside these thick centuries-old walls, there is early morning peace. In the apartment just above me, Madame Delhomme is baking bread again. The yeasty scent wafts out her open windows and blesses the courtyard with an aroma that has probably been present here for centuries, renewed each morning by this maven or that. Added to the baking bread is the subtler aroma of warm stone. It happens every morning as the sun climbs in the sky and illuminates the courtyard walls, adding a trill to the satisfying aroma of Madame Delhomme's hearth.

Monsieur Beaufort is turning the earth in the flower beds surrounding the still-sleeping fountain in the courtyard. I imagine I can smell that, too, for the earth is rich and black with the promise of spring blossoms to come. Sighing, I lift the small china cup in my palm to my lips to take a small sip of espresso so laden with sugar that it has been transformed into something more like coffee-flavored candy than a breakfast drink.

My neighbors have accepted me, albeit with predictable French caution. Since moving here I have been among them . . . but not of them. For the first two weeks, Mrs. Delhomme nodded when we met on the stairs, answering my greeting with a brisk *"Bonjour, Madame,"* that invited no further comments. In the courtyard, Monsieur Beaufort would shrug a greeting when I passed. He'd answered my question about the best place to buy plants for the balcony with a brusque comment about the shop I mentioned to him. *"It is a fashionable place for some. I personally never bother with those boys. They know nothing of my garden."* He'd then recommended a tiny shop I had never noticed tucked into a narrow street a few blocks away. The entrance was not promising, but the interior of the shop led to a doorway that opened to a courtyard filled with glorious green, blooming bulbs, and a few potted plants so large it would take a dolly and two men to move them.

The people who attend the little Protestant church I adopted for my own seemed glad for my presence. The woman behind the counter at the *épicerie* I frequent has learned to anticipate my likes and dislikes. Charles at the café where I usually drink an afternoon cup of coffee knows to douse it with extra cream. And yet, still I have felt very much on the outside looking in.

Luca has tried to explain their reticence. "It's not that we don't like Americans," he said, as if he were Parisian by birth, "but strangers—you must remember that France has been invaded by strangers many times over the centuries—create a certain caution. Consider that for us, today's stranger may be tomorrow's invading army. It births a reluctance you Americans can't appreciate. You are, after all only a couple of hundred years old . . . and neither of your neighbors are likely to try to conquer you and disassemble your government."

Luca's explanations helped me understand why I hadn't been welcomed by my neighbors with open arms. I even realized that it wasn't so very different from Omaha in many ways. The women at "the club" might have invited Mrs. Samuel Davis to lunch, but their friendliness never ventured past the surface. Not one had written since my move to Paris . . . unless I considered Meredith, who hinted that she was hoping I could give her some suggestions about *a place to stay.* Good old Meredith. The subtlety of an elephant. I began to think that perhaps I am not so unlike my Parisian neighbors, after all. I don't want my private home invaded either.

An unseasonably warm day just last week began to change things for me. I had opened my balcony doors and left them open to invite in fresh air, unaware that when I let the fresh air *in* and my violin music *out* . . . the invisible curtain my neighbors were content to leave between themselves and the foreigner in apartment number one would be rent.

The very next morning when I passed through the courtyard Mrs. Delhomme called down *"Vous aimez la brioche, Madame Davis?"*

Looking up at the rumpled old woman clinging to the iron railing around her tiny balcony, I reveled in the sound of my American name. *Dah-veece,* Mrs. Delhomme pronounced it. I smiled and called back, *"Mais bien sur."*

The old woman nodded. Wished me a good day. And when I returned from lunch with Annie Templeton, there it was, a *brioche* wrapped in one of Mrs. Delhomme's dish towels.

I savored the treat and returned the towel. When Mrs. Delhomme opened her door farther than a crack and I exclaimed over the stunning plasterwork in the hallway, I was invited in. It thrilled me only slightly less than an audience with the Queen of England would have. By then I had learned that living in Paris is one thing—getting to know Parisians is entirely another, and Mrs. Delhomme's invitation was accepted as the gift it was.

Mrs. Delhomme, it turns out, loves music. And while Monsieur Beaufort lacks Mrs. Delhomme's musical tastes, he likes Mrs. Delhomme, so when she said the American wasn't so obnoxious after all, he offered to help me resurrect the ailing fern he spied on my balcony late one sunny afternoon.

There is a chink in the armor, and it all began to happen *before* Jean-Marc arrived to charm Mrs. Delhomme. I am content. With many things. I have located a violin instructor who doesn't seem to mind my out-of-practice fingers and sour notes. Either he sees glimmers of the talent that has lain dormant for decades . . . or the glimmer of money enables him to endure. I'm not quite sure which it is, but I don't know that it really matters. I am enjoying my music again, not only because it seems to have bridged the gap between me and my neighbors, but also because . . . well, just because I love it.

Annie and Adolpho treat me like a combination surrogate mother and mature friend, and I gladly attend all their musical events. My faith is growing, although I wonder if I will ever be able to make Bible reading an automatic part of my day as does Luca Santo. So many distractions pull me away. I know it's important, but . . . with this part of my life, I am not content. I have wanted to ask Luca for advice. I scold myself about that notion. After making such a point about my personal independence . . . I should simply do what I know to be right. Long for the pure milk of the Word of God. Meditate on it day and night. For this, I should not need Luca Santo. Or any other human being.

I turn away from the balcony and retreat into the golden-hued room with soaring windows and a grand piano. Eschewing the violin this morning, I sit down at the keyboard and begin to play, quietly moving from a simple Brahms tune into a more popular song. I play the piano mostly by ear, and the ability to remember tunes—and go from one song to another—is returning. Sometimes when I play, I lose track of time, and my mind wanders into the past, bouncing from one memory to another. This morning as I play, the sun streams in the window. Looking up at the brilliant blue sky, I realize what a wonderful day it would be for a motorcycle ride. I smile at the contradictions of my life. I have been so intent to develop independence . . . and yet here I am wishing for something that requires a man. Foolish old woman.

"WHAT'S GEORGE KINCAID'S middle name?"

"Good morning to you, too," Mimi replied. "Except, it's . . . let's see . . . midnight there . . ." She paused. "What was it you asked me about George?"

"His middle name," Liz repeated. "Do you know it?"

"Thompson, I think. No . . . maybe Thomas. I'm not sure, but it's a *T* name. Why?"

Liz said nothing.

"Is something wrong?"

"No. Yes. I mean—" She heard her mother's doorbell sound in the background. "Answer the door, Mimi. I'll wait." As her mother went to the door, Liz listened. The voice was male. He was coming inside. She could hear her mother saying thank you, laughing. And then she was back.

"All right. I'm back. Now what's all this about George Kincaid? Is there some problem?"

"Who's there?"

"Jean-Marc," Mimi said.

"I didn't know he was back in Paris."

"He surprised me a couple days ago. I opened the door and *voilà*—a handsome man with his arms full of flowers. Not something an old woman expects to happen too many times a day!"

Liz could hear the joy in her mother's voice. Closing her eyes, she shifted gears. "Tell him hello for me," she said.

"Tell him yourself," Mimi said. And before Liz could protest, Jean-Marc was on the phone saying hello, sending greetings to Jeff, and reminding Liz that he was looking forward to introducing them all to the *Sea Cloud* next month.

How like him, Liz thought, to mention the ship—but not the other daughter. But the thought had barely formed when Jean-Marc said, "And Celine will be there, as well. I think she is more nervous about meeting you than she lets me see."

"Tell her—" Liz hesitated. "If you think it will make a difference, you can tell her I feel the same way."

"I suggested she use the e-mail," Jean-Marc said. "But she won't. She doesn't want to meet someone that way."

"I agree with that," Liz said quickly.

"You are coming, then? The business will allow you to get away?"

"I hope so," she said.

"But you were not expecting to talk to me," he said. "And I have taken too much time already. Here is your *maman*." And Mimi was back.

"Why did you need George's middle name, Lizzie? And . . . couldn't you just ask him?"

"I . . . uh . . . I'm having something monogrammed. To thank him for all his wonderful work on the project. I didn't want anyone around here to know. Thanks, Mimi," Liz said. "And have a nice time with Jean-Marc."

"Thank you."

"You really didn't know he was coming?"

"Not a clue. You should have seen me when he showed up at my door. My hair was a mess, and I was absolutely frumpy."

"She was not," Jean-Marc had leaned close to the phone. "Her natural beauty shines through always. And the hair was sexy."

Liz could feel her own cheeks coloring as he flirted with Mimi. "Well, I'm going to let you go, so you can keep him in line," she said, surprised that she was actually pleased—for Mimi's sake. Mimi hadn't said much, but she had to have been wondering about the man who had come for the Christmas reunion, reminisced about the past and spoken about a future . . . and then gone away and remained strangely quiet until now. What, Liz wondered, was the man up to, anyway?

"Are you sure everything's all right?" Mimi asked.

"Absolutely," Liz lied. "Wait until you see my new office. Mona's done another miracle."

"Have you and Jeff decided about the move?"

"Not yet. Things are . . . complicated. Jeff's been working long hours. They've sent him back to California twice. He hasn't had a minute's peace. I'll let you know when we know," she said. "Now give Jean-Marc a hug from me and have a good day. I love you, Mimi." She hung up the phone and realized she'd just sent her birth father a hug. That felt decidedly weird and was something she had never intended. Where did it come from? *The disk.* Somehow, the existence of that computer file made her feel like she had something to apologize for. Something to make up for. Had Daddy done more than just watch Jean-Marc David? He'd considered trying to break up her and Jeff. Had he ever considered meddling in Jean-Marc's life? The idea gave her chills. This was not the Samuel Frederick Davis Liz wanted to know.

THIN TO THE POINT of looking anorexic, Corbin Stewart entered Liz's office with the ease of a bulldozer. He did not walk. He lumbered. He sported a flattop and Birkenstocks with black socks. Then he tripped over his own feet and fell headlong. Liz looked on in amazement as he rebounded, standing upright so quickly she had to cover her hand with her mouth to keep from laughing as he pushed his glasses back up on his nose, straightened his tie, brushed off his sleeves, tugged at his pants.

"Y-you wanted to see me?"

It was too much. His voice actually cracked. Liz stifled another laugh by clearing her throat and offering to get him a cup of coffee.

"Thank you," he said.

Liz got up and went to the credenza. "Black? Cream? Sugar?"

"Yes. Uh. Black."

"Sit down, Mr. Stewart. And relax," Liz said while she got the coffee. "You aren't in trouble. I just need some advice."

She set the coffee before him and then went around to her side of the desk. She stifled a yawn. "Excuse me," she said. "I've been up late three nights in a row with a computer problem, and I'm hoping you can help me."

Stewart perched on the edge of his chair. "Problem? With Davis Enterprises computers? I wasn't aware of any—"

"No. It's with my computer at the home office." Liz sipped coffee. "Normally I'd just have one of you guys come out, but it's such a little problem I don't want to bother you. I think if you'll just answer a few questions . . ." It was obvious Stewart wasn't going to relax. He hadn't taken one sip of coffee. "I've been trying to look back at some old files, and I've come across a disk that is password protected." She made her voice intentionally casual. "It's not really all that critical, but I was just wondering . . . is there a way to get around something like that."

"Get around. . . ?" Stewart blinked. "Oh. You mean, like guess the password? Break the code? That kind of thing?"

"Exactly that kind of thing."

Stewart smiled. "I love things like that. If you'd like, bring me the disk, and—"

"No, no," Liz said—not too abruptly, she hoped. "I don't want to bother my guys at the office with it." She smiled. "It's really not worth all that trouble. I just thought maybe if you could give me a few ideas, maybe I'd play with it for a while—see if I could figure it out. If not, I'll just toss it out. It really isn't worth a lot of trouble."

"Well," Stewart settled back in the chair and shoved his glasses up again. He spread his fingers, pressed fingertips together, and rested his chin on the resultant "tent." With a smack of his lips, he began to talk. "People usually pick passwords that are easy to guess. So. If you know who made the disk, you just start playing with names and dates. Birthdays. Weddings. Anniversaries. Old addresses. Phone numbers. Social Security. That sort of thing."

"Social Security?" Liz said. "That's—"

"Yeah. Stupid. But people do it all the time."

"So you'd start with—"

"I'd just make a long list of those kinds of things."

"And just start guessing?"

Corbin nodded. "Educated guessing."

"That could take forever."

"It could," he said. "But it could also open the third time you try. That's the challenge."

Liz stood up. "Thank you." She nodded toward the coffee. "You didn't drink your coffee."

"That's all right," Stewart said, jumping to his feet. "I don't really like coffee." He hitched at his suit coat and nodded, then headed for the door. "If . . . uh . . . if I can help—"

"I'll let you know," Liz said. *Just as soon as I see a pig fly by the office window.*

## SIX

"WH-WHAT?" LIZ SPAT out her gum, ignoring the slight tweak of guilt as she opened her desk drawer and reached for the hidden pack of cigarettes. She scowled at Jeff, almost daring him to say anything as she took one out, tapped it on the side of the pack, and put it between her lips. "Don't say a word," she challenged as she lit it. Taking a drag, she sat back and stared at Jeff. When he didn't say anything, she crumpled the pack and tossed them into the trash can. "There," she said and got up to pace behind her desk. "Feel better?"

Jeff sighed and shook his head. "I don't want to fight about smoking right now, Liz. I don't want to fight at all."

"Good," Liz said, retreating into the tiny powder room connected to her downtown office, where she flushed the cigarette before calling out, "Then say 'Gee thanks, Henry. I'm grateful. Honored to be asked. But no, I don't want to move to California. My roots are here in Omaha. In fact, Liz and I are considering moving out to the Davis estate.'" She reappeared at the door to her office, raising one hand and bracing herself in the doorway. When Jeff didn't respond, she demanded, "Aren't we?"

Jeff cleared his throat. "I know *your* roots are here in Omaha. You've never lived anywhere else. Neither has your family. But I have." Hunching forward and resting his elbows on his knees, he looked up at her and asked, "Does it have to be an automatic no? An offer like the one Henry is making me isn't something to be declined lightly."

"It's not something to be considered, either," Liz snapped. She looked past Jeff toward the watercolor of the family estate hanging on the far wall. "I can't believe you'd entertain even the possibility." She looked back at him. "I can't leave Omaha."

He sat back up and gripped the arms of his chair. "Can't? Or won't? It's not like I'm asking you to sell off the company," he reasoned. "I'm just saying . . . can't we . . . think creatively? Maybe you could restructure. Delegate more of the day-to-day." His face brightened. "Maybe you could start a branch of Davis Enterprises out there. Expand."

Liz marched slowly back to her desk and sat down. Placing both palms atop her desk, she stared at Jeff. "So you want to move?"

"There are some positive aspects to consider. For both of us."

Liz got up and began to pace back and forth along the row of windows behind her desk. "I can see that becoming a partner in the law firm is great for you." She grasped the back of her desk chair and faced him. "But I fail to see what's in it for me." She had hurt him. She could see it.

"What's in it for you." Jeff repeated the words carefully. He took a deep breath and sat back in his chair. "How about this? What's in it for *you* would be the knowledge that you were supporting your soon-to-be husband. For a change."

*"For a change?"* Liz could feel her face flushing with color. "What is *that* supposed to mean?"

Sighing, Jeff looked away. He rumpled his hand through his hair. "I'm sorry. That wasn't fair. But if you look back over the last year . . ." He counted off things on his fingers. "The trip to Paris. The reconciliation with your mother. The sale of your condo. Your move home. The new office." He stopped counting. "We've been caught up in a lot of things that have to do with you and your family and the past." His voice was gentle. "Come on, Bitsy. Sit down and let's just stay calm and talk this through. You have to know this is the single most amazing job offer I am likely to get in my lifetime. Henry Widhelm is offering to make me a *partner*. He's selected me to head up the California division. Surely you can understand that's something I'd want to seriously consider."

Liz ignored the points he was making about his career. "It hasn't been just *my* personal life demanding time and attention from us lately." She stared at him. "I don't recall Henry Widhelm offering *his* corporate jet to enable a rescue mission to Danny's." It was a low blow, and she knew it. But she didn't take it back.

Jeff raised his eyebrows. He took a deep breath. "Let's keep Sarah and Danny out of this, shall we? All I'm asking at the moment is that we give as much energy to my career and my professional future as we do to the things that are important to you." His voice was pleading. "Come on, Liz. Can't we even talk about it? You know this is an incredible opportunity. You must see that. And"—he nodded—"of course I like the idea of being near family when we're ready to start our own."

Liz crossed her arms in front of her. "*Your* family. Not mine."

Jeff sighed. "Your mother lives in Europe, Liz."

"What about Irene and Cecil? They're like family to me. And California is just that much farther away from Mimi."

"So we buy a time-share on a faster jet."

Liz could hear his patience beginning to fray. She remained silent, waiting.

"Look," he finally said. "I'm not saying I'm going to *take* the job." He pressed his lips together and swiped across them with the back of his hand. He closed his eyes for a second or two, then opened them and stared directly into hers as he said slowly, "But I *am* going back out there to take a look around. And I'd like it if you would come with me."

"I am *not* moving to California. It's out of the question."

Jeff stood up. "I see," he said. "Well, then." He got up and walked to the door. "I guess I'll call you when I get back."

"You're going?" Liz demanded. "Even knowing how I feel?" She blathered, "Exactly how were you planning to fit a marriage, a honeymoon, and a new executive position halfway across the country into the month of May after you've already taken time off to go to Paris . . . and spent time with Danny and Sarah? And there's that wedding in Florence next month. And time with Jean-Marc. You've gone on and on about sailing on the *Sea Cloud*. What about that?"

Jeff's shoulders slumped. He turned around. "I don't know, Liz. I was thinking we'd talk about it. Come up with a plan that would work for both of us. Be *good* for both of us." He repeated with emphasis, "*Both* of us."

Liz sat back down. "There is no possible way to fit all of this into the next ten weeks."

"Not many couples take a three-week honeymoon," he said.

She frowned. "You were thinking of changing the honeymoon plans?"

He shrugged. "This isn't a plot, Liz. I don't have some hidden agenda I'm trying to coerce you to follow. I was just hoping you and I could discuss things with open hearts. I was hoping you'd be excited for me." He swallowed and stared down at the carpet. "I thought maybe we could take it one day at a time and just *think* about it. Together."

"What would be the point in taking time to think about something we both know we aren't going to do?" Liz snapped. "And it's not overreacting not to want to gallivant around Marin County. It's good time management."

He held her gaze for a long time. Nodded. "Right," he said. "I guess I can see how you'd feel that way." He cleared his throat and put his hand on the handle to the office door. He turned back. "You know, Liz, for your sake, I hope that someday you can stop trying to be the man your father never was." With a sad smile he left.

## *Mary*

MIMI.

The voice I hear is little more than a sob. "What is it? What's wrong?" My hand tightens on the telephone and I mouth Liz's name for Jean-Marc. We had just been getting ready to have a late dinner at my apartment on this Friday night when the phone rang. He comes to my side and puts his hand on my shoulder. I hold the phone away from my ear, glad he is there . . . wanting him to hear whatever it is Liz has to say.

"I—" Liz clears her throat. "I think Jeff . . . I think . . ."

I can sense her battling for control. "Is Jeff all right?"

"Yes. No." Liz groans.

Feeling my own throat tighten with emotion, I glance up at Jean-Marc. He frowns. Puts his hand at my waist and holds on. Comforted by his unspoken love, I force my voice to sound calm. "Take a deep breath and tell me what's wrong, Elizabeth." I realize I must sound just like I did back when she missed her curfew as a teenager. But maybe it would help my girl—young woman—collect herself.

"We've had a terrible fight," Liz says.

My timer sounds in the kitchen. Our dinner is ready. Jean-Marc motions that he will take care of it. I nod. Liz is sobbing now. "He—he's going to California. I think . . . I think maybe . . . the wedding . . . Oh, I don't KNOW."

Whispering a prayer, I hope my voice is completely calm when I ask, "Where are you?"

"Downtown. In my office. I've just been sitting here thinking and thinking. I didn't want to bother you, but—"

"Are you at your desk or on the couch?"

"My desk."

"Go over to the couch. Are you walking there now?" She assures me she is. "Good. Now take a deep breath. Another. Breathe in—one, two, three . . . Breathe out—one, two, three. Do it again, honey.

Calm down. Now, when you can, start at the beginning. Tell me everything."

While I talk Liz through the routine, I try to do the same on my end of the telephone call, moving to the couch beside the tall windows that look out over Paris. Street lights illuminate the neighborhoods that are becoming more familiar to me each day. Just across the street, a couple stands on their balcony, silhouetted against their brightly lit apartment. In the kitchen, Jean-Marc is grinding coffee beans. The aroma speaks *Comfort. Friendship.* I feel calmer. More in control. "We can talk all night if you need to, sweetheart. I'm listening when you're ready."

Jean-Marc hands me a cup of coffee across the back of the couch, squeezing my shoulder, then settles beside me with his own cup. As I once again position the telephone between us, I sense Liz regrouping, calming down.

"All right," she says. "I'm better." She pauses before blurting out, "Henry Widhelm wants to make Jeff a partner."

"Wonderful!" is the only honest reaction I can give.

"Not when you hear part B of the offer," Liz protests. "It means taking over the California branch."

"Partner *and* California head? That's really good!" Jean-Marc nods agreement.

"I guess they were already talking about him in the head office before they gave him that assignment out in Marin County. The way he handled that pretty well sewed it up for him. If he wants it."

"Does he?"

"Well, from the way he marched into my office a little while ago and announced it . . . and then went on and on about how wonderful it will be to live near Danny and Sarah . . . and how I shouldn't mind because, after all, my mom isn't even *in* the United States anymore . . ."

I don't know where it is written, but it seems to me that in some indelible place there is the rule that motherhood equals guilt. And here it is again. My daughter has a problem, and I am not there to fix it. Therefore, I am guilty. Of what, I'm not certain—maybe not living in Omaha for starters. Given a few minutes, I'd be able to compile a list. *This isn't about you. It's about Liz.* I try to return to the moment and challenge. "Jeff did that? He just marched into your office and told you he was taking the job? That doesn't seem like him." Jean-Marc scowls and looks dubious, too.

"Well, he didn't exactly announce it . . . but he . . . he wants to. I can tell. He wanted me to go out there with him so we can check it out. He was even hinting that maybe we'd have to put off our honeymoon, or at least shorten it."

"Why can't you go with him to check it out?"

"What's the *point,* Mimi? He can't take it. It's a waste of time for me to go out there. Don't forget I have an intern following me around these days. What's Ryan Miller going to do if I leave?"

She is trying to defend her position. I can't let her. "You aren't the only person in the universe who can teach Ryan Miller about commercial construction. You could have him reassigned with one phone call. But that's not the real problem here. Lizzie-bear, it's never a waste of time to show support for the man you love." While she absorbs the mild scolding, I decide to utter what she will deem ridiculous. "You could be surprised. You just might like it out there."

Predictably, Liz snorts, "Right. Have you *been* to San Francisco, Mimi? It's about as far away from Omaha as—"

"Paris? Don't shut yourself off to new possibilities." As I say those words, Jean-Marc nods and winks at me. And I can feel the blush rising. "Has Jeff said he wants to move?"

"Not exactly. But I can tell he's hoping I'll change my mind."

"How can you tell?"

"Because when I said I wouldn't go, he . . . he just got up and left. And he said he would call me when he got back." She is crying again. This is *not* the Liz Davis I know. "When he gets *back,* Mimi. He's going without me."

"Good for him."

"What did you say?"

"I said, good for him. Do you want a man you can drag around by the ring on his finger . . . or through his nose?"

When Liz doesn't answer, I continue. "The last thing in the world you need, Elizabeth, is for Jeff to make decisions based on fear of what you would think or say. You would hate that life. You'd lose all respect for Jeff, and you'd be miserable. The very thing that makes him refuse to let you push him around is one of the things that made you fall in love with him. It's also one of the things that is likely to make you into a better woman—and a happier one. Remember last November when he told you he was taking a step back? Aren't you glad he did?"

"That was different."

"Go with him."

"What?"

"I said, *go.*" I take a deep breath. "If you can't support Jeff in what he wants to do with his life, then you shouldn't marry him. Jeff deserves better than that, and if you can't see that, then . . ." I can't say what I am thinking, which is *then you're not good enough for him.*

"But, Mimi—the *company.* The oncology wing. The . . . the *estate.*"

"You can't snuggle up to a building on a cold winter's night, Lizzie." Jean-Marc is smiling at me.

"I cannot *believe* you are saying this!"

For a moment, I think Liz has hung up on me. Snuffling sounds finally come through, and I continue. "Go and see the lay of the land. Maybe there's a compromise. Maybe it doesn't have to be Omaha *or* California. Maybe you can find a way to do both. But if you can't . . ." I still can't say what I think. So I talk around it. "You know what I think of Jeff, honey. I already love him like he's a son. He's one in a million."

She is crying again, sobbing into the telephone. "I just don't know what to do."

This is a golden moment in a mother's life. A grown child is asking what to do. And I know what to say. "Call Jeff. Tell him you'll go with him to California. If he's already left, then go after him. Ask God to show you what's right."

"I think," Liz snaps into the phone, "that God has more important things to worry over than whether or not Liz Davis lives happily ever after."

I snap right back. "Happily ever after is a fairy tale, Elizabeth. This is real life, and you aren't the fairy princess living in Daddy's castle anymore. It's time to grow up. You have to decide what you want. Do you want the castles Daddy built or the prince riding off into the sunset?" I hand Jean-Marc my empty coffee cup. He kisses my cheek and heads for the kitchen. Is it the coffee or his cologne that smells so—comforting?

"I can't just suddenly decide to move. I know I'm not irreplaceable, but I'm not expendable, either."

"So," I remind her, "you delegate. Just because your father never trusted anyone else beyond a certain level doesn't mean you have to be that way. Isn't there some upcoming shining star who's caught your attention? Someone who could step into your shoes after a little extra training?"

"What about the house?" Liz snuffles. "We can't just sell it out from under Cecil and Irene."

"I don't know about the house." And I don't. But I have already made my choice between the mansion and my own happiness. Apart from the concern about Irene and Cecil Baxter, the only emotion I feel at the prospect of selling the estate is . . . relief. It saddens me to think that my own child hasn't learned from my example. "But I bet if we put our heads together we could find a solution."

"I can't believe you mean that," Liz sputters. "You really are *staying* over there, aren't you?"

"I'm thinking," I reply, "that if the estate is an albatross around our necks, and if it is coming between you and Jeff, then we should cut it free and be done with it. We don't *need* it. But you are right about Cecil and Irene. They would have to be part of any plan we make."

Liz explodes. "I do *not* want to sell my home! I want to get *married* there. I want to see my *babies* toddle across those floors. I want to—"

"When you marry, Liz, your *home* will be where your *husband* is."

"You know what I mean."

Unfortunately, I do. "Can I pray with you?"

"Sure. I'll take any help I can get to change this mess."

"It's my experience lately, honey, that prayer doesn't so much change *circumstances* as it changes *me*."

"If that's the best you can do, then don't pray." Her voice is angry. "I don't *want* to change."

It takes a moment for me to realize that my daughter has hung up on me. Leaning my head back, I close my eyes. I feel Jean-Marc's hand over mine. I open my eyes and smile at him, grateful for the gifts he offers. Silence. Friendship. Open arms.


"LICENSE. REGISTRATION. Proof of insurance, please." The officer leaned down to look in the driver's-side window.

"Can you turn that spotlight off?" Liz snapped. "It's glaring in my rearview mirror."

"Can you get out of the car?" The officer stepped back and looked down at her license. Then he bent to take a closer look. "Never mind about that. Something wrong, Miss Davis?" He flashed a smile. "You were fifteen miles an hour over the limit along here."

"I'm just . . . tired," Liz said. "That's all." *And the mascara running down my cheeks and the circles under my eyes are* not *a fashion statement.* Did they always have to ask such stupid questions?

"You stay in the car. I'll be right back," the officer said and retreated toward his cruiser.

Liz leaned her head back against the car seat. Forty dollars a tube and the mascara ran. At least this guy wasn't making her get out of the car. Moments later he was back at her window.

"I can't give you just a warning," he said, handing her the documents—topped with a ticket. He tipped his hat. "You be careful now, Miss Davis. By the way, my brother sure likes his internship with you."

*Oh, great. Just great.* Ryan Miller's big brother. *That's* why his smile looked familiar. She cleared her throat. "He's a good kid. Has potential."

"Yes, ma'am," the officer said, and grinned. "Sorry about the ticket. A man's gotta do his job, though. You can understand that."

Liz nodded. "Absolutely. A person's gotta do her job." She forced a smile. Waited for Ryan's brother to get to his cruiser and pull around her. He drove off with a wave. As soon as he was on his way, Liz put her Carrera into gear and pulled onto the pavement. Slowly. She drove the rest of the way home at precisely two miles an hour under the speed limit . . . until she was on the estate grounds. *"A man's gotta do his job."* The thought just made her mad. It was exactly that attitude that was taking Jeff to California. Macho Mania. Just inside the gate at home, she stomped the accelerator. The Porsche leaped ahead and careened around the curving drive toward the house. Liz gripped the wheel, relishing the idea of being "on the edge"—right up to the moment she misjudged a turn and the Porsche left the blacktop drive and peeled away several yards of Cecil Baxter's carefully tended lawn.

# ℒ SEVEN ℒ

"IF I WOULDA KNOWN you could bake cinnamon rolls that smell this good back in '78, I woulda proposed sooner."

At the sound of her husband's voice, Irene Baxter looked up from where she was standing at the kitchen sink washing dishes by hand and smiled.

"I couldn't bake cinnamon rolls that smelled this good back in '78," Irene said. "You are smelling decades of baking, finally perfected, old man. Now you take those muddy boots off before you step onto that tile floor."

"Yessum," Cecil said, closing the kitchen door behind him, and bending over to obey.

Seeing her husband grimace, Irene wondered at the old man's stubborn refusal to use the bench only inches away. "Sit down, you old fool," she said. "I love you, stiff knees and all. You don't have to pretend around me."

Cecil mumbled a protest, but he sat down, and the rubber boots came off with a minimum of grunts and groans. He nodded toward the back stairs. "Miss Lizzie been down yet this morning?"

Irene shook her head back and forth. "Haven't heard a peep."

"Hmpf," Cecil said. Putting his bony hands on his knees, he pushed himself upright. Going to the smaller of two refrigerators, he opened the door and poured himself a glass of orange juice, which he drank down in one long draught.

"Hmpf—what?" Irene asked.

"Hmpf—I wonder what's up," Cecil replied. "Someone slid off the blacktop and into the yard. Made quite a mess getting back onto the drive. Looked like they were mad or tipsy. I'm hoping for mad."

Irene wiped her hands on her apron. She reached for a hot pad just as the oven timer sounded. Taking the pan of cinnamon rolls out of the oven, she slid them on a rack to cool, then seated herself at the kitchen desk and opened the spiral notebook she used for grocery lists and every other detail of her housekeeping life. "I expect we'll know one way or the other before the day's out," she said, and added butter to the list.

UPSTAIRS IN HER ROOM, Liz groaned and rolled away from the ray of sunlight that had just slashed through a lovely dream with unwelcome reality. Jeff had been in the dream, and now he was her first conscious thought. He hadn't called since he walked out of her office yesterday. She didn't know when he was leaving . . . didn't know how long he was staying. "Checking things out" would likely mean meetings, tours of the office, and maybe even a talk with a real estate broker. He would be thorough . . . in a maddening, macho, male sort of way. More power to him. He was the one who was always talking about marriage being a partnership, how they would be co-chairmen of the board, and then, the minute she voted no on something important to *him* . . . he took off without her.

She closed her eyes. It was Saturday morning, she had worked hard, and . . . Mmmm . . . Irene was baking cinnamon rolls. If she could figure out a way to bottle and market the sense of *home* that crept through her when that aroma filled the air, she could retire. If she wanted to. The idea brought her back to the moment. An entire night of tossing around the lonely bed had made her no wiser. Sighing, she got up, wrapped herself in the chenille bathrobe Mimi had given her last year—*"made from a vintage bedspread, honey. Isn't that clever?"*—and headed for the kitchen.

Liz paused on the bottom step, enjoying the familiar sight of Cecil sitting at the kitchen nook . . . while Irene moved about the kitchen, rinsing this, arranging that. The Baxters' morning routine, coupled with the aroma of cinnamon and butter and fresh coffee were essential elements in Liz's definition of the word *home*. How, she wondered, could Jeff even hint that all of this be ended . . . for a job? And that's what would happen if they left Omaha. Mimi had called the house a mausoleum.

Whether it was because of Luca Santo or Jean-Marc or both or neither, Liz was beginning to accept the notion that Mary Davis would never again reside in Omaha. She would visit . . . but it wouldn't be home. And now Jeff wanted Liz to do the same thing as her mother. Leave it all behind. As if it were nothing more than a piece of property. But even as she thought it, she realized she was being overly dramatic. Jeff hadn't demanded anything. He'd only asked her to go with him to check things out. He'd said that maybe they could find a way, and she finally admitted to herself, Jeff was right—Henry Widhelm had made an astonishing offer. Sighing, Liz slid onto the bench in the kitchen nook opposite Cecil.

"You give up coffee?" Irene said as she lifted the stopper in the sink.

"Nope," Liz mumbled over the sound of draining water and gurgling soap suds. "Just . . . thinking."

Irene dried her hands on her clean apron. She opened the cupboard that held an entire generation of Davis coffee mugs and reached for Liz's favorite—the one heralding a *Bachelor Auction,* the local benefit where she'd "won" dinner out with Jeffrey James Scott. They'd met at a business seminar, and when he walked onto the runway at the benefit auction, Liz had bid high.

"You feeling all right this morning?" Irene's voice was concerned as she thumped the mug onto the table.

Liz took a deep whiff of the fragrant brew. Sighing, she brushed her hand across her forehead, swept her hair back off her face, and shook her head. She took a sip of coffee and apologized to Cecil. "I'm sorry about the yard."

Cecil shrugged. "I'll have Allison bring out some sod. It'll fill in. Can't promise it won't show at all come wedding day though."

"I won't whine if it does," Liz promised. "It'd serve me right for being so juvenile."

"You've got to settle yourself down, little miss," Cecil scolded. "That road rage nonsense is for the birds. Thank God, you didn't get hurt. If you'd pulled that stunt a few feet farther down, one of the berms could have sent you flying headlong through the library windows."

The idea was sobering. And Liz knew Cecil was right. Taking another sip of coffee, she got up and served herself a roll. "Tell me something, you two," she said. "What's the secret of a long marriage?"

Irene looked at Cecil, who was characteristically waiting for her to blurt out an answer before he gave his more considered view. "Don't know as there's any secrets," she said.

Cecil looked at his wife then, and Liz saw an unspoken something pass between them.

"Did you and Cecil *ever* have a fight?"

Cecil looked at Irene again and winked.

"Only one," Irene said, pausing before she added, "for about three years." At Liz's look of surprise, Irene nodded.

Cecil chuckled and nodded agreement. "First three years we were married were . . ."

". . . awful." Irene finished his sentence.

"I was a stubborn old goat," Cecil said, smiling love at his wife.

"And I was a headstrong woman."

"We butted heads so many times learning to live together . . ." Cecil said.

". . . for a while there we nearly forgot why we got married."

"Why did you?" Liz blurted out, then backpedaled. "I mean, what's one of the main reasons?"

Irene seemed flustered.

"The birds and the bees," Cecil said, "were pretty active back then, as I recall."

"Oh, *you*," Irene said, and shoved him playfully. She looked at Liz. "We both had good marriages the first time around. And I guess we met just about the time we both realized that wanting a partner for life wasn't being disloyal to the departed." She smiled at Cecil. "And when I met this handsome devil, those bees started buzzin' real loud."

Liz hid a smile. "But did you. . . ? Did you ever come close to . . . to breaking up?"

"Only once a day," Irene said. She looked down at her husband, who nodded agreement.

"I doubt we'd have energy to outlast all those fights now," he added.

"Well, Jeff and I are young," Liz said, "but I still don't know if we've got the energy." She paused. "It seems like we're fighting so much lately."

"No surprise," Irene said. "You two are like Cecil and me." She settled next to her husband on the bench. "So, let's hear it."

Liz poured it out, emphasizing Jeff's role as the obstinate goat even as she emphasized the impossibilities. "Not the least of which," she said, "is the idea that you two might have to move."

"Now, don't you let that affect your decision one bit," Cecil said quickly.

Irene agreed. "Not at all." She looked at her husband. "We've got our nest egg."

"The fact is," Cecil said, "my knees aren't what they used to be. Won't be long and someone younger is going to have to take on this place, anyway. Maybe this is all part of the good Lord's plan." He reached across the table and, in completely uncharacteristic Cecil

Baxter fashion, took Liz's hand in his. "You listen to me, little miss," he said, squeezing her hand and giving it a little shake. "Don't you dare let Irene and me be any part of a reason for you to fight with Mr. Jeffrey Scott."

Irene spoke up. "He's a keeper."

"I can't leave Omaha," Liz whispered. "I can't."

"Can't?" Irene challenged. "Or won't?" She waited for a minute, and when Liz didn't answer, she said, "You know something, Liz. Long about year three of that fight Cecil and I had way back when, I figured something out. Maybe you can learn from my mistakes and not let yours last that long."

"What did you learn?"

Irene spoke slowly. "Same thing I told you a few minutes ago. You love a man enough, you do whatever it takes to keep him around."

"Strong women don't do that," Liz said.

"That's what you think now," Irene said. "Because right now maybe you aren't being a strong woman." At Liz's look of confusion, she nodded. "Maybe right now you're being the obstinate goat." She leaned forward. "Sometimes, Miss Lizzie, it takes more *strength* to *give in* than it ever did to demand you have your way. And if you don't believe that, you just ask your mother."

Cecil looked at his watch and declared he had to get the call in to Allison about the sod. Irene stood up, and he unfolded his long legs with a grunt and scooted out of the nook. Arching his back, he said to the ceiling, "Don't know as I'd mind not having to trim hedges and prune trees all the livelong day." At the kitchen door he paused and, looking back at Liz he said, "I'm not generally one to say much, Miss Lizzie, but the way I see it, you've found yourself a real man. And there's not many of them around these days. The way I see it, that is." He closed the door quietly.

"Have you talked to your mother about this?" Irene said.

Liz nodded.

"And?"

*"Go west, young woman,"* Liz intoned.

Irene stood up. "You best be calling that pilot of yours," she said. "I'll pack up some of those rolls." She patted Liz's shoulder. "Another word to the wise, honey. It never hurts to feed 'em something sweet while you're eating crow."

LIZ'S E-MAIL TO her mother was brief. *Headed west. Talk later. Greet JMD for me.* Mimi would be pleased.

*JMD . . . JJS . . . GTK.* Sliding her desk drawer open, Liz retrieved the disk she couldn't read. She'd done what Corbin Stewart said and made a list of things Daddy might have connected with George Kincaid and used as a password. She tried the Kincaids' wedding anniversary date. Access denied. The street numbers for his old architectural office. Nothing.

Ejecting the disk, Liz set it aside and sent another e-mail, to Margaret, her assistant.

> *Called out of town unexpectedly. Clear Monday for me. Probably Tuesday. Have Ryan Miller meet me in office at 7:00 A.M. Wednesday. Tell him he'll be making a formal presentation regarding his idea for construction cost control at the Wednesday morning board meeting.*

That, Liz thought, would keep the overeager Ryan Miller busy until she returned.

Back in her room, she applied a fresh coat of Red Oblivion to her toenails while she thought over Irene and Cecil's advice. All Jeff was asking was that she check it out. It was, she realized, a reasonable request. There was plenty of time to come up with reasons for him to stay in Omaha. She'd overreacted—which was forgivable, considering the stress in her life these days. And when she showed up in California, Jeff would consider that and forgive her. That was one of the things she loved about him. He was a very forgiving person.

With a last dab, she finished refreshing her pedicure and stood up, catching a glimpse of red among the evening wear hanging in her dressing room. With the sponges still between her toes, she hobbled toward the red nightie. Irene was right about one thing. It never hurt to have a little insurance handy when a girl was eating crow.

WITH A GLANCE at her Porsche's speedometer, Liz flipped open her cell phone and speed-dialed California. "Hey, Danny," she said. "What time are you expecting Jeff?"

"What?"

"What time will Jeff be there?"

"Uh . . . Liz, I'm sorry, but . . . I don't know anything about Jeff coming back out here. Did we miss a call or an e-mail?"

"I'm sorry. I . . . must have misunderstood. He has some work to do out there. I'm coming, too, but we had to take separate flights. I just assumed he'd be headed to your place for the evening." Liz cleared her throat. She didn't want to lie to her future brother-in-law. But she also didn't want her personal life to be common knowledge. "Um . . . don't say anything, will you? If he wanted to surprise you he'll kill me."

"Sure, Liz," Danny said. "No problem."

"How is Sarah doing?"

"Pretty good, actually," Danny said. "She got a job."

"That's wonderful."

"And the kids seem to like their counselor. It's really great of you to be helping out with that, by the way."

"Glad to do it," Liz said. "That's what family's for. Right?"

"Well," Danny chuckled, "I do think that was the general idea God had when he created them. But I could tell stories about some of my clients out here—" He stopped abruptly. "But you don't want to hear that."

"Actually," Liz said, "I do." He sounded so much like Jeff. She didn't want to hang up. Not yet. She pulled the Porsche onto the shoulder of the country road.

"No specifics," Danny said. "I've just been an unwilling witness to some pretty sad stuff. You get into people's homes working on a fireplace or stone fountain and they tend to forget you're a person. You kind of fade into the background."

Had she ever done that? Liz wondered. Let out family secrets when a worker was around—forgotten they were there? She didn't think so. "That's not very kind of people," Liz said.

"Oh, I don't mind for myself," Danny said. "It's just that I don't like to watch soap operas—especially when they're real people's real lives." He paused. "Anyway, we'll act surprised if Jeff shows up on our doorstep."

"Thanks," Liz said. She forced a laugh. "You'll save me a scolding."

"Yeah, I know what you mean. Jeff can be really hard on you."

Danny's friendly sarcasm ended the conversation.

"IS THERE TROUBLE in paradise?" Sarah was standing in the kitchen doorway. As she talked, she pulled the sweatband off her head and chugged a glass of water.

"Diego and you have a nice walk?"

"The dog is a monster. He's going to kill me—or drag me around until I actually *lose* the weight." She went to the refrigerator and opened it. Taking out a can, she shook it up. "It's okay," she said to her brother. "This is allowed. It's my entire caloric intake for the next two hours. *Then,*" she said, reaching into the cookie jar, "I get *this* treat." She reached in and grabbed a small wrapped protein bar.

"You go, girl," Danny said, and kissed his sister on the cheek.

"I repeat," Sarah asked, "is there trouble in paradise?" She held up her hand, "I know, I know, that was not said with the full dose of Christian love I am supposed to feel for all of mankind. I can't help it," she said. "Elizabeth Davis isn't *man* and she usually isn't *kind*."

"Knock it off," Danny said. "Something wasn't right about that phone call." He grabbed the phone. Dialed. Waited. Frowned. "No answer from Jeff. No voice mail. Nothing."

Sarah shook her head. "Those two. I see what she sees in our brother. But I've got to tell you that apart from the figure and the face, I don't get it." She sighed. "But I guess it's not up to me to get it. I'm not the one marrying her . . . and Jeff seems really crazy about her." She sipped her canned shake.

"Just because you don't like Liz—"

"I do so like her," Sarah protested. "She's my future sister-in-law. I have to like her. Isn't that a law or something? And she's paying for counseling for my kids. And offered to hire day care. Why, if I depended on Liz, I'd hardly have to mother at all. She could buy substitutes for everything I do. And then I'd be free to do some-thing—as she so beautifully put it—worthwhile."

"She didn't really say that," Danny said.

"Maybe not," Sarah replied. "But she thought it." Without wait-ing for her brother to speak up, Sarah waved her sweat-soaked head-band in the air. "I know, I know. Whose approval do I want—Liz's or God's?" She shook her head. "I'd like both if that witch-on-wheels is really going to marry our brother. And before you scold me, I apologize for saying that." Her face sobered. "I really do have a bad attitude. She just makes me feel so . . . fat. Ugly. And like a complete failure. And," she said, finishing the shake, "did I mention *fat*?"

"Stop being so hard on yourself." Danny's voice was gentle. "Liz Davis is a very intimidating woman. No one can blame you for hav-ing mixed feelings about her. From what I can see, you've done a good job of standing your ground and letting her help where it mat-ters. I've had some of the same thoughts as you. All things being equal, I'd say you're doing quite well."

"Oh, yeah—I'm doing fabulous," Sarah said. She raked her fin-gers through her damp hair. "I've got two boys who are only happy when they hear their father isn't in the same county . . . and a daughter who's the queen of emergency preparedness."

"What does the counselor say about Hill's backpack fixation, anyway?"

Sarah shrugged. "To let it be. That if it gives her a sense of security to haul around a backpack, just let it be."

"What's she keeping in it, anyway?"

"A flashlight. Cheerios. Her baby blanket. That Bible story book you gave her. Phone numbers."

"Phone numbers?" Danny asked.

Sarah nodded. "Yep. Yours. Jeff's. My number at work. An old box of crayons."

"Crayons," Danny frowned. "I didn't think Hillary liked to color."

"But her brothers do," Sarah said. "Somehow—" she cleared her throat—"Hillary has this idea she might have to take care of them . . . again. Like she did that night while I was . . . out of it." Her eyes filled with tears. "I pray to God every day that Hillary never realizes what was really going on and that I was unconscious because her father knocked me out. She still thinks I passed out from the pain when I 'fell' and broke my arm."

Danny got up and went to his sister.

"Go 'way," Sarah said, swiping at the tears and waving him away. "I'm all sweaty."

"I'm not afraid of sweat," Danny said, and pulled her close to let her cry.

"DON'T LOOK AT ME," Sarah said as she filled Jeff's glass with milk that evening. "I'm the last person on earth to give marriage—or premarriage—advice. If you and Liz are fighting, you'll just have to flounder around in the dark like every other self-respecting man does in your situation."

"But you're a woman," Jeff protested. "Can't you help me see this from a woman's perspective?"

Sarah looked up at the ceiling for a minute. Finally, she looked back at Jeff. "Don't take this wrong, bro. But Liz Davis is another breed of woman from me. I can't help you understand her because *I* don't understand her. I've never wanted anything more than being a wife and a mom. And if I had a man like you ready to walk me down the aisle—I'd follow him to Timbuktu if that's where he wanted to live."

"Me too," Danny agreed. "About the not understanding women—or Liz—thing." He leaned back in his chair and hooked his thumbs in the loops of his blue jeans.

Jeff stared out the window into the distance.

"Eat," Sarah said, and handed him a plate of spaghetti. "Be glad the munchkins left some . . . and that they're in bed asleep. You'll have some time to think before they wake you up in the morning." She grinned. "They'll be thrilled you're back so soon, by the way."

"Thanks, sis," Jeff said. He picked up his fork and wound it full of spaghetti.

"Hey, you're good at that," Danny said. "You look like a real Italian—except you don't have the sunglasses and the guy named Guido standing behind you."

"The only Italian I know has white hair and not a bodyguard in sight," Jeff said. "He's the one who taught me how to do this." Jeff picked up a spoon in his left hand, the fork in his right, and spun another round of spaghetti."

"I'm impressed," Danny said. "But not as impressed as I'd be to see you actually riding one of those . . . Damati things."

"Ducati," Jeff corrected.

"Whatever," Danny said. "You really had a good time over there, huh?"

"It was hard on Liz, but I think she'd say now it was worth it, going through the tough stuff to get to where she is now with her mom. And there was a lot of fun, too. The motorcycles . . . the opera

New Year's Eve." The memory of Liz in the dark blue evening gown she'd worn that night and the passion it stirred in him came flooding back. "All in all," he smiled, "I'd have to rate Christmas—and New Year's—in Paris a definite ten." He stared back out the window. The sun had gone down, and shadows were gathering on the hills. Liz in that gown . . . yesterday's fight . . . Liz . . . Finally Jeff set his fork down. "I'm sorry, sis," he said to Sarah. "I really appreciate you heating this up, but I'm just not hungry." He stood up. "Think I'll go for a walk."

### *Mary*

THERE." I POINT to the screen and the words in Liz's e-mail, *Greet JMD for me,* before looking up at Jean-Marc, who is standing behind me. "Consider yourself greeted."

Jean-Marc smiles. "You must be pleased that she has taken your advice."

"I am. It's a rarity." I laugh softly. "Perhaps in my dotage I'm suddenly appearing wise to my own daughter."

"The rewards of growing older," Jean-Marc agrees. "My own Celine seems to have been affected by the same virus. Only last week she called to ask my advice about something . . . and then actually did what I suggested." He pauses, then nods toward the screen. "Does this mean you could perhaps come with me now? I know it's earlier than expected."

I shake my head. "The hotel isn't expecting me for another month."

He dismisses the problem with a wave of his hand. Luca's family owns a hotel in the Oltrarno district of Florence. He's sure something can be arranged.

I'm not convinced. "I'm Annie's surrogate mother now that her parents have raised such a fuss about the wedding." Even as I say the words, I know it's a weak argument. Annie Templeton would think my heading off with Jean-Marc romantic. But then, Annie Templeton isn't the one dreaming about Luca Santo. "It wouldn't be right for me to—"

Jean-Marc doesn't give up easily. "Annie will soon be in Florence herself. What could happen? And Celine and the boys are eager to meet you." He puts his hand on my shoulder.

I pat his hand with mine before closing out my e-mail and standing up. "I just can't spend a month in Italy," I protest. "Not now."

His Nordic blue eyes search mine. Finally, he smiles and shrugs. "Luca was right."

"What does Luca have to do with this?" I know it's childish, but now I'm feeling rebellious. Have the two of them been planning behind my back again?

"I told him I was going to convince you to come to Florence early. He said it wouldn't work. That you have a mind of your own."

"And what did *you* say?"

Jean-Marc shrugs. "That he wasn't telling me anything I hadn't learned decades ago." He leans close and kisses me on the cheek. Then, with a wink, he says, "But I didn't tell him I know the magic words to convince you."

"And what would those be?" I can't help it. I can't stay angry with him for long. He's too blasted charming for his own good. Maybe for my good.

"*Sea Cloud.*"

"I'm looking forward to meeting her," I agree. "But not yet. As I said, I can't go to Italy now."

"Wait." He taps the tip of my nose. "You haven't heard *all* of my magic words."

I fold my arms like a mother preparing to scold a child. "I'm waiting."

"*Bosendorfer.*"

"That's a wonderful piano. . . ."

"Yes. More than wonderful," Jean-Marc nods, stretching out his fingers and playing the air. "And Celine's occupies a salon in her villa overlooking Florence." He looks away from his hands and back at me. "Bring your violin. We'll make music together again."

I don't know if Jean-Marc is fluent enough in English to realize what he has just said. But before I can decide that, he says the last of his magic words.

*"Ducati."*

"What?"

"If you come to Florence, where it is warmer . . . we'll teach you to ride."

"We?"

"Luca and I. Hasn't he told you? Something came up with a renovation at the villa where his sister lives . . . where the wedding is to be held. He's leaving for Florence Monday morning."

He seems surprised I don't know. I am. Surprised . . . and a little hurt that Luca didn't tell me himself. But he's been very busy lately, and we haven't talked. Jean-Marc and I invited him to dinner last night, but he couldn't come.

"So . . . what do you say?" Jean-Marc says. "Do you trust two old racing buddies to teach you to ride?"

"By myself?"

He nods. "By yourself."

"I still have to check with Annie."

He hands me the phone with a self-satisfied smile. I know what he's thinking. He knew the magic words. *Sea Cloud . . . Bosendorfer . . . Ducati.* I tell myself those are the reasons I'm considering leaving early for Florence. The fact that Luca will be there is nice . . . but not the deciding factor. It isn't. It isn't. It . . .

# ⟡ EIGHT ⟡

"I'M SORRY FOR the inconvenience, Miss Davis," Dave said, "but I know I sent you a memo. It's scheduled maintenance."

Liz remembered and swore silently.

"You want me to see what else I can get you? Might be slim pickings at this late notice."

"No, that's all right," Liz said. "I'll check commercial flights first. Somebody will have a last-minute seat available."

Somebody did. For nearly twice what a first-class seat usually cost. And she had to change planes in Denver . . . and she wouldn't get into Oakland until nearly ten o'clock at night. But the blow was softened when she found a convertible available—with GPS. A drive up to Danny's in Mill Valley would clear her head. Being in a Mustang with the top down wasn't such a horrible prospect. As long as it wasn't raining. What would the weather be like? She checked the weather channel. Good grief. Was it ever winter in California? And with the GPS, she would at least be able to *find* Danny's house—no matter how late it was. She hoped Jeff would be sleeping with his cell phone by the bed. She hoped he'd answer it when it sounded "her" ring. Now that she'd decided to take Mimi's advice and go . . . the wait was driving her crazy.

"YOU HAVING TROUBLE with your laptop?"

Liz looked at the guy sitting next to her and shook her head. "I tossed it in my carryon at the last minute . . . forgetting that it doesn't adapt to 'ancient technology.'" She held up the disk labeled *GTK*.

The guy smiled. "Yeah, the bleep glops have fostinated and completely slam-dunked the market."

"I beg your pardon?" He hadn't really been talking gibberish. Liz knew Corbin Stewart would have understood every word this guy just said. But she didn't.

"I'm sorry," he smiled and offered his hand. "Gil Dayton. I'm sort of an IT guy. From the model of your computer I just figured you were an IT gal."

Liz shook her head. "Nope. Just a gal who doesn't want her equipment keeping her from being first in the marketplace."

"Bet you're your rep's favorite client."

"It's been said," Liz smiled.

"What I said was floppy disks are pretty much a thing of the past. There are more reliable ways to store data—and lots of it—these days." He reached in his pocket and held up a slim silver keychain drive.

"I've got one of those," Liz said. "A one-gig one, in fact." She held out her hand. "Elizabeth Davis." She tapped the floppy disk. "This was my father's. He passed away a couple of years ago."

"I'm sorry," Mr. Dayton said.

"Thank you. Anyway, I was finally cleaning out some old files, and I found this in his old office. It's password protected, and—"

"It's driving you crazy not knowing what's on it?" He smiled.

"Exactly. I doubt it's anything, but I'd like to know before I just toss it out."

"I know what that's like. You feel like you're throwing a piece of the person you loved right out the window."

"Your dad is gone, too?" Liz asked.

He shook his head. "My wife. Three and a half years ago." He shrugged. "And I still have every piece of jewelry I ever gave her. And the shoes. Haven't been able to part with that woman's shoes." He looked down at his hands and touched the gold band around his ring finger. "Silly, huh."

"Not silly," Liz said. "Sweet." She paused. "Your kind of loyalty—it's a rare thing these days."

"I noticed you're engaged," Mr. Dayton said. He hurried to explain, "Salesman's habit. It's called 'reading the customer.' I wasn't checking you out or anything like that." He shook his head. "I'm digging myself in deeper here. Let me rephrase that." He smiled. "Congratulations."

"Thanks."

"When's the happy day?"

"May 24. I hope." And with that, Liz found herself telling the widowed stranger, who looked more like a personal trainer than an IT guy, why she was on the plane, why she was flying to Oakland—and . . . he was listening.

"Wow," he said, "that's some story."

"I'm sorry," Liz apologized. "You've been so polite, and here I am boring you with my—"

"It's not boring. And I might be able to give you some ideas for that password. I'm kind of into that sort of thing, actually."

"Mister, if you can help me get past this password," Liz tapped the disk again, "I'll buy you a steak dinner. Or a Ferrari. Your choice." She was suddenly glad fate had dictated the corporate jet be getting maintenance this week.

"I'm a vegetarian," he laughed, "so be careful. I think Ferraris cost more than the average T-bone these days. Now, I'm sure you've already checked down a list of birthdays and wedding days and stuff like that. Right?"

Liz nodded.

"What about the 'sad' numbers?"

"What?"

"People tend to think that passwords are only built around the good numbers in a person's life. But right after 9/11, I can just about guarantee that thousands of new 'secret' passwords were created around those numbers. Or the fire department numbers . . . the flight numbers. Things like that. So, if you're checking 'happy' numbers and coming up with nothing, try a 'sad' number in the subject's life."

"I hadn't thought of that," Liz said.

"Most of us don't. We forget that things we mortals see as *negative* events are sometimes much more memorable than the happiest moments. We say we'll never forget a nice sunset, or a romantic moment. But the truth is, we will. But a tragedy like 9/11? Nobody forgets something like that." He looked down at the gold band.

She didn't even know why, but Liz asked. "Was your wife—"

He nodded. "North tower."

She closed her eyes. "I am so sorry," she said. Her voice cracked.

"Thanks." He continued, "I never thought about the password clue until then. But, suddenly, my kids were using those numbers—the date, flight numbers—for all kinds of things. It was like we were all haunted by them. So—" He stopped abruptly. "That's my idea for you. Look at the negative stuff."

Dinner arrived for the first-class passengers. Liz packed her laptop and the disk, and before long she and Gil Dayton were talking about movies and then travel. Gil had been all over the world. "Didn't like Paris nearly as much as Italy."

"Jeff and I are supposed to attend a wedding there next month," Liz said.

"Really? Where?"

"Florence."

"Ah . . . Tuscany . . ." He looked down at his plate of airline food. "Now *they* know how to cook. . . ." And he was off again, expounding this time, not on technology, but on cuisine. "Whatever you do, do *not* miss eating at Angiolino," he said. "It's a small *trattoria* just off the Via Maggio. Walking distance from the Ponte Vecchio." He put his fork down. "On a spring evening, you walk along the river at sunset . . . watch the lights start to flicker on . . . and then head down Via Santo Spirito. You'll think it leads nowhere. But then the neon light welcomes you to Angiolino." He pursed his lips and made a smacking sound against his fingers. "*Ottimo*."

"So," Liz said, "what do we order at Angelina's?"

"Angio-LEE-no," Gil corrected her. "You trust the waiter. Whatever the chef was inspired to make that day . . . that's what you eat. And the house chianti. Be certain you order that, no matter if you are accustomed to more expensive wines. They have their own label and—" He cleared his throat and shook his head. "Sorry. I tend to wax nostalgic about Florence."

"You're making me want to go . . . just when I'd about decided I wasn't going to be able to get away."

"Too much wedding planning?"

"Too much everything."

"Have a simpler wedding." He looked at her intensely. "Go to Florence, Miss Davis. It will change your life."

"All right," Liz laughed. "You've convinced me. Do you have any advice on how to make Omaha more attractive to my wandering fiancé?"

"None," Gil said. "But I'll say a prayer you work it out. I want you to remain successful, so if you end up reading that disk you really *can* buy me the Ferrari." He winked at her. "So, Miss Davis . . . I've been talking *way* too much." He handed his plate to the flight attendant and accepted a coffee refill. "Mind if I ask you a question? You don't have to answer if you don't want to."

Liz looked down at her watch. "It's not like I'm going anywhere for the next hour or so."

"Okay," Gil said. "Here's the deal: You're in Florence, and you've taken the advice of this guy you met on a plane back home and ridden the bus up to the top of the hill with the famous view of the city. You decide to go up the long—very long—stairway that leads up to the church. And just as you get to the top, the clouds come rolling in and it's like you're in another dimension. Angels singing, harp music . . . the whole thing. But you can't see what's at the top of the stairs anymore. For some reason, you're convinced that something wonderful—maybe even heaven—is at the top of those stairs. And you want to see it. Except just as you head up those stairs, a monk steps out from the clouds and asks for your ticket."

"My ticket . . . to heaven?" Liz asked with a short laugh.

"Yeah," Gil nodded. "Say it really is heaven at the top of those stairs. And the monk wants to let you in. He just needs to validate your ticket." He smiled. "What do you think? What would a nice girl from Omaha offer the old guy—assuming, of course, he was a vegetarian without a driver's license?"

STANDING ON DANNY'S deck overlooking the oasis his brother had created from a scraggly stand of grass, Jeff smiled. His brother had worked a near miracle, transforming a plain house into a comfortable home tucked behind a cedar fence barely visible beneath a weight of blooming bougainvillea, espaliered hibiscus, and white jasmine.

"You're still da man, bro," Jeff said as Danny joined him on the deck overlooking the broad valley below. He gestured toward the yard. "Doesn't seem all that long ago when all you had in your backyard was weeds."

Danny poised two cans of Coke on the top railing of the deck. Opening one, he handed it to Jeff. He laughed. "Never say impossible to a Scott."

Jeff took a deep breath. "Right."

"You gonna come clean with me about what's going on between you and Liz . . . or should I stay in La-La Land?"

Jeff looked at his brother.

Danny nodded. "Got it. La-La Land it is." Setting his pop can down, he pulled off his jacket and held it out. "Take it. You'll wish you had it when you get up on top."

"Thanks," Jeff said. The brothers stood shoulder to shoulder for a few minutes before Jeff headed out.

"Hey, bro," Danny called after him.

Jeff turned back.

"She worth it?"

"That's what I have to decide."

Danny nodded. Looked up at the sky. "Great night for a hike," he said, settling into one of the chairs on the deck. "When you get back . . . if you want to talk . . ."

"I know," Jeff said. "Thanks." He headed up the road. He knew which way to go—exactly which hilltop he wanted to reach—the perfect place to find the kind of aloneness he needed. He and Danny had spent hours hiking these Mill Valley trails since Danny had moved to California. But now, as he walked alone, Jeff realized he was out of shape for the steep climbs and not nearly as sure on his feet as he used to be. How fitting, he thought, as he began to ponder all the ways he'd been reeling off center since he first met Elizabeth Davis at that business seminar. He remembered what a shock it had been to realize what different worlds he and Liz had come from. He was reasonably certain that the entire house he'd grown up in could easily fit in the front foyer of the Davis mansion. As a boy, he'd learned to make whatever he wanted to eat. The main thing Liz had learned to make was reservations. Jeff Scott did his own laundry. Liz had grown up with Irene at her beck and call . . . and hired her laundry done after she moved out. When Liz wanted a room changed, she called Mona Whitcomb. Jeff went to the hardware store for drop cloths, paint, and new roller covers. These differences had caused their relationship to be rocky at times, but it had always been worth the ride. Until now. This time smoothing out the road toward a future with Liz wasn't just a matter of being flexible and learning a new way of doing things. This time . . . Jeff couldn't seem to find a way to bridge the chasm between them.

As the sun disappeared and shadows lengthened, he zipped up Danny's jacket, grateful for the flannel lining and deep pockets. He could feel the muscles in his upper back and neck stiffening. It wasn't from the cold. Tension always did that to him. It made him smile sometimes to realize that people really could be a literal pain in the neck to Jeffrey Scott.

There was so much to admire about Liz Davis. So much that was good. But the "bulldog" in her could also be maddening. She had a death grip on Omaha and Davis Enterprises. Jeff wondered if it were true what he had heard—that a bulldog could be decapitated and still not release. Not an image he wanted applied to his personal life . . . or to the woman he loved. He didn't want to force the issue. It hurt that he had to . . . It hurt to realize that Liz didn't seem to have the same kind of tenacity when it came to building a life with him. For him, love and marriage meant you did whatever it took to make it work. He was beginning to wonder if Liz had the same kind of commitment. Everyone said marriages were all about give and take. But where and when, he wondered, did one partner give so the other could take? The way things were looking, if he wanted this job, he was going to have to do it without Liz. And he didn't know if he could do that.

He had never felt so hopeless about their future. Just before the end of last year, when he thought Liz was mistreating her mother, he'd taken a step back, hadn't seen or called her for a while. It was one of the hardest things he'd ever done . . . but he'd been sure it would turn out okay. And when they finally flew to Paris, Liz proved him right. She reconciled with her mom, and he'd never been more proud of her. She leaned on him through the shock of meeting Jean-Marc David and the revelation that he—not Sam Davis—was her birth father.

He paused to catch his breath, looking up at the sky, wishing he believed in God the way Danny and Sarah did, wondering if everything he'd gone through with Liz was going to add up to nothing, afraid that in order to keep his self-respect he was going to have to do more than just take a step back. Was he going to have to walk away from the most alluring woman he'd ever known?

Where was the right answer in it all? He knew Liz would never respect a man she could bully into doing things her way, and he couldn't imagine married life with a woman who didn't respect him. Wasn't the kind of love that lasted at least partly dependent on mutual respect? But she'd said she wouldn't consider California. She'd demanded he respect her feelings, too, which when he thought about it, didn't seem unreasonable.

Sighing, he began to power walk. In a few minutes, he'd crested the hill, and there, in the distance, was the soft glow from the lights of San Francisco being cast toward the heavens. And such heavens. Tonight the sky was a vast cobalt-blue bowl inverted over a dark velvet valley with lights shimmering like diamonds strewn by a giant hand. His first thought was a wish—to share the beauty with Liz. Not just tonight but tomorrow, too. Not just this valley but all of Marin County. To somehow make her see the promise inherent in a life apart from her father's legacy. Apart from the mansion where Liz wanted them to live—permanently. Jeff had always known that marrying Liz Davis would mean being strong enough to stand in the shadows and cheer her on. He'd decided he wouldn't mind. But living in Sam Davis's shadow was another thing entirely. Jeff didn't know if he could do that—didn't know if he should.

It just seemed like something was wrong when a guy's widow was doing a better job of letting go and getting on with her life than his daughter was. Even now, thinking about Mary Davis made Jeff smile. The last time he'd seen her, she'd been dressed in those outrageous motorcycle leathers, walking along some fancy-named street in Paris on Luca Santo's arm, looking ten years younger. That's what he wanted with Liz. Not the motorcycle or the leathers . . . but that same kind of joy of living. Mary Davis had found it. Why couldn't Liz? Was there something he was doing wrong? Was he demanding too much . . . or too little? Should he have demanded she come to California, or had he been right to let her stay behind? They were both successful negotiators in their professional lives. Why couldn't they negotiate this?

*Because she won't. Face it. She's already made her choice. And it ain't you.*

What he needed, he decided, wincing with pain and reaching up to rub his neck, was a hot shower. And a stiff drink. He'd settle for the hot shower in honor of Sarah and Danny's religious leanings. Somehow, he didn't think gin and tonic was part of their program these days. He thought of the guy who'd been talking at the Bible study during his last visit and wondered what advice he would have for an engaged guy whose fiancée had planted her feet as willfully as Liz Davis.

*She's made her choice. Look around. She's in Omaha. You're in California.*

Heading back toward the trail, he paused and looked up at the sky again. A phrase from a poem—or was it something Danny's preacher had said weeks ago—came to mind. *"What is man that thou art mindful of him?"* Looking at the night sky certainly could put a man in his place in the grand scheme of things. Not very significant. Intelligent design made sense . . . and so did the notion that whoever or whatever had started the entire mess was regretting it. He almost wished Sarah and Danny were right—that God was personal—and interested in what happened on the hilltops and in the valleys around the world.

*So . . . if you're up there . . .* He stopped himself. Ridiculous, talking to the sky.

*She's made her choice.*

Hunching his shoulders, Jeff headed for the convenience store at the end of the trail and just up the road from Danny's. The kids would be delighted with doughnuts for breakfast . . . and Sarah would forgive him for inducing a sugar buzz. Sarah always forgave everybody. She even had kind words to say about her worthless husband.

He wondered how Liz would speak of him in the future. Somehow, he didn't think it would be something he wanted to hear. That was Bitsy. Fire and ice. A warm heart and an iron will. *Her heart belongs to Daddy. Give it up. Jeffrey James Scott cannot compete with Saint Samuel Frederick Davis. Wake up and smell the coffee, man. She's made her choice, and it ain't you.*

At the convenience store he got doughnuts . . . and Excedrin PM. Back at Danny's, he went around the house, opened the back gate, descended the stone stairs, and slipped inside through the door of the lower level. Diego greeted him soundlessly, pressing his cold snout into his hand and whimpering. Jeff stashed the doughnuts in the downstairs refrigerator and swallowed two of the pills. Stretching out on the couch, he closed his eyes. The last thing he remembered was Diego, snuffling his hair and then trying to lick the tears off his cheeks.

# NINE

THE BUZZING WOULDN'T STOP. First there was Diego
licking at his face and offering unwanted sympathy, and now this. Jeff
tried to ignore it, but the phone he'd left in his pocket last night
would not be ignored. He reached for it without opening his eyes,
squinting in the dark. Dark? It wasn't morning yet? He squinted at
the phone's blue light, blinking and then suddenly awake when he
recognized the number. He answered with one word. "Hi."

"I know I woke you," Liz said. "But I'm not sorry."

He glanced at his watch. "It's after midnight in Omaha. What's
up?"

"Actually," Liz said. "It's more like early Sunday morning. I'm
here. In Mill Valley."

"Here? Here . . . where?" Instantly alert, he sat up and looked
toward the ceiling, imagining Liz just upstairs, wondering how she'd
gotten in, why he hadn't heard anything. "At Danny's?"

"No, silly. At the bed-and-breakfast in town. The GPS on my
rental malfunctioned, and there was no way I was going to try to find
Danny's in the rain at two in the morning." She paused. "We . . .
need to talk. Can you come?"

"Now?"

"Should I have called ahead and made an appointment?"

Her voice was edgy. She was here, but she wasn't finished fighting. Or maybe she was just hurt that he was hesitating to come running. Or tired, like him.

He took a deep breath. "I've pretty much said what I have to say, Liz. Why don't you get some rest, and I'll come by after church tomorrow . . . uh . . . today." *The mention of church would tick her off. Oh, well.*

"Please, baby. Please come? I . . . I don't want this."

She sounded like she might be crying. Her voice was different. Softer? Was he hearing an apology? He thought of his almost-prayer only a few hours ago. Was this some kind of cosmic answer? Was fate finally going to do something for him? With another look at the time he relented. "I'll be there in about twenty minutes."

"You brought work." He could see the laptop sticking out of the carryon where Liz had opened it on the small table in the corner of the room.

"I just brought something to keep me entertained on the plane."

"What? David didn't stock the right movies?" Sarcasm. That wasn't good. Liz hated sarcasm—especially when it was at her expense. That was bad form. He didn't want to play it that way. He didn't really want to play at all.

"Actually," Liz said, "I flew commercial. The jet was unavailable." She paused. "Scheduled maintenance." She smiled at him.

Good heavens, what a smile that woman had. Part of him wished she hadn't come. Standing alone on a hilltop and convincing himself to stand firm was one thing. Doing it while she was a few feet away and he could smell her perfume was entirely another. He clenched his hands to keep from reaching for her.

"So I got this great last-minute bargain," she said, pulling him into the room and closing the door. "Only $1,300 for a three-hour layover in Denver and a rental—including a broken GPS." She smiled—the big, fake smile she often used when dramatizing a client's false joy when she had bested them.

"Sorry," Jeff said.

"No, baby," she said. "I'm the one who's sorry." She bit her lower lip.

It drove him crazy when she did that. He could feel his body responding to her. She put her arms around his waist and snuggled close, laying her cheek on his chest.

"Liz. I—"

"Shut up," she said. And kissed him.

Dawn found Jeff sitting on Danny's deck, coffee cup in hand, wrestling with a totally new feeling about his relationship with Liz Davis. Guilt. After all his talk back at the mansion in Omaha . . . he'd blown it. So much for speeches about respecting "old-fashioned values." So much for abstinence until the wedding. He was such a hypocrite.

He was supposed to go to church this morning with Danny and Sarah and the kids. *What would they think if they knew about last night? What would they say?* Actually, he knew what they'd say. They'd say it didn't matter what they thought. It mattered what God thought. Which was not something Jeff wanted to contemplate. He was pretty sure that if Danny and Sarah were right, if God really was interested in each human being in a personal way, he probably wasn't too thrilled with Jeff Scott this morning. It was a new sensation. Jeff didn't like it.

He got up and went back inside and helped himself to a doughnut. Liz would be here soon. Probably not for long, though, if he told her how he was feeling. They'd both always believed in monogamy, and they'd been faithful to one another. When he brought up the idea that he felt *guilty* about last night, she'd probably blow her temper in about forty-three different ways.

He was waiting out front when she drove up, and he unloaded the "new rules" all at once, feeling like a child confessing to his mother and promising never to do it again. "This can't happen again,

Liz. I love you. But this just—doesn't feel right. Anymore. It probably sounds holier than thou." He tried to laugh, but the sound was forced. "I'm pretty sure I'd feel that way if the tables were turned and it was you saying this to me. But I don't want to sneak around anymore. And I want us to respect Danny and Sarah's values, not to mention your mom and Cecil and Irene. So—"

"So . . . okay," Liz said and kissed him on the cheek. She looked past him toward the house. "Is there fresh coffee in there?"

For a minute, he was speechless. "Yeah," he said. "I . . . I made some a little while ago. Everyone else is still asleep."

She linked her arm through his. "So we can just tell them I surprised you and arrived late last night. I didn't want to wake everyone up, so I checked into the bed-and-breakfast up the road, and . . . whatever you think." She tugged him toward the house.

"Whatever *I* think?"

She laughed a little. "Don't rub it in. You heard me. Whatever you think. But we still need to talk . . . with words instead of rumpled sheets."

"I don't have anything new to say," Jeff said. "I still want to hear Henry out. And if he makes as good an offer as he can, then I'm going to want to consider the possibility of taking it."

Liz nodded. "I understand that. I still don't want to move. I can't even imagine it. But I'd like to come along. If you don't mind." She ducked her chin. Jeff could see it tremble. He didn't know this Liz Davis. At all. "You said we'd decide together. Try to come up with something that would work," she said, "For both of us." She shrugged. "When I finally got my emotions out of the mix, I could see that that's a reasonable request. If it was the other way around, and I was the one looking at the job of a lifetime, you'd do it for me."

Jeff let himself smile. She was trying. That was all he'd asked her to do.

"I don't give up easily when something's important to me," she said. "You know that. I hang on. Make impossible things happen. Mergers. Hostile take-overs."

"Which do you think we're trying here?" Jeff asked. "A merger or a hostile take-over?"

She didn't answer. "Remember that letter to the editor last year? The one that accused me of being like a bulldog because I wouldn't let go of something I wanted to accomplish?"

"I remember. They were talking about the hospital project."

She nodded.

"What about Omaha, Liz? Are you going to keep hanging on to that like a bulldog?"

"At the moment," Liz said, "I'm more concerned about hanging on to *you*." She looked toward the house. "So let's just call a time-out and . . . get some coffee."

"DOUGHNUTS!" JOSHUA SCREECHED. He stared wide-eyed at the box on the counter, but then, with a glance at Liz, he disappeared down the hall. Liz could hear him speaking in a stage whisper. "*She's* here."

Sarah mumbled something.

"*Her.* Uncle J's girlfriend."

There was a flurry of sound—doors opening and closing, voices—and then Danny came hurrying down the hall, appearing ridiculous as he attempted to try not to hurry, and ducked into the kitchen. "Well, this is a surprise," he said, and went to the counter and poured himself coffee.

"I flew in late last night," Liz said. "Wanted to surprise Jeff and come early. I guess he's told you what a witch I was." What was it, Liz wondered, about Danny's house that turned her into a bumbling idiot? You'd think she was facing an angry board of directors demanding explanations for plummeting profits and questionable bookkeeping. On second thought, that might be easier than facing

Danny and Sarah in the role of The One Making Jeff Miserable.

Josh came tearing back down the hall with Andy on his heels, obviously intent on the box of doughnuts, but at sight of Liz they both slid to a stop. Next to Danny. Waiting. Liz took the box off the table and held it out. "Here you go," she said. "I'll get you guys some milk."

"I want juice," Josh said. "Apple."

"You got it," Liz said. The boys each took a doughnut. Sat down at the table. And waited. Danny got glasses out, and Liz poured juice.

"Thanks," Sarah said, appearing at the door dressed in blue jeans, plaid shirt, and hiking boots.

Liz frowned. "I thought Jeff said we'd be going to church."

"We are," Sarah said. "Why?"

"I . . . I . . ."

Jeff came up the stairs from the lower level. "Remember last time we were here, sweetheart? It's casual. Relaxed. You can wear what you've got on."

Sarah's smile looked fake. "Yeah. Really. It's always a 'come as you are' kind of service. Kind of the way God does things."

"What?" Liz asked.

"Come as you are. To Jesus." Sarah looked at Danny, then Jeff, then back to Liz, "You guys explain it," she said. "I've got to convince Hillary that she shouldn't put a wet toothbrush in her backpack."

Sarah retreated down the hall. Liz looked at Danny. "Her backpack?"

"Later," Danny said, rolling his eyes toward where the boys sat. But Josh had already heard.

"Hilly keeps it packed so we have everything we need."

"Everything you need?" Liz asked.

"Yeah," Andy chimed in. "For Justin Case."

"Who's Justin Case?"

"He's not a *who*," Jeff murmured in her ear. He handed her a mug of coffee and motioned for her to follow him. In the living room out of earshot of the boys, Jeff explained. "Hillary keeps a backpack full of stuff she might need *just in case* she has to take care of the boys. *Just in case* their father tries to come and get them. *Just in case* something happens to Sarah."

Liz's eyes filled with tears. She cleared her throat, feeling stupid for being so emotional. "What's the counselor say about it?"

"To let it be," Jeff said. "To give it time. And surround her with responsible adults who don't yell and hit people, who love each other and come home from work sober and get meals on the table and laugh . . . and love *them*."

Sarah chimed in from the doorway. "And to hold them in the dark when they're scared and remind them that Jesus loves them and promises to never leave them or forsake them."

"Their counselor talks about Jesus?" Liz asked. "Is he—she—a professional?"

"It's someone at church," Jeff said.

"A professional? Or a nice Jesus freak who thinks Bible verses fix everything?"

"Relax, Liz," Sarah said. "Rachel has all the appropriate initials after her name to impress even you. She just also happens to believe in something even more trustworthy than all her psychology textbooks. That book God wrote—the Bible." Sarah's voice was defensive. "You've heard of that—right?"

"I'm sorry," Liz said. "I didn't mean . . . I just . . ." There she was again, on the verge of tears. What was *wrong* with her, anyway? "Look, Sarah. I don't know what it is about me that you hate so much, but could you give it a rest?"

"I don't hate you," Sarah said. "I'd just like it if you'd once in a while consider the idea that I might actually *have* a brain in my head. Not all of us are lucky enough to have Daddy hand us a company to run."

"Whoa, little sister," Jeff said. "Time-out. Are we going to *church*?"

The color drained from Sarah's face. She closed her eyes. "Oh, God."

Liz thought she was swearing . . . but as it turned out, she was actually talking *to* God.

"I'm sorry," Sarah said, looking up toward the sky. Her voice wavered. "Oh, God," she whispered.

Liz broke in. "Forget it. I asked for it."

"No," Sarah said. "You definitely did *not* ask for that." She looked at Jeff. It was her turn to tear up.

"Hey, Jeff!" Danny's voice called from the back door. "Would you help me lure Diego into the family room? If the neighbors file one more complaint about Sunday morning barking, I'm gonna get a fine."

"We'd better get going, too," Sarah said, "if we don't want Danny to leave without us."

"Let him go," Liz said. "I've got a convertible." She reached in her pocket and produced the keys.

"That's cool. For you. I've got some kids in a minivan to tend," Sarah said.

"Sorr-ee," Liz snapped.

"No, I'm sorry," Sarah snapped back. "Not about the kids, but . . ." She sighed. "Look, Liz, I just have trouble understanding you. I mean, what have you got to be so *stressed* about, anyway? I've got a fifteen-year-old minivan and three kids—and you've got Jeff and a convertible. And yet you're whining about how you might have to move to Sausalito. *Sausalito.*" She sang out, "*Hello-o.* Like it's such a *burden* to live in Yuppie Town and stroll down to Starbucks in the morning to drink coffee while you decide whether to buy one Chihuly or three for the office." Sarah looked at her. "Yeah. I know who Chihuly is. The arboretum at home did an exhibit last year. His glass flowers lighted in a real garden. It was astonishing. I had to practically hog-tie Hillary to keep her from picking one of the 'shiny blue flowers'—which, of course, cost more than my grocery bill for a month."

"I didn't know you liked . . . art," Liz said.

"I was an art major when I met Gary."

"I didn't know."

"That's just it, Liz. You don't know. Why not? You've known me for two years. And all you seem to *know* is that I have three kids and a worthless husband. You were amazed by Danny's house, weren't you? We call him the Mud Man, and you thought *plaster* and expected a trailer. I could see the surprised look in your eyes when you came through the garden gate the first time. My brother's an artist, too, Liz. The average dry-waller in Mill Valley makes about thirty-five dollars an hour. You know what Danny charges? Seventy. And he has a waiting list that will last him through the second coming, because he's that good. His client list looks like a Who's Who of San Francisco.

"But you don't know that because all you see when you're around us is the people who take Jeff away from you. Look around you, hon. The world is *enormous,* and it doesn't all revolve around *you.*"

With a sob, Sarah grabbed her Bible. She glanced at Liz. There was no anger in her voice when she next spoke. "I'm not as big a hypocrite as it looks like," she said. "I really do believe all the stuff about Jesus. I just do a lousy job of showing it sometimes. Especially with you, I guess." She sighed. "Look. Maybe we're about as compatible as oil and water. But we do have one thing in common. We both love Jeffrey Scott and want him to be happy. So . . ." She held out her hand. "Truce?"

"Sure," Liz said. Sarah was right. They were about as likely to get along as oil and water. It was obvious Sarah wasn't going to be thrilled about the idea of having her for a sister-in-law. But at the moment, Liz couldn't blame her. Every single thing she had just said was true. Embarrassing. But true.

"Thanks," Sarah said. Danny was honking the horn. The kids were yelling. Downstairs, Diego was whining and scratching at the door. The two women headed outside. "I'll give you one thing," Sarah said. "Thanks to you I'll be able to tell Dr. Lanning I'm dealing with some of my issues. Facing them head on . . . even if I do feel like a deer staring straight into oncoming headlights."

Walking to the Mustang, Liz thought about Sarah's analogy of being in the headlights of an oncoming car. And wondered if she was the one *behind* the wheel. Running over the competition in her industry was one thing. Lording it over Jeff's sister—who was already having a tough enough time of it—was another. She almost felt ashamed of herself. It was time to give Sarah a break.

"EXACTLY WHAT IS going *on*?" Sarah hissed at Danny on the way home from church. "And don't give me that look. You know exactly what I mean. She's being *nice* to me. She offered to tie Andy's shoes. She shared my *hymnal*, for goodness' sake."

Danny shook his head. "Don't have a clue. They're both acting weird."

"Dare we hope it's a *good* weird?" Sarah asked, then turned around and looked into the back seat of the van. "Joshua honey, don't put your rubber snake in Hillary's backpack. You know it freaks her out."

# ℐ TEN ℐ

FOOD POISONING. THE FLU. Whatever. As if life weren't hard enough. The rest of Sunday at Danny's was a blur. All Liz wanted to do was crawl in a hole somewhere. Instead, Sarah brought out a handmade quilt, piled Danny's oversized living-room couch high with pillows, and flitted in and out carrying trays of Sprite and crackers. Jeff offered back rubs. The boys tiptoed by the door with exaggerated steps that Liz could have sworn were louder than if they'd just thundered down the hall as usual. Even Diego was sympathetic, curling up next to the couch with a huge sigh and looking at her with mournful eyes. No, she didn't think she had a fever. No, she didn't want another pillow. No—no—no. What she wanted, Liz told Jeff, was to be taken back to the bed-and-breakfast and left alone.

"Not an option," Jeff said. "I want you where I can keep an eye on you." He was sitting on the arm of the old sofa where Liz had collapsed the minute they got back from church, trying to insist she was jet-lagged . . . and not fooling anyone.

"Just stay away," Liz said. "The last thing Sarah needs is for the kids to come down with whatever this is."

"Again," Jeff said, "not an option." He slid next to her and coaxed her to put her head in his lap. She closed her eyes, and he stroked her forehead, then gave her a gentle scalp massage. The next thing she knew it was evening, and she was feeling almost normal.

Sarah tiptoed in with yet another tray. "Jell-O," she said.

"Red or green?"

"Red."

"Thanks," Liz said . . . and there she was again, crying. "Sorry," she said, sitting up and reaching for a tissue. "I guess a girl never gets too old to want her Mommy on occasion. Mine always made me red Jell-O when I was sick."

"Cherry or raspberry?" Sarah asked.

"Cherry."

"Bingo," Sarah said, and put the tray down on the end table. "Our mom did the same thing."

"What was she like—your mom? Jeff doesn't say much about her."

Sarah perched on the edge of the overstuffed chair opposite the couch. "Tireless. Tender. Understanding."

"Stop," Liz said, taking a bite of Jell-O. "Another earth mother to be compared to—just what I need."

"Well," Sarah said, "if it makes you feel better . . . she could also be a real witch if you left dirty dishes in her sink." She put her hand to her mouth. "Did I really just *say* that?" She giggled.

Liz motioned to the cup of red gelatin. "Good stuff."

"Thanks," Sarah said. "I burned it."

"What?"

"You know how it foams up really fast—" She broke off. "I mean, when you make Jell-O, it foams up really fast—"

"Believe it or not, I have made my own Jell-O," Liz said. She knew she sounded defensive, but she didn't care. "I also know how to sew on a button. And mow a lawn."

Sarah nodded. "So, the phone rang while I was making this batch. I stepped away from the stove . . . it foamed up . . . and over . . ." She wrinkled her nose. "Thank goodness for air fresheners."

Liz sat up. "I should get back to the bed-and-breakfast."

Sarah shook her head. "Huh-uh. You're staying here tonight. Right on that couch. Where we can all drive you crazy trying to take care of you."

Liz sank back down beneath the quilt and murmured her thanks. She looked over her shoulder at the door to the room where Jeff would be sleeping tonight. "Tell Danny we'll be good."

"Oh, he knows that," Sarah said and smiled. "Jeff told us about your little talk."

Liz felt too tired to get mad.

MONDAY MORNING CAME far too soon. Liz wobbled to the breakfast table, and against all protests, insisted that she would be going with Jeff to meet Henry Widhelm in the city. After a rocky start and a trip to the bathroom to give up her breakfast, she began to feel better. As the morning wore on, it appeared that whatever bug had bitten her had left in search of another victim. Her physical well-being on the mend, Liz spent Monday and Tuesday having her emotional well-being sorely tested. Perfect weather, a charming office, a lively group of partners . . . and a salary beyond his wildest imaginations all combined to put a smile on Jeff's face and a knot the size of Omaha in Liz's gut. A ferry ride to Sausalito challenged her constitution . . . *and* almost convinced her that life in California wouldn't be all bad. She and Jeff meandered the streets, gazing in the windows of art galleries, and stopping for ice cream at a shop next to the pier.

"If your fa—Jean-Marc ever visited," Jeff said, "he'd like it here."

"What's not to like," Liz said, then shrugged at Jeff's surprised expression. "It's gorgeous." She took another spoonful of her sundae. "But I still don't want to move."

"I know," Jeff said. Later that day at the airport, he kissed her— like a friend—and said, "Henry said I could take some time. He knows this is huge. For both of us."

"Why does something that's hugely great for you have to be hugely terrible for me? That's not the way this is supposed to work," Liz said. Tears gathered. Again.

"You've got a big meeting tomorrow . . . and you still aren't feeling yourself. Get some sleep, Bitsy. Rest. We'll work it all out."

If only she could believe him.

### Mary

"YOU SHOULD GO," Annie says, and drops another lump of sugar into her tea.

On Saturday I had told Jean-Marc I needed to see Annie's face when I mentioned my leaving Paris early, and so here we are in our usual spot—the tearoom just off the Place de la Sorbonne. It's Tuesday evening . . . and the first minute Annie has had free since my call.

"Just like that?" I laugh and shake my head. "Oh, to be young and impulsive again."

Annie sets her teacup down. "If you were *impulsive,* you would have called me from the deck of the *Sea Cloud* yesterday morning," she says, then waves at me to be quiet as she rushes ahead. "I know, I know. You would never do that. Completely out of character. Especially when you were worried about Liz."

"She e-mailed me yesterday," I offer. "Her time in California went all right. At least she and Jeff are talking again."

"How long would you be gone if you go with Jean-Marc?"

"The trip from Arcachon to Livorno is a sixteen-day journey—if the wind cooperates. He said to allow for twenty because we'll have to put in to port a few times for 'technical matters'. And he made certain I knew we wouldn't be alone. His assistant, Paul, would be on board, too."

"Lovely," Annie says. "A chaperone." She sighs. "Really, Mary— three weeks at sea on a gorgeous yacht with a gorgeous man who loves you. What's the *matter* with you?" She takes a bite of pastry before going on, "You're great to be so conscientious about filling in for my mum, but I can manage a dress fitting without you, and everything else is coming together nicely." She swallows and then leans forward to say, "Go." When I don't say anything, her eyes narrow a little and she tilts her head. "What else is making you hesitate?"

"I don't know," I sigh. "It just doesn't feel . . . right."

Annie grimaces. "Let's review, *madame*. Your daughter reports that her trip to California went well and she and Jeff have kissed and made up. I happen to know that your violin instructor has left for his concert tour and won't be back until next month. You have a place to stay once you get to Florence and . . . let's see . . ." Annie makes a show of trying to remember another point. "Oh, yes . . . there is that little thing of two extremely handsome men eager to teach you to ride a Ducati. In *Tuscany*." She emphasizes the last word and rolls her eyes. "I can see how this is a terribly difficult decision."

I feel myself blushing. "All right, all right. I get your point." I lean forward. "But you can't assume they are *both* eager."

Annie leans back in her chair. "So *that's* it—Luca."

I shrug. "I know he's been busy. Something about a problem with some restoration work at the family house in Florence. It sounds very involved."

"Adolpho told me about it," Annie says. "And it is very involved. What Luca calls his 'family house' is an ancient villa. They were doing something in the chapel when the plasterers discovered some frescoes. They called experts in, and now there's a big debate over whether the painter was one of Botticelli's students or the master himself." At my look of amazement, she nods. "Yes. Botticelli. As in 1500. Birth of the Renaissance and all that."

"I had no idea."

Annie nods. "I know. Who would? Luca lives simply."

"If the discovery is in the chapel . . . what will that mean for your wedding?"

She shrugs. "We'll move it out into the garden. It's not a huge thing." Her face lights up with happiness. "I don't care *where* . . ." A shadow flits its way into the joy. "I only wish my parents . . ."

"I'm so sorry," I say. "When you said things went well at Christmas . . ."

"That was when we were going to wait a couple of years to get married."

"Your parents believe in long engagements?"

"I guess," Annie sighs. "But they also believe in grandchildren being born *after* their parents are married." She waves her hand at me. "No, no. I'm not. It's nothing like that. But I was trying to make the point for Mummy and Daddy that if they wanted the white dress to *mean* anything . . . we couldn't have two years of engagement."

"And they said?"

She sighs again. "Apparently Mummy hadn't quite computed the idea that her daughter was actually going to *sleep* with her Cocoa-Puff daddy." She grimaces. "Bad joke. Sorry. I'm trying hard to tell myself it is *not* the end of the world if my parents don't come to my wedding." She blinks back the sudden tears that surface. "All those speeches they used to make about race and society. . . ." She shakes her head. "Imagine my surprise when I discovered they didn't actually *believe* all their talk about the beauty of our diverse world."

"I'm sorry things have been so difficult for you."

She smiles again. "You've been great," she says. "And Adolpho's family is wonderful. They thought his mother was gorgeously exotic when she married into the family. And gorgeous she is."

"And they all like you," I remind her. "So you'll have plenty of support from family. In time I think your parents will come around, too."

"Thanks," Annie says as she takes another bite of her pastry before saying, "So let's review: My wedding details are falling into place. A few days ago you were worried about Liz—now you aren't. A minute ago you were worried about Luca Santo's silence, but I've just explained that." She leans over and says in a stage whisper, "Go to Florence." She winks. "The only thing left is to decide if you're sailing, flying, or taking the train."

"Train. I like to see the countryside go by."

Annie grins and winks. "Luca will be relieved."

"Don't be ridiculous," I protest.

"I'm not being ridiculous. I have eyes. Ears. A nose for romance." She pauses, and then with a little frown she says, "But I do have a question about the wedding."

"Of course." I am anticipating a request that I help with pouring punch or cutting cake.

"Land or sea?"

It takes a moment to realize Annie isn't asking about *her* wedding. "You," I scold her, "are incorrigible."

"Definitely," Annie agrees with a little nod of her head. "But I honestly can't decide which would better—a hilltop in Tuscany or a yacht in Livorno?"


"AND SO, AS YOU can see from these new drawings . . ."

Ryan Miller had drafted new blueprints. He apologized for their primitive look, but as he projected them onto the boardroom screen, Liz saw nothing requiring an apology. She did wonder if Ryan Miller had slept at all since receiving Margaret's notice about this presentation. The kid knew how to use CAD. And he had a prospectus ready—spiral-bound, with a cover that looked like a graphic artist had designed it. She hoped he realized the cost for that would be on him. She'd told him to prepare a presentation—not to spend corporate funds. As the meeting wore on, her irritation over the budget waned. Ryan Miller was increasingly looking like "the whole package" when it came to the commercial construction business.

His delivery was great. From the top of his head to the tips of his Italian leather shoes he had the look of boardroom experience combined with the air of success. Liz checked him out more than once—

reminding herself not to be swayed by the face or the body or the strong hands. She watched the way the board members reacted to him. Within the first few minutes of his presentation, the expressions on their faces changed from polite tolerance (*Give the boy a few minutes before we get on with the real business*) to disbelief (*Surely he doesn't expect us to believe he can really save us that much money*) to intense interest (*This guy is making good sense*).

His figures were indisputable. He seemed to have anticipated most of the questions that would be asked. And once, when Jamison Roberts asked something Ryan hadn't anticipated, the kid paused and said, "I hadn't thought of that. Can you explain that again?" He took notes while Roberts explained the reason for his question. Watching him, Liz could almost hear Ryan's internal modem processing information.

"I'm not quite sure about that," Ryan said. He looked around the room. "Anyone else have an answer for Mr. Roberts?"

No one did. Liz made a suggestion. Ryan explained why it wouldn't work. And then Jamison Roberts spoke up, proposed an answer, which Ryan didn't own until they had bantered back and forth for a few moments.

"How did I do?" Ryan said after the meeting was over.

"I think you know how you did," Liz said. "But if you need to hear it from me . . ."

"I do," Miller said. "You're the only one that matters, really." He waited a minute. Smiled. "I mean, you're the boss."

Liz had the vague impression Ryan Miller was flirting. Which she couldn't believe, given their age differences. She scolded herself for even thinking it. "Okay," she said. "Here's my review: Terrific. Thorough. Right on target. If you were applying for a position with the company, based on that presentation, I'd say you're hired."

"If you had a position open, I'd take it."

*Mary*

WHEN MY PHONE rings the morning after my tea with Annie, I am expecting Jean-Marc's voice.

"Is it true?" Luca asks. "Has Jean-Marc convinced you to come early to Florence?"

I hesitate, feeling self-conscious, worried that I'll hear something besides pleasure in Luca's voice when I say *yes*.

"Jean-Marc called me," Luca says. "Please tell me it is true and that you *are* coming early."

"All right. It's true." I hurry to explain. "But I'm not sailing. I . . . I'm taking the train." *Idiot. As if he cares about that.*

"Jean-Marc expects you will be on board the *Sea Cloud*," Luca says.

I shake my head. "No. I . . ." I don't know what to say. I don't think I was 100 percent certain about my decision until half a minute ago when I heard Luca's voice on the phone. The silence from his end of the conversation makes me nervous. So I hide behind my daughters, both natural-born and adopted. "Annie insists I should go, but I don't want to hurry off just yet. And Liz and Jeff have had some difficulties—"

"Nothing serious I hope?"

The warm concern in his voice helps me relax. "I hope not, too." And I find myself telling him everything. Every detail I know about Jeff's job offer, Liz's reluctance, the quandary about the house . . . everything. I finish with "I know Jean-Marc would do his best, but I don't want to have to wait to put in at a port and find a flight or a train if that situation blows up and I'm needed in Omaha."

"He will understand," Luca says.

"I thought I'd wait at least a couple of weeks before I head south." I hadn't really thought that. Until now. But as I say it, I feel myself relaxing with a sense that *this* is what I want to do. I don't want to leave Paris just yet. Later I'll analyze what it means. For now, I'm relieved to have made a decision.

"I can meet you at the airport," Luca offers.

"Train," I say. "I'd like to take the train. To enjoy the countryside."

"*Bene*. Everything will be ready."

"Everything?"

"*Sì*. Everything. Hotel . . . Ducati."

"You don't really have to teach me to ride a Ducati," I say. "Annie told me about the situation with the villa and the frescoes. Are they really Botticelli?"

He ignores my change of topic. "Is not a 'have to,' Mary," he reassures me. "Is a delight."

"I don't want to be a bother."

Silence. I close my eyes and remember exactly why it is I dislike the telephone. If I could see him, maybe I'd know what the silence means. There would be some clue, some expression, some . . . something. But now, there is only my hand gripping the phone while I wait for Luca to say something.

"You could never be a bother to me, *cara mia*."

I have goose bumps. I'm an idiot. An old fool. A . . . *moto maman*.

"You will bring the leathers, *si*? And you will call me with the time to meet you, *si*?"

I will. Oh, yes. I will.


BY WEDNESDAY EVENING when I meet Jean-Marc for dinner, I am more settled. We walk along the Seine, down the *quai* bordered by the Louvre, through an arched passageway and past the glass pyramid. After a long, but not uncomfortable, silence I ask him, "Has Liz invited you to the wedding?"

"She has," Jean-Marc replies, and leads the way past the pyramid, through another arch, and onto the Rue de Rivoli.

"And are you coming?"

Jean-Marc is quiet as we make our way toward the Champs Ely-sées. I can't tell if he's trying to decide or not. Finally, he says, "It would be . . . awkward . . . for her. Don't you think? Even if I am there only as your friend—which of course is all it would be."

I wonder if he's trying to lead me into a more personal discussion, but just when I begin to feel uncomfortable, he continues.

"I would, of course, be delighted to come. But I think perhaps the invitation was more *politesse* than any true desire on her part."

"I don't know what to tell you," I say. "Perhaps we should wait until we see how things go at Annie's wedding. As far as I know, she and Jeff are still coming to Florence." I sigh. "Although, when it comes to Liz, sometimes I'm the last to know what's really happening."

Jean-Marc takes my arm. "Perhaps you should go back to Omaha for a while. If you think it would help her."

"The thought has crossed my mind more than once. But I don't want to overreact. She e-mailed me when she decided to go out to California." I pause. "She could have called. I'm taking that as a sign that, while she wanted me to know what she'd decided, she was also sending an unspoken message."

"And that would be?" Jean-Marc asks.

"To let her handle things in her own way."

He pats my hand, nods, says something about the mysteries of communicating with grown children . . . and as we make our way down a familiar street, I realize that we have instinctively known we were coming here for this last dinner before Jean-Marc leaves Paris. Again. Luca and I have our favorite restaurants, and now Jean-Marc and I have ours, as well.

He speaks up. "Are you certain I can't convince you to change your mind and sail to Italy instead of taking the train? We could get an international cell phone. A satellite phone. The latest in *technolo-gie*."

"Thank you," I smile. "But no. Liz probably won't need me . . .

but *I* need to know that, if she e-mails or calls for help, I can get to an airport at a moment's notice without having to put into the next port and then transfer overland."

We order dinner. Jean-Marc tells me all about the plans he and Luca have for teaching me to ride in Tuscany. He refers me to the Ducati Web site to look over the new Ducati Monster that they both agree is a good motorcycle for me. The conversation meanders from one subject to another. At times there are silences . . . but they aren't uncomfortable. Finally, we finish dinner and head back toward my apartment. As we walk along, he tucks my hand through his arm and pulls me close.

We cross a bridge and head down the stairs to the edge of the river where last December Jean-Marc urged me to send my guilt and sorrow over the past down the river along with the blossoms plucked from a bouquet. We reminisce as we make our way back up another tier of stone stairs, along the now-familiar streets to my apartment. At the door, he leans down to kiss me. "I leave you to your daughters . . . and with the anticipation of introducing you to mine." He strokes the side of my face with the back of his hand. "It will be a great joy to finally have the dream come true," he says.

"What dream is that?"

"You. On the deck of my *Sea Cloud.*" With another light kiss, he whispers, "Less than thirty days." And he is gone.

BY FRIDAY AFTERNOON, Liz's life was back to what she defined as normal. She'd averted a few minor fiascoes on several projects at the office, traveled the company job sites with Ryan Miller, answered a dozen questions for the wedding caterer . . . and had come up with the perfect wedding present for Jeff, who was due back tomorrow from his "slower version" of the West Coast tour. A phone call to Mona had set everything in order at home. Mona had painters coming at dawn on Saturday, and had promised that everything else could be finished up so Jeff would be able to see his completed wedding gift by the following week.

And then, on Saturday morning, Liz turned on her office computer, popped in the *GTK* disk, and began trying passwords.

"Excuse me," Mona said from the doorway. "Consultation required, please."

Liz looked up. "You changed your hair."

Mona posed, one hand on her head and another on her hip. Her hair matched the outermost of her three shirts—the fuchsia one—and was piled atop her head, twisted into a knot held in place by a pair of red knitting needles. "Come, please," she said, making an exaggerated come-hither gesture that made her black-polished nails seem ominous.

Liz got up and followed her across the foyer to what had been the library only a week earlier. Now, the aroma of fresh paint hung in the air and, as usual, Mona was doing a miracle—transforming a dark and outdated room into an energizing work space more than fit for an up-and-coming attorney.

With a flourish, Mona opened the door. The toffee-colored walls in Jeff's new office were stunning. They surrounded a painting he had admired in one of the Sausalito galleries. Liz had called Tuesday night and had it shipped to Mona & Company. Jeff was going to be surprised—and Liz was certain he was going to love it. Hopefully more than California.

"What can I say?" Liz said, looking around the room in amazement.

"Astonishing. Stupendous. Mona my dear, you've done it again. It's a miracle. I can't *wait* to tell everyone at the club all about it." Mona batted her indigo eyelashes and laughed.

"The club? Who has time for the club?" Liz bantered. "How about I just take out a full-page ad in the *World Herald* shouting your praises."

"Original," Mona grinned. "I like it." She gathered up a stack of sample books, shooed Liz back to work, and said good-bye.

Back in her office, Liz returned to entering trial passwords created from the "sad" dates in George Kincaid's life. His wife's death. Her funeral. The address of the office he'd lost when his design debacle made headlines. And then she entered the date of the nationally televised event that had effectively ended George's career combined with the construction site address . . . and there it was.

She'd expected to see the same kinds of information Daddy had kept on Jean-Marc and Jeff. Dates. Narratives. Reports from private investigators. Instead, she got spec sheets. Drawings. Blueprints. Engineering comments. And notes that raised more questions than she wanted answered. Except, Liz knew, having come this far, she had to have answers. Because what was there could not be what she saw. She had to be misinterpreting things.

Leaning forward, Liz hid her face in her hands. She could hear her father's voice intoning, "Davis Enterprises will always have integrity as its highest aim." Another time when the company was having a tough time, Sam had said, "We may go down, Elizabeth, but if we do, it won't be because of dishonesty."

Was it all a sham? What was it Jeff had said that time. . . ? *I hope someday you can stop trying to be the man your father never was.* It made her physically ill to think Jeff might have known about this all along . . . and kept it from her.

She called Ryan Miller. True to his eager-intern genes, Ryan drove out to the house in record time, apologizing for his rumpled appearance as he rushed to her side.

"Stop apologizing and take a look at what I've loaded on this flash drive," Liz grumbled. "I need an engineer's opinion of what I'm looking at before I toss this out." She smiled then, hoping the smile didn't look as lame as it felt. She didn't want Ryan suspecting that she'd altered the files—which she had, erasing names and dates—anything she thought might lead to Kincaid Towers. "I just want to make certain that I'm not overlooking some brilliant innovation that might earn me a Ferrari and a beach house."

"Happy to do it," Ryan said, and dropped the flash drive into his pocket. "I'll take a look tonight."

"Just let me know what you think on Monday," Liz said, hoping she sounded casual. "Jeff's due in from a business trip in a few hours. I doubt I'll give it a thought until Monday." She rose. He followed her lead, and headed for the door.

"Sure you don't want me to call you right after I've taken a look?"

"Just bring it with you to the office on Monday." She hoped she hadn't snapped at him. She touched his arm, guiding him out the door. "Keep track of your time. Obviously you're earning double time for this. And have a great weekend," she said. They paused at the top of the sweeping stairs leading down to the circular drive where a small silver car—was it a Honda?—waited.

"You fit in that?" Liz asked, looking up at him.

"Well enough. More importantly it fits me and my budget."

Liz laughed. "I understand."

With a nod and a smile, Ryan descended the stairs, climbed into his car, and drove off.

LIZ HAD NEVER SEEN him fidget, but on Monday morning, sitting opposite her in the office, Ryan Miller was fidgeting. "So," she said. "Tell me what you think." *Lean back,* she thought. *Don't look so nervous.*

"You really don't know what this is?" he asked, holding up the flash drive.

"Don't have a clue," Liz lied. She forced herself to tease him. "Don't tell me I'm going to owe you a percentage of some great new discovery."

He shook his head. "Someone was playing around with support beams and load-bearing systems. What I don't understand is that the original drawings are great. But then there's a change about halfway through in the way one of the beams attaches. I went over it several times, thinking it had to be some kind of improvement I just hadn't seen before. But . . . there's really no doubt in my mind that, if that change were made . . . this thing wouldn't have . . . this walkway would have collapsed."

"Collapsed?" Liz held onto the edge of the desk with both hands. "Well, then. It's not an innovation at all. It's obviously inferior work, and I can throw it out." She stood up. "Thanks. It would have taken me hours to figure this out."

"Well, I didn't exactly stop with just that," he said.

"You didn't?"

He shook his head. "This kind of thing is sort of my area of interest. I've been trying to design a series of cantilevers that would enable a fully grown man—" He stopped himself short. "But you don't care about that. What I wanted to ask is, do you remember the hotel accident down in Kansas City years ago?"

"Who doesn't?" Liz said.

He nodded. "This is the same kind of thing. One little change an inspector might not even notice. But the walkway in these blueprints wouldn't have borne up under the stress of even fifty people."

"Well, then. Thank goodness these are just some not-very-good-builder's ideas and it never went further than an old computer disk." She forced a smile. "Thank you. Now I can toss this out without worrying I'm destroying my father's most brilliant piece of engineering—or some secret project that was important to him." She tossed the disk into the trash. "So, what's on the docket for you today?" Her heart was pounding so hard she thought surely Ryan must hear it.

"George Kincaid is taking me out to the hospital site," he said. "It will be interesting to hear from the architect's side. And we're having lunch with the decorator. And that should be a hoot from what I've heard about her."

"Ah, yes. My girl Mona." Liz smiled. "She's feng shuie'd the entire project to the point I don't know if patients will ever want to leave." She pulled open the center desk drawer and looked down.

"Greet them both for me," she said, while she pretended to scan the calendar. She stood up. "I've got a meeting in a few minutes, so—"

Ryan jumped up and hurried to the office door. "Let me know if there's ever anything else like that disk that I can do to help out."

"Thanks." She grabbed the phone. Finally, he was gone. Bending down, she retrieved the disk at the same time she dialed her assistant.

"Yes, ma'am." Margaret answered briskly.

"Would you have Billy in records retrieve some old blueprints for me, please. 1994. Anything George Kincaid worked on. And then call Jeff and tell him I'm working late and won't be able to do dinner."

"Yes, ma'am."

Was she imagining things or did Margaret's voice hold just a tinge of disapproval. Sitting down at her desk, Liz looked south toward Kansas City. Jeff was leaving the next morning for yet another week in California, but he would just have to understand. And her stomach wouldn't have tolerated dinner anyway.

LIFE AS LIZ DAVIS had known it ended at noon on Tuesday, March 16. She'd spent the morning at the *World Herald* reading microfilm. Now, back in her home office, as she hovered over an old set of blueprints, looking from the blueprints to the image on her computer screen, the truth was undeniable. The anomaly Ryan Miller had discovered on the computer disk was repeated on the blueprints on file—blueprints for Kincaid Towers, the innovative project that had landed George Kincaid's photo on the cover of *Architectural Digest* magazine . . . and made his name nationally known.

She'd been a freshman in college when it happened, and she remembered a lot about the towers. Their collapse in the early hours of a spring morning had caused Daddy a huge embarrassment—until it was discovered in the inquiry that Davis Enterprises was innocent. It was George Kincaid who was responsible for the faulty design.

George Kincaid who had inserted a last minute change in the way a certain walkway would be supported. George Kincaid who was wrong. Whose mistake led to a terrible loss—not of life, thank God, for the failure occurred when the construction site was deserted—but loss of money. Reputation.

As Liz sat at her father's old desk and followed the news story through issue after issue of the 1994 *Omaha World Herald,* she was surprised at how often a concerned Samuel Davis was pictured, his arm on his friend's shoulders, the epitome of loyalty. While the media feasted on George Kincaid, Samuel Davis remained the true, faithful friend who was sticking close by, no matter what.

Liz rubbed her brow with a trembling hand. Could George Kincaid have suspected he was sabotaged? What had led him into alcohol? Was it the failure of his building, or the betrayal of a friend? As her mind whirled from possibility to denial and back again to possibilities, she reached for the fountain pen on her desk, turning it in her hand, remembering how Daddy had told her all about the superiority of the fountain pen over the ball-point. He'd used his penchant for fountain pens as an illustration for *"how Davis Enterprises is all about excellence."* As she stared at the images on the computer screen, it took all of Liz Davis's strength to keep from grabbing it and driving its twenty-four karat gold tip into the leather ink blotter. Hiding her face in her hands, Liz wept.

# ELEVEN

SHE HAD TO TELL JEFF about the disk. She couldn't. But she had to. He deserved to know. Why did he need to know? What purpose would a scandal serve now? *A man's life was ruined. You have to make it right.* No, she told herself. She couldn't tell Jeff about that. He'd already accused her of trying to be the man her father never was. Whatever that meant to Jeff, if he knew this . . . it would give him even more ammunition for arguing the move to California.

Over the next few days, life seemed to steadily unravel. Liz snapped, "You should know that by now," at Ryan and sent him shuttling out the door on an errand that, while not a complete waste of time, wasn't nearly as important as she pretended. She argued with the wedding caterer when he said he'd have to charge extra for a chocolate fountain . . . and let that escalate until she heard herself say, "Just forget it. Cancel the whole thing. I'll find someone else." As she slammed the phone down, it dawned on her that the likelihood of Mona being able to find someone else—on such short notice—was very slim. She called back and apologized.

Things did not go well over the weekend when Jeff returned from California and finally saw his wedding gift. He was not nearly as enamored with Mona's toffee walls as Liz expected.

"It's . . . interesting," he said.

"But you *loved* that painting when we saw it in the gallery out there," Liz said. "It's perfect against that wall. Mona had the paint remixed *three* times before she got just the right shade to enhance the painting." He needed to know this hadn't just been an offhanded slap-it-together job, in spite of the time frame. She'd worked hard on this. And he wasn't impressed? She fought back angry tears.

"I said I liked the painting," Jeff said quietly. He shoved his hands in his pants pockets and circled the room. "I didn't say I wanted to live with it," he said, from the opposite side of Sam Davis's desk. Which, Liz realized, Jeff hadn't even noticed. She'd given him *her father's desk.* Didn't that mean anything to him?

"We haven't even decided we're living here." He studied her for a moment, watching her reaction. It was obvious he didn't like what he saw. "I see," he said, and exited the office by way of the door behind his desk that led out onto an expansive veranda stretching across the back of the house.

Liz marched after him. From the doorway she said, loudly, "You see what?"

He didn't even turn around and look at her as he spoke. "I see that you apparently *have* decided. The only thing left to consider was what color to paint the walls." He looked back over his shoulder at the newly painted room. "And now you've decided that, too."

"Don't jump to conclusions," Liz snapped. She stepped out onto the veranda and went to the stone railing, turning to face him from several feet away. "You said redoing my office was a good idea. That updating is never a mistake. What's so terrible if I went ahead and updated *two* rooms?" The fight escalated until they were battling back and forth like two swordsmen, each one intent on making the most savage cut.

Finally, Jeff held up both hands, palm out, like a mime erecting a wall between them. "This isn't solving anything."

"We've *tried* everything else," Liz shrilled. "I kept my word. I went with you. I even went to *church* like a good family girl. And *nothing* changed." It was as if she was standing outside herself, watching the scene. When, she wondered, had she become this . . . out of control *creature*? Her heart was pounding, and she was trembling all over. And yet, she felt powerless to change. "Maybe a good old knock-down-drag-out would do us both good!"

Jeff pressed his lips together and looked off toward the trees at the edge of the property. Taking a deep breath, he said, "Then knock-down-and-drag-out, Bitsy." His voice dropped a few decibels. "But do it with someone else, because I'm not playing." He headed back inside.

"And I'm not MOVING!" Liz yelled after him. The screech of her own voice shocked her. But she'd said it and she wasn't taking it back. As the words echoed in the entry hall, she stood, her hands clenched at her sides, trying not to cry—and failing. Bursting into tears, she ran up the sweeping staircase and fell on her bed. She waited for Jeff . . . and fell asleep waiting.

THE PHONE WOKE HER early Sunday morning.

Opening her eyes, Liz picked it up and sniffled. "I'm sorry."

"For what?"

It was Mimi.

"Oh . . . Mimi!" Tears began to fall again . . . and her stomach knotted up. "How did you know to call? Have you . . . have you talked to Jeff?"

"Jeff? No, I haven't heard from Jeff. Actually, I was calling to tell you I've decided to go to Florence early. But that can wait! Why would Jeff call me?"

"We had a fight."

Liz could hear her mother's sigh. "Oh, honey. I'm sorry."

"Everything's wrong," Liz said. "Jeff is mad at me. He doesn't like his new office. I bought a painting he liked, and then he said he didn't like it *that* much. And I almost fired the caterer . . . and . . ."

Liz recited a litany of offenses and problems, ending with a miserable, "I just can't keep all the plates spinning, Mimi. I can't."

"Elizabeth. You have no business taking on another redecorating project with Mona at this time in your life. And I told you to let Mona and me handle the caterer," Mimi scolded.

"I know, but I just thought . . ." Liz paused. "Where will you be staying in Florence?"

"The Hotel Lucia. Luca's twin sister owns it. I know, I know. Luca and Lucia—too cute. Liz, if you have a pen, I'll give you the phone number. E-mail is good, too. Luca's going to show me how to set up my laptop so I have e-mail access right away."

Liz took down the number. "I didn't know you were going down so early," she said.

"Neither did I, but we can talk about that another time."

Liz aired her problems, and as Mimi listened—and even said a short prayer for her over the phone—she began to feel calmer. "Thanks. I . . . I feel better." She blew her nose. "I'll be all right."

"Maybe you should cancel your plans for coming here," Mimi offered. "Everyone would understand. You can come later in the year, when things have calmed down a bit. After the hospital wing is dedicated, after your own wedding."

"No. That . . . that would just make Jeff even more upset. He's really looking forward to the trip . . . and the sailing with Jean-Marc. I can tell he's really excited about that. I don't want to be the reason for any more disappointments." Once again, tears threatened. "I don't know what's *wrong* with me. I cry at every little thing. And if I'm not crying, I'm mad about something. Is this typical for a bride-to-be?"

"That doesn't matter. It isn't typical for *you*." Mimi sighed. "You know what I think you should do? Call Dr. Reese. Get in to see him and tell him exactly what you've told me."

"I don't need a doctor," Liz protested. "That's just one more thing to do."

"Well, then, do it for me. Because as it is, I'm thinking I need to forget Florence and catch the next flight back to Omaha."

"Don't be ridiculous. You can't do that."

"I can do anything I want," Mimi insisted.

"Look . . . I'll call Dr. Reese. I will. First thing tomorrow morning."

"Don't forget how busy that office can be on Mondays. And don't give up," Mimi insisted. "At the very least he should give you something to help you deal with the stress until after the wedding."

"I don't need to be drugged to handle marrying Jeff."

Mimi's voice was firm. "Maybe not. But you might need some help dealing with the other things that are going on in your life. It's perfectly normal to feel overwhelmed just by the day-to-day responsibilities at work and a wedding, let alone all that you've been through since your father died. I remember reading somewhere that our bodies don't really differentiate between good stress and bad stress. You've had a *lot* to handle." She paused before asking, "I can be there by tomorrow. Shall I come?"

"Don't do the martyr thing, Mimi," Liz said wearily. "Jean-Marc e-mailed me about trying to get you to come early. I'm glad you two are spending more time together."

"I'm not doing the *martyr thing*. And Jean-Marc has gone back to Arcachon to sail the *Sea Cloud* to Livorno. He'll come up to Florence after getting into port. Until then, I'm going to do some sight-seeing on my own—maybe have dinner with Luca a couple of times. But none of that means I don't want to be there for you, Lizzie-bear."

"I know you do. You are. But stay where you are. Go to Florence. I'll see Dr. Reese. I've got your phone number. And if there's anything to report besides my usual lunacy, I'll call you."

"And you'll take whatever he prescribes?"

"Yes. I promise."

"If you aren't feeling a *lot* better within the next few days, I'm coming—whether you want me or not. There is such a thing as clinical depression, Lizzie—and it doesn't have anything to do with being weak. It just *is*. I've been there and done that, and I can tell you, if that's what's going on with you, then no organizational plan in the universe is going to help you feel better."

"Got it," Liz said.

"And then you call me—no matter what time it is here. The time difference is the same whether I'm in Paris or Florence. The Florence airport is smaller, but Luca would take me to Rome if I needed to get a flight out in a hurry."

"You won't need to," Liz said.

"Just so you know," Mimi said.

Liz teared up. "All right, Mimi. Thanks." Surprisingly, the idea of Mimi coming back for a while was comforting. At least until Dr. Reese could diagnose her "problem," and reassure her that everything she was experiencing was normal.

"I DON'T KNOW IF *I should be getting involved in this . . . but . . . here goes. . . .*" At the sound of Mary Davis's voice on his answering machine Sunday evening, Jeff dropped his car keys onto the end table and sat down on the couch. He didn't bother to take off his winter coat, but sat, elbows on knees, hands clenched, listening. *"I just got off the phone with Liz a little while ago. I gave her some advice. And I offered to come back to Omaha if she thought it would help. She insisted that I stay here. But I haven't been able to get the two of you off my mind. I hope this doesn't make me sound like a meddling mother-in-law, but . . . I just want you to know, Jeff, that if you disagree with Liz about that—if you think I should come back for a visit—I'll get on the first plane to Omaha. If you want to talk—if it would help at all—you can call me. Anytime. But, really, I don't want to meddle."* Her voice faltered. *"I love you, Jeff. And . . . I'm praying for you. For both of you."*

Mary had hung up, then apparently redialed to leave a P.S. *"You can call me even if it's two in the morning here."*

Jeff looked down at his watch. It was exactly two A.M. in Paris. He fumbled under the DVD player, looking for the Omaha phone book . . . and the country code for France.

"I'm sorry about the time," Jeff said as soon as Mary answered. "I just got in and listened to your message. . . ."

"I told you to call anytime. I meant it."

He didn't know how to start. There was a lump in his throat. He swallowed hard and reached up to loosen his tie.

"Pretend I'm your mom. . . . I feel like I already am."

Shrugging out of his coat, Jeff pressed the speakerphone button, sat down, and leaned his head against the back of the couch. "I don't know where to start. To be honest, I don't want to be railing against your daughter."

"Who better to rail to than me?" Mary said. "I know better than anyone else how . . . difficult she can be. But she does love you. And I don't want you to give up on her."

"I don't have any intention of giving up," Jeff said quickly. "I just . . . it just seems like giving Liz time to cool off has become a habit lately. Like every discussion ends up in a full-blown fight. And I don't understand why."

"She's under a lot of stress. The idea of moving away from everything she knows is frightening for her. Liz isn't accustomed to being frightened." Mary cleared her throat. "She isn't accustomed to not getting her way."

"Every time the word *California* comes up—or even nudges toward the surface of our conversations—her guard goes up." Jeff swept his hands through his hair and got up, pacing around the room as he talked, "I've got to tell you, Mary, that I'm tempted to think that her following me to Danny's two weeks ago was all show. It's as if she came out to gather information so she could build a more effective case for not moving."

"I don't think that's what was going on," Mary said.

"Good, because the idea that she'd play that kind of game makes me mad." He told her about the office Liz had redecorated without his knowledge. "It's like she's on a campaign to anchor me even more securely to her world here."

"Don't you like the new office?"

"It's great. You know how good Mona Whitcomb is. And Liz bought a painting we both liked out in Sausalito. The whole room is pretty much designed around it."

"But?"

"But beautiful things lose their appeal when they have strings attached, and I've got to tell you, Mary, that office has strings. Dozens of them."

"Have you . . . have you considered praying about all of this?"

"What?"

"Praying. There's some verses in Proverbs I really love," Mary said. "'Trust in the Lord with all your heart and lean not on your own understanding; in all your ways acknowledge him and he will make your paths straight.'"

Jeff was speechless, wondering if this was coincidence or the voice of God.

"Jeff? Are you there? I know I haven't really made an issue of it, but since coming to Paris I've become a follower of Christ. I don't mean to hammer you on the head with my faith, but the verses just sprang to mind, and I was hoping—"

"No, no. It's not that." Jeff sat back down, turned off the speaker, and picked up the handset. "Those are the exact same verses my brother, Danny, talked to me about before I left California."

"They are?"

"Yeah. He even wrote them down on an index card for me." Jeff reached into his shirt pocket. "I've got it right here."

"I didn't know Danny was . . . a spiritual person."

"Oh, he's more than spiritual," Jeff said. "He's a bona fide born-again Jesus freak—to quote your daughter." He paused. Swallowed. "Mary?"

"Yes, Jeff."

"I'm . . . Well, I don't know how to put this. It's all new to me.

But . . . when I was out there . . . I . . . uh . . . I changed."

Mary's voice was warm with emotion when she said, "Tell me about it."

"Well, I told you about Danny. He and Sarah have been going to this church with the kids. It seemed to be something they all depend on a lot. I was curious, and I want to do anything I can to help Sarah with the kids. So, it was only natural for Uncle J to go along. Liz even went with us when she was out there. I really didn't expect anything much to come of it. For me personally, I mean. I was just along for moral support for Sarah more than anything. I even went to a Bible study one weeknight evening. At first, I was uncomfortable. A fish out of water, really. But then some of the things people were talking about got me interested. It was like they belonged to a club I wasn't part of. A different lifestyle. I mean, I'd never given a thought to the possibility that there were people who actually *believed* everything in the Bible and tried to live by it. The Ten Commandments? Sure. But . . . these people are really *into* this stuff. It's changed their whole lives. At first it made me uncomfortable because I thought maybe Danny and Sarah were getting into a cult of some kind, but this past week the three of us went to the study again. I asked hard questions. More than once. We stayed up for hours going back and forth and back, and then it was like a light went on and . . . I just got it."

Mary was crying. He could hear her sniffling and blowing her nose. When she finally said something, it was just to tell him how happy she was and that she wished he was within arm's reach so she could give him a big hug. Then she asked, "Is *this* what you and Liz are really fighting about?"

Jeff shook his head. "Religion? Huh-uh. I didn't even get a chance to tell Liz about it. She was in such a hurry to show me the new office, and then we . . . I . . . I don't get it. I just don't get it. Christians are supposed to do what God wants, right? So . . . if God wanted us to move, wouldn't he change Liz's heart, too? Maybe it isn't God at all. Maybe it's just me wanting a fat salary—one that would impress even Liz. So that's my question for now. How does a person truly *know* what God wants, anyway?"

"Welcome to the life of faith," Mary said, "at least that's the one I know about. Lots of questions." She paused. "The answers do come. But for me, it's been very gradual. And I still have a lot that's unanswered. I'm like you, Jeff. Sometimes I don't know what God wants. Come to Omaha or go to Florence? My phone call was part of looking for an answer to that one."

"So how do you think God answers?" Jeff asked. "Do we just inherently know what to do? Or does someone tell us *for* God?"

"Yes. Both. Either. Neither."

"Thanks, Mary. That's as clear as mud." He laughed, realizing that he felt somehow better, even though he still didn't have any answers. When Mary remained quiet, he said, "You aren't going to tell me what to do, are you?"

"Nope," Mary said. "I don't think you need me to do that."

"If Liz knew how much I want to get her away from Omaha—" Jeff caught himself. "I'm sorry. I don't mean any disrespect to Sam— or you."

"I'm talking to you from *Paris,* Jeff. You don't have to apologize to me about wanting to cut Liz's unhealthy ties to the things around her."

"She's so *stubborn,*" Jeff said.

Mary agreed. "But don't give up on her because of that. Being stubborn is one of the traits that resulted in her waiting for you to show up in her life. She refused to settle for less than the best."

"Thanks for the compliment, but she may be starting to regret that decision."

"Do you still love her?"

"Yes."

"Then let's give it some time. And prayer. Lots and lots of prayer."

They prayed then, right on the phone. Mary assured him of her love for him. And somehow, when he hung up, Jeff felt better. For about five minutes. And then the doubt came rolling in. Again. It didn't seem right. He had an answer for *Where will you spend eternity?* But he didn't have a clue about the next fifty years. Somehow, he had expected being *forgiven* to make things easier.

LIZ HAD WANDERED into her mother's room and was sitting in the window seat watching snow fall when Irene opened the door.

"Here you are," she said. "Can I get you anything?"

Liz shook her head. "No, thanks. It's late. You and Cecil should get going before the driveway out back gets slippery."

"What about some hot cocoa?"

"I'll be fine." She turned to look at Irene and forced a smile. "Really. I just need some time to think."

"You want me to make some of my rolls first thing in the morning?"

Liz looked back out the window. "I don't think cinnamon rolls are going to solve this one." When her voice wavered, Irene crossed the room and gave her a hug.

"Doesn't seem all that long ago you were sitting right here letting your mama comb your hair or read you a story. You used to love to climb up here and watch it snow. Just like tonight."

Liz cleared her throat. She couldn't cry. If she started to cry, she might never stop.

Irene put her hand on her shoulder. "You and Jeff are going to be all right," she said. "You're just going through a tough spell, that's all. You'll work it out." When Liz said nothing, Irene bent down and kissed her on the cheek. "You know we love you," she said.

Liz reached up and patted her hand. "I love you, too. Both of you."

"You call us if you need anything, you hear?"

Liz nodded.

"Promise," Irene said.

"I promise."

With a last pat on Liz's shoulder, Irene left, closing the door softly behind her. Liz looked back out the window. The wind was picking up. Snow swirled across the landscape, whitening the lawn. Ice crystals pelted the windows. With a shiver, Liz pulled the chenille robe Mimi had given her tighter. She got up and headed downstairs, questions whirling around her. Why, she wondered as she passed the guest bedrooms, had Daddy never let them have company? Had Daddy done a "George Kincaid" on other people? Would it have killed him to let Mimi paint this back stairwell yellow like she wanted to years ago? Why hadn't Jeff called? How could she possibly go into the office tomorrow and pretend that things were normal?

As Liz made her way down the back stairs, through Irene's kitchen and into her office, the questions continued. Opening her briefcase, she withdrew the pamphlets she'd brought home from Dr. Reese's office today. She didn't need the desk light to remember the titles. With a little sob, she made her way back upstairs . . . back to Mimi's room . . . to Mimi's bed. Laying the pamphlets on the end table, she snuggled beneath the covers, thinking back over the unbelievable events of this afternoon.

"You'll be glad to know," Dr. Reese had said, "there's nothing wrong with you that time won't fix." And then, at Liz's quizzical look, he'd smiled and said, "I'd say sometime around September 15."

"What?" Liz still wasn't tracking.

"Your due date," Dr. Reese said. "You're pregnant, Liz. Congratulations."

"Are you sure?"

"Of course," he said. "Surely you suspected. You told me your cycle—" He regrouped and said in a tone that was less celebratory, "This surprise isn't . . . a happy one?"

"Yes. No. I mean . . ." She didn't try to hide the misery in her voice as she slumped back in her chair. "I don't know. The wedding isn't until May."

"You won't be the first bride to deliver 'prematurely'."

"But I don't want . . . I can't . . ." She bit her lip. Waited. "I'm sorry, Dr. Reese. I must sound like a complete idiot. But really, we took every precaution." *Except maybe once or twice.* She brushed her open hand across her forehead. "This just can't be. I can't have a *baby*. Not now. It's the worst possible timing. We've been doing nothing but fight for weeks. We haven't even *spoken* for days." She swallowed hard.

The doctor shoved a box of Kleenex her way as he slid open his desk drawer, flipped through a file, and withdrew some pamphlets. "You do have options. All are completely safe. And your privacy can be assured."

Liz looked down at the top pamphlet. *Adoption . . . Parenting . . . Abortion:* WHICH IS RIGHT FOR YOU? She shook her head and started to hand them all back to the doctor.

"Keep them. For later, when you've had a chance to adjust to the news and are thinking more clearly. What you choose is entirely up to you. If you are a religious woman, I'd encourage you to talk to your priest or rabbi. Or your minister. I think it's best to discuss things with your partner, but you seem to be indicating there are some problems there." He smiled kindly. "Not everyone is ready to become a parent, Miss Davis. Nearly half of all women in America will have had an abortion by the time they are forty-five. It's a relatively benign procedure."

Liz opened the pamphlet. Specially trained counselors were available at two different toll-free numbers to answer questions. Earlier was safer . . . and easier. The three kinds of procedures were outlined. She looked away. "I don't know."

"You don't have to know now," Dr. Reese said. "Just tuck the information in your briefcase. Get some rest. We can talk again—or you have the phone numbers there. You can call them twenty-four hours a day."

"Would I . . . would it require a hospital?" Liz asked.

He shook his head. "Nothing quite so institutional as that. The practice I recommend is located in a quiet neighborhood. The facility is very homelike. Comfortable."

Liz took the pamphlets, stuffed them in her briefcase, and left Dr. Reese's office as dazed and confused as she had ever been in her life. She hadn't gone back to work. Sliding into the driver's seat of her Porsche, she called Margaret on her cell phone, told her she wasn't feeling well, and gave Ryan Miller a pointless assignment. Then she drove home in a fog, dumped her briefcase on her desk, and dragged herself up the stairs. In her room, she shed her clothing, leaving them in a pile on her dressing room floor. Wrapping herself in the chenille robe, she'd dropped into the chair beside her bed.

But all these hours later, after reading the pamphlets and making excuses to Irene, after spending time alone and seeking comfort in Mimi's room, even now, she couldn't get her mind around even the fact of being pregnant, let alone decide what to do.

*Call Mimi.* She'd never been one to run to Mommy, but now every cell in her body wished Mimi were here. Lying beneath the covers, Liz opened her robe and lay her hand over her abdomen, trying to imagine it swelling in the weeks to come. If she stayed pregnant. An elaborate wedding would be a farce. If she stayed pregnant. Wasn't she the one who had said exactly that last year when one of her classmates from college got married and then delivered a baby six months later? The lucky girl was the body type that didn't show. Liz didn't think she was one of those. If she stayed pregnant, she would probably get as big as a cow.

She got up, turned Mimi's desk light on, and went back to the window seat, where she could look out on the snow-covered landscape, where she could read the pamphlets again . . . and think. There was a lot of information to absorb. She read a sentence, and thought of Jeff. With every new fact, every suggestion, every question . . . she thought of Jeff.

*Call Jeff.*

But the doctor had said her "partner" wouldn't have to know if she opted for abortion.

*Call Jeff.*

She couldn't. He was maintaining the silence. Lately it had become a contest of sorts . . . to see who weakened first. In this case, it had better not be her. Given the opportunity Jeff would do the right thing, which would mean marriage. He was such a Boy Scout about things. Dependable. Honest. Old-fashioned in some ways. Since he'd been spending more time with Danny and Sarah he was becoming more . . . spiritual. That was the word. *Spiritual.*

God. She hadn't thought about how God would figure in all of this. What if Jeff found out and decided this was God's will? That it was a sign or something? What if he made himself marry her . . . even when he didn't want to . . . because he thought God wanted it?

Maybe God *was* in this after all. Maybe he was punishing her for giving Jeff such a hard time these past few weeks. Maybe God had decided that Jeff was on his team. Maybe he was showing Liz Davis who was boss.

Looking out the window, Liz sighed and shook her head. Typical first days of spring in Nebraska. Snow. In the morning there would be white crystals clinging to the yellow blossoms on the forsythia bush out back. Planted next to the garage's stone wall and absorbing warmth from every hour of sunlight, it always burst into bloom early. And then was often blasted by a snowstorm. More often than not, the blossoms on that one bush were short-lived. Just like the plans she and Jeff had made. She could feel them shriveling and dying.

# ❦ TWELVE ❧

JEFF THOUGHT SHE WOULD call on Tuesday. Forty-eight hours or so was Liz's typical cooling-off period.

She didn't call.

Okay, he reasoned. It had been a bigger fight than usual. Irene and Cecil had even heard them yelling. He knew that because, when he'd left the estate on Saturday night, Irene bustled out to the car with cinnamon rolls. So he'd give Liz an extra day. On Wednesday she would call. He'd wait until noon, and then . . . he'd call her. That wasn't being a puppet. It was being in love and missing the woman you loved.

On Wednesday afternoon he got Liz's answering machine at the office . . . and her voice mail at home and on her cell phone . . . and . . . she didn't return his message.

On Thursday, he left a more . . . intense . . . message. He sent flowers, with a note. It didn't say he was sorry . . . but it *had* taken him three calls to find someone who had apricot-colored roses, which Liz knew were harder to find. She would appreciate the effort.

She didn't call.

He considered calling Mary for more advice. But she was supposed to be heading to Florence tomorrow, and he didn't want her to change her plans. He also didn't want Liz to feel like they were ganging up on her. No. Mary should stay in Europe and pray.

When he dialed Liz's office on Friday morning, Ryan Miller answered the phone.

Instead of shouting *What the heck are you doing answering my fiancée's private line?!* Jeff acted like he wasn't in the least bit surprised. It was hard, but he ignored the tiny needlepoints of jealousy pricking his brain. He was polite. He left a message—which apparently the Boy Wonder failed to forward because by noon . . .

She hadn't called.

So he took a long lunch and walked down to the Old Market building, where he saw Liz's Carrera parked in her spot, and bought more roses—red this time—and headed up to her office, where Margaret gave him the biggest smile ever and ushered him in, saying Liz was at a meeting just up the street but would be back soon and he should wait. Which he did, settling on the leather couch and trying to pray, but instead kept remembering the past and thinking about the future—both of which involved kissing Liz on this very sofa.

Wilted roses weren't going to make much of an impression, so he got up to get the vase he knew Liz kept under the sink in her private bathroom. Someone opened the office door. Ryan Miller.

"Nice," the kid said, leaning on the doorframe and nodding at the bouquet. "She'll like those."

"Yep."

"I was just leaving some reports on her desk." He got the hint and retreated.

Jeff listened for the door to close, then reached for the vase . . . and sent it crashing to the floor.

Frustrated with himself for being such a klutz, and ashamed that his tongue was apparently not yet as completely redeemed as his soul, he pulled the stopper in the sink and ran some water to maintain the roses while he cleaned up. As he dropped the remains of Liz's favorite vase in the porcelain wastebasket, he saw it. The box . . . the instructions . . . the verification. He stared at it for a long time. Pink for positive. Pink for . . . parenthood.

JEFF WAS RELIEVED when Danny answered the phone after the second ring.

"Hey, bro," Danny chided, "how are things in Richville?"

"Complicated," Jeff said. "Where's Sarah?"

"Enjoying Mom's Night Out. Well, I hope she's enjoying it. She didn't seem to know what to do with herself. She tried to stay home, in fact. But I sent her packing."

"That's good," Jeff said. "Good. The kids?"

"You sound like a robot checking off a list," Danny said. "What's up?"

"I need to talk to somebody."

"I'm somebody. Talk."

"Are you . . . are the kids—"

"Safely tucked in bed."

"This early?"

"Baby-sitter's prerogative," Danny said. Jeff could hear dishes rattling in the background. "So now I've got a cup of coffee and . . . I'm walking . . . onto the back deck . . . and sitting . . . watching Diego sleep down by the sandbox . . . so . . ." He sighed. "I repeat, what's up?"

Jeff sat down on the end of his bed. "Liz is pregnant."

After a long silence, Danny said, "Man . . . oh . . . man."

"I was hoping you'd have something more helpful to say."

"Are you calling for advice or needing someone to listen?"

"Both," Jeff said. He talked for several minutes—about their disagreement over his job offer, Liz's moods—ending with their most recent blowup over "his" new office at the mansion.

"What did she say when you told her about your conversion?"

"I never got the chance," Jeff said. When Danny didn't react, he added, "Okay, I chickened out. It seemed like we were already disagreeing about enough without my suddenly springing Jesus on her." He waited for a response, but none came. "I chickened out. So shoot me."

"You don't have to get defensive," Danny said. "We're all new at this. I'm certainly no expert. Do you still love her?"

"Do you have to ask that?"

"Not really. Just checking the state of the union—in light of recent events."

"I love her. I admire and respect her. I want to live the rest of my life with her. Children, mom, and apple pie—the whole American dream thing."

Danny was quiet. For a long time. Finally, he said, "Do you think Liz shares your children, mom, and apple pie vision of a happy life?"

"I thought she did," Jeff said. "Deep down. I thought we'd find a way for her to have the company, too. I told her she could delegate and run it from a distance—maybe even start a branch in California."

"Jeff," Danny said, "a business start-up is hardly a career path to children, mom, and apple pie."

"But she wants kids. We just planned to wait awhile. And I still believed that with some creative thinking, we could work out my promotion and her corporation. But now . . ." Jeff went on to describe the week of silence, the roses . . . and his discovery. "And I still haven't heard from her. Does she know I know? Do I drive out to the house and confront her? Do I wait for her to come to me? Do I call her and pretend I don't know?"

"You're asking *me*?" Danny said. "I said I would listen. I never pretended to understand women. Maybe you should be talking to Sarah."

"I'm talking to you," Jeff said, slightly irritated. "Man to man. Brother to brother. Believer to believer. You converted first. I figured you know more."

"So now you want spiritual advice," Danny said. "What would Jesus do? Is that what you're asking?"

"I guess I am," Jeff said, realizing that spiritual guidance was exactly what he had been wanting, whether he had acknowledged it consciously or not. He just didn't know how to ask for it.

"I don't *know* what Jesus would tell you to do . . . except to love her. The *agape* love."

"The *what*?"

"The Bible talks about different kinds of love. I don't remember all the Greek words, but there's 'sexual' love, which obviously you both have down. Then there's 'friendship' love, and in spite of the past few weeks, I'd say overall the two of you are good friends. In fact, that's probably what's kept you together through the recent stormy weather. But the best kind of love in the Bible is *agape*—God's kind of love. That's the one that does what's best for the other person, even if it requires personal sacrifice."

"Easy for God," Jeff said. "He always *knows* what's best for the other person. In some ways, I think it would be best for Liz if I broke everything off and let her stay where she loves it. She's good at being the queen bee—and she knows it."

"You really think that's what's best?" Danny said. "I respectfully disagree. I bet you anything that, if you asked her, Liz would tell you the most fun she's had in a long time was giving her mom that apartment and the violin. And when she was out here and got so sick, Sarah was under the impression Liz almost *liked* being treated like one of the family instead of visiting royalty.

"I don't know, Jeff. Maybe all of that has been God's way of warming her up to the idea that giving something besides money—and heaven knows motherhood requires a lot of giving—is one of the best gigs in the world." He paused. "I don't know what else to tell you. It sounds like a cliché, but the bottom line is she's like the rest of us. She needs Jesus more than anything. I wish I could reassure you that Liz is going to come around and you're going to get married and live happily ever after with a woman who has suddenly discovered her purpose in life is to mother your children. But I can't lie to you. I just don't know. But I do know that God isn't sitting up in heaven wondering what to do now. I mean, somehow it's all part of the plan. He'll give you the answer. You just have to wait. And you know I'll pray you have wisdom. And I mean that."

Jeff knew that should be comforting. It wasn't. Not really.

"I'm thinking your silence indicates a lack of enthusiasm about my platitudes," Danny said.

"It's all right. I didn't really expect you to have a solution. Thanks for listening. Tell Sarah whatever you want. And if she has some great bit of wisdom for me, tell her I'd appreciate a call."

"Maybe you should check in with a pastor there in Omaha."

"Maybe," Jeff said, "except I wouldn't have a clue where to start. I might as well tape the Yellow Pages to the wall and throw a dart for all I know about churches."

"Let me call my pastor here," Danny offered. "Maybe he'll have a connection. Or at least be able to tell us what to look for."

Hanging up the phone felt like cutting a lifeline.

### Mary

*"Italy is thousands of years deep."* I am sitting on the train reading Frances Mayes' book *Under the Tuscan Sun,* which is, I suppose, being a typical tourist. But the countryside she describes and the experiences she shares resonate with me. I look out the window, just in time to see a medieval church perched on a hilltop at the center of an equally ancient village disappear from view as quickly as it came. I sigh. It has been this way since the train left the station in Paris this morning—village after village, each one with its own story. France, too, is thousands of years deep.

I am grateful for the fact that coming to Europe has rebirthed my enthusiasm for my own story. I wonder as I sit on the train, alternately reading and gazing out the window, just how traveling to Florence will edit the outcome. Part of me is looking forward to the now-familiar smile that will greet me at Santa Maria Novella Station in Florence. Part of me is a little afraid. I said no to Jean-Marc's invitation to sail with him because I had to be more accessible to Liz. And that's the truth, but there is more to it than that. There is Luca.

I've been avoiding trying to understand how I feel about him, telling myself I am blessed to have two male friends who seem to enjoy my company and who offer delightful diversions. But in three weeks, Jean-Marc will be in Italy. And then I may need more than casual observations about friendship.

If Italy is thousands of years deep, perhaps while I am in Florence I can unearth the fragments of my life and find, at last, a way to make the uneven edges fit back together again—like an archaeologist restoring an ancient earthenware jar. Liz helped me begin the process when she provided the enchanting apartment in Paris and the Amati violin. And how I want her to piece her own future together. With Jeff, of course. But more importantly, with God. As I have prayed and thought about Liz and Jeff, I've become even more convinced that my Lizzie-bear should let go of the company. Davis Enterprises is a relic whose time is past, at least for the two of us.

Some pieces in my past, I know, will never be repaired. They grieve me. One of the things coming to faith has done is to aggravate my sense of painful loss when I think of Sam. I wonder where he is . . . and I shudder and repeatedly have to give that over to God. Will I ever see him again? Is he in heaven? Pieces of verses Luca once showed me float in my memory. *The secret things belong to God . . . leave this in the hands of a righteous God who judges fairly.* I cling to them. And hope.

There are other mysteries in the past, too. Riddles I probably won't ever solve. There was so much about Sam I didn't understand. I tell myself to let them go, and I'm beginning to be able to do it. Increasingly, I'm able to liken those niggling things from the past to the filler the archaeologists use to re-create an ancient piece of pottery. Missing shards don't always prevent their display, and missing pieces of my past won't keep God from using me now. *"Forget what lies behind,"* my pastor in Paris says, *"and press on."* It's good advice. I'm working on that.

As I ponder the past and watch it go by outside the train window, I'm trying to ignore a shrill voice that sounds from the seat behind me. A thirty-something woman is expounding on the beauties of Siena and complaining about the lines at the Uffizi in Florence. She has a plan. A better way to handle the museum lines. And she doesn't understand why "someone" doesn't "do something" about it. Why, she says, should it be so difficult to get your name on a list to see the Vasari Corridor? Why should it be so involved? And as she whines, I wonder why it is so often an American voice that comes through in this overloud, domineering voice that knows a better way. It makes me flinch. I want to apologize to the woman sitting next to me. *We aren't all like that,* I want to say. I look at her and smile and shake my head. We commiserate without words. She points to the guidebook sticking out of my bag.

"*È Americana?*"

"*Sì. Habito a Paris.*" Just when I think I make no sense at all with my feeble attempts at the Italian I've learned from a phrase book, her face lights up.

"*Alors . . . vous parlez français, madame?*"

Oh, yes . . . I do speak French. I am able to tell her we aren't all like that in French, and she nods. She knows. She's had American guests in her *pensione* in Lucca for years, she says. And for the next half hour she provides me with the kind of interchange that lifelong memories are built upon. When she learns that I am musical, she suggests that I might enjoy the free concerts offered at St. Mark's Episcopal Church on the Via Maggio in Florence. Nearly every night, she says. Opera . . . piano . . . and, she says, occasionally, a performance by a ten-year-old violin prodigy. Her daughter, who lives high above Florence in a villa, has told her about the child. The woman leaves the train in Lucca. But she wishes me well on my Florentine adventure.

The train rolls into the station in the early afternoon. With the help of my guidebook I have had time to plot at least a week's worth of wandering Florence on foot. Though Luca is here, I must not presume that he will have much time to spend with me. He has family, an ongoing restoration project, a wedding site to prepare. And if

I know Luca, he'll find a reason for at least one drive to the Ducati factory, Bologna.

I descend from the train, my small piece of luggage in tow. And there it is. That smile.

# THIRTEEN

JEFFREY SCOTT COULD MANAGE a high-pressured meeting at his law firm without a hitch. But on Sunday morning when he visited the Omaha church Danny's pastor had recommended and found himself asking a complete stranger—albeit a stranger identified as *Reverend* in the church bulletin—for a meeting about faith and marriage, his outstretched hand shook and his voice cracked. He was sure he sounded like a two-year-old. But Reverend Dayton—who ordered Jeff to lose the title and just call him Gil—didn't seem to notice. He grasped Jeff's hand firmly, patted him on the back, and agreed to meet with him that evening. Jeff spent the day alternating between wishing Liz would call and being relieved she didn't. There was something to be said for him having time to sort things out—if their problems could be sorted out. Jeff was beginning to doubt the possibility.

When Gil showed up for the Sunday evening meeting dressed in a T-shirt and jeans, Jeff assumed their appointment had called him away from his family and apologized. "I'm sorry to upset your Sunday evening. I can come back on my lunch hour tomorrow, if that's better for you."

"Actually," the pastor said, "I learned a long time ago that Sunday evening is a good time for me to be available to people. So I usually just consider all of Sunday as a work day, and use Friday, after my kids get out of school, through Saturday night as my weekend."

"Oh." Jeff loosened his tie. He followed the pastor through a maze of halls. He had no idea this church had so many additions. None of them showed from the street.

"Don't worry," Gil joked, "I won't let you get lost in the catacombs." He turned right, took out his keys, and unlocked a door. "The Lord has blessed us with lots of growth, but as yet no new site so we can expand in a way that makes architectural sense." He pointed to a plan mounted on foam core hanging on the wall behind his desk. "That's the dream," he said, then gestured around him. "This is the reality." He turned around and opened a cupboard, revealing a small refrigerator. "Can I offer you a bottle of water? I've got Evian in here. A couple of other brands. And Pellegrino, if you like sparkling. Or—gasp—Coke." He grinned. "Although the latter is an obvious betrayal of my personal health-nut code."

"Evian," Jeff said, trying to mask his surprise at the idea of a pastor with imported water in a hidden cooler.

"One of the things I liked most about Europe was the variety of healthy stuff to drink. Did you know there are dozens of kinds of mineral water? And each one has its own unique taste."

"Actually," Jeff replied, "I didn't know there were dozens. But I was in Paris over Christmas with my fiancée, and I tried a few."

"Paris," Gil said. "Beautiful. I'm partial to Italy, though. My wife's family won me over." He smiled. "Her maiden name was Arezzo." He pronounced it perfectly, as far as Jeff could tell. "I love Europe. Used to travel all over before I had kids." He opened a bottle of Pellegrino and sat down. "So, Jeff, you wanted to talk about. . . ?"

He began where Danny had said he should—with himself, his background and recent change. But the longer he talked and the more he explained about Liz, the more he realized what a mess things were. He hadn't gotten to the pregnancy yet when he broke off. "I feel like I have an infinite list of questions and no answers. I mean, I think I get the basics. I'm a sinner. The cross is how I get forgiven. I have a new relationship with God. But . . . I'm pretty much lost when it comes to what I do with all that now. I mean, life has gotten really complicated. The light has gone on for me—but not for Liz. Honestly—" he took a deep breath—"I haven't even told her about my conversion."

"Well," the pastor said, "let's start with the basics—about what exactly happens to a man when the light goes on about his spiritual need." As he talked, Dayton sketched simple diagrams, introducing words like *regeneration* and *sealing, old man* and *new man*. He knew how to define and explain the new terms without insulting Jeff's intelligence. And he had answers for all of Jeff's questions. Finally, he paused and sat back. "You seem pretty hungry to learn. If you can make it, I meet with a bunch of guys on Wednesday mornings at the Starbucks on Dodge Street. We're a diverse bunch. And it's early— 6:00 A.M. But—"

"I'll be there," Jeff said.

Gil grinned. Nodded. "Great." He paused. "Now, I feel compelled to give you the same advice my grandmother gave me not long after I came to faith. *Never* confuse Christians with Christ. Christians are an imperfect bunch of morons, sometimes. So . . . if you come to Starbucks expecting us to be perfect, you'll be disappointed. But, overall, if you give us time, we'll do our best to charm the socks off you."

Jeff laughed in spite of himself. "I'll be sure to bring an extra pair of socks," he said.

"So. Let's get to the rest of the story," Gil said. "You have a beautiful fiancée and a promising future. But. . . ?" He waited for Jeff to complete the sentence.

"I love Liz with every part of my heart. But these past few weeks it seems like everything I do is wrong. For her. I've just been offered a promotion that's the dream of a lifetime. But it means leaving Omaha. And Liz has made it clear that if I take it, we're through." He drew in a ragged breath. He talked about California. Danny and Sarah. Josh and Andy and Hillary. And the job.

"I thought it was the perfect opportunity for Liz and me to get a fresh start—to stop defining our lives by Sam Davis and do something of our own. But Liz . . ." His voice wavered. "She won't budge. At first I thought she'd come around. But now I don't know. And that's not even the worst of it. It's more than choosing between Liz and a job." He paused, swallowed hard, and then told Gil about the revelation in Liz's office. "She's pregnant. But she hasn't told me. And I don't understand why."

Gil was quiet for a few moments. Finally, he opened his Bible. "I'd like to share some things with you that help me when I don't have answers. Do you mind if I just read to you for a bit?"

Jeff shook his head. "I'm open to anything."

Gil looked down at the Bible. "Someday you'll have your own passages that have special meaning to you. But you're new to this book . . . so I'll just share some of mine. 'And we know that in all things God works for the good of those who love him, who have been called according to his purpose.'" He turned some pages and read, "'I have been crucified with Christ and I no longer live, but Christ lives in me.' That means that when you gave your heart to Christ, you gave him your life, too. He takes that commitment very seriously, and sometimes the changes he makes hurt. But we don't have to be afraid." He looked down and read again. "'I sought the Lord, and he answered me; he delivered me from all my fears.'" You don't have to be afraid, because whatever God does is for our good."

"I don't see how my losing Liz—and maybe my child—could possibly be good."

"Honest question. I felt the same way." He told Jeff about his wife's death.

"I'm so sorry," Jeff said. When Gil just nodded, he went back to the subject at hand. "So . . . what's the answer? How can God be working when it's all going downhill?"

Gil took a deep breath. "God isn't a magician." He held up his hands and pretended to wave a magic wand. "Poof! Problems all gone!" He shook his head. "Christians aren't exempt from tough times. And we don't have all the answers. But the promises are still true. God works it for eternal good. And we don't have to be afraid. We look at the trial, we look at what the Word says, and . . . we 'faith it.' God wants us to replace our very natural, very understandable, human fear with supernatural faith in the knowledge that he has it all under control. In every circumstance, every day."

"I can't," Jeff said, shaking his head back and forth. "The way I see it, things are completely *out* of control."

Gil nodded. "Again, I understand what you're saying. Been there, done that. But the truth is that human logic doesn't always work for spiritual realities. We give our weakness to God and trust him . . . and he gives us the strength to endure. We realize we can't . . . but God can. We find our strength in him. In our humanity, we are weak, but as God's children, we can be supernaturally strong.

"It's not something we learn overnight, Jeff. It's a process that takes time. And it's ongoing. You take a baby step with the faith you have today. And over time your faith grows."

"Well, I don't have a lot of faith at the moment," Jeff said. "Like I said, things seem to be pretty much out of control. And I don't see God doing anything in Liz's life."

Gil sat back with a smile. "Really? Well, bear with me while I tell a story. Okay?"

Jeff nodded.

"The board here at church decided to send me to a pastor's conference that was held out in California a few weeks ago. And one of our members decided to surprise me with a first-class ticket. As it turned out . . . my seat was next to a young woman who was clearly having trouble with her laptop. Before going to seminary, I used to sell computer software, so . . ."

A few minutes later, Jeff was blinking back tears as Dayton concluded. "I can't tell you a thing about that computer disk," the pastor said. "But I can tell you this—God is at work in your life, and in Liz's. Hang in there, bro. Hang in there."

GEORGE KINCAID HAD ONCE owned the house in Regency that everyone talked about. When it was first completed, it was the destination point for many Sunday afternoon cruisers—some of them from as far away as Lincoln. Daddy had scoffed and muttered when a newspaper article appeared about the fabulous new home. *"Rubberneckers. Can't find anything better to do than drive fifty miles to stick their noses through those iron gates?"* He'd had more unkind things to say, but Mimi had ways of hushing him up or shuttling Liz out of the room. When she thought back on it now, with her new understanding of Sam Davis, Liz realized her father was jealous. Jealous that someone else in Omaha would one-up the Davis estate.

As she approached George Kincaid's modest ranch-style home on Sunday evening, she realized that no one would envy George now. While his fall from the pinnacle hadn't come immediately after the Kincaid Towers' collapse, it had been inevitable. The loss of his reputation led to the loss of his business and, eventually, the loss of his ten-thousand-square-foot home. Rumor had it George had been drinking for quite some time, but eventually he had sunk into alcoholism. *All of it put into motion by Samuel Frederick Davis.*

Standing beneath the yellow porch light waiting for George to come to the door, Liz trembled. Everything in her life might be falling apart, things might be out of control, but this—this one thing— maybe *this* she could make better. If she told George, he would hate her. But he might regain his faith in himself. The tower collapse had nothing to do with him. It wasn't his fault. Maybe, Liz had decided, just maybe it would give George something of a new lease on life. If ever he was tempted to doubt his abilities again, Liz thought, she could at least spare him that. It was one part of her father's mess she could clean up. Still, she trembled at what lay ahead on this beautiful Sunday evening in Omaha, Nebraska. Facing George Kincaid was at once the most difficult—and perhaps the most important—thing she had ever done.

Maybe, she thought—almost begged—maybe he wouldn't be home. Then she could retreat and think it over and perhaps talk herself out of it. But he was there. He came to the door, opened it. . . .

"Liz? What's—"

She had to begin twice to make her voice work. "I have to talk to you," she said.

"Come in," George said. He reached for her. "Goodness, girl, you're shaking all over. What is it?"

He was fussing over her like a mother hen, drawing her into the living room, making her sit down, bustling into the kitchen with a promise of tea—and all the while Liz could not help but think that this was the worst moment of her life. Worse than when Daddy died. Because, she realized, after that death, part of him had lived on in her heart. Now she was facing the possibility that the Sam Davis she had worked so hard to keep alive had never even existed. Looking up at the family portrait over George Kincaid's fireplace, Liz fought to maintain control.

George came back into the room, steaming coffee mug in hand. It was cracked, the paper label of the tea bag hanging over the side. "I'm sorry. I forgot napkins." He looked toward the kitchen. "I'll—"

"No, George. Please. Just. Sit." She set the mug of tea atop an old copy of *Architectural Digest*. George scooped it up and handed her another. It was only then that Liz noticed the cover. *George Kincaid: Midwestern Panache Meets Old World Charm*.

He seemed embarrassed. "It's . . . well . . ."

"I remember how excited my parents were for you," she said. She closed her eyes. Actually it had been Mimi who was excited. Daddy had taken it all with a cool air that confused Liz back then. Now, she understood. Jealousy. Again. Daddy was jealous of George's success. But why?

"I—" Liz leaned over and rummaged in the orange canvas bag at her feet. "I have something to give you," she said. She grabbed the disk and handed it to him. As he turned it in his hands and stared at her, clearly clueless, she blabbered. "I found it hidden—in my father's office. It's . . . it's something about the Towers. S-something . . . my father—" She broke off, inhaled a ragged breath, and then blurted out the story between sobs. She explained. Everything. How she'd pieced it all together.

"He had enough engineering in school to figure it out—to know exactly how to change the blueprints. And then . . . the change was so slight the construction crew wouldn't have questioned it. And then Sam 'just happened' to be at the site when the inspectors arrived. It would have been easy for him to distract them and, after the fiasco, to point back to the good blueprints and make it look like you were responsible for making an unauthorized change." She broke off and swiped at the tears streaming down her face. "It was your word against his . . . and he won."

She took in a ragged breath. "I'm sorry," she said. "So . . . very . . . sorry. I won't blame you if you want to kick me out. Or if you want to stop helping with the hospital project. I wouldn't blame you for anything you do. I wasn't going to tell you. But then I thought, what if he's still doubting his abilities? What if he's turning down projects because of—" She wiped her nose. "I decided you deserve to know."

Having blurted out the truth, she sat, her knees together, her hands clasped, her lower back throbbing. She couldn't bring herself to move but sat as still as possible—waiting . . . waiting . . . waiting . . . while George stared down at the computer disk like a child inspecting an unfamiliar toy.

"So," he finally said, smiling sadly and dropping the disk onto the coffee table. That was all. Just "so." He leaned back and stared off into the corner of the room for a moment, and when he spoke, he didn't make any sense at all. "I'm so sorry, Liz."

"*You're* sorry? But—"

"I knew there had to be evidence somewhere." He shrugged. "I assumed Sam destroyed it long before he died. I was bitter for a long while. Intent on proving it. On finding something like what's on that disk and exonerating my name, once and for all." He sighed, shook his head. "But I never wanted *you* to know. And I'm honestly very sorry you found that." He gestured toward the disk.

"You . . . you know what's on it?" Liz needed clarification. Surely George Kincaid couldn't know about this. He couldn't.

George leaned back, pondering. Finally, he slapped his knees with his open palms. "I'll tell you what, Elizabeth. Let's have some real tea." He stood up and extended his hand. "Follow me to the kitchen?"

While George made tea, he talked. "Sometime back in the early 1990s, your father got the crazy idea that I was trying to woo Mary away from him. I don't know where it came from. The only thing I could ever come up with was one Christmas Eve when I asked her to dance. Your mother was a wonderful dancer, and my Betty had just died, and one dance became another and then another." He paused with the teakettle poised in midair while he enjoyed the memory. "Anyway, along about the fourth dance, Sam broke in. I've never seen such a murderous look in a man's eyes." He set the tea-kettle on the stove and looked toward Liz, who had seated herself at the kitchen table. "Did you know your father was a jealous man, Elizabeth?"

She shook her head, then nodded. "Until recently it never entered my mind. What did he have to be jealous of?"

"Exactly," George said, turning the burner on beneath the kettle of water. "Never was a woman more faithful and true than Mary Davis." He sighed, opened the cupboard to the right of the stove, took out two porcelain teacups and saucers, and after a huge yawn, said, "It's sad." He shook his head back and forth. "So sad. He never knew what a jewel he had." He looked quickly toward Liz. "Sorry, my dear, to burst your bubble, but . . ." He went back to brewing the tea. Liz noticed his hand shake a little as he poured hot water over the tea ball. It was a ritual he must be familiar with. The kitchen was silent, but it wasn't unfriendly. How, Liz wondered, could this red-and-white kitchen with the white-haired man in a plaid wool robe be anything *but* comfortable. Still, her heart was pounding.

George didn't speak again until he was seated opposite her, telling her to trust him and try it even as he poured milk into her cup, added a lump of sugar, and stirred. He waited for her to sip the concoction, waited for her satisfied murmur, and then went on with the discussion. "Of course you know I didn't take things quite so philosophically back then. Time was," he said, "I would have hid a little bottle of brandy up in that cupboard." He pretended to pour a shot of liquor into the tea. "And you would have been none the wiser." He nodded. "Thank God that's over."

It was just then that Liz noticed a beat-up book at the opposite end of the table. A Bible. George reached for the book. "But times change. And, it appears, you truly can teach an old dog new tricks— with a little supernatural assistance."

He patted the book and continued. "There was a lot more wrong with me back in those days than a failed project. When Kincaid Towers came down, that was simply the event that opened the world's window onto the reality of what was going on in my life. I was crumbling. The Towers might have hastened the process, but I won't blame them." He paused, and then looked straight into Liz's eyes. "And I won't blame Sam Davis."

"Did you know?" Liz blurted out the question.

"I knew he wanted revenge for some imagined offense. Perhaps it was the dance. Perhaps something else. I never understood it. But your father was . . . careful . . . about your mother. He always seemed to need some kind of reassurance about her. Why, I can't imagine. As I said, she was devoted to him, and no one ever questioned it— except Sam." He sighed. "Poor Sam." He reached across the table and squeezed Liz's hand.

Liz brushed her hair back out of her face with her free hand. "I don't know what to do," she muttered.

"I think I do," George said. He got up. He was gone for only a moment before returning with the disk in his hand. Going to the stove, he turned on a burner. Laid the disk in a skillet. Watched it melt.

# ℘ FOURTEEN ℘

SHE DIDN'T REALLY BELIEVE in miracles, but as she drove home Sunday night Liz realized that, if she did, she would think she had just witnessed one. Instead of indulging in the murderous rage he was due . . . George Kincaid made tea. And talked. Convincingly.

"You must believe me, Liz, I harbor no animosity toward your father. I was bitter for a long time. But then I began to realize that Sam Davis wasn't the one who took my life away. I did that to myself with years of bad decisions. And even if what you and I both think we know is true, it doesn't change a thing. I've lived long enough to realize that those towers collapsing was not the beginning of the end for me. It was the beginning of the real beginning." He had drawn a dot on a piece of paper. "This is now. My entire life." From the dot, he extended a line into an arrow. "That's eternity. That's the part I'm concentrating on now."

George Kincaid said he was a happy man, and after looking into his eyes, Liz had to admit he seemed to be telling the truth.

If only, she thought as she rounded the last corner for home, if only—

Flashing lights brought her out of herself and into the moment. *Oh no, not again!* If this was Ryan Miller's brother again . . . she was tapping her left foot against the car floor when the cop leaned down. Thank goodness it wasn't him.

"Evening," he said. "Do you know how fast you were going?"

"I'm sorry," Liz said, trying to sound contrite, hoping he didn't notice how her hands were curled into fists. She couldn't look at him. He'd read rebellion in every line of her face. Just once—just *once* couldn't they let a Porsche go by without honing in with a radar gun? "I wasn't paying attention. I just had a stressful meeting, and—"

"Yeah," the officer said. She could hear the sarcasm and see him smirk. "Those Sunday night business meetings are killers."

If he was going to be that way, she was finished with nice. Snatching her license and registration out of the glove box, she handed them out.

"Proof of insurance, please," he reminded her.

Liz fumbled for it. Found it. Thrust it through the window. While she waited for the cop to walk back to his cruiser and slap her with yet another hefty fine, she heard George Kincaid's voice saying, *"Look at me, Liz. You are looking at a happy man. I don't need a new project or an architectural firm to define who I am."* He had an interesting way of putting it. *"I am George Kincaid, converted reprobate, doing his best to give an ear to God and do his bidding."* She wasn't going to pretend she understood it, but she had to admire it.

All the way home, and even after she had climbed the stairs to her room and fallen into bed, she thought about her time with George. It was one of those amazing events in life a person thought might be a dream. She'd probably spend most of Monday morning convincing herself it had really happened. George Kincaid knew . . . and didn't want revenge.

When Monday came, however, Liz didn't have time to ponder George Kincaid. She was too busy throwing up. She hadn't even decided if she was going to go through with this pregnancy, and already it was making itself known . . . in very unpleasant ways. Irene was only going to believe she had the flu so many times. What *was* she going to do? With a groan, she fumbled for the phone to tell Margaret she would be late. An hour later, having convinced Irene to just let her sleep, she called the office again.

"Short of a miracle, I'm not going to make it in today at all. I'm going back to bed. Call me if there's anything I need to know about."

"Your calendar's clear," Margaret said. "But you already knew that. Ryan Miller checked in. He went out to the hospital site early and called a little while ago to say the foreman was going to put him to work out there today." Margaret paused, then asked, "Should I have Mr. Scott dial you at home, then? He's called for you several times this morning. Said you weren't answering the cell phone."

Liz hesitated. The title of one of the pamphlets from her doctor caught her eye. OPTIONS. She had options, it said. She could feel her stomach roiling. Again. Margaret was wondering what was going on. She was tactful . . . but she was wondering. "Tell him I'll call him later. But don't you dare tell him I'm sick. I don't want him coming out here. If I'm contagious, I don't want Jeff getting sick, too. I just need some peace and quiet." She hoped she sounded convincing enough to satisfy Margaret's curiosity. And she hoped Jeff didn't call. Not for a while, anyway. She needed time to think. *Options . . . miracles . . . Kincaid Towers . . . babies . . . Jeff . . . California . . .* Some of the pamphlets were tucked away in her mother's desk. She should get those out and put them back in her briefcase—as soon as she felt like she could make it downstairs without another dash for the bathroom. Her mind was spinning . . . but not nearly as fast as her midsection.

### *Mary*

"HAVE I DIED and come to heaven in Italy?" I feel like an awed child as I look around my hotel room at the frescoed walls, coffered ceiling, arched windows, and elegant furnishings.

Luca laughs. "My sister Lucia insisted you have the finest room in her hotel. I'm glad you like it."

"Like it?" Behind me a bellboy sets my suitcase down, waits for Luca's tip—which I notice is paper not coins—and exits. "This is for visiting royalty. I can't stay here."

"As a matter of fact," Luca says, "I believe the King of Spain did spend a night here once. In the 1500s. The building used to belong to one of the Medici. But it's been a hotel for a long, long time now. Long before our family purchased it and named it for the only daughter in the family. I'm glad you approve. Welcome to Hotel Lucia." He bows before crossing the room and pulling on a golden cord to draw back the drapes.

Looking at the view, I gasp with delight. The old section of Florence lies before me. Luca points out the various church domes, reciting names, "West to east, you have Santa Maria Novella . . . San Lorenzo . . . the baptistry beside Santa Maria del Fiore . . . in the distance, San Marco . . . and finally, farthest to the east, Santa Croce." He jokes, "It is not Paris, but we also have a few churches to keep you from despairing, eh?"

"I already know which one I want to visit first. The guidebook says Santo Spirito is a favorite of architectural purists. They consider it one of Brunelesschi's masterpieces. Right?"

He shrugs. "Far too gloomy for my taste. And as to Brunelesschi, if you want to see the real masterpiece . . ."

"The Duomo?"

"*Sì*." He nods. "Our churches are nothing like the gothic cathedrals in Paris. I'll be interested to see what you think. If you don't mind my doing the tag-a-long as you see the sights?"

"I don't expect you to do that," I protest.

"And I," he says, flashing a smile, "can't think of a better way to spend the days while Lucia drives everyone crazy with the wedding preparations."

"Should I be helping with that? I'd enjoy it."

"You," Luca says, "should be staying as far away as possible. Lucia is . . . Well, to explain my sister is impossible. When you meet her you will see what I mean. And in the meantime, until Jean-Marc arrives, I will take pleasure to show you my city."

"I don't expect you to baby-sit me every minute. From what I've seen in my guidebooks, Florence is a very walkable place. I already have at least a week's worth of sight-seeing to do, all of which would probably bore you to tears."

Luca protests. Boredom, he assures me, is not possible in Florence.

"So you don't mind standing in line with me to see *David*?"

"You call and make an appointment. No line," he explains. "And while I grew up with the *David* just across the street, almost, I still have appreciation. They have moved him since I was last here . . . and I'm told that four of my personal favorites by the master line the gallery on the way to *David*."

"What about the Uffizi? Another line, yes?"

"Unless you phone for a prearranged entrance time. And maybe a short line even then. But not a very long one this time of year, and while we wait *I* could bore *you* with my lecture on the Italian masters."

"You have a lecture on the Italian masters?"

"Most definitely," he jokes, "beginning with Ducati leading right up to Moto Guzzi—with a few remarks on the foreigners, Hyabusa and Honda."

"Motorcycles again," I scold him. "I knew it. You *do* have motor oil running in your veins."

We laugh, and then he says, "And when you tire of walking Florence, decide where else you would like to go—Siena, for example—and I will take you."

"I don't know where to begin," I say, quoting the novel I've been reading. *"Italy is thousands of years deep . . ."*

"If I may suggest," he says, asking permission with his eyes.

"You may."

"You begin with the thing that most calls to your heart." He smiles. "Will you have dinner with us this evening. At my family villa?"

The moment I accept his dinner invitation, he says something about Jean-Marc's trip and expected arrival date, looking out the window as he talks. He concludes with, "You would have loved the sea voyage. And he was so disappointed when you said the *no*."

There it is again. That resentment I feel at the idea of Jean-Marc and Luca discussing me. Why exactly does that bother me? "I wasn't comfortable being out of touch with Liz. Of course Jean-Marc promised that wouldn't really be the case, but you know how it is with Jean-Marc and sailing. Anything could happen."

Luca nods agreement and echoes, "Anything."

The silence between us isn't exactly awkward, but it is longer than usual. Do I imagine it, or does he sigh before telling me he will return for me around seven in the evening. At the elevator he turns to say that he suggests he come early so that he'll have an hour or so to help me with my computer and e-mail hookup before we leave for dinner. I decide that adjusting to Tuscan time is going to be fun. And then I notice. Luca Santo is no longer wearing a wedding ring.

I AM STILL IN AWE of the beautiful view from the entry-way to the Santo villa when a large, stunning woman opens the door and swoops down on me, engulfing me in her arms and kissing both my cheeks, before shooing Luca out of the way so she can take me on a tour of the villa. Luca was right when he told me his sister, Lucia Maria Lungarno Biacci, was a woman who could not be explained but must be experienced. I'm left breathless, both by Lucia's energy and the questions that interrupt her tour-guide litany.

"And this is our beautiful little chapel, which we are trying to restore, but now they have uncovered that awful painting." She leans toward me and lowers her voice to a stage whisper. "I don't *care* if it's Botticelli, I hate it." She sighs. "But of course, it must be preserved, so I will be cursed to endure it for the rest of my days. I ask you," she says, gesturing toward the wall where I can barely see a wan female figure who appears to be in the throes of revelation from an angelic figure.

"It's the visitation?"

"*Sì, Sì.*" Lucia nods. "*Esatto.* The blessed virgin accepts it so beautifully, don't you think. But that angel! Who wants to live with such an angel?!" And she is off on a tangent about some artistic detail that at once fascinates me and reminds me how ignorant I am. I don't really see all that much to dislike about the angel.

One thing I quickly realize about Lucia. She needs only a good audience. I am that because I am, plain and simply, dumbfounded at the woman's obvious knowledge of art history. Is this what growing up in Florence does? Is art so prevalent that it permeates the lives of those who grow up here? Do they learn these things by osmosis? Or is Lucia special?

By the time we have gone through the first floor of the house, I feel like a child being led through a wonderland castle. Luca's childhood home is stunning. Marble floors, fountains, gardens—all enhanced by a view of the valley that sweeps toward Florence. Off to the left is a fortress. I am told part of its walls form the border to the Boboli Gardens. In the center of the panorama, the Ponte Vecchio crosses the Arno River in picturesque glory. The domes of all the churches of Florence glow deep orange as the setting sun throws its last rays of light against their tiles.

Dinner is friendly bedlam. Lucia's children arrive along with a dozen grandchildren, and everyone is seated as Lucia orchestrates. And then comes the food—*antipasti* followed by a first course, followed by a second course, and yet another. *Contorno,* Luca calls it. The portions are small, but still I think I may explode. Finally . . . dessert . . . *dolci.* There is laughter and noise, and it's so wonderful that suddenly, when Lucia bends over to pinch a child's pink cheeks and plant a kiss, my eyes brim with tears. I miss Liz.

Luca puts his hand over mine and leans close, "We can leave whenever you've had enough. I know it's overwhelming."

I shake my head. "No. It's not that. Just a flicker of jealousy. All this family. Wonderful. I'm beginning to regret that I only had one child. And to wonder exactly why it is I've moved so far away."

Lucia's husband, Donato, a quiet man—which probably assures his survival in this rowdy family—with wonderful dark eyes and a completely bald head, raises his glass and proposes a toast. To me. I can feel myself blushing. I have no idea what he says, but Lucia butts in, stands up, and finishes for him. Everyone at the table is suddenly laughing. Luca refuses to translate. He scolds his sister, but his expression is adoring.

"All right, all right," Lucia says, waving her napkin to silence her family.

They quiet gradually, but I can hear a stifled giggle here and there as Luca protests—loudly—for Lucia to stop. "You are embarrassing our guest," he says, "Enough!"

Lucia tosses her head so that her wonderful black hair is back behind her shoulders. She lifts her glass high, and says in English, "As I have said these many years, my friend Sophia—" she crosses herself and looks to heaven—"may the dear Lord rest her soul in peace and bring us all to dine with her in the heavenly home. . . ." She clears her throat again. "My dear friend Sophia spent far too many years teaching Luca how to be a decent husband for it all to go to waste in a Ducati shop in Paris!" She nods at me. "May your friendship be blessed, even as I sense Sophia's blessing upon you!" And with that, Lucia takes a drink and sits down.

Next to me, Luca raises his right hand to his brow, pretending to hide his face. But he peers at me from beneath it.

I lean toward him. "I see what you mean about Lucia."

THE MORNING AFTER LUCIA embarrassed me in front of Luca's entire family, she appears at the hotel to apologize. "Luca is very upset with me," she says. There are actually tears in her eyes. "He tells me I have mortified you and you will likely not want to return to dinner soon. You must allow me to apologize."

"You don't owe me an apology," I say quickly. "I loved being with you. With all of you."

"You are very kind, *signora,*" Lucia smiles. "You must know that for as long as we have been born, I am the . . . um . . . guarding dog . . . for my twin brother. Sometimes maybe I am too much guarding. Luca is grown man. And I . . . um . . . I stir the soup that is not mine. Maybe too much."

"Thank you. But, really—"

"And so, you will let me make you up. Today, you go here." She hands me a gray booklet advertising a spa, with a stylized swan and the word *Fonbliù* on the cover. "I am not coming. Too much wedding things. But Tomaso will take very good care. And now, I go. *Ciao.* And Luca comes for you at the spa this afternoon and takes you to dinner at wonderful trattoria. No menu. You sit, chef cooks, you eat. *Perfetto.*" She presses her fingertips together and smacks them with a kiss, wishes me a good day, and is gone.

In Lucia's wake I am . . . breathless. This, I think, is what Liz would have been like were she born in Italy. I look at my watch. It's too early to call her. She won't be up for a couple of hours yet. So I sit down to look at the brochure, wherein Lucia has noted what she has ordered for me. *Relaxing, detoxifying, and reenergizing . . . utilizes heated stones of lava. . . . The method has been passed down by the American Indians.*

I chuckle. I'm in Italy being pampered by a Native American tradition. Lucia has also ordered *a complete two-hour treatment that regenerates and purifies the face and body . . .* with something called *Boue Marine du Mont St. Michel mud.* Mont St. Michel is a medieval city on a tiny island in the north of France completely surrounded by the ocean every time the tide comes in. A fortress that was never conquered. A medieval wonder. I've always wanted to see it. Maybe being covered in Mont St. Michel mud is . . . the next best thing?

Last night when he said good-night at the hotel, Luca told me that beneath the "guardian dog" persona, Lucia is a woman with a heart the size of Italy. "And when she takes a person into that heart of hers . . . they are blessed." I do believe him. I just never expected being blessed with Lucia's friendship to include being covered with mud and pounded with hot stones.

## ꕚ FIFTEEN ꕚ

IF HER FIRST DAY at work was any indication, Alessandra Buonartti would not be working long at the Fonbliù spa. She'd done everything possible wrong. The bookings were a nightmare. One wrap took twenty minutes, another treatment took forty. And that beast Tomaso expected her to know everything—all of it—as if she had been working here for years, instead of hours. She was close to tears when the scream sounded from the pool. *What now?* was all she could think, but the next breath of the screamer was a cry for help. Alessandra jumped up and bolted down the hall and . . . clutched the wall in horror staring at the spot where two spa customers were dragging a limp woman out of the water. Blood—there was blood everywhere. And Alessandra couldn't cope with blood. Except she must. She must.

Grabbing a towel, she rolled it up as she went to the woman's side. She'd banged her head. "Here," Alessandra said, pressing the towel over the wound which would, she saw quickly, require stitches. For this, she knew what to do. A girl didn't grow up with brothers and not know how to handle a bump on the head. Still the woman was unconscious. And American. Tomaso would be beside himself with anger. They'd be sued . . . they'd. . . . Jumping up, she went to the phone and called for an ambulance before going back to the woman's side, where a small group of patrons had gathered.

No one knew the woman. Alessandra nodded at a co-worker. "Break into her locker. Get her identity."

"Tomaso knows everything," another girl said. "Signora Biacci sent her to us."

Alessandra closed her eyes. Could it possibly be worse? The American brought in by Lucia Biacci? Alessandra saw her job dissolving before her eyes. Just then, the woman groaned. Alessandra spoke to her, but there was no response. She could hear the ambulance blaring up the street.

"Here," someone handed her the woman's wallet. There was a note. In English. But she recognized the words *In case of emergency*. She knew who to call in America. She'd do that first. The daughter first. Then Signora Biacci. And if she could not reach her, someone at the Hotel Lucia would know what to do next. And then—only then—would Tomaso be notified.

IRENE FROWNED AND SHOOK her head as if the caller could see her. "What? Yes, yes. I mean, this is where she lives. But she can't come to the phone. She's got the flu. Give me the message." She pressed her lips together. "You aren't listening to me. I said that Miss Davis has the flu. She's not coming to the phone. Give me the message. And could you talk slower? Shouting isn't going to make me understand your Eye-talian accent any better. I'm old, but I'm not deaf. What? What? You don't understand? Well, neither do I, honey. You just call back after you've found somebody who talks like I do."

Irene slammed the receiver down with more than her usual insistence. "Some snooty youngster needs to have a knot yanked in her tail," she grumbled. "Yelling over the phone like a lunatic."

From where he sat reading his paper and drinking coffee, Cecil spoke up. "And you're just the woman to do it, hon. Except for the fact that you can't exactly reach over the Atlantic Ocean." He chuck-led.

"Very funny," Irene said. She bustled to the back stairs. "I'm just going to go up and see if Lizzie needs anything. Maybe she's ready for some red Jell-O." She grumbled all the way up the stairs about life in general. She had never thought things would come to this. The house little more than a museum, with her and Cecil rattling around while Liz came and went. And the girl had been fighting off the flu bug for days now, but she wouldn't listen to a thing Irene said. She wanted to be left alone. She didn't want to see Jeff. She didn't want her mother to know. It just didn't make sense.

Irene had just hit the top of the stairs when the phone rang again. She went past Liz's room and into Mary's to pick up the phone.

"Elizabeth Davis?" It was a man's voice this time. Another Eye-talian.

"No," Irene repeated. Without trying to sound any less irritated than she was. "I already told someone that Miss Davis is sick and isn't coming to the phone. If you're not going to talk to me, either, you can stop calling because I'm not—" Irene closed her eyes so she could try to concentrate. This one she could understand. "What did you just say? Mrs. Davis is . . . at *what* hospital?" *Oh, dear Lord.* She slumped against the edge of the desk. "Just a minute. Hold on. Let me get a pencil and some paper." She fumbled in Mrs. Davis's desk drawer, grabbed a piece of scrap paper, and began taking notes.

"All right," she said. "All right. I've got that. Let me read it back to you." She read back the name of the hospital. This wasn't scrap paper. It was some kind of . . . *Oh, dear Lord.* "What did you say happened? A fall?" *If you are facing an unplanned pregnancy . . . you are not alone.* She tried to pay better attention to the phone call. She scrawled the word *unconscious.* That could be bad. *Broken bone.* She read the phone number of the hospital back to the man, who wasn't quite so abrasive now that she was listening better. *Please, Lord . . . clean break. Good doctors.*

But she couldn't help but think back to two years ago when the housekeeper for the Zimmermans had broken her foot. It had turned out to be one long year of casting and surgeries. The poor woman had to retire—with so many pieces of metal in her foot that she now set off alarms in airports.

With the phone call over, Irene looked the pamphlet over more carefully. It explained a lot. About a lot of things. Liz's moods. Why she'd been coming in here to her mother's room late at night. It was sweet—and heartrending at the same time—thinking of Liz being drawn to her mother's room. And it made sense to put this trash in the desk in here, where Irene only dusted surfaces and maintained status quo. There was no expectation of Irene ever opening one of Mary Davis's desk drawers. Liz probably had that all figured out. Liz had a lot of things figured out, it seemed. Surely, Irene thought, abortion wasn't one of them. If Mrs. Davis ever found out . . . And what about Jeff? She had thought better of Jeff. This just didn't make sense at all. *Except it does. If Jeff said he doesn't want a baby . . . if Jeff broke it off . . . if Jeff is moving to California.*

"LIZ. WAKE UP." Irene was standing over her calling her name. As she came out from under the canopy of dreams that weighed as heavily as any pill-induced sleep she'd ever had, Liz heard the tone. This was not Irene's I-will-try-to-fill-in-for-absentee-mother voice. Turning over, Liz opened her eyes. She was afraid to lift her head off the pillow, in spite of the fact it seemed her stomach had settled in the last couple of hours while she slept.

The minute Liz opened her eyes, Irene said, "There's been an accident in Florence."

Dread washed over her. Instantly alert, she bolted upright in bed with no thought of morning sickness. "Is she . . . is she all right? What happened?"

"If you'll hush, I'll tell you," Irene said. "She was at some fancy spa and slipped and bumped her head. They said she's unconscious. I think she cut something. And broke something, but the Eye-talian wasn't sure of that." Irene looked down at the paper in her hand. "They gave me a phone number." She shoved the paper toward Liz.

She couldn't look Irene in the eye for a long time. Instead, she looked down at the floor. One of Irene's shoes was beating a rhythm into the carpet.

"I didn't snoop, if that's what you're thinking. That young man was talking, and I had to take notes, so I opened the middle drawer of your mother's desk and grabbed the first thing handy. I suppose I should have come and gotten you, but you've been battling the *flu* for so long and you seemed so *sick,* I didn't want to bother you. I thought you'd want me to take a message."

Liz slumped over and rested her forehead in her hands. How, she wondered, was it possible to sleep so deeply and still feel so weary? "No one's accusing you of snooping, Irene. Calm down." She shook her head. "I can't talk about this now. I've got to—" Her mind shifted gears. She looked at the phone number Irene had written down. Luca Santo's number. "I've got to call Luca. He'll know what's going on." She pushed the down comforter down and slid her feet to the floor.

"You still feeling sick?" Irene said.

Liz shook her head. "No. It's better."

Irene put the pamphlet down on the night table and headed for the door. Just outside the room, she turned around. "You liberated women always say you don't need a man to help you be successful in the world. Isn't that right?"

"You could put it that way."

"No," she snapped. "*I* can't 'put it that way'. *I* don't *think* men are accessories you wear when you like them and discard when the shine wears off. But that's not what I'm talking about." She took a deep breath. "If Jeffrey Scott doesn't want a baby, then you're well rid of him." Her voice wavered, "But remember what you said, Lizzie. You said you don't *need* a man to help you be successful." Her chest heaved with emotion as she blurted out, "We can raise that baby, Lizzie. All of us together." Her chin trembled. "You *know* I love little ones. Me and Cecil both love children." Tears spilled down her cheeks. "Don't *do* it, Lizzie. Please."

Liz couldn't face her. She was trembling on the edge of decision . . . at the worst time to make a decision. Mimi was hurt. She had to think of Mimi. Swiping at the tears on her own cheeks she nodded. "Thank you, Irene. That . . . that means a lot."

"You're going to Italy?"

"Of course. Unless Luca Santo or Jean-Marc or someone can tell me exactly what's happened. Unless I can talk to Mimi myself."

"I think I have some vitamins that might help you feel better," Irene said. "And if you keep soda crackers handy—sometimes if you just eat one or two in the morning before you even raise your head off the pillow . . . sometimes that helps."

Liz cleared her throat. "Thank you, Irene. For . . . for everything. Really." But Irene was gone. Liz wondered if she had fled down the hall for fear of what Liz might say next. By the time she had her cell phone in her hand, she had a mental list of what to do. Luca Santo's number was in her briefcase. On the way downstairs she decided that, whatever else happened, by the end of the next day in Florence, Mary Davis would own a satellite cell phone. *Which would do a lot of good if she's unconscious.* The what-ifs began to pepper her thought processes. *Focus. This is not the time. Focus.*

She called Margaret. "Get online or on the phone and find a way to get me to Florence, Italy, as quickly as possible. My mother's had an accident. If Dave can fly me to Newark, and that lands me in Florence faster, call Dave and get him started on a flight plan. If I can't reach someone in Italy who knows what's going on, I'll be in my car on the way to the airport in twenty minutes. Call me on my cell phone and let me know if I'm headed to the Davis hangar or the terminal." What a blessing to have someone like Margaret at times like this. *Great. You're around Danny and Sarah for a few days and you've got religious vocabulary. Since when have you ever thought of things as bless-*

*ings, anyway? You are lucky to have Margaret.*

Margaret spoke up. "Got it. I'm already online. I'll call you in a few minutes. You want me to bring some euros to the airport?"

"You're a genius," Liz said. "Yes. Thank you. Two or three hundred."

"And your passport. I've got it right here. I pulled it while you were talking."

"You're a goddess," Liz said.

Margaret ignored the compliment. "Do you want me to call Mr. Scott?" When Liz didn't answer, she said, "He'd want to know."

It was not like Margaret to give personal advice. Was Liz imagining things, or had Margaret's tone of voice changed with the words *he'd want to know.* Was it a double entendre? Had Margaret seen the home pregnancy test? Good old Margaret . . . super efficient. . . . Sometimes she took to cleaning when Liz was out of the office. And she'd been out a lot this past week. . . . Liz closed her eyes. Took a deep breath.

Why had she thought it necessary to second-guess Dr. Reese, anyway? How likely was it for the lab results not to be accurate? But no, Elizabeth Davis couldn't take her own doctor's word for it. Elizabeth Davis had to go out and buy her own test—double-check things. What an idiot. And then she'd left the evidence in the trash. Liz argued with herself. She'd been upset. And it was, after all, her *private* office. She'd meant to take the test with her when she left for her meeting, but then it got late and she wasn't feeling well, so she didn't get back to the office at all.

"Don't forget the roses," Margaret said.

"Roses? What roses?"

"The ones Mr. Scott left in the sink in your powder room."

*Oh . . . no.* Jeff had brought her roses? Jeff had been in the powder room?

"I brought in another vase, by the way."

"Another vase?"

"To replace the broken one. The pieces were in the trash."

*Broken vase. . . . trash can . . . powder room . . .* The truth hit home. They know. They both know.

*Focus . . . focus.* "I didn't know about the roses," Liz said. "I didn't get back to the office that day. I never saw Jeff."

"That explains a lot," Margaret said.

*I can't deal with this now. I can't . . .* Liz cleared her throat. "I can't deal with Mr. Scott right now. You can call him and tell him about Mother *after* I'm in the air. Tell him I'll call him when I know something. And . . . thank him for the roses. No. Don't. Don't mention the roses." If she mentioned the roses . . . She shook her head. No. If he wasn't talking, then neither was she. At least not yet. With Margaret on task and Irene finding saltines and vitamins, Liz took three deep breaths and went to pack. Periodically she dialed Luca Santo. More than once she tried her mother's cell phone. Mimi would have turned the phone off if she was at a spa. She always did that when she wasn't going to answer it. To save the battery, she said. It drove Liz crazy. She couldn't just leave a message and wait for Mimi to turn the thing back on. If Mimi was badly hurt. . . . *Focus.*

Two black skirts, three blouses, a spare pair of shoes, makeup, grab-and-go bag. She was glad she'd learned that trick. From Mimi, actually. In Paris. Mimi kept a small travel bag packed with her toiletries so she could grab-and-go without taking time to collect eyeliner and tweezers and all the other essentials of feminine life. It was a great tip, and they had shared a laugh at the idea of Mary Davis advising Elizabeth Davis on how to organize for a business trip. As she grabbed the black bag, Liz blinked back tears. *Please let her be all right.* She brushed her open hand across her abdomen. *I need her. I know what she's going to say . . . but I need to hear her say it.*

"I'M SORRY, OFFICER," Liz said, as she rolled down her window and started pleading her case before the cop had even reached her car. "I'm not trying to be smart. Really. I'm telling you the truth. My mother is in Italy, and I've just received a phone call that she's been injured. She's in a hospital over there, and I've got to get to her. I'm headed for the airport. To catch a commercial flight— my pilot couldn't get everything ready as fast—if I can only get there while they're still boarding. Please. You've *got* to believe me! Please let me go. I'll never speed again. I'll promise you on a stack of Bibles . . . I'll buy a hundred tickets to the policeman's ball . . . but—" She burst into tears.

The officer leaned down to look at her through the window. "Hey now, Miss Davis. There's no need to get hysterical."

Liz turned to face him. It was Officer Miller. *Thank goodness.*

"You say your mother's in the hospital? In *Italy*?"

"Yes," Liz said. "I don't know what's wrong with her. She fell. She's unconscious. And I can't get a call through to anyone she's with."

"You follow me," he said, and stepped back from the window.

"What?"

"I said, follow me. When I pull around."

She looked up at him, blinking away tears. "Really?"

He nodded. "Really." He leaned down and looked her in the eye. "You calm enough to drive safely?"

"Yes." She nodded, sat up straight, gripped the steering wheel.

"Then let's get you to the airport." He paused. "How soon did you say your flight is leaving?"

"Sooner than I can probably make it now," Liz said, her voice miserable.

"Maybe not," Officer Miller said. He nodded at the car. "We'll go straight to the loading zone. If you can bring yourself to trust me with your baby's keys, I'll park her for you . . . and deliver the keys to your office when I'm off duty."

Liz took in a deep breath. She nodded. "Thank you."

ONE OF THE GREAT THINGS about living in Omaha,

Liz realized anew, was the airport. No long lines. Efficient. Pleasant security. The two-hour window of time required elsewhere could be shrunk considerably here. But not, Liz realized as she stood in her stocking feet and held out her arms for the TSA employee to wand her, for people who booked last-minute international flights. Margaret might be a genius about collecting passports and compiling travel itinerary, but "last-minute" raised a red flag no amount of influence in the post 9/11 world could change. So there she stood, looking like some kind of scarecrow, when Jeff walked up and set his carryon on the conveyor belt. He was getting searched, too. They were going through every compartment in his carryon. Liz was beginning to think maybe she could scoot away without him seeing her. Elizabeth Davis never traveled in jeans and tennies. Elizabeth Davis was never seen in public without her makeup and never went anywhere with her hair pulled up into a ponytail. Maybe he wouldn't . . . But here he came—they were going to wand him, too.

One of the worst things about living in Omaha was the small airport. With nowhere to run and nowhere to hide, Liz decided to take the offensive. "I didn't know you were headed to California again so soon," she said, hoping she sounded casual . . . friendly. Except that her voice wavered when she said it. For a fleeting moment she came dangerously close to falling apart. Now that he was here in front of her, all Liz could think about was pieces of a broken vase and roses left to wilt in the sink at the office. He couldn't know she hadn't known about that . . . He must be hurt. Or angry. Was that it? Was he angry? How she longed for him to reach for her . . . to somehow find a way to scale the wall of secrets between them, put his arms around her, and make everything better.

"I'm not going to California," he said. He met her gaze briefly, then glanced away as he said, "And hello to you, too." He sat down and took off his shoes.

Liz bent down to tie hers. She bit her lip to keep from saying anything. *Not in the middle of an airport.*

The security guard was instructing Jeff to take off his belt, to check his pockets again.

With a grim smile in Liz's direction, Jeff pulled the pocket linings out.

"You can go, ma'am," the security guard said to Liz.

"He's my fiancé," Liz said. She didn't sound very convincing.

"Traveling together?" the guard asked.

"No," Liz said.

"Yes." Jeff contradicted her and explained to the frowning security guard. "It's a surprise."

The guard smiled. "Well, have a good trip," she said, and nodded at Liz as she waved Jeff toward the gate.

Liz bent down to pick up her bag. Jeff reached for it.

"I'll carry it," he said. "Unless that somehow disempowers you."

"Thanks," she said. "I'm . . . we're . . . at gate 6."

"Yeah," he said. He looked down at her. "I know you don't need me. You probably don't want me. But I love Mary, too."

Her voice cracked. She couldn't look at him. Still, she asked. "How did you—"

"Irene. Margaret. They both called me." He set the bags down in a vacant seat and changed the subject. "You mind watching these while I get some coffee?"

She shook her head. "Go ahead."

"You want anything?"

"Coffee sounds good."

"Decaf or leaded?"

"Leaded. When have you ever known me to drink decaf?"

He opened his mouth to say something, but then seemed to think better of it and just shrugged and walked away.

*He knows.* Leaning over, Liz rested her head in her hands. She couldn't think about this. Not now. They couldn't possibly talk about it. Not in the middle of an airport . . . not now, when . . . *Focus on Mimi.* She was trembling all over. Terrified. She looked toward the gate. When were they going to start to board the plane, anyway?

They'd told her she probably wouldn't make the flight, and now . . . delay. Jeff came back with the coffee. When he handed it to her and sat down beside her, she closed her eyes, trying to concentrate on the coffee. But try as she might, she could not keep the tears from slipping down her cheeks. She started to get up.

"I have to . . . have to go—"

"No," Jeff said. "You don't." His voice was gentle. He pulled her back down beside him, took the coffee out of her hand, set it on the carpet beneath her seat, and wrapped his arms around her. "It'll be all right," he whispered. "It'll be all right, baby girl."

She shook her head. "You don't . . . you don't—"

"Shhhh. Shhhh. Let's just concentrate on getting to Mary right now, Bitsy. That's enough trouble for today, don't you think?" He held her tighter.

"Don't let go," she whispered.

## ℘ SIXTEEN ℘

*Mary*

I WAKE UP IN THE AMBULANCE. The first thing I see is . . . very little. Bandages obscure my vision, and my head feels about twice its normal size, but not all from the bandages. The incessant pounding has its effect, too. And the siren. And the excited chattering of the paramedics riding with me. When one of them notices my eyes are open, it induces new activity. I feel the blood-pressure cuff tightening. Another paramedic leans close, shines a light in my eyes, and says something. I don't know if he's talking to me or not. Just in case, I manage *"Mi dispiace. Non parlo italiano."*

The paramedic starts, looks at me, and then, pointing to himself, says something about his ability to speak English. I think he said that my Italian is better than his English. When I smile, he seems reassured as to my condition. I catch the word for *hospital* in his next sentence, and decide to wait. Likely someone at the hospital will speak English or French. If not, I'll write Luca's name on a piece of paper and make them call him. I close my eyes. Note to self: Never try to do an aerobic workout on a hydrocycle after a two-hour massage. Noodle legs make climbing out of a pool impossible. I hope I haven't broken anything. . . .

When I awaken next, I am disoriented and afraid. And I hurt . . .

everywhere. My head, my back . . . and my right—no, left leg. I walk myself through the same routine I've always used with Liz. Breathe . . . breathe . . . one, two, three . . . in, one, two, three . . . out. Lamaze breathing is useful for a lot more than childbirth. With my eyes closed, I reconnect with my body and take inventory. My head is bandaged. I must have bonked it good when I slipped getting out of the pool. I wouldn't be surprised if I have stitches. My neck is stiff, but it works. My lower back is killing me. The right leg is fine. I can flex my ankle, bend my knee, wiggle my toes. But the left one is a different story. Any movement at all is excruciating. I'm grunting with pain when I hear Luca's voice out in the hall. Luca . . . and Lucia. They are having an animated conversation with someone else. A man. A doctor?

Lucia sweeps into the room and flits to my side. It is hard to believe a woman her size can flit, but Lucia can. She's graceful and stunning. Which does nothing for my morale as Luca joins her. Lucia takes one look at me and bursts into tears. She is sorry . . . so sorry. It is all her fault. Tomaso should have told me about the effects of his treatments, should never have left the spa while a new client was there. . . . She chatters on and on, and every time she looks at me there is a new flood of tears.

"I must look much worse than I feel," I protest. "Really, Lucia. It's not that—BAD." I grimace and nearly shout the last word, because I've tried to rise up on my elbows to prove my point, and when I do, the bottom of my left foot hits the bed railing. I look at Luca. "Is it? That bad?"

"You have broken the leg," Luca explains. He shakes his head. "No, not broken . . ." He gestures, looking for the word, then looks at me with a question. "Crack-ed?"

"Fractured?" I supply the word.

Luca nods. "Sì. Is only fractured."

I lie back flat and reach up to touch the bandages wrapped around my head.

Luca takes my hand. Smiles. I feel better. "The head is all right.

A few stitches. A black eye. That is all."

I have a black eye. Charming. I am suddenly very much aware of the two beautiful people before me. I try to joke. "You know, seeing you both from this angle makes me see how much you really do look alike." I say to Luca, "I had trouble imagining you as a woman when you told me you had a twin sister."

"I am thinking this is good thing," Luca teases back. He puts his arm around his sister's shoulders and leans his head toward her. "But you see now. Beautiful man, beautiful woman." He winks at me.

The doctor comes in. Luca translates. Apparently I have a very slight fracture in one of the leg bones just above my ankle. The doctor beams with good news. It won't require surgery. In fact, after the swelling goes down in a couple of days, they will fit me with some kind of boot that will enable me to walk. I may not even need crutches. They will keep me here "under observation" until the day after tomorrow—more because I was knocked unconscious than because of the fractured bone. Then the doctor shines a light in my eyes, has me follow his hand, and count his fingers.

"So I can plan on being back at the hotel by Thursday?" I ask.

"No hotel," Lucia says. In a flurry of Italian, she explains something to the doctor, who nods with satisfaction and leaves. Lucia beams at me. "You will come to my house."

My protests are pointless.

Luca encourages me. "Please, *cara mia*. Lucia feels responsible." Behind him, I can see Lucia nodding. "She is going to pamper you, no matter what you try to say. If you are under our roof, it will make things easier for her. You will be saving her the trips down to the hotel."

"All right." The pain pill I've taken is beginning to make me feel drowsy. I smile at Lucia. "Whatever you say. You're the boss."

Lucia beams. "I am . . . de boss." She wears the title well even as she orders Luca to make certain I have some soup. I didn't even notice the container on the bedside table.

"I'll feed you soup later," Luca says. "Why don't you let your eyes close for a while."

I close my eyes. "Luca," I murmur.

"*Sì, cara mia.*"

"Don't let anyone call home about this. Until tomorrow." I fall asleep before he can answer.


JEFF LINGERED AT THE top of the ramp, wondering what he should do. They'd been seated several rows apart on the flight, which had been good. He hadn't had to keep up the pretense of ignorance for long. But, they had a five-hour layover until the Lufthansa flight took off. He might have been able to play the knight-in-shining armor for a few minutes in Omaha . . . but he didn't think he could do it indefinitely. How long was she going to pretend, anyway? She had to know he knew. She'd seen the roses. Even if she hadn't been back to the office . . . Margaret would have mentioned them. Wouldn't she?

As passenger after passenger filed past him, Jeff's mind raced from one impossible scenario to the next. The situation was unbelievable. Focusing on the passengers filing off the plane, he forced himself to think about Mary. He would tell Liz they should keep trying to get hold of Luca in Florence. Maybe Mary was fine. Maybe the whole trip would be unnecessary? He said as much when Liz caught up.

Opening her cell phone, she dialed Luca Santo's number. "He isn't answering," she said and swore softly. She left a message and then nodded toward a row of empty seats in the waiting area. "I'm going to go over there and hook up my laptop. See if anyone has e-mailed."

"Let me do that," Jeff said. "You don't look so good. Why don't you go on to the lounge and see if you can find a place to stretch out."

"I'm fine," Liz insisted.

"I *want* to do this," he snapped. He sighed and looked up at the ceiling for a minute. *Help*. Taking another deep breath, he lowered his voice. "Look, we declared a truce in Omaha. At least I'd like to think so. So let's make this about Mary and not about us. Once we get to Florence and see Mary, and I know everything is all right, I promise to disappear if that's what you want."

"Nobody ever said they wanted you to disappear," Liz said. "It seems to me you pretty much decided to do that all by yourself." *No. You helped create this mess*. But she wasn't going to go there. Not now. She grabbed her bag. "I'm going to check my e-mail."

Jeff looked down at her and forced himself not to jab back. She was pale. With her hair tied back in a ponytail she looked vulnerable. It was all he could do to keep from pulling her into his arms again. "I'll get you something to drink. Does anything sound good?"

"Something sparkling. But not sweet. Sweet makes me gag."

He nodded. "All right, then. Nothing sweet. No gagging." He headed off in search of sparkling water. A few feet down the concourse he turned to watch Liz make her way across the waiting area. *Hello? God? Are you listening? I need a big dose of patience here. Five hours' worth, please. Sometimes I want to choke her. Sometimes I just want to hold her close and tell her I hope the baby has Nordic blue eyes. I doubt either one is a very good idea right now. Help*.

He opened his eyes and saw a cooler. With Pellegrino. Sparkling. Not sweet. It was a funny way for God to answer his prayer, but he'd take it. Buying two bottles, he ambled back to where Liz sat with tears in her eyes.

"What is it?" He handed her the Pellegrino.

She shook her head. "Irene," she said. "Just a very sweet note from Irene."

"I didn't think Irene liked computers."

"She doesn't. And that makes this even sweeter." She took a sip of Pellegrino. "But she hasn't heard anything." She looked worried, almost frightened.

"Let's get you something to eat," Jeff said.

He managed to ignore the *thing* looming between them for several hours. When Liz fell asleep on his shoulder in the lounge, Jeff indulged in the idea that maybe things were going to work out between them after all. But she woke up in a surly mood. And after she tried and failed several more times to get hold of Luca Santo, things slid downhill. No one at the hotel in Florence knew anything. She called three times and got the same answer. "Call Mr. Santo. Mr. Santo knows everything." On the last call the concierge told her that Mrs. Davis had been checked out. Her mood hit bottom.

"You don't have to carry my bag!" she snapped when she and Jeff left the lounge and headed for the gate and their next flight. She grabbed the bag off his shoulder and stormed off. In the wrong direction.

Jeff watched her stomp away with a sigh. He begged God for more patience and headed toward the gate without calling after her. She caught up a few minutes later.

"I'm sorry," she said. "That was . . . not nice. You're right. We should just pretend to be friends. I never would have yelled at Ryan Miller that way."

"Of course not," Jeff muttered. "Wonder Boy would never do something so politically incorrect as to offer to carry his boss's luggage." He pretended to have a eureka moment, raising his eyebrows and hitting his own head with his open palm. "That's it! I'll just pretend you're my boss, and I'm twenty years old."

Liz glowered at him.

"When were you going to tell me, anyway?" He said it so abruptly he surprised even himself. But it was the question that had been branded on his mind for days now.

"When was I going to tell you *what*?" She feigned ignorance.

What did she want from him, anyway? "Forget it," he said. "Just . . . forget it." He gave in to his own emotions and, grabbing her hand, pulled her into a seat beside him just around the corner from their gate. "No. I take that back. Don't forget it." He took a deep breath and then launched into a retelling of how he'd discovered the pregnancy test in her private office powder room.

"Well," Liz said, looking away. "At least now I know for certain why I haven't heard from you in the past few days." She glowered at him. "Margaret told me about the roses. The broken vase." She bit her lip. "I thought you might have seen—" Her blue eyes reddened, and for a moment Jeff thought maybe if he put his arms around her . . . But the thought was barely formed when Liz straightened her shoulders and looked away. "It's just as well that you didn't say anything," she said, and started to stand up.

"What does *that* mean?" Jeff stood up beside her, resting his hand on her forearm to keep her from walking away. "I didn't say anything because I was waiting for *you* to say something."

Liz shrugged. "I didn't know you'd been in the office. Anyway . . . there wasn't anything to say." She glanced toward the waiting area where other passengers were beginning to collect their things. "I still haven't decided what to do."

"What . . . to . . . do?" Jeff frowned.

"I'm not ready to be a mother. Surely that doesn't surprise you." She paused. "This isn't the Dark Ages, Jeff. Women have options."

When the meaning of what she was saying hit home, rage flowed through him, so hot it was all he could do to keep from slapping her. How could she say that? How could she even think it? *"Women have options." God, is she really saying that?!* And then, as suddenly as the anger had arrived, it melted, leaving in its wake a chasm of hurt so deep he knew that nothing between them would ever be the same. He'd held out hope for them until this moment. But if this was how she really felt about his baby . . . He swallowed hard. Cleared his throat. God must have put a mute button in the air. Somehow he managed to say it quietly. "That's not an *option* inside you, Liz. It's our *child.*" He might not have raised his voice, but he felt like he'd just screamed the entire length of a football field. Dropping his hand from her arm, he stepped back. Turning away from her, he stumbled off down the concourse. At the first men's room sign, he turned in.

His hands were shaking as he leaned over a sink to splash cold water in his face.

WHAT KIND OF PERSON inflicted pain like that on someone she had once loved? As she watched Jeff stumble away from her, Liz felt something inside her crumble. All her resolve to be strong and all her insistence about *options* gave in to something else she had never in her life acknowledged. Fear clutched at her gut. Wanting to run after Jeff was her first instinct. But she had to run for the women's room instead. She gave up her lunch and stood trembling in the bathroom stall, feeling cold . . . and very alone. This, she realized, could not be fixed. She had finally done it. Finally screwed everything up so completely that it could not be fixed. Her engagement ring weighed heavy on her finger. She should give it back.

"Last call for Lufthansa flight 8817 departing at 2:45 P.M. for Frankfurt. Last call for . . ."

They had apparently fought right through the announced boarding of their flight. He'd said they should call a truce for Mimi's sake. But then he'd told her he knew. Why? Surely he didn't really believe she was considering her "options." Did he? *Why wouldn't he think that? You never did tell him. He found out. When he brought you* roses *that you never even acknowledged* . . . And in spite of all of it, here he was, trying to help her through this new tragedy. He'd held her and let her cry. He'd told her it would be all right. *Mimi.* Was this going to be a tragedy? *What if—* Grabbing her bag, Liz flung open the door to the stall and ran for the gate. Jeff was right about one thing. This had to be about Mimi. Not about her. In a few hours, she'd know what was going on with Mimi. In a few hours . . . her life could change again. What if . . . what if . . . what if the worst happened?

Settling into her seat on the massive jet, Liz tried not to cry, but she didn't succeed. If the worst happened to Mimi, the first thing Liz would want . . . was Jeff. If something happened to Mimi, she'd be all right if Jeff was there.

*Dear God. What have I done?*

JEFF SCOTT HAD EXPECTED a lot of things when he signed on with Jesus. A ruined life was not one of them. Pastor Dayton had warned him that some people made overzealous promises when they told their conversion stories. "Of course these things do happen. Alcoholics are delivered from their addiction. Marriages are healed. But I'd be doing you a disservice if I told you that if you come to Jesus everything is going to be just great. The truth is, Jeff, there's a cost for following Christ. You may lose some friends over this. I had a buddy who wrote me off. Told me that if I ever did anything besides going to church to give him a call. I never heard from him again. Your brother and sister are believers, and that's great. But your fiancée may not be at all enamored with the idea of your new faith. She might despise you for it—unless you keep it a secret. And you shouldn't do that."

He'd been struggling with how to tell Liz. Maybe now he wouldn't have to. It had been taken out of his hands. He didn't know if he'd ever be able to look at Liz again after what she'd said, much less have a talk about Jesus. *"Women have options."* That sentence would likely be branded in his memory for the rest of his life. Maybe that was a good thing. It would make ending things easier.

As the plane approached sunset and the horizon glowed red, Jeff realized with bittersweet tears that his prayers for direction about his job had finally been answered. He would call Henry Widhelm from Frankfurt and accept the job in California. Henry had generously told him to get on the plane to Italy and be a good husband-to-be. "We've been purposely lightening your case load, hoping you'd be leaving for the West Coast soon. Go. I'll take care of everything." A guy couldn't ask for a better boss than that. Jeff would find a way to tell him that . . . and try to emulate him in the office in San Francisco.

Maybe God had to pry a person's fingers off things before he could work in their life. Maybe that's what he was doing. What was it Pastor Dayton had said? *"All things for his eternal glory and your eternal good."* *Eternal* was a good word. Maybe he'd been too short-term in his thinking. Maybe once he got away from Omaha he could start learning to think more in light of eternity.

He began to think about the good things about leaving. Not having to read about Liz and Davis Enterprises was high on the list. He'd miss Mary and Irene and Cecil. But he wouldn't miss those toffee-colored office walls out at the estate. He fell asleep as the plane soared into indigo skies.

# SEVENTEEN

LIZ HAD AN HOUR to try to reach someone while they waited for their connecting flight from Frankfurt to Florence. Luca's phone was busy—busy—busy. When she finally got through, he had already talked to Jeff. He repeated the news that made Liz sigh with relief. Mimi had a black eye, some stitches, and a fractured bone in her leg, but she was doing fine. In a couple of days, when the swelling went down in her leg, she would get a special boot and be able to walk. She might even be released from the hospital today. His sister was handling everything, and Luca would be at the airport to meet them. He had even managed to reach Jean-Marc and tell him, not only about the accident, but also that she and Jeff were expected in Florence today.

As soon as she hung up, Liz looked around for Jeff. But he was nowhere in sight. When they boarded the plane, she had already put on her seat belt before she saw him coming down the aisle. When their eyes met, his were stone cold. It made the hair stand up on the back of her neck. He settled in a row nearer to the cockpit.

For the entire hour flight to Florence, she was painfully aware of his presence. He tended to play with his hair when he was tired or pondering a problem. All these hours of transatlantic pondering had raised a few "tepees" at the crown of his head. She remembered how the habit used to annoy her. How she used to harp on it while she'd reach up to smooth them down. Now she didn't know why she had made such a big deal of it. It really wasn't all that important. In fact, it was kind of cute.

He didn't wait for her in the airport. She thought he must be hurrying ahead to get their luggage and look for Luca. But inside the airport, which was little more than a long Morton building—funny that the Florence airport made Omaha's look huge—she saw him talking to Luca, and then he left without looking back. Once again, she felt that chill. She hoped he hadn't gotten airsick. She remembered that time down at Worlds of Fun in Kansas City . . .

"Elizabeth," Luca said, his dark eyes sorrowful. "I am so sorry you have made this trip all the way for such a small accident. We will go first to the villa with your luggage and you can rest for a while, or I will take you now to the hospital. Whatever you want." He paused and then said gently, "Jeff tells me a little of your difficulties. He kindly requested about a hotel and will go ahead. I will get his baggage . . . and yours. If you can tell me, please, what they look like."

"I wrapped the handles with orange tape," Liz said. She held up her hand. "About this tall. Both black. Hard cases . . . not soft."

With a nod, Luca was gone . . . but not before pressing a note into her hand. "From Jeff" was all he said.

> *Sometimes it takes me a while to face reality.*
> *You aren't the only one with options. Good-bye.*

LUCA MUST HAVE KNOWN what the note said. He was at once a good friend and, when she thought about it later, almost like a father with a wounded child. He retrieved the luggage and led her into the waiting area, which was little more than a snack bar with a few benches. Liz was grateful one was empty. She dropped onto it and leaned over. When Luca leaned down she whispered for a bath-room.

"Right behind you, *cara mia*."

Somehow she made it. Morning sickness. Again. She exited with a paper towel in hand and forced a weak smile, mumbling something about airline food and anxiety. Luca made her sit down, retreated to the snack bar, and came back with a small piece of bread and a bottle of Pellegrino, which he insisted would help. She forced down the bread and sipped Pellegrino while they walked through the doors to Luca's car—a sleek black Mercedes that had been left unattended and was about to be towed.

Luca fired a volley of Italian and shooed the tow-truck driver away. He said something to the policeman in the process of writing a ticket. The officer peered at Liz. She decided she must look even worse than she felt, because he tucked the ticket in his back pocket without finishing it, climbed into a white car marked *Polizia,* and sped away.

*You aren't the only one with options. Good-bye.*

He couldn't mean that. Could he? Not the options part. The other part. The good-bye. They were here *together.* Mary would expect to see them *together.* What was happening? Another wave of nausea hit.

"Pull over," she gasped, knowing even as she said it, it was impos-sible. Luca had been weaving in and out of traffic, darting here, changing lanes there, narrowly missing a car . . . a bus . . . a pedes-trian—and all the while chattering away about how nice it was that traffic wasn't so bad this time of morning. He used the control on the driver's-side door to roll her window down . . . just in time. At least she didn't ruin the interior of the car. Could anything be worse than leaning out the window of a car. . . ? Yes. Of course. This was noth-ing compared to . . . *Good-bye.*

"Everything will be all right. He loves you very much. I know it." Luca reached into his jacket, pulled out a silk handkerchief, and handed it to her.

Liz tried to wave it away.

"No, no, you take it. I have dozens. Breathe in the fresh air. You will feel better soon. Breathe, *cara mia,* breathe. . . ."

Closing her eyes, Liz leaned back against the leather upholstery and concentrated on slow, even breathing. She was finished throwing up. For now. But Luca was wrong about one thing. She didn't feel any better.

*Good-bye.*


## Mary


I DON'T KNOW what is more surprising to wake up to in the morning—seeing Lizzie or seeing Lizzie cry.

"Goodness, don't cry," I mumble. "It's all right." I look past Liz to Luca. "Tell her it's all right." Back at Liz. "And what are you doing here, anyway? Didn't Luca *tell* you it's nothing? A few stitches . . . a minor fracture—nothing permanently damaged but my pride."

"You know me," Liz says, sniffing into what I realize is one of Luca's silk handkerchiefs. "Always tearing around like a madwoman. Never waiting to get the facts . . . just reacting." She blinks back more tears. "Anyway, Jeff and I got on a flight about an hour after the spa called the house."

"The spa called . . . *you?*" I shake my head. "And Jeff came . . . too? What a sweet guy."

Liz sobs. Luca puts his hand on her shoulder and steps closer. "I was following instructions to the letter. Waiting, just as you said, *cara.* But the new girl at the spa—she was so worried about following the rules, thinking only to keep Tomaso from firing her. She called to Omaha—but I didn't know until it was too late. Already the plane was in the air on the way to Frankfurt."

"I'm so sorry," I say to Liz. "What a waste."

"Don't say that," Liz interrupts me. "I'm *glad* I came."

She sniffles again, which makes me wonder something. I look at

Luca. "Am I really all right? Is there something . . . wrong . . . you aren't . . . telling. . . ?" I can't seem to help it. I am sinking back into slumberland again.

"Sleep, Mimi," Liz says and puts her hand on my forehead.

"Good," I say. "That feels . . . good."

IT IS MUCH LATER in the afternoon before I am awake enough to finally remember things so Liz doesn't have to keep repeating them. I will be released the next morning, and Lucia has arranged everything.

"She's quite . . ." Liz pauses, searching for the right word.

"Domineering," I fill in the blank and chuckle. "But charmingly so. She's completely won me over."

"She's the perfect hostess . . . and so *together*. We'll practically have our own wing of the villa," Liz says.

"Too bad Jeff couldn't come with you," I say. "If you have to be here, you might as well be together. I have an appointment to see the *David* at the Academia for . . . Saturday, I think it is. The two of you could have gone. I suppose Henry Widhelm wouldn't hear of it, though, it being so close to your wedding."

Liz looks down at her engagement ring and says something non-committal. That's when I remember, or think I remember. . . . "I was so woozy earlier . . . did you say you *and* Jeff are here?"

She nods.

"So . . . where is he?"

She bites her lower lip. She won't look at me. Tears spill down her cheeks.

LUCA SANTO WAS A great guy. He didn't ask questions.

He scratched a note on the back of a business card and told Jeff to take a cab to the Hotel Lucia. "They will take care of everything," he said. "Your luggage will come soon." He promised to arrange for Jeff to see Mary alone, took the note for Liz, and left. He hadn't called trying to fix things, either. Jeff really appreciated that. He needed some time to figure things out. And so, after washing his face and trying to slick down the village of tepees at the back of his head, he went downstairs and out the door.

The Hotel Lucia was on the opposite side of the river from most of the main sites. He headed west and across the first bridge he came to and walked past a string of boutiques with names like Ferragamo, Gucci, Prada, Valentino . . . Versace. Liz would love it here. He could imagine how things would have gone "in the old days." He would have pretended to try to drag her away, would have said they had to watch their budget . . . and then he would have delighted in following her into some of those same shops and seeing her model the clothes. He would have especially liked her in the short skirts and high-top boots that seemed to be fashionable. *Pregnancy would have cramped her style. She wouldn't have liked having a bulging belly. She would have looked in these windows and . . .*

Turning away from the designer shops, he walked west. The commercial area reminded him a little of Paris, with tall, old buildings, narrow sidewalks, and wide windows beckoning the herds of tourists inside for shopping. There was some kind of amazing church up ahead, though, completely filling the visual space at the end of the street he was on. He headed for it . . . and soon was standing, staring in openmouthed wonder at three buildings unlike anything he had ever seen—a marvel of pink, green, and white . . . marble, he thought. With—terra cotta?—bas-relief sculptures in a row. The cathedral was obvious, but he wondered about the smaller octagonal building . . . and the tall one, which he decided must be a bell tower, although it seemed odd to have it detached from the cathedral.

Walking around the small octagonal building he spied the entrance—pairs of doors with relief in what he thought must be brass or bronze. Again, unlike anything he'd ever seen. Inside he picked up a brochure written in English. He was inside the *Baptistry of Saint John*. The ceiling was dominated by a mosaic of the risen Christ. That, at least, he could understand. The rest of the ceiling reminded Jeff of his ignorance of the Bible . . . and made him wish he knew more. *Liz would know. She grew up in Sunday School. She would know these stories.*

Leaving the baptistry, he crossed the open plaza and paused to look up at the outlandish . . . overdone . . . fabulously beautiful cathedral. He walked the perimeter more than once, pausing often to stare up at the angles, the columns, the incredible detail in every row of marble. *Davis Enterprises never built so much as a square foot of anything as gorgeous as this.* How long, Jeff wondered, would it be before he stopped relating everything in his life to Liz? With a sigh, he stuffed his hands in his pockets and headed past the statue of Dante, up the broad expanse of stairs, and inside the cathedral.

The free pamphlet at the entrance told Jeff he was in the Duomo. *The cathedral we see today is the result of 170 years of work. The first stone of the facade was laid on September 8, 1296 . . .* The inlaid marble floors showcased designs so intricate, it was hard to believe a man could have created them. Toward the back, a stairway led down to a small shop which shared space with Santa Reparata. Signs said the crypt contained what was left of a fourth-century church *and the remains of Roman houses on which Santa Reparata was erected.*

*I'm looking at . . . Roman houses,* Jeff thought. *Roman* houses. It was too much for his brain to take in. He thought of the architects he knew back in Omaha. What would George Kincaid think of this? Coming up from the crypt, he turned to go. And saw the small statue near the back. It was probably only three feet high, a man with a monk's bald pate and a full beard, a simple robe belted with a piece of rope . . . standing with both his arms and his face raised toward heaven. Jeff stood for a long time, staring at that statue. He even positioned himself so he could look up . . . at whatever the statue was positioned to see. It was nothing. Just space . . . and a clear window. Not even stained glass.

*Look up. Come to me. My burden is light. Lean on me. Cry to Jesus.* Phrases from songs or verses . . . rumbled around in his head as he stood there. Some of it probably wasn't even really from the Bible. But between those phrases and the little statue at the back of the great cathedral, Jeff got the message. Sliding into a pew, he looked up. *It hurts.*

There were four "candle trees" at the back of the church, masterpieces in themselves, made of dozens of thin rods of iron coming up out of an iron "wicker" base, the tip of each rod forming a platform on which sat a small candle. He wasn't Catholic, but he thought it was pretty obvious that lighting one represented a prayer . . . a burden . . . something someone needed to show God. On impulse, he bought a candle. He was thinking of Liz. But then, as the flame flickered and he placed it on its platform, the idea of the life that might never be lived overwhelmed him. He stood at the tree of lights, blinking back tears.

## Mary

I AM SITTING up in bed the next morning when a male hand thrusts a bouquet of flowers around the corner and waves them in the air to get my attention. I laugh. "Good morning to you, too, Mr. Santo." But the face isn't Luca's. And it isn't happy, in spite of the plastered-on smile. "What a delightful surprise." I accept the bouquet and inhale with appreciation. "Where on earth did you find lily of the valley?"

"I didn't," Jeff says. "Luca seems to know just about everyone in this entire city. He asked me if I knew your favorite flower . . . and then he took it from there. But"—Jeff smiles again—"he was nice enough to let me be the delivery boy." He sits down in the chair at the foot of my bed and leans forward. "So, they are coming to collect you soon, I hear. And your leg is better, right?"

"The leg will be fine. The cut will heal. The black eye will fade. So . . ." I lay the bouquet across my lap and fold my arms. "Stop the small talk, and tell me what's happened."

He takes in a deep breath. He doesn't even pretend he doesn't know what I'm talking about. "Some things . . . just aren't meant to be."

"True. But I'm not willing to admit your marrying my daughter is one of them. I know her pretty well. And I know what kind of man she needs. And you're it."

He clears his throat. "Thanks for the vote of confidence. I was inclined to agree with you until . . . well, until recently." He gets up, walks to the window, and stares down into the street. "I'm sorry, Mary. I really have learned to . . . love you." He turns to me with the saddest smile I've ever seen, then comes to my bedside and kisses me on the cheek. "You've been great. I'll never forget you. It was going to be great to have a 'mom' again." His voice breaks. His shoulders slump—and there I am, hugging him and wishing I could be Irene just long enough to "yank a knot" in Liz's tail. When I tell him that, he laughs and stands up. "I'm quite certain Liz is past that kind of thing. She has . . . plans . . . I can't be part of."

"She can restructure Davis Enterprises to accommodate a move to California. And she knows it. She's just being stubborn. Give her time, Jeff. She'll adjust."

He shakes his head. "That's just more living in the shadow of the great Sam Davis—no disrespect intended." He adds the last for my sake and tries to lighten the conversation. "And I can't handle an office with toffee-colored walls, no matter what Mona says."

"Nothing you've said is a reason to break off an engagement, Jeff. Let me talk to her. I know she's stubborn, but I've seen God working . . . pulling things away to make her look to him. Sometimes, we have to lose everything to find what really matters."

"You're preaching to the choir, Mary," he says. "I agree with you. Or did. And I thought that maybe if I prayed hard enough and waited long enough, God would reward me. But even I have limits."

"Love doesn't have limits," I say—a little more harshly than I had intended.

"Then maybe I never loved her. Because I'm moving to California when I get back home. Alone."

"Get out of here," I say.

His eyebrows go up.

"You heard me," I am already putting the flowers aside. "Go out in the hall while I get dressed. I'll call you when you can come back in."

He's staring at me, but he isn't moving.

"Jeff, I've spent too many years sitting around waiting for Liz to make the first move and come to me, and I'm not waiting any longer. So are you going to help me get out of this hospital or not? Either way, I'm leaving."

"You can't—"

"Yes. I can."

And I do.

## ℐ EIGHTEEN ℒ

IT WOULD NOT HAVE surprised Celine Dumas to learn that her father had children all over Europe. The young Jean-Marc David had broken his share of hearts as a young motorcycle racer. It was a fact he acknowledged with a shrug of the shoulders. And so, when her father returned from the mysterious "Christmas in Paris," and told her about Mary Davis and the "other daughter," Celine took the news in stride. It was, as she told her father, no surprise.

What did surprise Celine was that, after decades of barely knowing one daughter, in this case herself, Jean-Marc now seemed bent on having something of a traditional father-daughter relationship with not only her, but also "the other." He credited a new belief in God for the change, and while it was Celine's experience that nothing her father promised or claimed remained that way for long, this change was at least pleasant.

The less self-centered and tamer version of Jean-Marc David was a welcome addition to Celine's life for more than just herself. Her twin sons, Xavier and Olivier, had always adored their grandfather—whether he deserved it or not. And sometimes he did not. But since claiming religious conversion, Jean-Marc was returning his grandsons' affection with more than empty promises. The boys were blossoming, and Celine was cautiously grateful to whatever had caused their grandfather to notice. Perhaps it was God, as her papa insisted. She was more inclined to credit Mary Davis. And for that, she would thank her. Should they ever meet.

As for the "other daughter," Jean-Marc had been e-mailing her since January. He'd made it no secret, and had even shared some of their correspondence with her. Elizabeth Davis seemed nice enough, Celine told her father. Yes, she said, perhaps they would meet. Some-day. What she did not say was that she sensed a certain . . . cau-tion . . . in this other daughter's tone that reminded Celine of herself. Elizabeth Davis was keeping herself at a distance, much as she herself had learned to do over the years. They at least had that in common.

Life for Celine Dumas had not always been simple. The product of her father's short-lived passion for a café singer, she was early aban-doned by her mother and claimed by Jean-Marc, who treated her more like a beautiful and very spoiled poodle than a child. When she grew old enough to compare her life to that of other children, she began to make demands. For life on land, school, a predictable schedule . . . and a father who, if he really did not intend to settle down, at least didn't flirt with *all* her schoolmates' mothers. Some demands, he met. She went to school on land. Boarding school, so Papa wouldn't have to stay put. His choices hurt, and finally, there was a split.

From the time she was seventeen until she was expecting twins, Celine had little to do with her father. And then, he resurfaced just in time to rescue her from a horrible marriage to an older man and to hire the right lawyer. Ironically, it was her father Celine had to thank for her current circumstances, which included a lovely, albeit small, villa in the ancient city of Fiesole near Florence, and a monthly stipend that enabled her to answer her calling in life—to mother her boys.

And so it was that, through all her father's varying appearances and disappearances in and out of her life, the adult Celine Dumas did her best to accept who he was, to love him when he visited, and to refuse to resent him when he disappeared, sometimes for months.

Loving Jean-Marc David was an exercise in unselfishness, and Celine had decided that a father on *his* terms was better than no father at all. She had adjusted.

And now it was almost spring, and as Jean-Marc continued to be the "perfect" grandfather, Celine maintained a cautious optimism, feeling something like the mouse who tests the cheese only to be trapped when he assumes that *this* time, it really is without cost. If Jean-Marc failed this time, it would involve more than just her. This time, he would hurt Xavier and Olivier. That, she would not abide.

Only two weeks ago, Jean-Marc had told her he was going to Paris, in hopes of convincing Mary Davis to sail with him when he made his annual spring trip from Arcachon to Livorno. A few days later, when he called from Paris, his voice was sad. No, Mary wouldn't be with him. Elizabeth needed her. He and Paul would cast off alone. Celine noted the date on her calendar and went about her life. The boys practiced piano on the Bosendorfer in the sun-filled room that overlooked the site of ancient Roman baths, and Celine took her morning walk to collect the ingredients for the day's meals, met friends for coffee, went to mass on Sunday, and expected her father in about sixteen to twenty days . . . with reservations.

And so it was, that when Jean-Marc called her a week before his expected arrival date and said he was at Santa Maria Novella Station in Florence and would be staying there for a few days . . . Celine was left speechless. Jean-Marc not sailing exactly according to schedule was normal. Jean-Marc abandoning the ship and staying on land was *not*. Hearing sadness in his voice, she hung on to the telephone receiver and waited for some kind of awful news.

"Hello? Hello? Did you hear me?"

"I heard you," Celine said. "But . . . what's happened? To the *Sea Cloud*?"

"Nothing. I hired a crew to bring her the rest of the way. Luca Santo called. Mary came to Florence early, and she has fallen and broken her leg. So . . . is it possible for you to make up the cottage or shall I stay here in Florence?"

"Don't be absurd, Papa," Celine protested. "Of course you will stay here with us. It's nothing. It won't take me two minutes." His next words made her hesitate.

"Luca has told me that the injury is not severe. If that is true . . . would you . . . I'd like everyone to meet. Sunday afternoon. At Gilli."

"Everyone?"

"Yes. Everyone. Elizabeth and her fiancé have come to Florence, as well. You could meet them all."

Celine closed her eyes. She had agreed to meet Mary and Elizabeth Davis mostly because she didn't believe it would ever really happen. And now here they were . . . Mary . . . Elizabeth . . . even the fiancé.

"Please, *mon petit choux*," he pled. "I know it isn't the most ideal circumstance, but . . . she's someone I've loved. We—"

"It's all right, Papa," she interrupted. She drew the line at hearing more of Papa's colorful history. She might be reluctant . . . but she was also curious. Something about this woman was obviously different from all the others. Meeting Mary Davis might be awkward, but it would also be interesting to see the woman who had affected such a change in Papa. And as for meeting Elizabeth . . . When she really thought about it, Celine reasoned that the both of them likely shared similar emotions about the situation. "The boys can play at Gérard's for the afternoon. What time do you want to meet?"

He mentioned a few details, and they soon finished their conversation. She hung up the phone, and smiled in spite of herself. *I know it isn't the most ideal circumstance.* Exactly what would *be* an ideal circumstance for meeting your father's former lover and the "other daughter"?

She walked down the hall to her room and looked in the mirror. Other modern women wanted so many things. They ran companies, pursued careers, broke glass ceilings . . . and sometimes found time for husbands and children. Perhaps she was a woman out of time. All she had ever wanted was a quiet family life. A husband to support her and children—a dozen, had God granted them. Father Ambrosio said that God always knew what it was that he was doing. Celine knew that truth in her head. But what, she sometimes wondered, could he have been thinking planting a girl who wanted what others thought boring . . . in the life of a man like Jean-Marc David?

"I'VE GOTTEN YOU this far," Jeff said, opening the taxi-cab door and helping Mary out. "The rest is up to you." They stood looking up the stone stairway toward the villa gate.

While the cab driver retrieved Mary's overnight bag from his trunk and carried it up the stairs and rang the bell, Jeff helped Mary hobble up the front steps. "Maybe we should have taken the offer of the crutches at the hospital," he said.

Mary shook her head. "From what the doctor said, I won't need them as soon as I get used to this boot. And I'm not exactly going to be running around Florence in the next few days, anyway." At the top of the steps, she turned to Jeff. "Kiss me good-bye," she said. "And remember, you promised to stay in Florence until you hear from me."

"I'll keep my promise, Mary," Jeff said. He bent to kiss her on the cheek before heading back down the stairs. "It won't do any good, but I'll hang around."

Whoever answered the doorbell must have raised a general alarm, for suddenly there was a flurry at the door. Glancing back, Jeff saw Luca and his sister . . . and then Liz, looking pale and strained, even from this distance. Turning around, he headed down the road on foot.

## Mary

ADRENALINE IS A good thing. I say that because I am running on it as I stifle a grunt and make a show of stepping inside the doorway, all the while joking about the fashion statement I'm making with my new boot. But Luca isn't fooled.

"Get the cane," Luca calls up to Liz, and she brings me a beautiful black walking stick with a carved ivory handle. Soon I am ensconced on the loggia and not oblivious to the fact that Liz is ill at ease. Or ill. I can't decide which. I am determined to find out, but she slips away, and then all my plans dissolve with the unexpected arrival of Jean-Marc.

He comes to my side, kisses the back of my hand and, leaning down, whispers, "You see, *ma chère* . . . that an old dog can learn new tricks." At my look of confusion he smiles. "I was on board the *Sea Cloud*. We had put into port for a small repair and Luca called me about this." He points down at my leg. "And I told my sea mistress good-bye."

I want to scold Luca for bothering Jean-Marc about nothing, but he's left the room—as has everyone else. Lucia returns with Pellegrino, cheese, and bread. "I could kiss you," I say. "No more hospital food!"

Lucia blushes, although I realize it is more because Jean-Marc is mercilessly complimenting her beauty than from my comment. As Lucia sweeps out of the room, Jean-Marc asks me about joining him Sunday afternoon for tiramisu . . . and to meet Celine.

I tell him yes . . . and ask if the invitation includes Liz.

"But of course. Where is she?"

"She just slipped out. Hopefully, to go after her fiancé." And I explain what has happened, according to Jeff. It feels good to share the parental burden. Until Jean-Marc tells me what he thinks we should do—which is, essentially, nothing.

"They are adults," he says gently.

"They aren't *acting* like adults. They're squabbling like children."

"I don't know," he says, looking out over the valley as he talks. "Children squabble over what game to play. Who gets the largest piece of candy. The problems for Elizabeth and Jeff are much more profound."

"But the solution is the same. Stop being selfish. Do what's best for someone else."

"Lose your life to find it?"

"Exactly." A little thrill runs through me to hear this beautiful man speaking of the words of scripture . . . as if he believes them.

"But it takes some people a while to learn that. For me, it took half a century."

He reaches over and takes my hand.

SHE COULDN'T CATCH UP. He wouldn't let her. But still, Liz tried, hurrying down the winding road like her life depended on it. And maybe, she thought . . . maybe it did. She couldn't live the rest of her life with the memory of that hurt look in Jeff's eyes . . . and that note in her mind. She couldn't. There had to be something . . . something. . . . And so she kept going down the road, hoping to catch up to him. Finally, she came to the famous overlook. She'd seen this view on postcards and prints. Florence lay below her, with russet church domes and tall towers . . . and in the distance, rolling green hills in a clear blue sky. But she didn't have time to notice any more than that . . . because just around the corner . . . there was Jeff, heading up a long flight of stairs leading up the hill toward . . . What else could it be in Florence but another church—this one of gray and white marble.

Up and up she climbed . . . through iron gates . . . up and up . . . until she couldn't breathe. Did *all* pregnant women completely lose their ability to *breathe* this early? Or was it a sign of a panic attack?

Breathe . . . two . . . three . . . breathe . . . two . . . three.

"Jeff!" she called. "Jeff! WAIT!"

He either didn't hear her or he didn't want to. He just kept climbing.

*"You aren't the only one with options. Good-bye."*

At the top of the last set of stone stairs, she paused. Had he gone into the church . . . or into the cemetery? From down below, you'd never guess there were all . . . these . . . graves. Scanning the burial grounds to the right and left and catching no sight of Jeff, Liz hurried inside the church. She had to pause just inside the door to give her eyes time to adjust to the gloom. High above her Christ, depicted in a gilded mosaic with his right hand raised, looked down on worshippers. . . . But the church was nearly empty, and the dull light was oppressive. Turning to go outside, she was startled when someone, somewhere, turned on electricity, and the artwork above and in some of the naves was at once illuminated.

"Jeff?" she called in a stage whisper, and headed toward the altar. If her heart were pounding any harder, the sound would be echoing off the walls. She crept toward the front of the church . . . around the back of the altar where an elderly couple stood. They nodded and smiled and moved away. The lights went off. That's when she saw the small box along the wall. For one euro the lights came on for a few minutes.

Going back outside, she stood for a moment, watching as people descended the hill. There was no sign of Jeff. She sat on the stairs. Her stomach rumbled. She was tired of being a victim of her bodily functions. One minute she was starving, the next throwing up. How long did this kind of thing last, anyway?

Getting up, she wandered down the stairs. There was no hurry now, and the burial grounds around this church were filled with sculpture. She descended into one and wandered from grave to grave. It was so different from anything she'd seen before, no grass, only stone, and graves only inches apart, but many of them boasting life-sized busts or bas-reliefs or photographs. And flowers everywhere— tucked into crevices, plopped into the intricate brass holders.

Off to the east, the hillside was covered with mausoleum spaces. Drawn to a bronze on one of those spaces, she walked over. Although she could not read Italian, she knew this was the grave of a beloved brother killed in World War I. The scene was dramatized—soldiers rushing forward in formation while one fell back, mortally wounded.

To the left, life-sized angels watched the scene and prayed. Liz's eyes welled up with tears with sudden, overwhelming sadness at the lost hopes and dreams. Someone was still grieving this boy's death. Fresh flowers had been left in a bouquet at the base of the bronze bas-relief.

Heading for the stairs that would take her down the hill, Liz left the burial ground. But across the way she saw more sculptures. She crossed in front of the church and descended into the area, this one apparently for wealthier families. There was carefully trimmed grass framing each grave. Niches in the far wall proved to be room-sized family mausoleums, some with little altars and chairs where, Liz supposed, mourners still came to pray. Some had left behind photographs. Notes. Letters. The one with a 5x7 portrait of a young woman and an elderly one laughing brought more tears. Two potted hydrangea bushes in full bloom had been placed here recently, and the small altar was adorned with crocheted lace and five imposing candlesticks, each with a white candle. But it wasn't the hydrangea or the candles that moved her. It was the single red rose lying before the photograph—that was what got her. That and the hormonal soup.

In every direction, angels of every size and style imaginable in bronze and marble, floated above doorways, looked down mournfully at names, held scrolls, raised holy hands . . . smiled serenely in the face of death. Turning to go, Liz had to walk right by one of the larger sculptures in the section. She'd hurried by it before, but now she stopped, and the more she looked at it, the more impressed she was by the life-sized depiction of a woman dressed in a softly draped gown, simply belted at the waist, her long hair parted in the middle, a thick braid encircling her head like a halo. Her arms were outstretched, and in each hand she held the corner of a fabric drape that went behind her entire body like a shroud. She held it high, as if preparing to enfold the four children clinging to her. The oldest couldn't have been more than four. They stood looking up at her, linked to one another by a hand on a waist or an arm. One hid his face in the folds of her skirt. The other three were looking up at her . . . beseeching. And the baby . . . the bare-bottomed toddler, held both hands up, imploring. Liz could almost hear him calling for his mother. She stood transfixed, staring into the woman's classically beautiful, completely serene face. This was a mother who would whisper as she enfolded them in cloth, and brought them close, "It's all right, children . . . Mama's here. . . . It'll be all right." This was a mother who sang lullabies in the night. Who saw to it that everything *was* all right. You could see it. Sense it. And at the idea that such a woman had perhaps left such babies behind . . . Liz began to weep.

The sun was out. The woman's face shone bright white against the clear blue sky. Swiping her face, Liz gazed past the life-sized sculpture toward Florence in the distance—more churches . . . more faith . . . more belief in the future. Alpha and Omega . . . beginning and end. Angels keeping guard, collecting souls, watching . . . *It's all right . . . everything will be all right.*

Off to her left was another life-sized sculpture of a woman. This one was in bronze, and the woman had fallen to her knees. She was lifting her emaciated arms to heaven, her palms pressed together, her eyes closed, her mouth open. *Supplication* was all Liz could think of. *Help,* she seemed to be saying. *Help.*

Looking back over her shoulder and up the hill, Liz pondered the mosaic of Christ high on the facade of the marble church. Going in, she had barely noticed it. Now, it called to mind fragments of a phrase from somewhere in the past. *I will lift my eyes up to the hills . . . from whence cometh my help. My help comes from the Lord . . . who made heaven and earth.* As she looked up, she laid her open hand on her abdomen . . . and chose.

*It's all right . . . Mama's here. . . . Everything will be all right.*

# $\mathcal{V}$ NINETEEN $\mathcal{V}$

*Mary*

ONE THING IS CERTAIN about parenting—nothing is ever certain. Just when you think you know what to expect, a child tosses something new at you. Parents expect this to happen less frequently as their children mature. Sometimes things only get more surprising.

Jean-Marc and I are still on the loggia sipping Pellegrino when Liz returns. To my surprise, she goes to him first, and kisses him on the cheek. He flushes with pleasure and looks at me, wondering if this is my suggestion. I shrug and shake my head.

I have never seen Liz so nervous. She is pale and brushes her forehead with a trembling hand. "Are you comfortable?" she asks me.

"I'm fine," I say. "Worried about you. I'm glad you've decided to talk about it." Of course the "it" I am expecting her to talk about is her engagement.

"I know you're worried," she says, and immediately looks away. She clears her throat. "I have . . . some things . . . we need to talk about."

Jean-Marc begins to rise, but she asks him to stay. "Some of this . . . is about you." He sits back down next to me.

"I'm going to run this sort of like a meeting, if that's all right with you," she says to me. "I know that's weird, but I'm not trying to be bossy. Really. I just . . . I need to say a lot of things without any interruptions or I may not make it through."

"All right, Lizzie," I try to reassure her. "We're on your side."

Jean-Marc nods.

Liz sits down facing us, bends forward, laces her fingers around her knees, and begins to talk. "Last month after that dealer bought Daddy's vinyl, something happened I didn't tell you about."

Jean-Marc looks at me for a translation of this use of the word *vinyl.*

"Vinyl recordings," I explain. "Records. Music."

He nods.

"About a week after he'd come to pick everything up, he sent me a padded envelope with three computer disks in it. He said he found them in one of the covers marked *Breakfast at Tiffany's.* He didn't mind not having that record, the issue was the disks should come back to the owner. I think he was worried I would accuse him of stealing personal data or something. There were three disks, all three labeled by Daddy. J–M–D, G–T–K, and J–J–S."

She pauses and looks from Jean-Marc to me. "Did you know Daddy kept track of Jean-Marc for years after you and Daddy were married?"

I frown. "Why would he do such a thing?"

"I don't know," Liz says. Her voice is miserable.

I shouldn't be defensive, but I can't help myself. "I *never* gave your father any reason to doubt my loyalty to him. Until this past Christmas I had no idea where Jean-Marc even was or what he was doing. I kept my promise to your father."

Liz reaches over and takes my hand and gives it a squeeze. "I know you did, Mimi. I believe you. And even if I didn't, the proof is on that disk. Daddy kept a very thorough account."

I suddenly understand the times over the years when I wondered about little things—thinking I'd turned my computer off and finding it in sleep mode instead. Finding things left out that I thought I'd put away. And those times when I came into our bedroom and found

Sam using my computer. He always had an explanation. But now . . . now I know the truth. Poor Sam. I can't muster the energy to be angry. All I can feel is sorrow for a man who had every reason to be happy and chose, instead, to be miserable.

"The second disk was about Jeff," Liz says, looking down at her hands while she talks. "Daddy had him followed, too. Investigated. Background checks on Danny and Sarah. . . ."

"No!" I don't want to believe it . . . but I do.

"Yes," Liz says. She looks up at me with a sad smile. "Eventually, Jeff passed inspection. From what I could tell, it was about the time Daddy started calling him Jeff instead of Jeffrey. I remember that because he let us take the Austin Healey out for a date. That was a *big* deal."

"Oh, honey, I'm so sorry."

She tilts her head a little and asks, "Can you guess G–T–K?"

I remember her phone call. *"What's George Kincaid's middle name?"* "The only thing I know about George Kincaid and your father," I say, "is they were good friends. George was one of the few people your father let into his private world. One of the few men he trusted. Goodness, he even asked George to stay at the house once when you were little. You were sick, and Sam had to fly out to the coast to avert some business crisis. George was the one he called to stand in for him. He stayed in the guest house for nearly a week. The doctor wanted to put you in the hospital, but I wouldn't hear of it, so George and Betty came and stayed so you could have round-the-clock care right here at home. Betty had been a trained nurse before marrying George. I don't know what you think you've discovered, but George Kincaid was your father's best friend."

While I've been talking, Liz has gotten up and begun to pace back and forth on the loggia. When I finally stop, she blurts out, "Daddy ruined him."

"What?"

She sweeps her hair back out of her face. "I don't know why, but I've checked the details on what happened to George. It was Daddy."

"Don't be absurd." I'm a little angered by her dramatics. "Your father loved George Kincaid. George was ruined by alcohol. I can recount lots of times when Daddy refused to pour George a drink—scenes at the house, things you just don't need to know."

"Of course he didn't *make* George an alcoholic," Liz says. "I'm talking about—"

"I don't want to hear this." I hold up my hand to signal her to hush. "Whatever you think you've found—it isn't true. Sam Davis was many things—and not all of them good—but he was an honorable man who kept his word."

"You're half right, Mimi," Liz says. "He certainly did keep his word—to himself. He committed to making George pay—and he did it."

"You aren't making any sense. What on earth could there have been between George Kincaid and your father?"

"You." Her blue eyes are calm. And cold.

"What?"

"You heard me," Lizzie said, glancing from me to Jean-Marc and back again.

I shake my head. "I repeat—you aren't making any sense."

Jean-Marc stands up abruptly. "This is nonsense, Elizabeth. And you must know it."

Jean-Marc may get it, but I don't. "What *are* you talking about?!"

"Daddy thought you and George—" Liz doesn't finish the sentence. "And he made George pay. And eventually it ended up destroying George's architectural firm. It was all on the disk."

I shake my head. "Whatever you think you have found cannot be true. Sam just wouldn't have done that. Not to George." My head is spinning. What on earth could any of this have to do with the problem at hand? Her fiancé has broken off their engagement . . . and Liz is talking about Sam?

Jean-Marc steps behind me. His hand on my shoulder helps me calm down. Faithful friend. Thank you, Lord.

"Ryan Miller checked some things out for me, and . . . and . . ."

She turns away. Her face is in profile as she says, "My father changed something on the engineer's copies of the blueprints for the Kincaid Towers. Something the inspectors probably wouldn't notice. And they didn't. And the buildings came down during construction." She swallows hard. "And the great Samuel Frederick Davis made it happen."

"Elizabeth. You are talking about breaking the law. If anyone had been hurt—"

"But no one was. Except George Kincaid." She inhales. "All those lies." Turning back to face me, she mimics her father's voice. "'Elizabeth, we may go down . . . but if we do, it won't be because we've compromised our integrity.'" She looks from Jean-Marc to me and back again. "I have ruined my future because of loyalty to a legacy that's a complete . . . lie."

It is quiet on the loggia for a long, long few minutes. Jean-Marc sits back down. Liz finally returns to the chair opposite him and me. He is the one who speaks first. What he says amazes me. "From all that I know, Elizabeth, Samuel Davis was a good father to you." He looks at me. "And, in his way, he was a good husband. He was faithful to you both. And loyal. There is no point in ever speaking of these things again."

"Except . . . poor George," I say miserably. I could cry for George. How will we ever face him?

"Yes. That's what I thought, too . . . But . . ." And Liz recounts her visit to George Kincaid.

"Praise God," is all I can say when she is finished. "And may he bless George tenfold for his amazing example of forgiveness."

"I think God's looking out for George pretty well," Liz says. "Through you, Mimi—when you asked him to work on the hospital project. Although I'm surprised he wanted to work with anything with the name Davis on it, I'm glad he did. And glad you insisted on it. There is some satisfaction in thinking that, while my father masterminded George Kincaid's career debacle, I've . . . we've"—she motions between herself and me—"been part of his new beginnings.

It isn't enough. But it's something."

My beautiful, strong daughter puts her palms to her knees, gets up again, and walks back toward the edge of the loggia. She puts her hand atop the waist-high stone wall and, looking toward the hilltops in the distance, abruptly shifts gears. Her voice is calmer when she says, "When I went running after Jeff earlier, I didn't find him."

"What were you going to say to him?"

"Probably the wrong thing," Liz says with a little shrug. "That's all I've done lately—say the wrong thing. Everything has been such a . . . mess. I've been hanging on to everything Daddy started, from the company to the house to his old office—building a monument to a man who never even existed." She gestures helplessly. Her voice is bitter as she says aloud, "The Samuel Frederick Davis Memorial Oncology Wing." She grunts and makes a face like a child finding something suspect in her food.

"Come back and sit down, *ma chère*," Jean-Marc says gently. To my surprise, Liz obeys. He reaches over and takes both her hands in his, holding them while he says gently, "No person on this earth is so simple as to deserve unmitigated hatred . . . or blind worship. The man who was your father, Elizabeth, deserves to be remembered. As does the man who provided so well for your mother for so many years. And the rest—" He looks at me and smiles. "The rest you send down the river, eh?" He drops one of Lizzie's hands and reaches over to squeeze one of mine before sitting back and waiting while Liz blows her nose. "You would, I think, enjoy talking to my daughter Celine. She has much experience with accepting a father who has many flaws."

I find my voice. "Is this . . . is this information about your father the reason you've pushed Jeff away?"

"Partly," Liz says. "Mostly. Maybe." Her lower lip trembles. "Maybe not. Believe it or not, the great Elizabeth Davis, hard-driving business woman . . . is . . . afraid. I don't know how to start a life somewhere else. Omaha is all I've ever known."

"You told me you think the Bay Area is beautiful. And there's family nearby. Something tells me that in time, you and Danny and Sarah and those kids could get along just fine. The only question you really need an answer to right now is, Do you love Jeffrey James Scott?"

She closes her eyes, and the tears spill down her cheeks. "Oh . . . *yes.* But I've hurt him, Mimi. So . . . badly."

"Hurts heal," I say. "And, just as I told Jeff at the hospital this morning, love forgives."

Liz shakes her head. "Not always. Not everything. Some things probably go beyond a human's capacity to forgive."

"Then we tap into *God's* capacity to forgive," I say gently. "Look around you, Lizzie-bear. Have you really *seen* Florence? The promise of forgiveness is everywhere you look." She isn't getting it. So as gently as possible, hoping I'm not preaching too much, I say, "The *cross,* honey. The *cross.* There's nothing you could have done that God cannot forgive . . . and nothing he can't enable Jeff to forgive. Look what God did in and through George Kincaid. The man made you *tea,* Lizzie. He designed Sam's memorial wing. There's nothing you could have done that's all that terrible."

"I've made him think I won't have his baby." Her hand goes to her abdomen and she bursts into tears. "I didn't mean it. I didn't mean it. I never really meant I'd do it. . . ."

I am momentarily frozen in my chair while my brain absorbs the word *baby* and translates that to conscious thought. And then there is the rest of what Liz has just said. *"I never really meant I'd do it."* Do what? *"I won't have his baby. . . ."* She's pregnant? She's been contemplating abortion? Without talking to anyone?

In the instant of time it takes me to process all these thoughts, Liz covers her face with her hands and slumps down onto her knees. I reach for her, but my leg is propped up on a cushion, and when I try to move, pain shoots into my knee, and instead of my hand going to my daughter, it goes to my knee. Once again, I am thankful for Jean-Marc, who does not hesitate to pull Liz into his arms. And if I ever was tempted to think my adult daughter doesn't need her parents . . .

I see before me the proof that I was wrong.

Liz hears my gasp of pain through her tears. She peers at me over Jean-Marc's shoulder and for a split second she forgets herself and her troubles in her concern for me. "Mimi—"

"I'm all right."

"*Chérie?*" Jean-Marc turns around.

"I'm all right."

With all the exclaiming and caring and sobbing things get a little maudlin. Jean-Marc and Liz help me reposition my leg, and while Jean-Marc goes off to fetch more water so I can take the next dose of pain medication, Liz and I have a moment alone.

"I'm sorry," she murmurs, looking down at her hands.

"So am I."

She looks up at me with a little frown. "What do *you* have to be sorry for? *I'm* the one who always told you that you were being old-fashioned when you warned me about overnights. Who told you not to worry, that Jeff and I knew what we were doing? That it's the 'modern way?'"

"Sshh," I say and shake my head. "I was apologizing because I was *here* in Europe when perhaps I should have been *there* in Nebraska."

"I'm twenty-nine years old, Mimi," Liz mutters. "I should be able to cope with life. And even if you had been living in Omaha, I wouldn't have listened to you. When did I ever listen to you?"

"In 1987. When I told you orange wasn't one of your best colors." Where on earth the ability to laugh came from, I don't know. Well, yes, I guess I do. God's grace. Liz gives one little, heartbreaking laugh, and then tears fill her eyes again. "Come on now, Lizzie-bear," I plead. "We're past all that, you and me."

She makes a face and shakes her head. "For all my brilliance and looking down my nose at who I thought you were . . . I've done nothing but repeat your mistakes."

"Don't call yourself a mistake," I insist. "The circumstances of your birth might have been less than ideal, but you were a blessing.

And yours and Jeff's baby will be a blessing, too. Let's decide that right this minute." I shake my head. "To think that you were thinking—"

"I wasn't. *Thinking,* that is." Liz sniffles. She dabs at her eyes with a tissue. "Here I go again."

Lucia sweeps in, Jean-Marc in her wake. She bears a tray of fruit and cheese, two more bottles of Pellegrino, and an expression of grave concern. "You must tell me what to be done," she says to Liz and me. "Anything you need. I am hurting with you."

"You've done it," I assure her, gesturing around the loggia. "You've shared your home with us and made us feel welcome. I can't thank you enough."

"I know it!" Lucia says, her face lighting up with a smile. "I am calling once again the spa—"

"No," I say—perhaps a bit too quickly.

Lucia gestures at me. "I know, I know. You not want to go back there. Is not necessary. Tomaso comes to you. Tomorrow." She beams at Liz. "And to you. First thing. Here on the loggia. Is beautiful place for relaxation massage. I am telling Luca, and he will go down to see the details." She flutters out of the room.

Having decided she will have Jeff's baby and likely agree to follow him to the ends of the earth—in this case, California—Liz continues to obsess. "What if he won't forgive me? What if he's already left?" It takes all of my persuasive skills—"He promised me he wouldn't go anywhere until he hears from me"—and reassurances from Jean-Marc—"He won't go until I take him aboard the *Sea Cloud*"—to convince her that Jeff is planted solidly in Florence for the next few days and that she needs to regroup instead of taking charge.

Liz has wept for another quarter of an hour in Jean-Marc's arms when she slides back into a chair on the loggia with all the energy of a wet noodle. When I explain to her that it is perfectly understandable for her system—which has been "overfiring" for several weeks—to completely shut down, she gives herself permission to ignore the clock and heads for bed in the middle of the afternoon.

Jean-Marc stays for a while, but he is restless. We make small talk—regretting that I won't be able to learn to ride a motorcycle as planned, estimating when the hired crew will make landfall with the *Sea Cloud,* wondering how Lucia will cope with moving Annie's wedding to the garden. He offers to go with me to see Jeff but immediately agrees when I tell him I think it would be better if I did that alone. When Luca arrives and offers to drive me to Jeff's hotel tomorrow morning, Jean-Marc heads for Celine's. He will pray, he promises. He will call.

I start awake, realizing as I look down at my watch that I've been asleep in my chair on the loggia for nearly an hour. Luca is lounging in a chair across from me, with reading glasses perched on his nose, an oversized book spread out on his lap. When he senses movement in my chair, he looks over with a smile. "Liz-bet sleeps again," he says. "I have just checked in for you and found her awake. She was restless, so we talked a little. She told me about . . . things." He smiles. "I convinced her that God and her mother have things under the control, and that what she must do is to rest so that she is ready for the blessings tomorrow will bring."

He may not have had children, but it would seem that Luca Santo has the heart of a father.

He frowns a little. "Are you certain you have energy for this meeting with Jeffrey yet today, *cara mia?*"

"I'm certain," I say. Indeed, the nap in the chair, the fresh air on the loggia—and perhaps, Luca—combine to give me renewed energy for the task at hand.

"I was going to say we could have some dinner down in the city, but I think . . ."

Dinner with Luca—the time alone, not the food—is especially appealing to me. I don't dare try to analyze that. It just is.

"Are you sure there isn't anything wrong?" I ask. Luca has been unusually quiet as he drives us down to the city.

"Of course not," he says. "What makes you ask?"

"You haven't swerved or honked once. And you're yielding to pedestrians." There. That smile. I love that smile.

"The experts have not made their decision about the fresco in the chapel . . . and it weighs on Lucia. She wants everything perfect before the wedding."

"She's been so gracious about having house guests," I offer. "But I loved the hotel, too, and you can see I'm doing fine. Perhaps Liz and I could move back in the morning . . . if there's a room."

He smiles. Again.

I'm feeling much better now.

"There is one room most certainly available, and you may have it at your disposal."

"I don't need the penthouse," I joke. "I only *pretend* to be the Queen Mother."

Another smile. Even a chuckle.

"That's better," I tell him. "You had me worried."

"Don't worry about anything," he says, and reaches across the seat and squeezes my hand. "Enjoy Florence."

At the mention of Florence, I remember. "Oh no. I forgot about the appointment at the Academia."

"When is it?"

"Saturday afternoon. I want to see the *David* . . . but . . . I don't think I can handle that much walking. Not yet. And Jeff and Liz must come first. If I can't keep the appointment . . . is it . . . proper to call and cancel?"

"You could. But you could also let me take you in the chair with wheels."

I shake my head. "I don't mean to seem ungrateful. But I just don't want to be seen that way. I wouldn't mind with a cane—and in a few days I'll be ready to do it. On my own two feet."

He says something about the Queen Mother not wanting her subjects to see her limping before asking, "If you think she wouldn't mind, I'd be honored to take Elizabeth on Saturday. It would perhaps give her something to do besides to worry?"

"Mind? What's to mind?"

"That I'm not Jean-Marc," he says. "Perhaps she would rather spend the time with him. We could call him and ask . . . on her behalf."

I shake my head. "He needs time with his grandsons and Celine. And I know he's hoping to head down to Livorno. He expects the *Sea Cloud* any time now, and he wants to be there. I don't think he trusts his hired crew as completely as he's been pretending."

We pull up to the hotel. Luca helps me out and into the lobby. "I'll find parking and check back with you in . . . an hour?"

"I'll be in the atrium. Say a prayer that Jeff is with me. That will be a good sign."

SCUSI. SIGNORINA.

Liz swam up from the depths of sleep and opened her eyes.

"What time is it?"

The housemaid shrugged and held out the phone.

Taking the phone, Liz squinted and read . . . *12:00 P.M.*

"What day is it?"

The housemaid beamed. "Thursday, *signorina. Sì, Sì.* Is Thursday."

How was that possible? She'd slept . . . the entire night through . . . and half the next day? Mimi wasn't kidding. Her system wanted to shut down. She put the phone to her ear. "Liz Davis here." *Stupid. The automatic office voice isn't required in Florence.*

"Jeff Scott here."

She brought her other hand up to the phone—as if by holding on with both hands she could somehow keep him longer. "Really?"

"Really. Did I wake you?"

"Yes. No. I mean . . . yes, but it's time someone did."

He didn't waste time on small talk. "Mary tells me you've made a decision."

"Yes." She swallowed hard. "I . . . I never really meant . . . I mean, I never would have—"

"That's what Mary said. But you sure had me convinced."

"I . . . That was wrong. I'm sorry. So . . . very . . ." She gave a little hiccup, fighting back the tears.

"I didn't call you to make you cry," Jeff said. His voice was friendly, but not . . . quite . . . her Jeff. "I called to tell you that Jean-Marc has invited me to go to Livorno with him to welcome the *Sea Cloud* into port. If you're okay with that, I'd like to go. I'm thinking we could both use some time to sort through things . . . and make sure."

"Oh, I'm sure," Liz said. "I'm sure. I'm having this baby. I love you. I want to do . . . better. To be with you."

"That still means moving."

"I know that. I expected it."

He was quiet. She knew he was thinking. One of those things that was at once admirable and maddening about him. Finally, he spoke up. "You hold that thought. Until I get back. I want you to have a chance to unwind and rest." His voice changed—she could hear the emotion now. It sounded like . . . *hope,* although some doubt and uncertainty remained. "Because I don't think I can survive Act Two of what we've just put each other through."

He said a few more things. Kind, meaningless things about how he hoped she would enjoy seeing Florence with her mom and Luca . . . and how, when he came back, they would talk. She did her best to hold back the sobs. To believe him. It took all her willpower to avoid begging him to come to her. Right now. Elizabeth Davis wasn't the kind of woman people told to wait. But Jeffrey James Scott wasn't the kind of man a woman could manipulate. Not if she wanted him around for long.

"I understand." She said it because he expected it of her, not because she really did. This, Liz realized, was going to be hard.

Maybe the hardest thing she had ever done. How on earth would she possibly survive until Jeff returned to Florence?

"Jean-Marc said to tell you that, once we are back in port, he plans on arranging an excursion on the *Sea Cloud* with everyone. He hadn't mentioned it to you yet, but apparently he'd talked to Celine about meeting all of us over the weekend. Maybe now we'll wait to meet her when we go sailing. We'll just have to see what happens."

"Sailing with . . . everyone?"

"Your mom . . . you . . . Luca . . . Celine. I'm not sure who all would be included. But that's something to look forward to. Right?"

She forced confidence into her voice. "Absolutely."

"All right, then. You rest, and . . . I'll call you when we get back."

"Jeff, I . . . I love you."

"I believe you. Would you do something for me?"

"Anything."

"Keep your eyes and your ears open when you go sight-seeing. And your heart. Try not to worry about California. Be here now, Liz. In Florence. For all you're worth *be here now*."

# ℘ TWENTY ℘

THE LINE AT THE Academia, home of many works of art, including Michelangelo's *David,* snaked out the door and halfway down the block. As she and Luca approached the long line, Liz's heart sank. She was still tired, and the thought of waiting in that line . . . If she hadn't promised Jeff to really *see* Florence, she would have stayed back at the hotel. In bed.

"Thankfully," Luca said, seeming to sense her mood, "your mother made an appointment. We will be going to *that* door."

"Good," Liz forced a smile at the sight of half a dozen people waiting outside another door about half a city block away.

"Did you know," Luca said, "the *David* used to be just outside the Palazzo Vecchio?"

"*Outside?* In the open air?"

"*Si*. He had an arm smashed . . . some toes . . . but now he has his own room and guards who watch. When I was a boy—" Luca shook his head. "No matter. Today, I am looking forward to introducing a beautiful American woman to beautiful Italian boy." He winked.

Inside the Galleria, they walked first through a souvenir shop and then turned left, where, up ahead, a screen had been mounted and a video dramatizing Michelangelo at work had attracted a small group of Asian tourists. Following Luca through the doorway and past the video screen, Liz looked off to the right, and there, at the far end of a long gallery featuring unfinished sculpture, was *David,* his marble base completely obscured by a huge crowd.

"Tour buses," Luca murmured. "Three were parked outside. If you care to . . ." Taking Liz's arm, he led her toward the *David,* pausing at the first of four massive blocks of marble. Human figures seemed to be trying to free themselves of each piece, but none had succeeded. The marks of the sculptor's tools were evident on all sides.

"Just think," Luca murmured. "The tool that made *those* marks on *that* stone . . . was in the hand of Michelangelo."

Liz stopped to look up into a stone face. Suddenly the unfinished pieces were more than just blocks of marble positioned to distract tourists who had to wait their turn to see the *real* art at the end of the hall.

Luca explained, "There was disagreement during their creation. Michelangelo was, some say, a difficult man at times. As are we all, eh? Whatever the reason, the figures remain trapped in their marble cocoons."

"You know a lot about art," Liz said.

"I know a *little,*" Luca corrected her. He looked down toward the *David.* "In a few minutes, they will go, and we will have a better viewing. If you will permit me a small story?"

Liz nodded.

"This is only a story, *signorina,* so you must not quote me as if it really happened. I don't know. But the story is told that one day someone was watching the great master at work. This was after he had carved the *David,* whose marble cocoon lay for years unused because of a great fault. Leonardo himself had rejected the stone as impossibly difficult—almost worthless. Anyway, the story is that Michelangelo was asked how he could look at a block of stone and get out from it such a wondrous thing as the *David,* the *Pièta.* The master shrugged his shoulders"—Luca did an exaggerated shrug— "and said, 'Is easy. I just knock off what doesn't look like David.'"

Luca put his hands in his pockets and stood looking up into the face of the unfinished piece they had been studying. "I think it is in the letter to Rome that Paul writes of God determining to make us look like Christ. The phrase, I believe, is, 'conformed to the image of his Son,' and I am thinking that would be good . . . for me . . . to be loving and wise as was Christ. And then I realize, that is what is happening since I believed. God knocks off what doesn't look like Christ." He smiled and shrugged. "Of course, for God to make Luca Santo look like Christ is much more difficult than for Michelangelo to form marble into a beautiful man. For human transformations, it takes the whole of life . . . and"—he nodded—"sometimes it hurts like *heck*." He winked, looked past Liz, and took her arm. "Come now. We have good chance for walking all around His Majesty."

After seeing replicas of *David* and posters and postcards and drawings all over Florence, Liz expected seeing the actual sculpture to be anticlimactic. But as she stood beneath the towering, ten-foot-high masterpiece, she was entranced. Even the veins in his arms stood out in relief. It would not have surprised her if the statue had come to life. And, she could not help but notice the powerful back and *derrière*. When she covered her mouth to hide a smile, Luca nudged her shoulder.

"You women," he chided, "always thinking the same thing."

"You don't know what I was thinking," Liz protested.

"I know what my Sophia was thinking when she and I first saw *David* together. Because she told me." He leaned down and whispered, "Great buns."

Liz laughed out loud, then scolded, "What would Master Michelangelo say if he knew you were joking about *buns* right after giving a religious lesson taken from his own words?"

Luca seemed to ponder for a moment before answering. When he did, he pointed toward the ceiling of the vaulted dome above the *David*. "I am most fortunate. The true Master is very forgiving."

"CELINE . . . DUMAS?" Liz didn't try to hide the surprise she felt when the caller identified herself.

Musical laughter sounded over the telephone. "Yes. Celine Dumas. The *other* daughter."

Liz made a face at Mimi, who had just come out of the bathroom, red-faced from leaning over the tub to wash her hair without getting her boot wet.

"Our dear papa has, quite characteristically, decided to go off to his precious *Sea Cloud* and cancel our meeting," Celine said. "I don't think a change in Papa's schedule needs to affect those of us who have a life on dry land. We can enjoy tiramisu at Gilli without him. What do you think?"

What could she say? "I think . . . yes. Jean-Marc has talked quite a bit about you—and Xavier and Olivier, too. We'd like to meet you all." *Like,* Liz thought, might be a little strong. But . . . it had to be done. And she did like the idea of meeting Celine and her children without an audience.

"Oh, I wouldn't subject you to so much all at once," Celine laughed again. "As a matter of fact, the boys went with Papa and your fiancé to Livorno. He is quite charming."

"Yes . . . yes. He is. I'm glad you aren't too upset with him for the postponement."

"Not Papa," Celine chided. "Your fiancé. Signor Scott."

"Thank you," Liz said.

"Would you and the Mrs. Davis I have been hearing so much about have time tomorrow afternoon?"

"Can you hold on a moment while I check with her?" Liz covered the mouthpiece with her hand. "She's inviting you and me to meet, anyway. Without Jeff and Jean-Marc."

"When?"

"Tomorrow afternoon."

"I don't see any reason why we can't," Mimi said. "In some ways it might be better." She sat down on the edge of the bed and began to comb out her hair. "Simpler. Fewer personalities around the table. Less of an audience watching to see how we all do."

Liz nodded and accepted Celine's invitation.

"Gilli is not so far from your hotel," Celine said. "But you might want to take a taxi, anyway. I don't know about your mother walking that far? Or would you rather I come to the hotel? Whatever is easier."

She was being so considerate. She sounded really nice. Liz assured Celine that she and Mimi were looking forward to Gilli, arranged to meet her there at two in the afternoon the next day, and hung up with a sigh.

"What?" Mimi asked, shaking out her damp curls.

"You heard. Tomorrow afternoon at two." Liz flopped down on the couch. "Is it hormones or Italy that's turned me into a nervous, exhausted, stuttering scaredy-cat?"

"You, my dear daughter, will never be a stuttering scaredy-cat," Mimi said. "And being nervous is normal. I am, too." She forced a smile. "It's not exactly the most predictable meeting we've ever been involved in." She paused before adding, "I feel like I should apologize for putting you through this at all. You'd have a right to feel off-center whether you were pregnant or not. But it's also true that pregnancy adds another level of tired."

"How long is *that* going to last?" Liz grumbled, punching one of the bolsters and settling it beneath her head.

"Fifty years," Mimi called from the bathroom where she had retreated to dry her hair.

"And just for the record, stop apologizing," Liz said, before asking where her mother and Luca were going that night.

"Some small trattoria his family loves. Angelina's, I think he said. We can walk from here. I guess it's on this side of the river, even."

"Angio-LEE-no's?" Liz asked.

"Yes. That's it. Why?"

Liz closed her eyes and shook her head. "This is just too weird."

And she told Mimi about meeting Gil Dayton on the plane . . . his computer knowledge . . . and his recommendations for Florence.

"Well," Mimi said. "I'll let you know what I think. I'm famished, so it had better be good."

*Mary*

THE APPROACH TO Angiolino is not promising, save for the fact my hand is tucked under Luca's arm. The street is nearly deserted and boasts only one or two shops, both closed. There is no traffic and only dim light, until we reach the small double-paned window with a bright-pink neon bar illuminating the painted word *Trattoria*. The display in the window is an amusing collection of wine bottles and fake food, with a four-foot-tall ceramic pig dressed as a chef.

"We're very early," Luca says, even though it is seven in the evening. "They've just opened. That's good. I didn't make a reservation, and it can be difficult . . ."

From the bar just inside the front door, a woman calls a greeting. She knows Signor Santo by name. Perhaps I am imagining things, but it seems to me that I receive more than a cursory inspection as Luca guides me past the bar and toward the narrow doorway that leads into the dining room.

I hear *"Buonasera"* as a balding older man, sporting thick glasses and a white apron, appears at the door and leads us to one of no more than a dozen tables in a room about the size of the living area in my apartment in Paris. From my chair I have an unobstructed view of the kitchen, where a portly man dressed in white—complete with foot-high chef's hat—is carving a slab of meat. The wide window into the kitchen is hung with dried onions, red peppers, and strings of fresh vegetables. Piles of plates to one side, a bunch of fresh herbs . . . bottles—it is very picturesque.

"Yes. Picturesque," Luca agrees when I tell him what I think. "But just wait . . ."

With a wave of his hand, he rejects the offered menu, saying something I don't understand to the waiter, whose name is Paulo. The dream begins. By the end of the first course, I realize I am in the presence of an artist. The chef manages his kitchen like the conductor of an orchestra, turning this, spicing that, all in rhythm, so that each dish is presented at the perfect moment. As other diners arrive and the room gradually fills, a helper steps in, dipping sauce, swiping out pans . . . but the only one to actually prepare the food is the moustached chef, who handles a dozen orders and as many different dishes with finesse, never seeming to hurry, sending rapid-fire orders to his assistant, without raising his voice.

"I would applaud him," I say as I savor what Luca reminds me is the *secondi piatti,* "but I'll explode if I move that fast."

Luca laughs and pours more Chianti. He reminds me to take my time and to savor each bite. As the voices of fellow diners fill the room with laughter, I do just that. I relax. And realize that I am savoring my time with Luca as much—perhaps more—than the meal. While part of me basks in his attention, the other part seems to be standing apart, observing this night. It's as if there is a running commentary inside my head.

*The attraction is more than physical. The two of you are on the same page spiritually, too. He's so at ease with himself. So relaxed in his skin. He hasn't looked at his watch once. It's as if he has nothing else in the universe to do. He has a business waiting for his attention, but he isn't wondering how things are. Or, if he is, he hides it better than—You should stop comparing them. They are both good men. Both good friends. Both—*

I suppress the inner commentary just as Paulo brings two small glasses of clear liquid and sets them before us.

"Beware," Luca warns me, although he upends his without hesitation.

"What is it?"

"*Grappa.*"

"What's . . . *grappa*?"

"Taste," Luca encourages me. "But just a tiny bit at first."

I taste . . . blink, cough a little, wipe my watering eyes . . . and we laugh.

"You can have the rest," I hold the small cordial glass out to him.

"Oh no," Luca waves his hand in protest. When Paulo serves coffee and dessert, Luca leans toward me and says in a conspiratorial tone, "It's really a *French* pastry." He looks up at the scowling waiter and says a little louder, "Although the French stole it from the Medici kitchens several hundred years ago." Paulo nods agreement and hurries off to answer a question from a diner across the room.

"So," Luca asks when we have finished dessert, "what do you think of Angiolino?"

I don't have to think to answer him. "Healing," I say. "This entire evening has been healing. Relaxing. A welcome respite from the fray."

He frowns. "I am sorry to hear that you come to my home and find . . . a fray."

"It's nothing you've done. You are doing everything possible to make it a delight." It seems quite natural for me to reach over and touch the back of his hand as I say, "Celine called. Even though Jean-Marc and Jeff are not here, Liz and I are meeting her tomorrow afternoon."

Luca covers my hand with his and pats it. "Ah," he says, then looks at me with a smile. "For this you have no need to worry. I am certain Jean-Marc has said wonderful things about you both to his daughter, and I am just as certain that she will be delighted with you both."

"Have you met Celine?"

He shakes his head. "I was like you. Without a clue as to what had become of our friend. Until he came to Paris." Taking his hand away, he smiles. "To *you*."

He glances toward the door. "I see people waiting to be seated. Would a walk be welcome . . . or torture?"

I try not to feel hurt that he has pulled his hand away, and I force a smile as he helps me with my chair. "I'd rather not have to be *rolled* down the aisle at either Annie or Liz's wedding, but if I eat too many meals like this, that will be a serious possibility. A walk is a very good idea."

We make our way up the street, along the river, toward the Ponte Vecchio. I am unusually aware of Luca's hand only inches from mine as we walk. I wonder if he thinks I'm purposely staying close, hoping he'll take my hand. I wonder if he's wishing I'd pull away like he did just moments ago at dinner. My inner monologue returns. *Don't be an idiot. Why are you so self-conscious? You're acting like a teenager. Maybe you should just rest your hand on your shoulder bag. Maybe you should stop obsessing about this. Good grief, woman, you'd think you were in high school. Grow up!*

When we pause to rest on a bench beside a small fountain, Luca points up to the tower at the end of the bridge, where a lean-to of sorts has been added around the base of the tower. He explains that this is part of something called the Vasari Corridor, built by request of the Medici when they ruled France in 1565. "When we are on the bridge," he says, "you will notice a long row of windows above the shops. Is part of this enclosed passageway leading all the way from Palazzo Signoria"—he points across the bridge toward the tower in the distance—"then to the Uffizi Palace . . . toward the river . . . across this bridge . . . around the tower you see . . . and on up the hill behind us, all the way to the Pitti Palace. This is so the Medici could make their way from building to building, in any weather . . . and never mingle with the peasants while they kept the eye out." He pauses. "We should check to see if they are giving tours tomorrow. It is not always open. It would be something special for you and Elizabeth." He is quick to add, "The walk is long. I don't know in miles. But again, I would suggest the chair with wheels which I would happily pilot." Flustered, I protest about taking up too much of his time. He nudges my shoulder, "Consider this, *cara mia*. To push the chair is much easier than to push the Ducati."

I frown. "You think I'd be that bad—that you'd have to *push*?"

He explains. "Is how Jean-Marc and I planned it. First, we push you while you learn to sense the——" He searches for a word, mimicking falling to one side or the other.

"Balance?"

He nods. "*Yes*. The balance."

"Where, exactly, was this ridiculous lesson going to take place?" I'm suddenly self conscious at the idea of two middle-aged men pushing a gray-haired woman across a parking lot. And, when I think about it, I'm clueless as to where they'd find a parking lot big enough. Where *do* people learn to ride motorcycles in this country?

Luca taps the tip of my nose. "Have a little trust, please. There is a plan for when the leg has healed." He stands up, extends his hand to pull me up beside him, and we head across the bridge.

As we make our way through the maze of people staring in windows at the vast array of jewelry, Luca is once again my tour guide. "These were all butcher shops until one of the Medici wearied of the smell of . . ." He hesitates, searching for the word, then says, "Carcasses. He decided to kick the butchers out, send them to the edge of the city, and invited the goldsmiths in."

I've been doing my best to pay attention. As if there might be questions later. But it's hard. Because he hasn't let go of my hand.

He pauses before one of the windows. "Would you like to shop?"

I shake my head. "I wouldn't know where to begin. But we'll have to make certain Jeff brings Liz here. She will love it."

Halfway across the bridge Luca insists that I sit down to rest. Seeing my cane, a young couple vacates one of the few benches. Luca sits down next to me and explains that the bust in this mini-plaza at the midpoint of the bridge is a tribute to a famous goldsmith.

When I ask about the dozens of locks attached to the iron fence around the sculpture, he shakes his head. "Something about if you put on the lock you will return to Florence. I'm not sure." As we look out over the water he recounts the destruction of all the bridges of Florence in World War II. "Except this one," he says. "It is said that the only reason this one survived was that Hitler chose to stand here to watch the rest fall."

When I shiver at the thought, Luca puts his arm around me. *Nice trick,* my inner monologue scolds. The river's surface is an indigo reflection of the night sky. While Luca and I sit together, streetlights and shop lights begin to come on, casting broken threads of light on the water's surface. I murmur, "Enchanting."

"Completely," Luca agrees, so close I can feel his breath on my cheek.

"The river . . . or the sky?"

"Neither . . ." he says, before standing up and extending his hand. He smiles. "When you talk to him, you must tell our friend Jean-Marc that, if he knows what is good for him, he will waste no time in returning to Florence. These lights . . . this city . . . they stir things in a man. I just might decide to challenge your Frenchman's charm."

"Not to worry," I tease him. "Clearly, Jean-Marc has not cornered the market on charm." When Luca slips his arm around me again, I pat it like a mother showing affection for a grown son. The gesture does nothing to calm my emotions. "And now, if you really want to impress me . . ."

"Take you back to the hotel?"

"Actually, I was thinking more in terms of *gelato.*" *And anything else that might prolong the evening.*

"I thought you were full to burst!"

"I was, then . . . but now I'm not." *Liar.*

"You will not be allowed to blame me if you roll down to the aisle!" he jokes. But he agrees that *gelato* is a good idea. And he takes my hand again as we walk.

We amble back across the bridge and settle at a café, where I decide that *gelato* is like eating a cloud. We indulge in more coffee . . . more talking . . . And the running commentary in my head goes into overdrive.

*For a woman with a French sailor in her heart, you seem awfully happy tonight. Holding hands with this guy is not exactly the way to control things. Do you want to control things?*

I refuse to think past this moment. But in this moment I know one thing—I don't want to say good-night. I'm delighted when we reach the hotel and Luca prolongs the evening by leading me out onto the balcony overlooking the river.

He raises the subject of Celine again. "From what Jean-Marc has said, I think your Liz-bet will be much surprised at how much she is like Celine—in spite of the different careers."

"You think of Celine's decision to stay at home as a career choice?" I don't hide the surprise from my voice. *The man is too good to be true.* But with Celine and Liz as the topic of conversation, Jean-Marc is also present, at least in my mind. I wonder if that is exactly why Luca has brought it up.

He shrugs. "I cannot speak for others, but I know that I was a full-time career for my Sophia." He grins. "She used to tease that she had no time for other children besides me."

"I know what she meant," I say. "Keeping Sam *almost* happy was an entire career for me."

He's facing me with one elbow resting on the iron railing. For a long moment he stares at me, then reaches up to trace my jawline with his hand. "I am thinking it is safe to say that if Signor Davis was unhappy, it had nothing to do with his wife. And while it may not be polite to speak ill of those who have passed on, I will tell you that I also think he was a fool if he did not realize what a treasure he had."

My heart is pounding. I close my eyes, concentrating on the sensation of Luca's hand caressing my cheek. When he pulls me close and kisses me, I silence the inner voices long enough to kiss back. With enthusiasm.

He pulls away. "Forgive me," he begs. "Forgive me, please, *cara mia.* I didn't mean—"

I put my hand on his arm. "I *did*," I whisper. "Every minute of it."

He covers my hand with his, but he looks away, across the river, and I can sense a battle going on. It is all I can do to wait, motionless, hoping he doesn't move away from me. But he does. Ever so gently, he takes my hand and places it on the railing before us and, with an affectionate little pat, increases the distance between us. It's a tiny distance, but it might as well be a mile for the depth of the chasm I sense between us now. When Luca speaks, his voice is controlled with what I think is a bit of resignation.

"I do a great disservice to Jean-Marc in this moment. He is my friend. He loves you . . . and I have no rights."

*Jean-Marc.* I close my eyes. I nod in agreement, willing myself to choose what I think is God's will. *Help me not to hurt him again. I love him. Of course I do.*

Reaching out to frame Luca's face with my hands, I search his eyes for a moment before turning and walking away. At the door of the hotel, I realize that I've left my cane leaning against the railing. I'm limping along like an old woman, which, I decide, is fitting. I feel ancient . . . decrepit . . . sad.

There is always something for which to be thankful. Tonight, it is that my room at the Hotel Lucia is serviced by a private elevator. When the tears come, I can let them fall. Please let Liz be asleep.

## ℣ TWENTY-ONE ℣

"REALLY, HONEY," Mimi said from beneath the down comforter, "there's nothing wrong at all. I'm just exhausted. It's *my* turn, you know. You go on. Enjoy your morning in Florence. Luca said there's a huge open-air market over around San Lorenzo church. It's on the map inside the guidebook. Easy to find. Not much of a walk. Wander back around lunchtime. Maybe we can have a quick bite together before we go to meet Celine."

"If you're sure," Liz said from the doorway.

"I'm sure." Mimi snuggled deep into her pillow. "This is divine. It's *good* to be queen."

With a small laugh, Liz drew the door closed behind her. On her way out she hung the *Do Not Disturb* sign on the doorknob and headed downstairs. *"Do me a favor,"* Jeff had said. *"Open your ears. Open your eyes. Open your heart."* She was going to try to see whatever it was he was talking about. But first . . . she was going to . . . run back inside and throw up.

She used to say she was about eighteen when she gave herself permission not to love her mother. How thankful Liz was, this morning in Florence, that that was in the past. She was almost thirty years old now, and as she headed up the street away from the Hotel Lucia toward "Michelangelo's Bridge," she decided she was now going to give herself permission to be *like* her mother. Mimi had developed a knack for enjoying wherever she was. For seeing little things. For pausing and listening and learning. Maybe, Liz thought, maybe you just needed to have the time. She had never seemed to have enough time. This morning, as she crossed the bridge and headed toward the marketplace Mimi had mentioned, she had nothing but time. Whatever it was she was supposed to see or hear, she hoped it would show itself. Today.

No one had told her about *this* part of Florence. Like ducks in a row, the great Italian designers had lined up shops along this street. Fashion to die for . . . but, Liz realized, not fashion to pay for when her body was going to be changing so radically. She paused before one window, ogling a pair of bright green and gray and black tights on a size-zero mannequin. On impulse, she went inside and bought two pairs of a different pattern in the largest size available, one for Margaret, the other for Irene. It was going to be fun teasing them about chartreuse polka-dot legs.

Farther up from the river, the streets narrowed. Liz took a turn, thought it might be wrong, decided to take Jeff's advice and go with the flow, and ended up walking by a tattoo parlor with a Harley Davidson parked in the window. What, she wondered, would Luca Santo, who lived and breathed Ducati, have to say about *that*?

With her stomach beginning to settle and rumble with hunger, she got up the courage to go into a tiny corner coffee shop. And she was glad, as the array of pastries inside was mouth-watering. Thanks to her time with Luca yesterday, she knew to order *latte macchiatto*. Pastry in hand, she scooted outside, where the *barista* had said he would serve her coffee, and sat down, leaning back, closing her eyes, and lifting her face to the morning sun. *Listen,* she reminded herself. *Savor.*

Just across the street a young mother was grinning at the toddling steps of a blond-haired little boy making his way along the narrow sidewalk. *I bet Jeff looked a lot like that.* Just as she thought about Jeff, the little guy lost his balance on the uneven sidewalk and fell down. His mama swept him up in her arms, whispered something, kissed his cheek, and set him back down. Tears came to Liz's eyes at the realization that, in a couple of years, *she* would be the one who could make everything all right. She thought about the statue of the serene woman up on the hill. *Mama's here. Everything will be all right.*

The *barista* brought her coffee as Liz nibbled at her pastry. Next door to the little café, a shopkeeper was opening for business. He set a small table in front of his store so the young woman following him out could put her armful of scarves and umbrellas down. The minute her arms were empty, he grabbed her and planted a kiss on her cheek . . . her forehead . . . her lips.

With a smile toward the *barista*, who was now smoking a cigarette while he leaned against the doorframe of his business, Liz headed off.

"*Arrivederci, signorina*," he called after her. She waved in response, but then he said something else.

Liz apologized, "I'm sorry. I don't speak Italian."

The scruffy-bearded man winked and said in English, "Enjoy my city, *signorina*."

"I am," Liz answered.

By midmorning she had located the market, bought three new pairs of shoes, a leather backpack—for transporting the shoes—and an elegant journal with the Florentine *fleur-de-lis* engraved on the cover. She was sitting on the steps that led up to—what else—another church, when another tourist walked by.

"Now, this church is all right," he was saying, pontificating, really, "but not really remarkable. No really *important* art. Simple. Bland. And look at the facade. It isn't even *finished*. . . ." His companion was nodding, taking in every word. "There is a sandstone staircase designed by Michelangelo . . . but they won't even let you *in* the library to see the desks and the ceilings he designed. And besides that, Michelangelo is everywhere in Florence. . . . There's really no reason to go in. We have so much to see today!"

As the too-loud voice faded into the distance, Liz turned around.

From what she could see, the man—however annoying—was right. Compared to the pictures she'd seen of the other churches and cathedrals in the city, San Lorenzo wasn't much. But the fact that the know-it-all tourist was talking it down made her curious. She would go in.

Liz wandered inside the "simple, bland" San Lorenzo for over an hour, going slowly, taking in every work of art, every side chapel, alternately amazed and taken aback by the paintings and tombs inside the church.

At one point, organ music began to play, and Liz realized mass was being conducted in a side chapel that was roped off to keep tourists out. But no one ordered her to leave, and she was grateful as she continued her self-guided tour.

Above one marble casket in a side chapel, a larger-than-life angel was holding on to a human form that appeared to have just been extracted from the casket beneath their feet. A silver filigree box on the wall opposite the angel turned out to be a casket . . . with its resident's bones visible through the opaque rose-colored liner. Was it glass? Liz wondered. Whatever it was, she thought it a bit macabre and hurried away toward the altar—in front of which a simple stone slab marked the grave of the founder of the Medici dynasty. Mimi had said the message of resurrection was all around you in Florence, if only you took time to see it. As she made her way around the interior of San Lorenzo, Liz realized that Mimi was right. Death and resurrection went hand-in-hand for the faithful, one just as certain as the other.

In the side chapel past the altar, Liz encountered her first representation of the resurrected Christ in the form of a statue, probably of carved wood. The Christ was so lifelike, Liz found herself looking away from his eyes, rubbing her forearms to rid herself of the goose bumps. Moving past the rest of the artwork, she made her way to a rear pew and sat down. She'd seen the painting on her left when she first came in the church, but now as she sat and stared up at it, she was newly captivated by the interpretation of a very human Jesus in Joseph's workshop. Joseph looked on as the child—Liz guessed him to be about three years old—bent down to pick something up. Joseph's expression was loving, but behind the love was something else. A burden. An awareness, Liz decided, of what was to come for this beloved child. The artist had painted a piece of lumber jutting into the scene from the lower left corner, continuing it up into the sky behind the figures of Joseph and Jesus to form a cross that loomed over the child. The imagery was breathtaking.

The painting brought to mind so many things she'd never really thought about. She put her hand over her own abdomen, thinking for the first time in her life about Jesus' mother, Mary. How helpless she must have felt at times. How agonizing to watch as her son was mistreated . . . tortured . . . buried. Jesus had been a real little boy— although probably not blond—toddling along the streets just like that little guy she'd seen earlier. A little boy who played and burped and fell down and reached for his mother. . . . And in the end, Mary had had to give the baby boy back to God *so that he could die.*

Blinking away her tears, Liz looked away from the painting on her left toward the one on the right, where Christ hung on the cross, looking down on a woman clinging to his feet. Her face was not beautiful physically . . . and yet, it was beautiful. She was actually smiling a little. As if some great burden had been lifted, some new peace imparted. Liz could almost hear her whispering *Thank you.* She turned again to look at Jesus the little boy and then back again to the dying Savior, and up ahead, to the right of the altar, at the resurrected Lord. *"The promise of resurrection is all around you."* Liz glanced back toward the woman at the feet of Jesus whose face reflected the very thing she wanted most. *Peace. I want peace.*

What was it Gil Dayton had said on the plane? Something about thinking about all of today in light of eternity—that if we knew we had eternity locked up, we could weather anything life threw at us. He'd talked about things Liz didn't want to hear. Things like sin and God's demands for perfection, and what he believed was the only way to forgiveness. He said forgiveness was free. That people couldn't earn it, but they could accept it as a gift. She'd listened politely back then, not wanting to make the plane ride uncomfortable for either one of them. But she'd been more than a little irritated by his assumption that everyone had what he called a "sin problem" keeping them from God . . . and that no one was good enough to fix it on their own.

Looking back toward the adorable child with the cross looming in his future, Liz decided it must be true. She couldn't fix it. But Jesus could. Looking down, she noticed the kneeling bench. She gladly used it.

*Thank you. Thank you.*


## Mary

I WAS A fool to think I'd get some rest this morning. Lucia Biacci, dear as she is, has apparently never accepted the concept that there are people in the world who get energy from time spent alone. She calls three times in the first half hour after Liz leaves. First, with an invitation to come up to the villa for a late morning treat. Next, to invite me to lunch or for tea in the afternoon. Finally, she offers to call the spa and send her favorite esthetician to the hotel, "for hand massage and manicure—is wonderful." It takes most of my already depleted emotional energy to reassure Lucia that the thing I want most in the world at the moment is to spend my Sunday morning in Florence alone. I hint that I've sent Liz out the door, at least in part, so that I can have some time to myself.

Finally, Lucia relents. But not until I promise to call her if I need anything. I promise. And wish she would have said something about Luca. But she didn't.

After unplugging the phone, I muscle a chair closer to the window, prop up my leg and settle in, recounting my litany of problems to the disgustingly clear blue sky, telling myself I am praying.

Actually, I am whining. I have a mental list, and I am determined to review it.

*I'm tired of limping around.*

*If a person can be killed with kindness, I'm going to die at the hand of Lucia Biacci.*

*What's going to happen between Liz and Jeff? And why hasn't he so much as called her? Off on the high seas with Jean-Marc. What kind of advice is he going to get from him?*

*What's going to happen with Liz if Jeff doesn't . . . I don't even want to think about it. But I might as well face it. I'm going to have to move back to Omaha. I guess that pretty well takes care of my personal struggles regarding Luca and Jean-Marc.*

I sigh. Reach for a tissue. Blow my nose.

How can I be like this? Of course I'll move back. Liz will need my help with the baby, and it'll be great. There's nothing to compare with a grandchild's love. And Irene and Cecil will be thrilled—which also takes care of the question about what to do with the estate. Liz can have my room, and I'll. . . .

I know my worrying is pointless. I have those Bible verses in mind about not worrying and letting God handle things. But this morning, I can't quite seem to apply them to my life. I am supposed to be trusting God. About everything. Liz. Jeff. Baby. Luca. Jean-Marc. But I can't seem to trust God with a single one of them. I want Liz to know Jesus, to marry Jeff, and to bring a healthy baby into a Christian home. I want to live in Paris . . . and I want Luca to . . .

*Father. Help. I love Jean-Marc. I do. But it's not . . . It's not the same as what I feel for Luca. What am I going to do?!*

When a bell announces the arrival of the elevator, I limp to the bathroom as quickly as I can. I'm a mess. My hair hasn't been combed yet, my face is streaked with tears, and looking in the mirror confirms my worst expectations about my appearance.

"Just a minute, please," I call through a crack in the bathroom door, hoping whoever it is speaks English. All I really want is for them to leave me in peace. I turn on the water to mask the sound and blow my nose. Again.

They don't get the message. There's a knock on the door. *Pushy*. Just what I don't need this morning—a pushy hotel employee. Dabbing my face with a towel, I jerk the door open and blurt out— Nothing. Because it isn't a hotel employee.

"Mimi," Liz says, her blue eyes radiant, her cheeks flushed with pleasure. "Oh, Mimi . . . I *get* it. The things you've been talking about . . . and Danny and Sarah and Luca . . . and Jeff and . . . Mimi, I *get* it." She blinks back tears and clears her throat. "I went inside a church and there were two oil paintings and . . ."

I've been sniffling most of the morning. But the well isn't dry. It is said that God works in mysterious ways. Apparently that would include fractured bones to bring a daughter to Florence, and absent fiancés to get her attention, and unexpected babies to bring her to the end of herself, and centuries-old churches to speak without words and to make sense of mysterious things like sin and redemption, faith and resurrection, old stories and new life.

FROM ACROSS THE arrangement of mostly empty tables, Liz and I see a stunning raven-haired woman raise her hand. When she calls our names, we duck under the canopy that provides shade for the tables scattered along Gilli's storefront and head in her direction. Celine stands up and extends her hands to us both. Her laugh is melodious. A bit nervous, perhaps, but genuine. And she kisses us on each cheek before gesturing toward the other two chairs gathered around a small marble-topped table. When Liz settles a small shopping bag on the ground, Celine speaks up.

"I see you've been enjoying my favorite hobby," Celine said. "Is it shoes?"

Liz nods. "I bought three pairs at the market this morning. But then we passed this shop on the way over here . . ." She shrugs as she removes her sunglasses.

"You walked, then?" Celine says, and turns to me, removing her sunglasses as well.

I forget her question beneath the gaze of those unbelievable eyes. I've seen them before, of course. Liz and Celine look at each other and say in unison, "You have my eyes." They laugh—nervously.

I recover first, remembering Celine's initial question. "You asked if we walked," I say. "Yes."

"I am pleased to hear it," Celine says. "Tuscany agrees with you. And the leg is doing well?"

"Oh," I say, reaching down to tap my knuckles against the boot. "I'm sick to death of limping around. But everyone has been very kind."

"Papa was very disappointed, you know, to think that the Ducati lessons will be postponed."

I feel myself blushing, which is ridiculous. I am old enough to be her mother. Why should I feel self-conscious? *Because she has it.* My inner monologue reminds me. *That indescribable European flair. Style. Grace. And you don't. Not a single drop.*

Celine waves a waiter over, asking us as he approaches, "We decided on tiramisu, *si*?"

Liz nods. "I hear it's wonderful."

"*Tiramisu tre,*" Celine said. "*Una espresso per me e. . . ?*" She waits for us to respond.

"Espresso is fine," Liz says.

I order decaf coffee. My nerves don't need a caffeine overload.

When the waiter retreats, things get quiet. Very, very quiet.

"This is . . . strange," Liz finally says, looking from Celine to me and back again. "Who could ever have imagined something like this?"

I am fidgeting with my scarf. My eyes wander toward the beautiful building housing Gilli. I say something lame about the display of gourmet candies in the window.

"Gilli is something of an institution in Florence," Celine explains. "Since the eighteenth century." She pauses, then says to Liz, "I owe you my thanks." She turns to me. "Actually, I owe you both my thanks."

Liz frowns. "For what?"

With a smile, Celine lowers her voice. She leans forward. "For being part of the change that actually gave me a father . . . and gave my two sons a grandfather. I had come to almost accept that Jean-Marc David would never take the time for them." She looks at me. "But ever since you came back into his life . . ." She smiles. Sits back. The waiter brings our order, and after we add sugar to our coffees and exclaim over the tiramisu, Celine adds, "I hope you mend quickly, Madame Davis. Papa so looks forward to sharing his *Sea Cloud* with you."

"Mary," I say quickly. "Please. Call me Mary."

"Mary, then," she says, nodding my way and then taking a tiny bite of her dessert. She wants to know about Davis Enterprises and expresses admiration for Liz. "I can't imagine running such a company," she says, "and I applaud you." She is articulate, bright, and content with her life. She spends her time at home, raising her boys, marketing, doing charity work. In many ways, Celine Dumas is a wealthier, and hence more stylish, Sarah Henderson, translated to another culture. I wonder if Liz realizes it.

"We are all looking forward to having you join us for dinner some evening," Celine says. "And then of course there will be the pilgrimage 'To The Ship.'" She says the last three words with her hands clasped in feigned adoration.

"I've never gone sailing," Liz says. "But I've seen the magazine cover Mimi found. The *Sea Cloud* is a gorgeous yacht."

"Magazine?"

Celine doesn't even know about it. When I tell her about seeing it in a musty shop in Nebraska, she shakes her head in amazement. "Papa didn't tell me," she says. "But you said it was an old magazine?"

"From a few years ago."

"That explains it. I used to hate the *Sea Cloud* with all my might. The magazine probably came out during those years when Papa and I barely spoke." She takes the last bite of her tiramisu and gestures with her spoon. "She was always the mistress Papa wouldn't give up. For a long time I couldn't forgive him for that."

"What changed?" Liz asks.

Celine pauses, thinking. She gives a little shrug. "Certainly not him. Not then." She smiles. "I changed. And realized that having Papa on his terms was better than having no papa at all."

Somehow, Celine's openness about her strained relationship with her father seems to break down what remains of the awkwardness between us. I ask about her boys. She has photos. They are as different as can be—one dark, one fair. But both are beautiful. And both have those eyes. We talk music, and Celine mentions that her father has been practicing the accompaniment to a violin concerto. And the girls talk shopping. Celine offers to take Liz on a guided tour of the best shoe stores in Florence. And she offers to help us procure the very best seats to a performance of *La Traviata* at the Teatro Communale. And while she is aware of the concerts the woman on the train mentioned to me, she hasn't personally attended. "Don't tell Papa," she says and winks at us, "but I much prefer American jazz to the classics."

While we are all together, I forget to be stressed about Jean-Marc and Luca. The cloud doesn't descend again until Liz and I are back in the hotel lobby. Liz wants to sit in the lounge and watch the light change on the water as the sun goes down. I plead fatigue.

She frowns. "I hope you aren't coming down with something."

"I'm fine. But you know me. Stress wears me out. And while I can't imagine how things could have gone better with Celine . . ."

"I understand," Liz says. "But it's so early. Why don't you call Luca and see if he wants to meet us for dinner?"

I shake my head. "I can't imagine eating another thing. And besides that, Luca won't want to come."

"What do you mean, he won't want to come?" Liz cocks her

head and asks, "Have you two had a misunderstanding?"

I shake my head again, "Just the opposite. We have an under-standing."

Liz frowns. "An understanding that says you don't call him?"

"Look," I say, pointing toward the buildings along the opposite riverbank, where the setting sun has painted the ancient walls in a palette of warm color. I put my arm around Liz's waist. "Right now," I say, "what I'd like to do is spend a quiet evening in my hotel room without having to answer any questions about Luca Santo."

"What about dinner?"

"If we get hungry, I happen to know about a little trattoria just up the street. . . ."

FOR ALL MY WORRY and sleeplessness, it seems that God does have a plan—at least when it comes to some of the things I have been worrying about. I really am blessed. Liz and I are very different people, and yet we are managing to make some wonderful memories while she waits on Jeff and I wait on . . . Well, I just wait.

Following Luca's advice, on Monday morning I call the Uffizi Palace and, after a few incidences of misdirection and an hour or so standing in the wrong line, Liz and I get on the list that enables us to see the Corridoio Vassariano. I don't know what I enjoy most . . . seeing the display of artists' self-portraits mounted on the walls, or listening to the delightful accent of our tour guide, a graying charmer who imparts his passion for art with a constant stream of adjectives. "And here, we have the beautiful rendition of the superb artist . . . and now you are looking at the delightful portrait by the wonder-ful . . . and you will see next the splendid work of the fantastic and beloved . . ."

After a while, I forget to listen to the details and simply enjoy the lyrical voice and the fact that my daughter is with me and we are, for the first time in our lives, *in tune* with one another.

On Monday afternoon we return to the row of designer shops and head down a side street where we discover a tailor who makes men's dress shirts. Liz wants to bring Jeff here and order a dozen, but the minute she says it aloud she tears up.

"Love forgives, Lizzie," I remind her. "It's going to be all right." I wish I was as convinced about that in respect to my own life as I sound for hers. Looking at shirt fabric I am torn between envisioning Luca in the red pinstripe or Jean-Marc in the blue.

On Tuesday, after sleeping late, we call to make an appointment to join a small private tour of some of the artisans' workshops in the Oltrarno District. We visit a silversmith and a bookbinder. The tour finishes with our small group standing in an obscure back alley, ringing the bell at a massive wooden door where a man opens a small iron-grated opening and only admits us after he has recognized our tour guide. Inside, we mount several flights of stairs past a fresco recently discovered as part of a planned expansion. I think of Luca's family villa and remind myself that I need to call Annie Templeton and make certain everything is all right with her. She and Adolpho will be arriving in Florence soon. It will be a welcome distraction.

At the top of the goldsmith's studio stairs, we are admitted through another heavily locked and bolted door. My leg is killing me, and I am sorry I have come—until the goldsmith begins to explain his work. As he demonstrates refining gold in a furnace, the spiritual analogy isn't lost on me. Liz and I talk about it all the way back to the hotel—how God is at work in our lives, and the fact that it hurts should just serve to encourage us that he is making something beautiful. We both sleep well.

We are forcing ourselves to enjoy being tourists, and there is no lack of wonderful things to see in Florence. On Wednesday evening we will go to a concert at St. Mark's Episcopal Church on the Via Maggio. Liz walks over to the church while I rest during the day. When she returns, she reports that the handbill posted just outside the church door looks promising. And it is wonderful—one of my favorite Puccini arias is on the program. On Thursday, Lucia sends a car to take us back to the spa and then, in the afternoon, to Fiesole, where we see Roman and Etruscan ruins. I can't quite wrap my brain around the concept of sitting in a stadium on the very same stone where a Roman once took in a play. But that's nothing compared to the mental gymnastics required when Lucia mentions—assuming I know—that Luca has gone to Bologna on business.

When I tell Liz, she frowns. "Luca left town without talking to you? What *is* going on?"

"Stop worrying, honey. There's nothing going on."

Of course, that is precisely my problem. I haven't seen or heard from Luca since last Saturday evening. I don't know what I expected, but it wasn't this. There is nothing going on, and I am running short of wisdom and patience.

THE PHONE RANG late Thursday night.

"We're back," Jeff said.

Liz gripped the phone and mouthed his name to Mimi, who clasped her hands together as if she were praying and disappeared into her bedroom, closing the door behind her.

"How . . . how was it?"

"Unbelievable. Fantastic. I don't even have words," he said.

Liz made what she hoped were encouraging noises and then fell silent.

"How's everything in Omaha?" he asked.

*Omaha?* "What?"

"I know better than to think you haven't talked to Ryan Miller and Margaret at least twice a day since you've been in Florence," Jeff said. He didn't sound upset about it, but Liz wasn't sure. Was this a test?

"Well, then, you may find it hard to believe when I tell you that I haven't talked to either of them."

"Right," Jeff said. "Only once a day?"

"At all," Liz said. The silence on the phone almost made her angry. Did he think she was lying? She took a deep breath. "There have been more important things going on than business meetings. I've checked my e-mail a couple of times. Made some suggestions to George Kincaid. Put a little more responsibility on Ryan Miller's shoulders." She added quickly, "He can handle it. And I don't want to be bothered with the details. I realize *you* probably don't believe that, but it's the truth." She bit her lip to try to keep from saying the next thing that came to her mind, but didn't succeed. "So . . . what's next, Jeff? What's going to happen now?"

"Well," he said. "I'm not sure. But we . . . we do need to talk. I'm sure about that."

She was shaking all over. She sat down. Closed her eyes. Willed Elizabeth Davis, business maven, to come to the forefront. "The ball's in your court, Jeff. You set the time and the place, and I'll be there."

"The hotel lobby. Tomorrow at noon."

Fear clutched at her midsection. He was going to tell her they were finished. That had to be it.

"Did you hear me?"

"I heard you," Liz said, hoping she sounded more in control of her emotions than she felt.

"Did you and Mary have something planned for lunch tomorrow?"

"It's fine." She tried not to snap. But she didn't think she succeeded.

"How is Mary?"

"Fine. She's fine. Healing. Resting. Shopping. Touring. She's fine."

"Good. Would you give her a message from Jean-Marc? He has some business to attend to first, but then he'd like to bring her down to the ship on Sunday if she's up to it. Tell her that, unless she says differently, he'll pick her up about ten in the morning."

"Why doesn't he talk to her himself?"

"Because he had a meeting to hustle off to. I'm sure you can understand that."

*Ouch.*

"Hey," he said, his voice gentling. "I didn't mean that the way it came out." When Liz didn't respond, he repeated his reassurance. "Really. I didn't mean it that way."

Her voice wavered. "Okay," she said. This was just too hard. She couldn't stand not seeing his face. He was being so . . . businesslike. She had so much to tell him, but she couldn't do it this way.

Jeff cleared his throat. "So . . . I'll see you tomorrow?"

Liz nodded. As if he could see her.

FRIDAY MORNING WAS the longest morning of Liz's life. In between bouts of morning sickness or plain nerves—she didn't know which—Liz did her hair three times, changed clothes at least twice, and fidgeted through Mimi's praying for her. She paced up and down the bank of windows in the suite's living area until Mimi teased her about having to pay for new carpet.

"I was hoping that would make you smile," Mimi said.

Liz just shook her head and kept pacing. Finally it was time. When the elevator doors opened, Jeff was right there in the lobby, holding a small box wrapped in brown paper.

"Not yet," he said, when she reached for it. "Luca's taking us."

"But . . . Lucia said he was gone."

"He was," Jeff said. "But now he's back. And he's driving us."

"Where?"

"You'll see," he said, and took her hand and led her outside. They slid into the backseat. Luca greeted her with a big smile and a kiss on each cheek. He asked about her health, and then settled behind the wheel of his Mercedes, whistling as he pulled out into traffic and headed off, driving like a crazy man. Why hadn't he gone up to see Mimi if he was so happy? And how could he be this happy when he had to know Mimi was miserable? Or had they talked, and Liz just didn't know about it?

Jeff must have sensed her tension, because he reached over and took her hand. It helped. A little. But not as much as refusing to look out the windshield. They were headed up into the hills somewhere, driving past a beautiful place called Villa Cora, rounding a turn—and Luca screeched to a halt, got out, opened the door for her, bowed like a chauffeur, and drove off without a word. He hadn't asked about Mimi once. Liz was beginning to think Luca Santo wasn't quite as nice as he'd made Mimi think he was.

"Hey, beautiful," Jeff said gently, putting his hand on her shoulder. "I'm over here." When Liz turned toward him, he took her hand and led the way into a restaurant where the *maître d'* took them to a table by a window with the view spread before them.

Jeff sat down opposite her, the box on the table between them. "Now," he said.

"It's gorgeous," Liz said, as she unwrapped a clay sculpture of a dancer poised on her abdomen with her back arched so that her legs came up over her head. She had contorted herself nearly into a circle. Between her toes, she held a mask of some kind over her face. "But . . . I don't understand."

Jeff pointed to the mask. "It's an Etruscan theatrical mask," he explained. "I saw it in the window of a gallery—one of those days after you said . . ."

"I'm so sorry," Liz said. Her resolve to be calm today was quickly folding. She squeezed her eyes shut, trying to stop the tears. "I am so sorry for . . . for everything."

He didn't acknowledge what she said. Instead, he looked down at the sculpture, touching it gently and turning it slowly as he talked. "I looked at it for a while, thinking—very bitterly, I might add— about all the masks you had worn to draw me in." He looked up at her then and said, "I wasn't feeling very complimentary toward you."

"You had every right to hate me," Liz said.

"Oh, no. I didn't." He stared into her eyes. "Love forgives, Bitsy.

It believes all things and hopes all things and endures all things. At least," he said, "the kind of love Danny and Mary both told me I needed does." He looked out the window and back at her. "It's called—"

*"Agape."* He frowned a little with surprise. She nodded. "It's a new word for me, too. Mimi told me about it. A new kind of love from anything I've had—or thought about. Until now."

"Now?"

She nodded. "Well, to be exact . . . until Sunday morning."

He sat back and stared at her. "Sunday morning? This past Sunday morning?"

She nodded, looking down at the sculpture. "I've worn so many masks, Jeff." She swallowed. Took a drink of water. "When I followed you out to California, I didn't really have any intention of moving out there. I was just gathering evidence for my argument against moving. Playing along until you came to your senses." When Jeff started to talk, Liz held up her hand. "Please. Just let me finish with this. You deserve to hear it all." She took another drink of water. "And most of my show of friendliness toward Sarah and the kids—it was just that. Show." She looked down at the sculpture. "Another mask. But then, this past Sunday morning, I tried to do what you said. I tried to open my eyes . . . and my heart. And then I wandered into this church and . . ." Twenty minutes later, she finished by pleading his forgiveness—again.

Jeff looked a little shell-shocked. Instead of sweeping her into his arms, which she had spent plenty of time envisioning over the past few days when she wasn't panicky with worry, he said gently, "Well, that makes it easier for me to tell you."

He'd had a similar experience with God . . . and he'd wanted to tell her. But he'd let everything else stop him.

"You're not the only one who needs to be forgiven, Bitsy." He smiled slowly. "I didn't have the guts to tell you about any of this. And I haven't been completely honest with you. I didn't actually lie about how I felt, but I didn't tell you about my encounter with God.

I didn't tell you how much I wanted to move. How much it bothered me to think about living at the estate." He glanced away, then back at her. "How tired I've been of competing with Sam Davis for your affection and your respect and loyalty." He shook his head slowly from side to side. "I was afraid I'd lose you if I said all those things. And then I nearly lost you anyway."

He reached out and turned the sculpture so that Liz could see the dancer's feet removing the mask from her face. "So this," he said, "is our reminder. From now on, no matter what contortions are required, we take off the masks. With God's help."

He reached across the table and grasped her hands so that the statue was inside their linked arms. "I love you, Elizabeth Samantha Davis. I've loved you well. And I've loved you poorly. I've loved you for the wrong reasons and in the wrong way. And I've loved you for the right reasons in God's way." His eyes welled up with tears. He swallowed. "But in and through it all, I've known that, however I love you . . . it's forever. Will you marry me, Bitsy?"

Liz choked back her tears and forced a smile. "I'll do more than that," she said, "I'll follow you to California." She paused and looked down at her stomach. "Correction," she said. "*We'll* follow you to California."

## *Mary*

ANYONE WATCHING SURELY would think us mad. A gray-haired man and an equally endowed woman, the latter blind-folded—and sporting a cane.

I chuckle and hold out my hand. "All right," I say, adjusting the blindfold around my eyes.

"Not to peek," Jean-Marc says, and taps me on the nose.

I shake my head. "Can't see a thing." I run my fingers across his calloused palm. "I feel the hands of a seaman."

"An age-ed sea-man," Jean-Marc says, accenting each syllable.

"I don't know about that," I answer, touching the blindfold again. "Seems to me you're still young where it counts." I throw my shoulders back and salute. "Lead on, *mon capitain.*"

He is so careful, leading me along the dock. "One step up . . . Careful, it's rough here. . . . Stay close, the dock narrows . . ."—and, finally—"All right." He steps behind me and puts his hands on my shoulders. "Are you ready to meet one of the other women in my life?"

"Ready." I put my hand to my heart. "You'd think I was being introduced at court. My heart is pounding."

*"Voilà,"* Jean-Marc says, and removes the blindfold.

And there she is . . . much more impressive than anything I

expected. The *Sea Cloud* on a magazine cover is beautiful. The *Sea Cloud* in reality is majestic. Her hull is black. The polished wood-grained cabin literally glows in the sunlight, and the deck is spotless. I grab Jean-Marc's arm. "Stunning. Absolutely stunning."

He is studying my reaction, his blue eyes serious. "Come aboard," he says to the deck and opening his arms.

I lean forward, first handing him my cane, then allowing myself to be lifted onto the deck. Like an excited child, he leads me—reciting work he has done, improvements he has made since the purchase—and then once again takes me in his arms to help me below, where he has retrofitted a berth for his grandsons. He tells me how he matched the exotic original wood after an exhaustive search of old shipyards.

I wander belowdecks murmuring, "I can hardly believe it. All those years I've tried to imagine you like this . . . and now that it's reality, it's difficult to take it all in."

"I've imagined you here," Jean-Marc says. "Just like this. Alone . . ." He leans toward me. Taking both my hands in his, he smiles down at me. My heart thumps—but for the wrong reason. *Don't let me hurt him, God. Don't let him say it. Please.*

We have dinner on board the ship . . . out on the deck . . . by candlelight, even though it is early evening and the effect isn't quite what Jean-Marc probably hoped it would be. The *Sea Cloud* and this setting are everything a woman could possibly dream of . . . if only . . . I set my fork down and look toward the horizon.

"You are thinking . . . of . . . life on board a yacht," Jean-Marc teases, reaching over to trace my profile with the back of his hand.

I close my eyes to fight back the tears. I am thinking, not only of how much I do not want to hurt this man, but also of Luca, whose touch I will never know.

"And, I think . . . you are wondering how it could possibly work." He gets up and walks toward the prow, pauses, and with out-stretched arms, says, "We did it, Mary." His voice is warm with affection. "We found each other again. After all these years. Life is good.

Very good, indeed. With the return of you, God has also given me a second daughter. And soon . . . another grandchild. He is very good."

"He is," I agree. But in the face of Jean-Marc's joy, I am miserable.

"I have waited a very long time to have you on board my ship, Mary," Jean-Marc says. "And there is something I want to ask you."

"Don't. Please." I rub my forehead with both hands. I bow my head and beg him, "Just—don't."

"Shhh . . . Let me talk, *chérie*."

I get up and try to limp away, but he catches me from behind and wraps me in his arms. His embrace is loving . . . and I don't have the heart to fight my way out. I close my eyes. *I asked you not to let this happen. What possible reason could there be for breaking this wonderful man's heart . . . again?*

"As I have wanted to say for a long time, Mary," Jean-Marc whispers, "I have loved you for years."

*Get it over with. Just get it over with. . . .*

"And now that I have you and the *Sea Cloud* in my life at the same time, I want to ask you to do me the honor of hosting your wedding on board my ship."

"What . . . did you . . . just . . . say?" I spin around in his arms to face him. His blue eyes are serious . . . and there is no hint of pain in them.

"I asked you for the privilege of having the wedding—yours and Luca's—here. On board the *Sea Cloud*." He smiles down at me. "You were expecting something else?"

"But . . . I thought—"

"So did I." He nods. Shrugs. "For a while. But I'm wiser now. And you deserve a man who will give you his whole heart. God forgive me, part of mine will always belong to my sea mistress. And finally, I have realized . . . that is who God made me to be. It's not so bad, is it?" He releases me and steps back a little, waiting for my answer.

"No," I shake my head. "It isn't bad at all. It's who you are. And you are . . . wonderful." I kiss him on both cheeks. It doesn't seem enough. We hug. Even laugh a little. Both of us are relieved.

"And I can give you this gift? This wedding?" Now he sounds eager. He hurries to explain. "There will of course be the civil ceremony in Florence. But then . . . your minister . . . here on my ship . . . and so . . .

"My dear, sweet, beloved friend . . . you amaze me."

"That's good, yes?" He winks at me.

"It's very, very good," I say. "Except for one thing."

"Tell me," Jean-Marc says. "If it is in my power to do . . . I will do it."

I shake my head. "You can't do this."

"What?"

"Produce the groom . . . change his mind . . . rule his heart."

"As to the changing of his mind," Jean-Marc says, "when I saw him only yesterday, his mind was not in need of changing. The rule of his heart is God's alone. And again, when I saw him only yesterday, I was glad to learn that God has given Luca Santo's heart to you, dear Mary."

I am hearing the words . . . but having difficulty believing them. Jean-Marc isn't quite finished. Sauntering over and picking up his coffee cup, he gestures toward the pier. "And as to the producing of the groom . . ."

I hear an engine rev, and as I turn toward it, a red Ducati roars into view and screeches to a halt at the end of the pier. The rider is a beautiful man with a glorious smile. I am blinking back tears as I look back toward Jean-Marc. There must still be a question in my eyes. He comes to me and kisses both cheeks and my lips. Lightly. And then he laughs.

"For you . . . for learning . . . we decided the red Monster was the best."

"That's . . . for me?"

The Nordic blue eyes smile. "Yes, dear Mary. *All* of it is for you.

The motorcycle . . . my friendship . . . and Luca's heart. You have only to claim them." He turns me around and gives me a little shove toward the pier.

There is one thing they didn't tell me at the hospital when they fitted me with this boot so I could walk while my leg healed. If one is determined, it is quite possible to actually *run* short distances with it on. Say, for example, into the arms of the man you love.

# TWENTY-THREE

*Mary*

I WAS WARNED. Luca told me that any wedding reception planned by his sister would continue until the guests were begging for mercy and refusing more food.

"For Lucia," he said, "love and food are linked with a chain no one can break."

As I sit between Luca and Jean-Marc at Annie and Adolpho's reception dinner on the loggia, I witness the proof of Luca's prediction. I thought I knew all the courses of a formal Italian meal, but Lucia seems to have invented more. We've been at table for over two hours. Between each course there has been a pause for music—first from a stringed quartet that is part of Adolpho's chamber group in Paris, then from various relatives, and finally from a local tenor who gives a rendition of *"Ti Adoro"* that sends chills down my spine. Or maybe it's the fact that Luca reaches for my hand during the song.

Annie and Adolpho slip away without much fanfare. Jean-Marc is talking to Liz when Luca nudges me to follow him. We make our way to the front door, where Adolpho and Annie are waiting. They want Luca to photograph the departure. It's no wonder. Annie tosses me her bouquet, tucks her dress up, hops behind her new husband, and away they go on Adolpho's motorcycle. The last thing I see is Annie's white veil flying in the wind.

Back inside, I am barely seated at the table when, with a wink at Jean-Marc, Luca stands up and calls out that he has a belated toast. *"Lu mio cumpare ha uno cervellu finu,"* he says, nodding at Jean-Marc.

When Jean-Marc shakes his head and everyone laughs, I demand a translation. At Luca's insistence, Jean-Marc tells me Luca is quoting a well-known poem. He translates for me. "My close friend has a very fine mind."

Luca continues, *"Che tutto il mondo ha girato assai . . ."*

"He has traveled the world over."

*"Precio' questa faccenda me rovina. . . . E inao na mugliera ho da tro-var."*

Jean-Marc smiles as he says to me, "I have this problem that is troubling me. . . . I've got to find a wife."

Liz and Jeff are grinning at me, and I can feel a blush creeping up my neck as Luca continues in English. "We did not wish to take away from the wonderful day for our beloved Adolpho and Annie, so we have agreed to keep the secret. I wish now to share with you all—" He is forced to pause, because at the far end of the table, Lucia has let out a little screech and a stream of praise to several saints. Luca says something in Italian that makes everyone laugh—including Lucia. And then, he turns to me and extends his hand. "Once in this lifetime, God blessed a crazy young man with the love of a woman he did not deserve. And he truly is a God who does beyond all that we ask or think, for he has blessed me yet again." When he looks at me, I see tears in his eyes. He puts his arm around me, clears his throat, and continues. "I wish to share with you all the happy news. Mary Davis has consented to become my wife."

If there is any doubt in my heart as to how my French sailor feels about this news, it dissolves when Jean-Marc rises and embraces both Luca and me. It is he who first offers congratulations, who tells everyone how he and Luca plotted and planned for me to be on the *Sea Cloud* that day, who offers first a toast and then a prayer of bless-ing, who introduces Lizzie and Jeff to everyone. As Luca and I are engulfed in a sea of well-wishers, I am suddenly aware of Liz hugging

Jean-Marc. And I hear her say the beautiful word. *Papa*. She calls him *Papa*. And two pairs of Nordic blue eyes fill with tears.

## *May 1, 2004*

GEORGE KINCAID STOOD at his front door, morning newspaper in hand, staring at the driveway. Dressed as he was, in rumpled pajamas and a worn plaid bathrobe, he was reluctant to be seen tripping down the front porch steps, but some things had to be investigated. Dropping his paper on the floor, he stepped outside. He went down the stairs, past the beds of blooming tulips, and across the thick spring lawn. When he reached out to touch it, the thing on the driveway didn't disappear. It was real. Silver and white two-tone . . . rag top . . . wire wheels—a classic in every way. Only the red bow tied to the hood didn't make sense. Well, actually, nothing about it made sense. He reached for the note tucked under the windshield wiper. Keys fell out.

> *The title is in the glove box, and it has been signed over to you. Mother said you used to love this car. Now you can love it more. Happy May Day, George.*

It was signed *Liz Davis*.

"Well, well," George said. "Well, well." He looked back at the house. He should get his wallet. His license. *Pshaw*. Who would care if an old man took a spin in his classic Austin Healey on a Saturday morning? He got in. Started it up . . . and smiled.

"I KNOW YOU'VE heard this before, but it's the truth," Liz said, pulling her checkbook out of her handbag in hopes it would eliminate any doubts. "You are the only one who can do this the way I want it done." She stared across the desk at Mona Whitcomb. "Name your price."

Mona clicked her desktop with her black-and-white-polka-dot fingernails. She made a face and chewed the end of the pen in her mouth for a moment. "You want to open *when*?"

"A year from this fall."

"And who's the liaison after you're in California?"

"George Kincaid," Liz said. "He's doing it *pro bono*. But obviously you'll be working closely with Irene." She smiled. "Believe it or not, I've realized I'm not Superwoman. I'm going to *delegate*." She ignored Mona's amused little snort. "But I want it done right. And you're the woman to do it right."

Mona reached behind her and grabbed a wire-bound sketch pad from beneath a pile of catalogues on the lateral file behind her desk. Flipping it open, she grabbed a pencil and began to draw, turning the open pad sideways on her desk so Liz could see what she was doing. "What would you think if we did handprints on the walls . . . and, maybe . . ." She glanced over the rim of her rhinestone glasses at Liz. "Now don't yell. Think about this." She scribbled on the paper. "What if we had permanent markers . . . all colors . . . for auto-graphs." She laid her pencil down and leaned back in her chair. "And, I think, the toffee walls in the library-slash-office could stay. *Someone* will need an office. Won't they?"

Liz nodded. She pointed to the sketch pad. "I love it. Do it."

Mona blew a bubble and popped it. "What about your mother?"

"What about her?"

"She won't have a cow?"

Liz shook her head. "No cows." She broached the next topic with a bright smile, hoping Mona didn't notice it was a bit forced. "I'd like you to do something else, too. It's a little short notice."

"I may not be a real wedding planner, darling," Mona said, and cracked her gum. "But everything's under control. One more thing or three isn't going to cause a meltdown." She grabbed a pad of elec-tric blue sticky-notes. "Fire away."

"Actually," Liz said. "We want to cancel the production."

Mona blinked. Slowly. Several times. She cocked her head. "You're canceling your wedding?"

"Not the wedding. Just the production."

"Well, thank goodness for that," Mona said, patting her chest with an open palm. "You nearly gave me heart failure. For a minute there, I thought maybe Jeffrey Scott was back on the bachelor market."

Liz laughed aloud. "Sorry."

"Does he at least have a brother?"

"Actually, he does," Liz said. "In California."

"That's perfect," Mona batted her false eyelashes. "After you move to California, I'll do your first decorating job free—if you'll introduce me."

It would almost be worth it, Liz thought, to see Danny Scott's reaction to magenta-maned Mona. Of course, she realized, Mona's hair might not be magenta in, say, three hours. Liz shook her head from side to side. "What can I say?"

Mona threw her head back and laughed. "All right, all right. Back to serious wedding talk. Tell me what's up."

"What's up is we're doing something smaller for the wedding. In Tuscany, actually."

"Am I in a fairy tale?" Mona quipped. "Are you *kidding* me?!"

Liz shook her head. "Nope." She smiled. "It gets better. It's on board a yacht."

Mona fell against the back of her chair and let her mouth fall open. "You *are* living a fairy tale, girl. For real." She leaned forward again on her elbows. "So . . . what's all this got to do with Mona and Company?"

"We'd like you to plan an informal—and I do mean *informal*—celebration out at the house. Sort of a combination wedding reception and introduction of the new project. In late June."

Mona glowered. "You mean plan another party?"

"Jeff's brother will be there."

"You'll need tents," Mona said.

"You can do tents," Liz nodded with a smile. "You can do anything you want as long as it's relaxed."

"Relaxed as in 'no tie'?"

"Relaxed as in T-shirts and blue jeans," Liz said, laughing again when Mona peered at her over the top of her glasses.

"This," Mona said, taking off her glasses and resting her chin in her palm, "I've got to hear."

Liz told her about Mary and Luca, about that Sunday morning in Florence, and with a gulp, about the baby. She ended with "So . . . can you do it?"

"Liz . . . dahling," Mona said, with an exaggerated flourish, "when have you *not* loved Mona's denim soirées?"

*Omaha World Herald*
*June 13, 2004*

    *A yacht off the Tuscan coast was the setting for the June 5 wedding of two prominent Omahans. Mrs. Mary Davis, widow of Samuel Frederick Davis, married former world champion Ducati racer, Mr. Luca Santo, currently of Paris, France, where the couple will reside. Miss Elizabeth Davis, president of Davis Enterprises, married Mr. Jeffrey James Scott, also of Omaha. The couple will reside in Sausalito, California.*

    *After a brief civil ceremony in the city of Livorno, the couples exchanged sacred vows on board the yacht Sea Cloud owned and piloted by family friend, Jean-Marc David. A reception was held at Mr. Santo's family villa near Florence. Following their wedding trips, the couples will host a second reception on the grounds of the Davis estate here in Omaha.*

*Omaha World Herald*
*August 1, 2004*

   *Davis Enterprises has announced the appointment of Mr. Ryan Miller as an interim member of the Board of Directors while the company undergoes internal adjustments, due to the recent marriage and subsequent relocation to California of former CEO Elizabeth Davis Scott. The former Ms. Davis and Jeffrey James Scott of Omaha were married this past June. Mr. Scott has taken up responsibilities in the San Francisco offices of Widhelm, Capshaw, and Gross. Mrs. Scott would not comment on rumors that Davis Enterprises will open a California branch sometime in the next fiscal year.*

## September, 2004

   THE FALL AIR IS crisp and clean as two Ducati motorcycles round the curve leading into the vast park around the castle at Chambord. Inside the park gate, the motorcycles slow down, cruising slowly down the blacktop road. At one point, one rider motions to the other. They glance left, where a clearing in the forest provides a brief glimpse of King Francis I's "hunting lodge," a 440-room castle with over 350 chimneys. Pulling into the parking lot, the riders take off their helmets, unzip their leather jackets, and are laughing and talking about the wonderful weather when a cell phone rings.

   "Is it?" Mary asks.

   Luca peers at the caller ID. "I think so." Luca answers. "Hello? Yes . . . yes . . ." He smiles and hands Mary the phone. She listens and begins to cry and hands it back to her husband.

   "Yes . . . sure . . . all right," Luca says and looks down at Mary. "They're going to try to broadcast a picture."

   Mary and Luca lean close . . . peering at the phone screen. Three tiny faces . . . two wreathed in smiles . . . and the third . . . a newborn baby boy. Blond, like his father. Beautiful, like his mother.

"Yes, yes," Luca says. "It's wonderful. Congratulations. She can't talk—she's crying too hard."

Finally, Mary calms down enough to take the phone. "Eight pounds, five ounces," she repeats. "Oh, I'm so happy, Lizzie-bear. Yes. That's how it was with me, too. Yes, sweetheart . . . I know. You'll be able to tease him for missing it for the rest of his life. Aren't you glad you had Sarah go to those classes with you? California traffic . . . you can't account for it."

They talk for a while longer. Mary cries. Luca smiles. She hangs up. Sighs happily, snuggles against Luca.

"You didn't ask the name!" Luca exclaims.

"She told me," Mary says.

"Well, what is it?"

"I think there's a new family tradition," Mary smiles, counting off, "Jeffrey James Scott. Jean-Marc David, Luca Ilario Santo." She touches Luca's cheek. "The baby's name is John Luke Scott."

Together, the grandparents whisper, "Three first names."


*June, 2005*

*Mary*


"I HAVE BEEN SENT below to see what is wrong with the matriarch," Luca says. He has just descended from the deck of the yacht and stands silhouetted in the doorway.

I look up from where I am sitting at the table. I've been writing furiously in my journal. "I just had to get it down," I say. "There's nothing wrong. Everything is so right . . . I . . ." I clear my throat and shake my head, smiling at my husband and wondering how to express what I am feeling. "Sometimes," I say, "there just aren't words."

Luca nods. "I know."

Behind him, up on deck, there is the sound of childish laughter.

Sarah and Danny are here with the children. Liz is up there, too, cradling the most beautiful baby boy the world has ever known in her arms. He's threatening to walk soon. Growing up too fast.

And then there is Jeff, who, at this moment, is back at the stern immersed in some discussion with the man who has come a very long way to teach him how to sail his new yacht. He's a handsome sailor, with gray hair and Nordic blue eyes.

"It is overwhelming, sometimes, the goodness of God, is it not, *cara mia*?" Luca sits down next to me and kisses me on the cheek.

"Thank you," I say.

"For what?"

"For agreeing to spend our first anniversary here. In California."

"It's important to be with family," Luca says. "And this is when they could all come together at once. These times we will cherish. Maybe even a little more than the surprise I have for next week."

All my begging is to no avail. He won't tell me what he has planned, although he hints at lovely views of beautiful valleys in the wonderful state of California. And although he won't say, I am quite certain the surprise includes a motorcycle. Probably two.

### Fall 2005

T HIS CAN'T BE IT," Joe said, pulling over to the side.

"That Pastor Dayton said it was a nice place," Millie replied. She leaned over and looked out the window of the rusty Camry.

"Well, that may be . . . but this can't be it."

"Drive in, Joe." Millie looked in the backseat. "He's sleeping, but we need to get settled in case he needs something tonight."

"All right," Joe said, shaking his head and gripping the wheel. "But this doesn't look right."

The Camry crept up the winding blacktop drive, past a pond and around a corner. When the house came into view, Millie put her hand on her husband's shoulder and said, "You were right. We'd better get going. These folks aren't going to want us snooping." It was too late. Someone was opening the front door . . . coming out . . . and *waving* at them. An old woman with a big smile. She was wearing an apron and looked more like someone's grandmother than the housekeeper for a place like this.

"Sort of looks like Grandma Hillis," Joe said. "And look . . . that's got to be her husband."

The woman came down the stairs and called out. "You the Boyces?"

Joe leaned across Millie. "We are," he said.

"Welcome to your home away from home," the woman said.

"Glad you found us. They keep telling us the sign is on its way, but then that's construction for you. Lots of promises and lots of delays." She broke off. "But you don't care about that." She came to the car and bent down so she could see them both through Millie's window. "I'm Irene Baxter." She nodded toward the mansion's front door, where the elderly gentleman was waiting. "And that handsome devil up there is Cecil. His knees don't do these stairs so well, but he's too stubborn to use the new ramp. So you'll forgive him if he doesn't climb down. He'll meet you in the back and show you where to park the car," Irene said. She turned her head and looked in the back window at the sleeping child sprawled on the backseat. "What a beautiful little lamb," she crooned. She reached in her pocket and handed Millie a crocheted cap. "This is a nice home, but the Nebraska breezes are a little chilly sometimes. You be the judge, though."

"Mama?"

"Hey, sleepyhead," Millie said. "Look what this nice lady just gave you. Why don't you put it on. Wind's blowing. It'll keep your noggin warm."

The boy pulled the cap over his bald head and smiled.

"Now, if you don't like that color," Irene said, "you just let Irene know, 'cause we've got a whole rainbow of hats, and you can have any one you like. Okay?"

The boy nodded. "I'm five," he said, holding up his fingers.

"I'm a hundred and twenty-three," Irene joked, winking at Millie. "But don't you tell. Promise?"

"I won't."

"That's good. Now. You know what I know?"

The boy shook his head.

"I know your name is William Arnold Boyce. And you like cinnamon rolls."

"How'd you know that?"

Irene shrugged. "Grandmas just have their ways," she said. She held out her hand. "If your mama says you can have one, we'll go get one right now."

"He can have anything he'll eat," Millie said. "He's nothing but skin and bones."

Irene opened the back door. "Well, come on, Mr. Bones," she said, and held out her hand.

Billy took it and slid out of the backseat. He wobbled a little but got his balance. Looking up the long flight of stairs to the front door, he looked doubtful.

Just then, a magenta-haired woman appeared at the top of the stairs. In her polka-dot glasses and chartreuse sweater, she was what Mrs. Baxter called "a vision of . . . what, I'm not sure—but a vision."

"Hey, you in the red hat." She called down to Billy.

Billy looked up.

"You know how to ride a horse?"

Billy shook his head.

"Time you learned." She bounced down the stairs, got down on all fours, and whinnied—badly—before ordering him to climb on. He did. And none other than Mona, of Mona & Company, who was running behind on this project and had come out to check on her crew, stood up and carried the first resident of Sam's Place up the stairs to where he would sign his name on the handprint-covered foyer wall . . . and start a legacy of hope for patients and their families who traveled to the Samuel F. Davis Memorial Oncology Wing at Creighton University Medical Center praying for cures . . . and needing a home away from home.

*And now, to him who is able to do*
*exceedingly abundantly above*
*all that we ask or think,*
*to him be glory in Christ Jesus for now and evermore.*
*Amen.*

# ✌ ACKNOWLEDGMENTS ✌

*In the midst of book tours and trying to balance appearances on the* Today Show *and* Oprah *. . . Mel Gibson called. We were supposed to have lunch to discuss his playing the lead in the movie version of my latest book . . . but, as I told Mel, life gets crazy sometimes, and lunch would have to wait.*

Sometimes people tend to think a writer's life is like that. I suppose some writers' lives *are* like that. Mine isn't. The writer's life I know involves no book tours, no television appearances, no movies . . . no Mel. (Well, actually . . . there is a Mel, but his last name isn't Gibson.)

The writer's life I know is simpler. And better. Because . . .

- Agents like Janet Kobobel Grant help their clients plan careers in light of eternity.

- Publishers like Carol and Gary Johnson encourage writers who want to use politically incorrect words like "sin" and "salvation" and "Lord Jesus Christ."

- Editors like Dave Horton and Ann Parrish and Karen Schurrer brainstorm and question and correct until this book is the best book—so far.

- Artists like Paul Higdon design gorgeous covers.

- Families like mine support and encourage and accept simpler dinners and living with "attack dust bunnies" when I fail to keep all the plates spinning.

- Famous writers treat decidedly *not* famous writers like me as colleagues. (Thank you for suggesting *Florence . . . Oltrarno.*)

AND . . .

- Chili beans are ingredients for fellowship . . . instead of soup.

Thank you, Father . . . for the gift of story.
Thank you, Bethany House . . . for the gift of being published.
Thank you, Reader . . . for the gift of your time.

# Discover a *Fresh* Voice in Inspirational Fiction

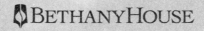